INDEPENDENT
LEGIONS
PUBLISHING

000 INDEPENDENT
LEGIONS
PUBLISHING

MONSTERS OF ANY KIND

EDITED BY
ALESSANDRO MANZETTI AND DANIELE BONFANTI

ISBN: 978-88-31959-10-0
COPYRIGHT (EDITION) ©2018 INDEPENDENT LEGIONS PUBLISHING
OCTOBER 2018
COPYEDITING: DAVID THOMAS
COVER ART: WENDY SABER CORE
INTERIOR ILLUSTRATIONS: STEFANO CARDOSELLI

000 INDEPENDENT
000 LEGIONS
PUBLISHING

SUMMARY

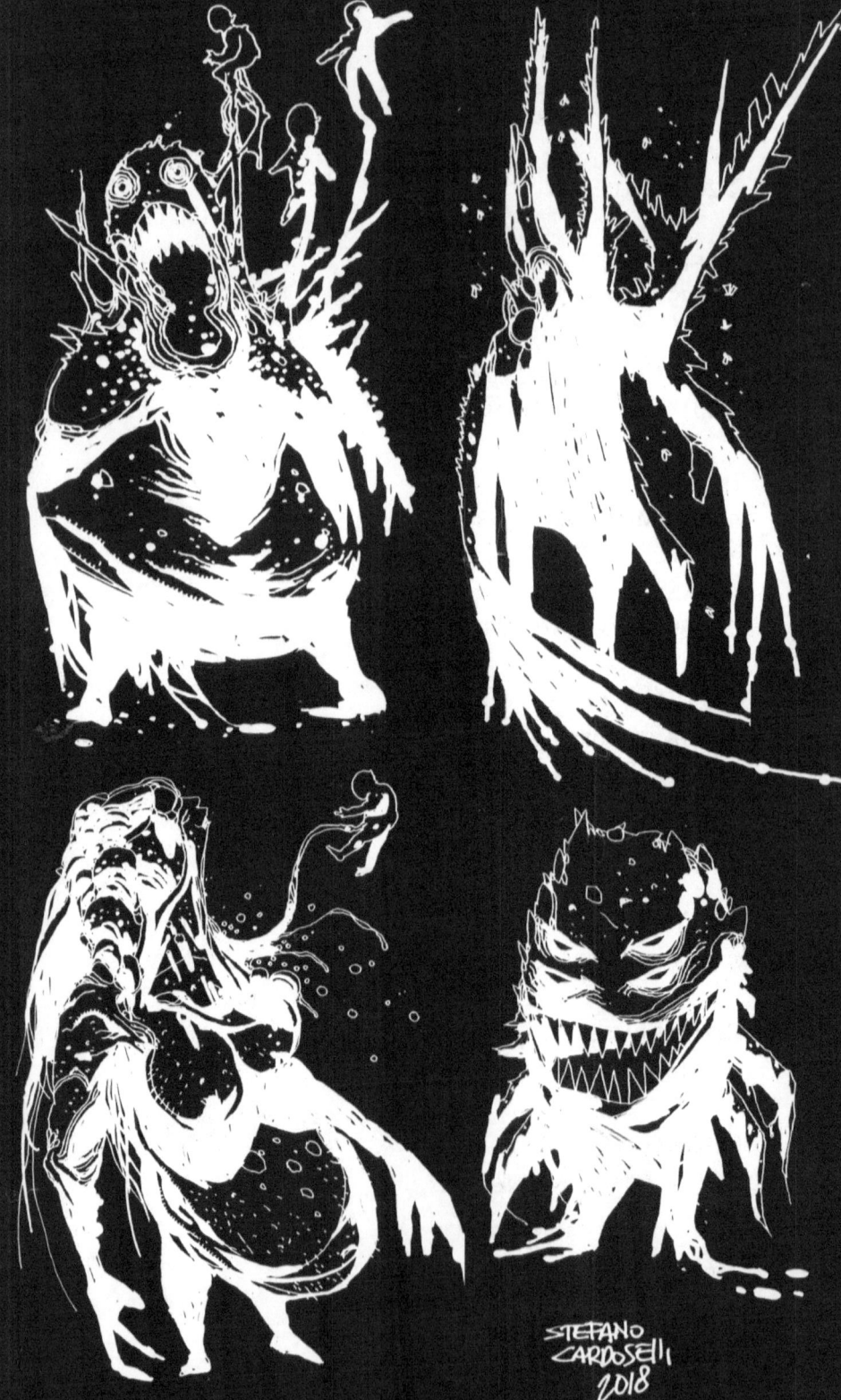

INTRODUCTION

by Daniele Bonfanti and Alessandro Manzetti

It's always a little offensive when the word "monster" is used for murderers and criminals. Let's face it: those are human.

And they're the exact opposite of monsters, as they are not only very human, but sadly very *ordinary* in their evil; while monsters are awesome. Literally. The word "monster" comes from Latin, *monstrum* (trust us, we're Italian: we speak Latin all the time), which means something prodigious, exceptional, completely beyond normality. So: *awesome.*

As you see, something very noble.

Monsters are difference, change, deviance. Life force.

And in a society striving to flatten every difference down into cultural baby food, thinking of nature as a machine to exploit for our (mostly counterfeit) needs—the fear and respect that kept us alive, until now, hidden behind the arrogant delusion of power and control—monsters are maybe the last line of defense against self-annihilation.

If they want to survive, men need monsters.

MONSTERS OF ANY KIND

EDITED BY

ALESSANDRO MANZETTI
DANIELE BONFANTI

MONSTERS OF ANY KIND

CODY GOODFELLOW

PERPETUAL ANTIMONY
by CODY GOODFELLOW

They come sneaking up the stern and bow steps of my houseboat simultaneously, so the boat scarcely rocks in the stagnant current. I'm too impressed to blame them. They must've been walking all night on the river, on their outlandish snowshoes. For their ingenuity alone, they deserve better than they're going to get. Nature may be cruel in its using, but we can all of us hope only to be useful.

My late-model Sunstar is mired in the middle of the thickest patch of the Columbia HAB, or Harmful Algal Bloom, off Frenchman's Bar, a quarter mile downstream from the mouth of the Willamette. Damming the river from four miles upstream to another two below my home on the state line, the bloom is thought to be an invasive species brought in with ballast water from the Panamax freighters out of China, and like the gator-sized amphibious snakeheads in the shallows, mutated into an ecological catastrophe by runoff from the Hanford nuclear site, two hundred miles away.

Luridly scarlet stalks and purple-black float bladders interwoven into a dense carpet steeped in clouds of luminous crimson dinoflagellates. If it came from China, they spliced the worst traits of a dozen aquatic plants into its genome before sending it over.

Thick enough to choke the props on one such gargantuan freighter, which straddles the Willamette–Columbia confluence, and has become quite popular with squatters. That's probably where they came from. The south shore is farm collective territory, with more booby traps than all of Vietnam amid an impassable junkyard of cargo boxes, city debris and the aforementioned snakeheads. The Washington shore is fenced, mined and patrolled by a militia group called the Vancouver Regulators.

They made it on those ridiculous snowshoes, so they know the river, know the treacherous liminal terrain of the bloom. Looking for food or salvage, or maybe, like they know the river and the factions and the rest, maybe they know about me.

Four of them, with axes and knives. One carrying a rifle like it might still have bullets in it. Creeping across the bloom in the predawn light towards my house, skulking through my dank parlor, pulling faces at the library, at the obscene uselessness of all these damp books, at the pervasive, cloying rot and the moist touch of clammy curtains dividing the rooms.

I was going to slash my wrists and throat and set off the thermite charges, sending this boat to the bottom. Thank goodness they removed the ethical quandary of suicide by coming to kill me. Whatever happens next will be not a tragic accident, but an act of will.

I was always of two minds about whether I wanted to survive this. But to let someone kill me, even when I'd abandoned myself to this, is still unacceptable.

We have never backed away from a fight.

I come from willful people. Self-made men.

My great-grandfather came from nothing to found a trash collection business in Portland that grew to become the largest waste disposal concern in the Pacific Northwest. Spare with his fortune and absolute in his scorn of loafers, he had all but disowned his pill-addict son, and ran his grandson half to death almost before he became my father. I saw a lot of the Portland dump, because when Mom kicked Dad out, he lived in a camper on the lot. "If I don't own anything," he always said, "she can't take it away."

I remember the first time we went to visit Great-Grand, the first time I saw the house. Mom was afraid of him because she was going to ask him for money. She called him a skinflint and a monster. While she smoked a joint in the car to settle her nerves, I was set loose in the backyard, which was a rambling, partitioned affair, a series of puzzle boxes; beyond a secret gate lay the lawn of spiky Japanese grass and the sand garden, and beyond that, the koi pond with the tiny pavilion on an island in the center, and beyond that, the shrine with the green idol under the mulberry trees; and beyond *that*, an afterthought even I as a small child saw as a perverse non sequitur, a horseshoe pit and a gazebo overlooking the perilous slopes of Forest Park.

I was feeding the koi when the crane came. A big stately, strange saurian thing, it took no notice of me as it stilted across the still green water, gulping down carp the size of my arm. I ran to tell the servant, who was already coming out the back door with a shotgun.

The bird ignored the servant but took wing just before the first shot, which sheared off its head and a good six cobalt blue inches of its serpentine neck. The body nearly cleared the fence, but flopped back into the pond. The servant took the greedy bird by its clawed feet and shook it until an adult carp and two babies slithered out of the decapitated bird and returned to swimming, none the worse for wear.

The silent servant brought me inside and left me to look at the antique toys in the parlor while my mother cried in the kitchen.

Even then, the house had a green smell, like an old church. Spotless, but still you could smell nature eating it, like early cancer on a loved one's breath.

The whole house throbbed with the melancholy reeling notes of a grand piano. That's how I first saw him, with his back to me, hands stamping up and down the keys, playing something of Debussy, if memory serves. I retreated for fear of bringing that furious attention on myself, into the drawing room, and something wonderful.

The glass cases that were the only furniture here displayed ornate pagodas with trees, every leaf rendered in creamy bone; mountains wreathed in ossified mist that seemed to part under my gaze; cranes, whales and octopi; a hollow sphere with a smaller sphere within it, and through portals in its crosshatched surface, yet a smaller sphere, and within *that*—

I remember it was this, which tempted me to press my nose to the glass, which so engrossed me, that I failed to notice when the music had stopped.

The hand caught mine in a grip like driftwood. The fingers went round and round my skinny arm like segmented snakes. "You were instructed not to touch."

Mother was still crying, the echoing house making her sound like a lost, lowing cow. It hadn't worked with Dad, so why it would have any effect on this creature...

His eyes widened, like sleepy animals slithering out of their burrows to menace me. His smile was a pure agonistic display of health and menace. "The distinctive features are apparent enough," he said, "but are you a boy or a girl?"

I told him I wasn't going to decide until I got married, which made him laugh. It wasn't supposed to.

Mom hated him for a hundred reasons, but my parents argued about his capacity for saying mean things. Upon first meeting my mother, he described her to her face as "pretty as a freshly peeled potato," and professed bewilderment when she burst into tears. Father said he didn't mean to be cruel. Mother kissed me on the forehead and told me Beauty is in the eye of the beholder.

He asked me if I liked his collection, and I did not have to lie. He told me that they were ivory, but not from whales or elephants, and that the spirits of the animals they came from had cursed them.

"Go ahead," he said, "and touch one." Even then, somehow, I knew he wasn't sharing with me, but watching me to see if I'd pass a test.

I reached up and took hold of a sphere textured like a sea urchin, with ports cut out of it allowing you to see another sphere trapped within, and another within that one, and so on... It was warm and creamy smooth and strangely light, yet harder than my bones.

"Everyone in this family thinks they're clumsy," he said, "but I'll tell you the truth. Everything they do, their shadow spoils it. Everything they reach for, something inside them tries to knock it over, break it, hurt them. They cover up their self-loathing with self-regard, but it isn't hard to see, if you have to clean up after them. Why your mother gives me such fits. She wears her self-loathing on her sleeve, so something even nastier must lurk underneath, I don't wonder..."

Taking the sphere out of my hands, he wagered me a gold double eagle I couldn't see what was in the top display case, which was nearly five feet above the baseboard upon which I was perched by my toes. Laughing breathlessly at my comical efforts to wrench myself taller, he asked me how the giraffe got his long neck. Not quite through kindergarten and terrified of him, I said, "Stretching?"

"That only gets you so far, though..."

"Growing?"

"How fast can you grow?"

I strove even harder to grow, to no lasting effect, but he liked my antics enough to give me a prize, anyway. Reaching up onto the shelf, he took down a tiny tin, the size of a fuse kit, and put it in my hand.

I rattled it eagerly, thinking I'd gotten the coin and mother would be so proud, and our money troubles were over, but inside was only a single metallic pellet, leaden gray with a dull silverfish luster.

I think he believed that I, alone of all his descendants, would see the value of his one true treasure. "Nature hates us," he said, "because we know a better way." Showing me his hands as if I should be impressed and not terrified by them, he wiggled them and even then, I noticed how his pinky finger was longer and thicker and split off from his palms much lower than they should, so they looked like mirror thumbs.

For a short time, I was convinced that I'd been taken into a forbidden secret of the sorcery of adulthood. But it was not until the rest of the world had begun to die, perhaps not until it was too late, did I come to learn how hard it really is, to grow.

Just as even most westerners got their misunderstanding of how karma works from hippie pop songs, even the few scientifically literate among us in the last bright days seemed to get their grasp of genetic mutation from monster movies. Generally, radiation recomposes DNA in much the same way that rocks thrown at a stained glass window creates a new work of art. Any phenotypic changes resulting from this damage are passed on like karmic debt to the next life, and any useful mutation is like the proverbial hurricane in the junkyard assembling a working passenger jet.

That astronaut who returned from a thirty-month mission on the International Space Station, and had his DNA sequenced and compared to his identical twin... Besides the extensive chromosomal damage that almost insured any offspring he had would suffer untold genetic maladies, there were extensive stretches of introns—junk DNA—absent from his previously homologous sibling. Science journos speculated that the extra junk was inserted by viruses mutated by cosmic radiation, despite no such contamination being recorded on the ISS at the time.

What they didn't know, what they couldn't know, was that the bath of cosmic radiation had given the astronaut's genome the plasticity to begin to write itself according to the astronaut's deepest unspoken desire, to be unique. Given enough time, observers would record that the astronaut either succumbed to systemic cancer and died within weeks, or began to undergo massive phenotypical changes, radical gene therapy administered by the suppressed id, until the astronaut bore little outward resemblance to his secretly despised twin.

It would be lovely to know how the astronaut's story ends, but that was the year NOAA predicted mean sea levels would rise three feet in the next decade, and they went up almost four feet before Easter. Waves of migration from famine and plague-wracked equatorial regions accelerated a collapse almost insured by global economic and energy policies. Dirty bombs went off in D.C., Manhattan, L.A., Chicago, Phoenix, Seattle, with retaliatory missile attacks on conservative strongholds in the south.

Bathed in and melted down in the radiation of change, America chose cancer and death, and oblivion for the many mutant offspring stirring in its corpse.

⚬

I was seventeen and packing for college when my great-grandfather died. Mom and Dad sat at opposite ends of the auditorium-like office.

"I tender my most humble apologies for any culpability I might bear, in shaping you into what you have each become. Though I strove always to make you take responsibility for your respective flaws, yet, to my mind, it was always *I* who failed you; failed to instill in any of you the ambition to make your own marks upon the world, to shape it or to adapt to its adversities and so become more than a parasite upon your antecedents. Truly, I must have misjudged your mettle, and by extension, my own. I cannot condemn your respective failures, but no more can I reward them with the fortune that cost me so dearly, in the earning."

To no one's surprise, the financial assets were dispersed into a variety of charities, environmental causes and trusts. The sprawling estate went to my grandparents, who had always coveted it. Most of my great-grandfather's collections went to my aunts and uncles and cousins. The ivory went to my mother, who would find it impossible to sell legally, and who steadfastly refused to have any scientific tests done to find out what they were made of. Control of the family business went to my father, though in such a straitjacket of conditions that he was all but denied any income from it.

I had not expected anything, but I received my bequest from the attorney when my relatives had retired to their respective watering holes to curse the dead.

I was to receive an undisclosed sum held in trust for a period of twenty years, from which I would be allowed to draw an annual income of not more than two hundred thousand dollars, so long as I met the conditions.

The gray-faced attorney took my arm and stressed how emphatically my great-grandfather wanted me not only to receive this, his most precious gift, but to benefit from it, and grow. That was exactly what he said, in the same candied monotone with which he'd read the will.

But the conditions must be met. Was I still using the pill?

It was nothing less than a miracle. I reached into my pocket and showed him the tin pillcase from the old days of traveling patent medicine shows and snake-oil peddlers. The label was scuffed blank, but the embossed title of the product was still somewhat evident, when held up to the light. *Doctor Boniface's Perpetual Pill Of Antimony.*

Perhaps one of Great-Grand's cruel jokes, but I'd kept it, hid it from Mom, who would have angrily thrown it away. I kept it with those other things that acquire totemic significance in childhood, and I chanced upon it when I was getting dressed for the funeral, but I had not opened it.

The lawyer eyed the tin with a gravity I could not begin to appreciate at the time. Going to the sideboard, he filled a glass of ice water and brought it to me, waiting expectantly until I took it.

Inside, I found exactly what it said on the tin—a single, slightly imperfect sphere of lustrous silvery metal, exactly the size of a common garden pea. Cold and slightly tingly on my tongue, it went down without a hitch. The lawyer shook my hand, presented me with a pen to sign a contract I did not read, a bank passbook, and a handwritten journal.

I had, naturally, some vague idea of what it was. Though antimony was used in the Middle Ages as a murder weapon, it was believed quite efficacious as an irritant to move stubborn bowels. Until the Victorian era, such pills as I had just ingested were used to aid digestion by the suggestible and miserly, for the perpetual antimony pill was meant to pass unaffected through the guts, to be retrieved from a chamber pot and washed for reuse. An antiquarian's perverse curiosity, antimony pills were frequently passed down through generations.

Needless to say, I did not try it, not even after discovering the note secreted inside the tin.

Folded seventy-two times, the tiny, fussy handwriting must have been copied by hand from the document that originally accompanied this medical wonder of the boldly idiotic era when so many miracle health cures involved direct exposure to radiation.

As proven by the inheritance theories of Lamarck, the toil sowed by the specimen is reaped by the offspring. To this SCIENCE must be added what might otherwise seem magical, for the unique properties of the Perpetual Antimony Pill of Dr. H.W. Boniface, derived from a previously undiscovered isotope of pure antimony and its uniquely beneficial radiation, cleave to no known natural philosophy but their own.

Skeptical or not, so long as I continued to "use" the pill, I would not have to work. I resolved to humor them, even going so far as to use a bedpan and a magnet to retrieve it, but I had no luck finding it. I could not be blamed for losing it, so I confidently reported to my first annual physical with a ready explanation.

Imagine my surprise when the physician probed me with a wand that emitted a low, uneasy grumble as it passed over my abdominal region. He checked off a box indicating I was still using the pill, and impatiently told me that yes, that was a Geiger counter.

The nightmares that plagued me as a child abruptly returned. In them, I am wandering through Great-Grand's endless house, seeking to find or escape the source of the maddeningly intricate piano music, but I am not myself. Sometimes I am the crane, and the dream ends with the servant cutting off my head to retrieve the koi, only now it was the pill she sought.

But most times, I am the piano.

⸺ ⸰⸱⸰ ⸺

Like so many of my age, I began to do research on the topic only once it was inside me.

Dr. Boniface's Pill of Perpetual Antimony was one of the last wave of patent medicines to flourish before the Great Depression. The "previously undiscovered isotope of pure antimony" promised to destabilize the structure of genes, yoking their form and function to the motor of the individual will.

Never very popular, already an icky anachronism in the age of indoor flush toilets, the pill was removed from shelves soon after release when it was linked to several dozen deaths by cancer, mostly in the southeast. Dr. Boniface, if he ever existed, completely vanished, his lab a false name with a fake address. A class-action lawsuit, almost obligatory now, went unfiled, and in an era when factory workers still wet their brushes on their tongues to paint radium numbers on watch faces, many more deaths probably went unreported, or were not connected to the innocuous little gray pill.

I didn't know and never thought to ask if any of my relatives also received an antimony pill and a similar allowance, but I began to wonder two years later, when I woke up one morning and found myself the sole survivor of my great-grandfather's legacy.

One summer after inheriting it, my grandfather stroked out while battling the invasive Japanese knotweed, black mold and Chinese ailanthus that had overrun the property soon after Great-Grand's death. The expense crippled them, but my grandfather felt he'd won a war, and wouldn't be moved. Gran found him facedown in the backyard koi pond. All the fish were gone, and so were his eyes. Gran put the estate on the market, only to find the knotweed had undermined the whole foundation. The house was unsalable, so she got good and drunk and tried to burn it down in the middle of a thunderstorm, which took some gumption. She only destroyed the east wing, and she forgot to leave.

My father was killed in a dispute with a disgruntled trucker at the Wilmington depot. His autopsy showed he was riddled with cancer, so bad they gave up trying to figure out where it even originated. That he'd been living for years in a camper in an industrial dump site was tacitly avoided by everyone, but he was another head on Great-Grand's wall.

In a panic, Mother donated the ivory collection to one museum after another, only to have it refused without comment. Everyone told her to harden up, it was all in her mind. Turned out they were right. Inoperable brain tumor killed her eight months after my dad.

The first I heard of it was a call from the family lawyer, who had to remind me of the will reading, the last time we'd crossed paths. There was now the matter of, as he described it, the "terminal bequest." As the last named survivor in the will, I was entitled to claim the remaining financial estate out of the labyrinth of trusts in which Great-Grand had hidden the family wealth. There was only one outstanding criterion to be satisfied before the estate could be executed.

Was I still using the pill?

What a remarkable question. I almost answered reflexively in the negative, but caught myself. Not if I still possessed it, but if I was still *using* it... I told him that yes, of course, I never went anywhere without Great-Grand's trusty alimentary aid. Good, because they'd test me.

One could make a case that Great-Grand had murdered his family, that he had murdered me. For all I knew, the pill was still inside me, lodged or hiding somewhere and wreaking havoc on my chromosomes, or diffused into my mildly radioactive blood.

But one could also argue that he had never forced us to take his test, that he offered us the chance to grow, and the others had failed. Perhaps his perfidy would have become a scandal worthy of TV coverage, if the world did not also begin to die in earnest, that same summer.

I had inherited a ruin. My lawyers instructed me to have it razed and rebuilt, or simply to abandon it. Instead, I moved in and commenced excavating my family's hidden past.

My great-grandfather kept a journal, an account he no doubt expected would one day be made public as the world demanded the remarkable story of his family's ascendance beyond mere humanity.

A fiend for self-improvement, he consumed correspondence courses instead of sleeping, read every piece of inspirational crap that he could get from the library. "I have always believed," he grandly states in the conclusion, "that Man is a malleable animal, reshaped by a combination of chance and will from that of an animal. A man becomes what he says and does, but only by reduction. Only by will alone can he begin to become much more than a Man."

By fate or chance, he purchased and became a fanatical believer in Dr. Boniface's Pill of Perpetual Antimony. He didn't throw it out when the pill was withdrawn from the market, after the deaths. Because, as his journal blandly, exhaustively detailed, he was getting results.

He timed everything he did, and tried to do more of everything quicker, and noted progress in his reading speed and retention, ability to calculate and recall sums in his head, to remain underwater, to run around the block or across the city. Each day, he plotted goals to push himself, to stretch, to grow.

When he noted a vacuum in the waste disposal market and started his company, he became obsessed with environmental issues, things like lead poisoning, mercury, radon, but rather than invest his burgeoning profits in green technologies or conservancies, he began consuming lead, mercury and radon.

Stretching.

He noted that he experienced chronic "hurtful growths in my abdominal crevices," but developed the ability to expel them, much like a cat coughs up a hairball. But he also bragged of having his driver's license photo rejected by a traffic cop, so radically had his facial features changed.

But he lamented in his conclusion that he had not gone far enough, that his vanity had prevented him taking the experiment as far as he could. Perhaps someone less enamored of themselves, more hungry for essential transformation, might go further than he, and it was in that spirit that he commended his research to the reader.

By now, I had begun to keep a journal of my own. I tracked my diet and excreta with a minute fervor that would've shamed Howard Hughes. I used a Geiger counter to monitor the pill's presence in my body. Now, I was afraid of losing it, afraid that it would animate and actuate some deep seed of self-destruction in me before I could find my higher purpose.

Does it hinder this narrative that I have not described myself to you? I never thought of myself as the fat, plain person in the mirror, the sinusoidal monotone I heard on my voice memos. But what was I? Fish or crane, or just another cursed acquisition of a toxic family fortune bought with trash.

I could spend the apocalypse in relative comfort, working on my physique and learning the piano and generally becoming a perfect emblem of meaningless privilege, but there was no one left to tune it, and the world was dying.

We managed the Hanford contract when it was declared a Superfund site by the EPA, and then crowned the most toxic place in the western hemisphere by the media. I could wallow in my own hollow self-improvement, or I could try to give something back, and perhaps do more than heal what we'd destroyed. Perhaps I could give it the chance to grow.

It might seem as if I retreated here to surrender, to marinate, to die as far away as I could isolate myself. But nothing could be further from the truth. I came here to prepare for the battle of my life; to meditate, to vegetate, perhaps...but not to die alone, or even to become something unique.

I came here to be useful.

Eventually, they find their way to the bedroom, to the bathroom, to me.

While two knock over shelves looking for a wall safe and another ransacks the closets, the fourth comes in and sets down his rifle, unzips and uses my toilet, no doubt reveling in the novelty.

Then he sees me.

It's dark in here. The windows barely let in a trickle of crimson-stained light through the same algal growth everywhere outside. It fills the bathtub to the rim and spills over onto the sodden floor in thick, feathery red tufts that he takes in with utterly uncomprehending eyes. How could he know what he's seeing, even when he recognizes my vague outline nested in the depths of the overgrown tub. Only my nose breaks the stagnant surface, half scummed over with secondary growths. My breathing quickens, my nerves spark, my limbs spasm, sending waves of frigid river water over the gunwales of the tub.

The looter takes up his rifle and points it at me, fires, fumbles with the lever, fires again, backing towards the doorway and missing it, shouldering the door shut in its warped, waterlogged frame.

With one arm half torn away and a lung collapsing in a torrent of blood, I come staggering out of the tub not to attack or to surrender, but to prove something to myself that Mother was wrong.

Beauty rests not in the eye of the beholder. I am beautiful precisely because I make him sick to his stomach, fill him with the rage to destroy me, simply for existing in his rotting, moribund world. I am not this body, I silently tell him. He cannot comprehend my beauty, cannot begin to appreciate all the work that has gone into it. But he will.

He shoots me twice more, in the belly and the leg, because he's worried I'm still coming towards him. The others come running and set to with their weapons, chopping me down like a tree.

They are here because I needed them. To do this, to help me prove this to myself. I came as far as I could with Great-Grandfather's pill. My vanity persisted, though not nearly so much as his. I needed this to make me decide, what I am, what I will be.

They stand over me and speculate on what was wrong with me. The weed, they conclude, got into my brain and worked me like a puppet. That's the only explanation they can muster for the misfired flora-fauna hybrid growths blooming from my back, the thick stalks snaking away from my spine and down the drain. This, with particular nasty specificity, they make sure to sever, thinking they have done for me, whatever I am.

They come away from my attempted murder disappointed. The books and the cursed ivory collection are the only fortune I took from my ancestral home, and the premises are quite inundated with heavy metals, PCBs and low-level radiation. Already, they wheeze as they lace up their snowshoes. The first two to step out onto the bloom find it buoyant enough, but when the third joins them, he simply sinks out of sight.

The bloom closes over him, then takes the other two with greedy slurping sounds. Sucked under and entangled in prehensile vines, they thrash and scream bubbles in the icy depths like flies in a web. Perhaps, in the last moments before surrendering to the pressure and drawing in burning breaths of deoxygenated water, they behold the vastness of my new body—my true body—and find me beautiful.

The fourth, the one with the rifle, stands on the aft deck, looking out over the river, at the rippling waves of red weed contracting like a muscle.

He actually shoots at it, when it's too late to do anything else. As before, I admire his grit, his determination to die fighting. I close my grip on the houseboat and pull apart its rotted keel so it subsides like a bad soufflé into my embrace. The last of them screams for help, empties his gun and then gets off a flare before the houseboat sinks completely into the river.

Into me.

Now, there is no going back, if there ever was. I am one with the dead river. I am its new life. Free from the senses, the burdens of my old form, I can begin my work in earnest.

Great-Grand's work was never done because he missed the point.

His self-improvement was never complete not because he loved himself too much, but because he loved no one else. Nature doesn't hate us because we know a better way, but because we have refused to serve Her.

The toxins from the Hanford site flow through me like poisoned blood, and I filter them through the eccentric kingdom that is my glorious new body, where by molecular alchemy I transform them, shaving off protons and adding neutrons and releasing them into the water, into the land, into the life, into farms and into people tested and winnowed down to those with the will to adapt and survive, as a river of antimony.

They will stretch, will grow, into a new world, a better world. A world without us.

And I will be with them, running in their veins.

For I am a river to my people.

MONSTERS OF ANY KIND

DAVID J. SCHOW

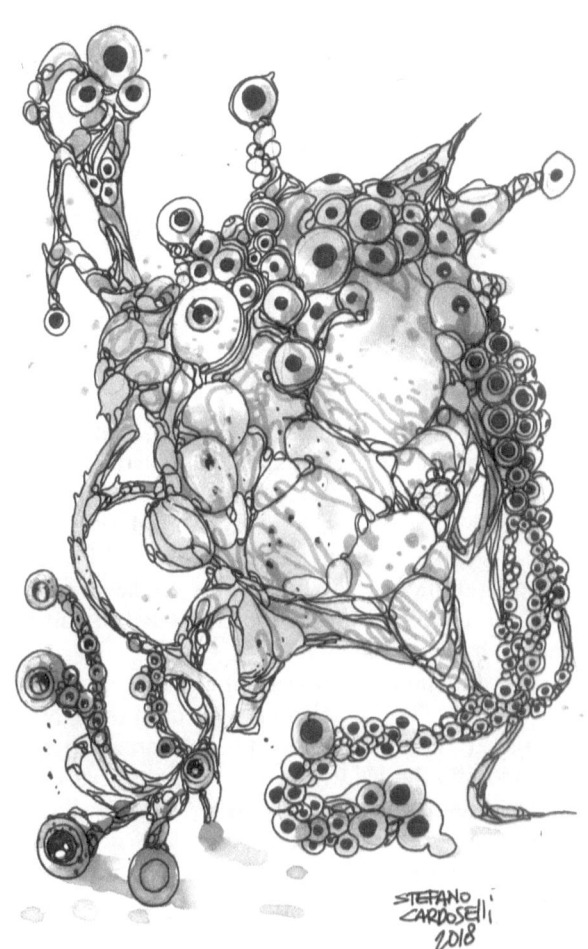

THE THING TOO HIDEOUS
TO DESCRIBE...
by DAVID J. SCHOW

...slapped a pseudopod across the SNOOZE button on Its alarm clock. It liked to be half-awake when midnight actually clicked over, so Its alarm was habitually set to 11:59 p.m. The blue glow of the numerals pleased It, reminded It of some of the biogenous hues It could produce in Its tentacled extremities when satisfied or amused, so It had appropriated the device during some predawn wander or other, from one of the townies who had been imbued in sufficient fear to abandon her bedroom in the middle of the night.

Its carapace was running red—glowing softly, from worry, taken to bed and slept on. It was not as young as It used to be (what on Earth *was?*); slithering to the sink was becoming a chore. It tried not to make the grunts and huffs the elderly use to punctuate every movement. It yawned wide instead, freeing a few flying insects who had invested sleeptime (Its own, not theirs) in the determined consumption of tartar flecks from Its back molars. The little monsters never drowned, they never suffocated, they were a nuisance, they were pestilent, riddled with germs, yet perfectly suited to their scavenging purpose.

Salve, for the burns. The Thing applied an herbal poultice to the gelid patches of still-healing flesh, repellently smooth and tender to the touch, like a bubo swollen with dead antibodies. Fire had purged detail from Its cratered brown exodermis, the way a child might use an eraser to obliterate portions of a photograph of the Moon's natural topography. It had lost a sucker from the tip of one of Its retractile protrusions. The wounds would scab thickly, then rearmor. They always did. Last night's close call had been nothing new.

Outside, the tarn beckoned. The Thing always felt better after a wakeup rinse and a bit of a roil in the sludge. It furled its feelers for the downhill roll, eyestalks whipping around and causing a roller coaster sort of dizziness. It flattened Itself to a glistening membrane on the surface of the brackish water, soaking up some lunar rays, and letting the tidal influences provide inspiration. When It rolled out, nearly all the water sluiced free. Its skin was not absorbent.

It was time to go find some teenagers.

Maysville was one of those antique, rural Kentucky bergs that rolled up the sidewalks promptly at dusk, and whose church steeple still constituted its highest structural elevation. The bell tower therein had been tolling the hour, and half hour, for more than fifty years without breakdown or incident. The church itself—alabaster, roofed in green shingles—glowered over the town square, where rustic benches and litter baskets were emplaced with the precision of chess pieces. The manicured, triangular greensward it faced was a sort of local picnic spot for those unimaginative enough to venture into the woods. It was near the business district at the intersection of Main and Center streets, where local merchants closed shop promptly at five in the afternoon.

At quitting time, the locals did familial rituals, talking ceaselessly about food or the weather, sitting on porches in rockers or swinging loveseats on creaking chains. Then they started drinking—most alarmingly, at a watering hole whose neon sign proclaimed it as BAR. If you telephoned the place, the proprietor, a burly ex-boxer with a buzzing, dysfunctional voice and only the vaguest grasp of the world beyond his batwing doors, would answer "Tommy's." The Thing had never called Tommy's; the Thing had no use for telephones, although It recognized that when one human or another grabbed one, it usually meant trouble.

Generally, the residents of Maysville kept to their homes (the better to service the exponential care and feeding of town gossip) and, at night, banded into drunken groups to hunt down the Thing once and for all. Maysville needed a monster, apparently, to rationalize its hidebound prejudices, its oddball religion, its social dynamic, and to unify the townsfolk against some common enemy...mostly so they did not tear each other apart.

The Thing Too Hideous to Describe did not know of any monsters in the vicinity; that was one of the reasons It had chosen the area for Its semiretirement. No werewolves or incubi, no demonic apparitions or defrocked Indian burial tracts. No real estate hauntings, no unspeakable, lowering molochs, and practically no children possessed by devils, although sometimes the Thing was not so sure. The kids here had inherited their progenitors' sense of superstitious paranoia and hidebound, inbred fear, and frequently they *acted* monstrously, but the Thing was capable of appreciating the difference. No real monsters...

...unless you counted the townsfolk, who got incredibly intolerant when they got liquored up at Tommy's. The formula was always the same: They complained, and drank, and groused, and drank, and started stamping their feet, while drinking some more, and before you could say *boo*, you had a gang of violent alcoholics storming up your nether port—drunk, deluded, waving torches and pointy farm implements, screaming with bloodlust in a democracy of madness and mob unreason.

There were already plenty of frightening things in the world, thought the Thing. Circus clowns, for example. Cartoonists and writers—creatures who invented the kind of lurid pulp that could inflame the basest frenzies of unthinking, potentially dangerous crowds. Such artisans of corruption sat in their high places, and distorted form, and made a mockery of all life, and did not care that their exploitative claptrap sank fear into the souls of the ignorant. The Thing had once seen a photograph of one of their minor gods. The portrait depicted some gloomy Gus, all hangdog and horrific and mostly hairless, his eyes broadcasting doom and cosmic apocalypse, hinting at a near-blasphemous tunnel vision that hated all it saw, and saw only that which could kindle the otherworldly passions resident in the fetid lobes of the man's dark and hateful brain.

The Thing Too Hideous to Describe spooked a couple of smooching high-schoolers, about a block from the town square, against a fence, behind some trees near the cemetery, where these nascent fornicators had assumed they might swap fluids and DNA unnoticed. It was a transient thrill. The humans emitted high, squealing noises and took clumsy flight, colliding with trees and each other in their haste to escape. That buoyed the spirits of the Thing only momentarily. Now the offspring would hurriedly report an extravagant exaggeration of what they had seen, amplifying the disgust factor to hide their own guilt in the shadow of the more sensational. Then the local authorities, the town leaders, and their parents would all use *that* as an excuse to partake of more abundantly available booze, and soon enough the whole process would culminate in smoking torches and riot behavior.

The mob would never cross the tarn, however—none of them would ever be that brave. There were too many hazards not governed by hysteria: bloodsuckers, quickmud, venomous reptiles; no streetlights or convenience markets. Beyond that, a treacherous maze of rocks and switchbacks, where precipitous heights waited to plummet the curious to broken-boned death on sharp rocks, or the lack of geographical benchmarks threatened starvation within a labyrinth. No, the mob would never manage to seek out the lair of the Thing Too Hideous to Describe, because indigenous legend had it that once you went in, you never came out.

Yet upon its return for lunch break, the Thing Too Hideous to Describe saw light. Human light, the artificial light of a battery-operated beam. Once, a group of besmocked know-it-alls in helicopters had buzzed unnervingly close, convinced that the Thing might be some sort of alien invader from another planet. They had given up and retreated to the safety of their grandiose theorizing. They always gave up, when it came to actually learning something. It was more profitable to fall back on whatever make-believe they were selling unwary consumers, this week.

Whoever had chanced upon the Thing's home did not look like a scientist, nor did he appear to be a representative of the military. He looked like a clerk. He was wearing a bulky down jacket and hiking boots. He wore spectacles and had a hairless face (the way humans scraped off their pelts had always made the Thing a bit queasy). It was comical to watch him feel around the edges of the nondescript cave that led down to the Thing's home. He did not appear repulsed by the slime coating the ingress. He sniffed it, from the tips of his gloves. His flashlight beam strayed wild again, as he consulted a big metal notebook he held crooked into one arm.

The Thing Too Hideous to Describe held steady and watched, as this Outsider—for that was definitely what the man was, not from around here—stiffened, the way humans always did when they felt there was some creepy lurker, monitoring them. Now would be an excellent opportunity to pull the old stalk-and-scare, making the guy look toward the most likely source of monsterishness, then drop tentacles down on him, from above. But before the Thing could indulge Itself, the flashlight ray crossed Its big, ebony orbs, causing a stab of pain like a migraine. Before the Thing could rally, the man-creature in the bulky coat spoke to It.

"Oh! Hi there...sorry, I hope I'm not intruding or anything..."

This struck the Thing as very odd. Usually, they ran away by now, or started shooting. Instead, this manling checked his book again—*a book! Another damned book! Oh, cursed item!* thought the Thing, steeling for the worst. But this did not appear to be a *book*-book, of the sort It reviled. No, it was a ring-binder sort of affair, its pages containing not hated text, and certainly not the most loathsome print of all, *fiction*, but graphs and charts.

And the man-creature was walking toward It, the tone of voice spewing from his mouth-hole not scared at all, but apologetic.

"Sorry to bother you, like I said, but my name is Steve Brackeen. I was going to leave you a note. Um...is this a bad time? I was hoping maybe we could talk a little..."

Worse, as the man-creature came closer to the Thing, his aura read decidedly cool, not a nimbus of red-hot fright or hatred. He pulled off one glove to expose his hand, that simian tool depending grotesquely from the end of his arm with its upsettingly snake-like five digits, pink and hairless. No slime.

It had been ages since the Thing Too Hideous to Describe had risked vocal contact with a human, and Its works seemed rusty. A lot of bug-infested mucus glopped out of Its face, plus bits of a turkey club sandwich It had enjoyed two days ago, but the man-creature broadcast no distress at this.

"I'm—I'm not a census taker or anything like that. I came here to talk to you, actually, if—if you think you could spare—"

He was flashing a laminated card that featured an inaccurate photograph of him, and his name, spelled out in modern English.

The Thing Too Hideous to Describe did not wish to shake hands with the man-creature, primarily because It disliked that sort of actual physical contact, but also because It had nothing a human could reasonably call a hand.

"Like I said, my name is—"

The Thing was perplexed. This was most assuredly outside the normal playbook. What could It do? It invited the guy inside.

—⁕—

"I'm a little grubby," said the man-creature named Steve. "You'll have to excuse that. This is a lot better than stomping all over Europe, lemme tell you." He spread a disposable paper towel over the glistening hump of rock near the Thing's firepit, then sat down, extending his booted leg appendages to compensate for the elevation of the rock. "Nice place. The fire is nice, too."

The Thing Too Hideous to Describe had to pause to ponder the word, one It had almost never heard. *Nice?*

"You know—homey. Anyway, I've been working on this big doctoral thesis. That's what all this hoodoo in the notebook is about. I've been documenting the weird crowd behavior of group insanity in small, isolated towns and villages, you know—the kind of places the world always seems to pass by? And some of the stuff I found out is pretty upsetting. Like in the Black Forest—rampant alcoholism, leading to berserk, antisocial group action. Apparently a lot of those villagers have nothing better to do with their time than invent wild stories about their betters, and use those stories to justify blowing up every castle in a hundred-mile radius. No, sir or madame, your hamlet is not being victimized by one of your own retarded halfwits…it must be a *vampire!* That's the way these kooks think. No, your cemeteries aren't being vandalized by teen punks or necrophiles…it must be that mean old professor up on the hill, who has more money and pedigree than you could ever imagine, why, he must be *stitching all those corpses together to make a big stupid monster,* yeah, that *must* be it!"

The Thing Too Hideous to Describe was forced to concur. Humans almost never behaved logically, or compassionately. They did bray a lot about tolerance, which exercise for their vocal cords was probably more economical than actual practice.

"I mean, you've seen some of those movies, right?" said the Steve-creature. "Who really makes out, every time the besotted Burgomeister decides, you know, to blow up another dam? Local contractors, funeral directors, hardware stores, the makers of pitchforks and rope, gun dealers and the distributors of ammunition, hell…monsters are great for their economy. They all get shitfaced at the inn until they're fizzed enough to see monsters, then they start grabbing for the dynamite. And who do you think gets first crack at developing the destroyed real estate? I mean, *where's the real problem,* here?"

The Thing Too Hideous to Describe had to nod in agreement, at that one.

"I guess the fundamental question is: What are these imbeciles smoking…and where can I get some?" The Steve-creature cracked a smile that bisected his misshapen round face into a leer, showing teeth. "Did you hear about the lunatics running the asylum over in Mapleton, USA? They think they're plagued by some mummy guy who crawls out of a bog every quarter-century or so to pick on the descendants of some heat-stroked, hallucinating Egyptologist who drank himself into a coronary before the Second World War! I mean, accounts vary, but the story stays the same: These people refuse to accept responsibility for their own lives. Nah, we were all abject failures in life because we were *cursed by monsters,* not because we're all so inebriated all the time we can barely tie our shoes!"

The Steve-creature flipped open his notebook. The Thing Too Hideous to Describe leaned forward to peruse the data in better light.

"See here? No matter how many times they wipe out these supposed monsters, those monsters always come back, even if they're, you know, utterly purged from the planet. See? It allows for the maintenance of a consistent level of mass psychosis. Pretty soon, your toilet doesn't flush, and voila—it must be the Mad Doktor's fault, or some monster that conveniently runs contrary to whatever religious derangement governs the town. Not only does it maintain the status quo and help the local economy, but it severely limits the employment opportunities for bona fide monsters. Look at this graph—see? Monster jobs and mean income level, down every year. I'm thinking of presenting some of my findings to Affirmative Action."

The Thing Too Hideous to Describe flipped to another page of facts and figures, using one of Its secondary pseudopods, the stumpy, more articulate ones. Yes, the bald information in black and white certainly seemed conclusive enough.

The Steve-creature reached into his shoulder bag. *Here it comes,* thought the Thing. *It's a trap. He's going to whip out a weapon and try to bushwhack me. Or worse, this has all been a setup, and he's going to try to sell me something.*

No, it was merely a little tape recorder.

"I just want to get some of your thoughts," said Steve. "Your angle on the whole phenomenon, and maybe ask you a few questions about your relationship with the population of Maysville, if that's not too intrusive or presumptuous of me. You'll be speaking on behalf of a very broad monster demographic—what you say may affect hundreds of others in the same position as yourself."

The Thing's eyes blinked in incomprehension, fluttering at the ends of their stalks. Not only had It not anticipated company, but there was nothing around that could qualify as refreshment, especially for this iron-blooded, bipedal air-breather. It sighed, making a congested, bubbly sound. It really needed to work on Its hosting skills.

Ominously pleasant, this talk in the dark. An exchange of ideas, seductive in its invitation...and almost promising some manner of betrayal as the final course. But I can smell human lies, the way I can sense deceit hidden beneath their too-thin, fragile skins. This one is compassionate and educated. If they were all like this one, never would I have to salve burns from the night before. If they were all like this one, the structure of our universe would not exist. I kind of like him.

But holy Peter, is he ugly! That jackstraw corpus, with its gangly, meatless limbs. Only two eyes, both the limpid color of poison. The rictus mouth with its nasty, square teeth. The absolute wrongness of his geometry brands him as an abomination, something the sane gaze instinctually rejects from view. I think that, were our stations reversed, I might derive pleasure from his extinction. I hope not, for that would make us both, as races, equally uncivilized.

Commotion, in the calm of night. The Thing Too Hideous to Describe was accustomed to such uproar, but this night, It was not the catalyst.

The Thing scuttled up a high tree in the woods and spread his pods out, spider-like, for stability. From here, Its vision, tuned to nonhuman frequencies, could perfectly make out, from this distance, the church steeple and town square. The *sounds* were familiar—inebriated raving, the crackle of firebrands, the hyperactive jostle of sweaty bodies lusting for a kill. All the trappings of a conventional Maysville monster hunt, with their preferred monster as absentee.

A large phone-pole crucifix jutted from a pyre of smashed furniture, the kindling provided by the rent bodies of those few books in town that had not been banned or burned already. Spiked to the pole, his wrists and throat engirded by barbed wire, was the Steve-creature, the human who had called himself Brackeen. The goodfolk of Maysville pelted him with rotten fruit and broken glass, from the bottles they had drained. His shredded notebook was utilized to ignite the fire. The lynch chaos of Maysville's drunken residents would not be denied.

He had been found out. He had ventured into the town to do interviews and take notes, and the innkeeper had poked into his guest's luggage, or, more likely, someone had just peered over his shoulder at an opportune moment. He had been damned by his own research. Maysville, ever on the lookout for mutants, would obliterate any aberration...especially when they could find no other one to torment.

The Steve-creature hollered in protest, at first. Then screamed curses. Then, merely screamed, before he fell silent and continued to cook. His unholy book was consumed by righteous fire. His head sagged and his hair vanished in a puff of greasy smoke.

The Thing Too Hideous to Describe averted Its gaze, with something like pity. They were not all alike, these humans. The Steve-creature had resembled those executing him (hell, they all looked alike anyway), but in no way was he the same as them.

With a measure of melancholy, the Thing Too Hideous to Describe slithered down from the tree and trundled wearily homeward. Tomorrow night, It really should sortie into town, to do what It did best, but It knew the task would come without verve or enthusiasm.

The human conceit of vengeance, however, might be adapted to fruitful use, on some other midnight, soon to come.

MONSTERS OF ANY KIND

JESS LANDRY

SILT & BONE
by JESS LANDRY

Empty-handed, Sergeant Michelle Seaton exited the last house on Heritage Lane. She let the old screen door swing shut behind her as she stepped out under the shelter of the roofed porch, one that had seen better days. Seaton took a deep breath, like all the books had told her to do when she felt that feeling rising inside her, and let it fill her lungs. She imagined it coursing through her body, forcing itself down through her throat, digging itself into the very tips of her fingers. She felt it touch her toes, though they were still soaked to the bone from the floodwaters that threatened Split Lake. Her hometown. The one she'd left all those years ago. The one she was in charge of evacuating.

You're right where you need to be, she thought, remembering how she'd poured through those books, highlighting and tagging all the lines that kept her sane. *Every day is a gift, remember that.*

A gift. She patted her damp clothes, in search of her own gift, and got lucky with the somewhat dry pack of smokes in her back pocket. She lit the cigarette and leaned against the grainy wood siding of the house, letting her head fall back. The rain pounded rhythmically on the tattered shingles above her. It didn't bother her much—she liked the rain, how it washed away anything in its path, even stains from the night before. Split Lake was a ghost town, but a few clicks north, Crossland still had civilization. And a liquor store.

How many houses had she been in over the past two days? Fifty? One hundred? She'd lost count after what seemed like the millionth winding gravel road, the same road that led to the same peeling white farmhouse, the same peeling farmhouse whose owners had left it all behind when the rain hadn't stopped after the twelfth day. The only thing missing from each and every house, aside from some clothes, were the crucifixes hung on the walls.

At first, Seaton tried to salvage what she could—collecting family photos off the floors, carefully placing them above countertops or on second floors in a bid to keep the water from ruining them. But memory after memory had been left behind with not a care in the world. *If they don't give a shit, why should I?* crossed her mind more than once. It wasn't like the water had come out of nowhere—it'd taken ten days for the Wapusk River to spill its banks, plenty of time for people to gather their things and be on their way. But no one seemed to be in a rush then. Only when the water seeped its way over the roads did they start to notice. Still, in the odd house, she found herself picking up family photos and placing them out of the water's reach.

Soon this house would be just like the photos left behind—a water-stained memory with nothing left to salvage.

A gunshot shattered the quiet; Seaton took another puff of her smoke.

Constable Kangee Brown emerged from the nearby barn, holstering his firearm. He waded over to Seaton, the water past his ankles, the ripples lapping dangerously close to the porch.

They were all that remained of the Split Lake branch of the Royal Canadian Mounted Police. The day everyone realized that the rain wasn't going to end, when they hugged their children and told them it would be okay, when they gave their pets a quick scratch behind the ear and drove off without them, that was the day Seaton pulled into work and saw Brown sitting in a sea of empty desks with a photo of his wife and son in his hands. The others in the precinct had run off to Crossland, where it was drier than the desert, where they didn't have to risk their own asses to save the people they'd sworn to protect. Brown had sent his wife and kid there, too. Told them he wouldn't be longer than a few days. Off they'd gone, his boy giving him a smile from the backseat, his wife watching him through the rearview mirror.

"So?" Seaton asked as Brown stepped onto the porch, shaking the water from his boots.

"Few cows were already gone," he said. "But whoever lived here had time to tie them all up low. I mean, real low. They couldn't stand, except one. She managed to stretch her rope out but sliced her neck open. She was bleeding out."

Seaton nodded, watching Brown as his gaze lost itself in the rippling floodwaters. His dark features, usually full of vigor, seemed dull.

"You did the right thing, Brown," Seaton said, hoping her words gave him some reassurance. "Let's move out before we can't drive through this anymore."

Brown stepped off the porch and headed for the cruiser, wiping his hands on his wet uniform. Seaton smoothed out her tight brown hair and placed her hat securely on her head. She pulled the dying can of spray paint from her utility belt and gave it a good shake. *One more down, only a handful to go.* The bright orange acrylic coughed out just enough to cover the front door of the house with an X.

<hr />

If there was one thing Seaton had taken away from the past twenty years, it was that time was not on her side. It never had been. The two cops rode in silence; Brown kept his face away from Seaton, staring out the passenger-side window. A wave of relief washed over her when the road veered left into a treed area, a dead-end ahead, and a roof peeking out from the greenery. *Last house in this area.*

As the cruiser plowed through potholes and rising waters, Seaton eyed the photo of her daughter that twirled from her rearview mirror. Chelsea, grinning at an unwrapped Christmas present, the multicoloured holiday lights behind her. Not even her one-lick-too-long bangs could mask the pure joy in her almond-shaped eyes. And Seaton behind her, smiling, a younger version of the old skin that looked back at her every morning, gazing at her child like mothers were supposed to. The fire rose inside Seaton then, the flames licking her guts, boiling her blood. She looked away from the photo, focused on the road, and took a deep breath.

I'm right where I need to be, she thought as they pulled into the last house on Valour Road. *Every day is a fucking gift.*

A two-storey Victorian rose from gravel like a tombstone. From the look of it, the house had once been white; traces of its former colour lingered behind the earth-stained wooden façade. The large double doors that led into the home swung in the breeze, carelessly left open. The windows were long broken, the surrounding trees had taken to growing in and out of them. Giant oaks loomed over the house forming a canopy from the rain, their roots protruding from the mud. The house stood on higher ground, the floodwaters inching closer and closer. Farther back, the trees gave way to a decrepit barn that had already succumbed to the water—it lay on its side, bits of the roof collapsed into the waters below.

"Let's make this fast," Seaton said to Brown.

"Yeah," Brown replied, leaning forward to fully appreciate the view. "And by the looks of it, no one's lived here for a long time. This'll be quick."

"Take the barn again," Seaton said, eying the house. "Guaranteed there's no surprises left in there."

"Yes, Sergeant," Brown said, exiting the car.

Chelsea's picture rocked back and forth from Brown closing the door. Seaton reached out to stop it with both hands, keeping the photo pressed between her fingers for longer than she meant.

<hr/>

"Royal Canadian Mounted Police, anyone home?" Seaton knocked against the door's frame and waited for an answer. When none came, she announced herself once more as she stepped in.

She stood in what was once a living room. Much like the exterior, hints of the house's former self were buried underneath years of wear and neglect. The wallpaper wilted like dying flowers. Roots sprouted from the fireplace, covering its intricate brickwork like a vine. The stink of musty earth lingered no matter which direction she walked. Brown was right—no one *had* lived here in a long time.

Beyond the living room sat the kitchen; to Seaton's right, a staircase leading up, the carpet permanently stained with God-knows-what; on the side of the staircase, a small door Seaton assumed led to the basement.

Seaton removed her hat and headed to the kitchen. The back door swung in the breeze, carrying with it the earthy stench of decay.

"RCMP, we need to evacuate immediately," she said, her wet, heavy footsteps weighing down the old floorboards. Seaton walked over to the back door and secured it against the hard breeze. Still, the wind found its way in through the only window in the kitchen, its glass shards on the counter below.

Seaton placed her hat near the sink and looked out the window. The trees practically stood side by side, rising from the floodwaters like they had just sprung to life. A tire swing hung off one tree, its rope lost in the thicket of branches above. Chelsea would've loved it. She had always been the first to run off and play. Seaton imagined Chelsea there in the green dress she'd sewn for her, a mess of fabrics and jagged edges.

I love it, Mama, Chelsea had said the first time she saw it. She'd worn it every day for an entire summer. Her laughter floated by Seaton's ears as though Chelsea were here with her now.

Maybe it could've worked here, once. But it was too late for that now. *What's done is done. I'm right where I need to be.* She breathed deep, because that was all she could do.

The floorboards creaked behind her. Seaton turned her head back.

A little girl—no more than nine—stood quietly; her wide eyes on Seaton.

Before Seaton could utter a word, the little girl bolted.

"Wait!" Seaton exclaimed, giving chase as the child ran up the stairs. She took the steps two at a time, trying not to lose sight of the girl, but the girl was small and fast. She ran into the last room on the left, slamming the door behind her. Seaton followed suit.

The door creaked as Seaton slowly opened it. The room had two windows—a large one that shone onto the wall closest to Seaton. Under the dark tree canopy, she could make out a name written over and over in an uneasy hand: Izabella.

A branch had grown through the other window at the far corner. It withered towards the floor, rainwater travelling down its limb and through its leaves, dropping onto the decaying hardwood. Hidden underneath the makeshift awning, the little girl cowered, her knees pulled to her face.

Seaton approached the girl cautiously, her footsteps feeling heavier the closer she crept. She got into a crouch position a few feet away as the child watched her with wide, dark eyes. Long black hair stuck to her face, her skeletal frame jutted out from the torn dress she wore, thick with mud just like the rest of her, her bare feet stained black.

"Hey, it's all right," Seaton said in the voice she had used to soothe Chelsea whenever she'd been frightened. It felt foreign on her lips. "My name's Michelle. Are you Izabella?"

The little girl wedged herself deeper into the corner, trying to meld into the walls.

"It's okay, I'm not here to hurt you. I'm a police officer, see?" Seaton pointed to the insignia on her arm. The girl's wide eyes shifted from Seaton's face to her arm to the door. "I'm here to help."

"Help?" The child's voice was tiny, fragile.

"That's right, help," Seaton said, smiling, slowly moving closer. "Is there anyone here with you? Your mommy or daddy?"

In the distance, a gunshot cracked through the rain. As Seaton's eyes automatically went to the direction of the sound, the little girl took her chance, darting past Seaton and out the door.

"Izabella! Wait!"

Seaton took off after her. By the time she reached the stairs, the girl was already on the first floor. Seaton leaned over the flimsy railing and watched the girl run into the basement, slamming the door behind her. The rail vibrated in Seaton's hands. She pulled her radio out of her belt when she reached the bottom step and went for the basement.

"Brown? Over."

Static.

"Brown, copy? Over."

Nothing.

"Kangee, if you can hear me, there's a young female in the house, approximately seven years of age. She ran into the basement, I'm in pursuit. Over."

Without waiting for an answer, she holstered her radio and opened the door.

Seaton gagged as the stink from earlier hit her square in the face. She pulled a flashlight from her belt and descended.

"Izabella?"

Seaton swept the flashlight beam around the room as she stepped into the centre of the basement and into a few inches of water collected on the floor. The walls had started to droop inwards under the pressure, though the problem had been addressed at some point— metal beams had been fastened vertically to try and keep the house from swallowing itself whole. But one bar had already come loose, and every drop of water that worked its way in threatened to bring it all down.

"Izabella!" Seaton shouted. "It's not safe here, we need to leave."

A noise from behind Seaton made her spin around. Out of instinct, her free hand found the butt of her firearm. The light found its way to the far wall behind the stairs.

A hole large enough for someone to crawl through met her light. The brick foundation had been chipped away around its diameter— jagged pieces lined the hole's entrance like a shark's mouth—and led into a tunnel. The roots from the trees above had found their way into the walls of the tunnel, of the house, of it all. They poked through the dirt-lined tunnel like fat worms.

Seaton stepped towards the hole, eyes watering from the stench, as she moved her light in to see how far the tunnel went.

Staring back at her was Izabella. The girl was on all fours, her pupils aglow in the flare.

"Hey, I have an idea," Seaton said, bringing her calm tone back. "Why don't we go play on your swing outside? I can push you really, really high. What do you say, Izabella?"

She had pushed Chelsea on a swing set, once. It'd been a few years after she'd lost her to Child and Family Services, when she'd finally started to get her life back on track. Seaton had been granted once-a-week visitation, and she made sure to take advantage of every moment, every memory. They'd walked to the park by her foster parents' house, a place in the nice area of town, the rustle of the fall leaves the only sound around them. Chelsea sat on the swing, her feet nearly scraping the tiny rocks below. Seaton had pushed her from behind while Chelsea stared ahead, her hands wrapped tightly around the swing chains.

Seaton reached her free hand out to Izabella. The little girl stared back, dropping her shoulders slightly. She appeared to be studying her, as though she'd been a witness to the same memory. Seaton heard something *plop* into the water behind her. Her eyes moved away from the girl for a split second. Time was running out.

Izabella took off down the tunnel. And without hesitation, Seaton crawled in after her.

The farther she crawled, the more twists and turns the tunnel led her down. She had lost all sight of Izabella, her light only illuminating a few feet ahead of her. Seaton's chest tightened, the tunnel getting smaller and smaller as she crawled deeper and deeper. The sharp tree roots cut into her skin, opening fresh wounds stung by dirt and sludge. She pressed on, though her knees popped and ached, and the hole shrunk to the size of her body. She wouldn't be the one to leave a child behind. She had done it once before. Never again.

Finally, the darkness ahead faded. Seaton turned one more corner and saw the promise of light. Her body numb, she dragged herself along the last stretch until she came to the end of the tunnel.

With a final heave, Seaton thrusted herself out of the narrow tunnel, tumbling into the cold, knee-deep water below.

She scrambled against the wall, chest heaving, limbs aching. She had fallen into an earthy circular chamber, the walls constructed of mud and roots. Water cascaded from a hole in the ceiling, spilling into the pool around her; the only source of daylight fought to make its presence known through the same opening as the water.

Izabella stood on a large pedestal at the centre of the chamber that looked to be a sawed-down oak; soaked from head to toe. In the light that emanated from somewhere above, she looked even thinner than Seaton realized. The water had washed away the dirt from her skin, she now appeared pale and sickly—the girl was a tiny bag of flesh and bone. Her hair clung to her head.

Beside her, what seemed to be a throne of branches and mud had been constructed. The twigs spread in every direction behind the chair like a thousand arms reaching out to the walls. Growths of moss and cobwebs littered the branches, the falling water wiping some of them away into the rising water.

On the throne sat a motionless woman who looked as though she'd been carved from a birch tree. Her delicate features and ashen skin shimmered in the struggling light; dark, horizontal lines and black knots speckled every inch of her visible surface, even her eyelids. Roots spilled from her head: five long, thick stems that thinned out as they joined the mosaic of branches behind her. Her arms lay on the armrests, strangely human yet twisted like intertwining branches, leading to slender fingers that extended into thin twigs sharp enough to slice through skin and bone. Her forehead extended past that of a human's, ending in a ragged, broken trunk—a crown of flesh and bark. A burlap robe lay across her body, the fabric eaten away by time; its hem resting at the pedestal's edge, nearly touching the dirty water that lapped at her feet.

Seaton willed herself to move, to grab the little girl and get out of there, but her momentum was gone. She shivered in the rising water.

Are you still where you're meant to be?

"P-please," Izabella stuttered, her body shaking. "Help."

Her eyes darted from Seaton to the woman. Izabella tugged on the woman's hand but it wouldn't budge.

"Help."

Seaton felt something in her guts, the fire inside climbing through her body. She took a deep breath in, just like the books had told her to do.

I'm right where I need to be, she thought.

Seaton stood up, forcing the weight of the water off her. She approached the throne and noticed all the roots were interconnected. How could she get the woman out of this flooding chamber? Seaton tried to get a hand underneath her to lift her off the chair but something was blocking. She then tried to get a hand behind the woman's back, and able to wiggle a few fingers in. Seaton pulled and pulled, but the woman did not budge. Izabella watched, keeping her hands against the woman's.

Just then a sharp pain stung Seaton's finger and she pulled back in alarm. Blood poured from her finger around the spot where a large splinter had pierced her skin.

The woman's eyes shot open.

Seaton lost her footing, falling back into the water. At that moment, the whole room came alive. The roots lining the walls pulsated, sending shockwaves through the water trickling down them. The walls themselves shuddered, shaking off loose chunks of damp earth. The hole above collapsed, sending a massive tide of water into the chamber but allowing more daylight to seep through.

Like a statue coming to life, the woman trembled, shaking off her body what had to be centuries of dust and earth. She rose from her throne, the mosaic of roots and branches behind her stirring to life, working her upwards like a marionette on strings. The draped fabric fell off her to expose her inner workings—the shape of a woman's body but no skin to mask what lay inside. Black, decaying roots slithered where organs should have been, wet and sliding up and under her birch limbs. Instead, where the skin should have covered her, a black edging circled as though she'd been stricken by a flesh-eating disease. She rose high into the air and her throne followed suit, dismantling itself into spider-like limbs. The branches twitched and groped at the air around them like a newborn child exploring the world around them for the first time.

Seaton waded backwards, stumbling through the rising water that was now up to her chin, keeping her gaze on the woman.

Izabella screamed, the walls coming down dangerously close to her. Seaton rushed to the girl's side, but the woman took notice of Seaton, and four slithering branches suddenly lunged at her. They grabbed hold of Seaton's wrists and ankles, lifting her out of the water like a rag doll. Seaton dangled in the air, splayed like the Vitruvian Man, as the woman brought her closer.

The smell of rotted earth stung Seaton's eyes. Through her wincing, she came face-to-face with the woman. Her eyes were two dark knots that caved inwards, revealing an equally dark interior. The woman blinked with heavy eyelids, a dim life somewhere inside.

The woman cocked her head to one side, a guttural clicking sound resounding from her open mouth; there was something bestial, something prehistoric hidden in it. Her breath was hot against Seaton's cheek, her mouth lined with jagged spikes of wood.

Seaton didn't try to struggle. She couldn't. The roots were wrapped around her limbs too tightly, their splinters penetrating her skin.

"I'm here to help," she said in her calmest voice. "Help."

The woman cocked her head to the other side like a curious dog.

"I'm not here to hurt you."

The woman stared at Seaton for a moment, the same contemplative look Izabella had given her in the tunnel. But then the woman let out a high-pitched screech, unhinging her jaw wide enough to swallow Seaton whole. Sharp branches rose up behind the woman like the quills of a porcupine, their tips glossy from the water. She aimed them at Seaton's face, scowling at her.

"Help! Help!" Izabella shouted below, tugging on the woman's roots.

"Help." Seaton coughed, the grip from the branches cutting off her circulation.

Suddenly, a large chunk of the earth above came loose, sending all its weight down upon the woman. She came cascading down, her roots and webs failing her. Seaton dropped into the water as the woman collapsed onto her pedestal.

As the woman lay there, the roots connecting the room to her body began snapping off from the walls, withering like dying insects.

Izabella threw her little body over the woman, wrapping her arms around her. The floodwaters spilled over the pedestal, following an invisible path until it reached the woman's lifeless face.

"Help," Izabella said between sobs, the water ready to swallow her whole.

In that moment, all Seaton could see was Chelsea's face the day she'd lost her: the tears, the hands grasping at something that wouldn't grasp back, the look of utter confusion as she'd been taken away from a mother that couldn't even raise her head off the pillow. A mother, a selfish drunk who'd thought time was on her side, who'd thought her daughter would forgive her when she had finally cleaned herself up. But the ice in Chelsea's eyes during every scheduled visit had told Seaton all she needed to know: she wasn't a mother. Not anymore.

She'd failed Chelsea. She wouldn't fail Izabella.

As the water engulfed everything in its wake, Seaton swam to the child, tearing her from her mother's lifeless body, wrapping the girl's arms around her.

"I need you to trust me," Seaton said, and for once, the words felt right.

The little girl nodded, burrowing her head into Seaton's chest. And as the walls collapsed around them, Seaton wrapped her own arms around the shaking child and let the water carry them to higher ground.

The rain was lighter now; it tapped gently against Seaton's wet uniform as she wrapped a blanket around Izabella's shaking body.

"I'll be right back," Seaton said, closing the car door, the floodwaters lapping against the cruiser's wheels. The little girl with the wide eyes said nothing, but brought her legs to her chin and looked down.

Seaton made her way out to the barn, calling Brown's name, the water past her knees. The barn door lay slightly ajar, just enough for Seaton to squeeze through.

The barn had been on its side for some time, its beams ready to snap. The grey shadow of the day found its way in through the holes in the roof, lighting up areas like slivered spotlights.

"Kangee!" Seaton cried out, pressing her legs against the force of the water.

The trees had found their way into the barn, their roots poking in and out of the water, lacing their fingers through the crooked and dilapidated walls.

Something pulled against Seaton's soaked pant leg.

She turned and saw Brown floating in and out of the spotlights. His head lay faceup to the sky. Long wooden slivers stuck out of his chest.

She reached down and put two fingers on his neck.

Suddenly, Brown's body lurched forward, his lungs begging for air. His eyes widened and shot to Seaton.

She watched in horror as the water lapped over him, spilling into his body through the holes in his chest. He glared at Seaton and gasped for air; a low, guttural sound that stirred something inside Seaton. She unholstered her weapon and clicked the safety off.

Brown gasped again and looked away, up to the sky.

When Seaton returned to the cruiser, Izabella had grabbed hold of Chelsea's picture.

"Pretty," Izabella said, pointing to the picture and looking at Seaton.

Seaton smiled, sweeping a strand of wet hair out of the little girl's eyes.

She started the car and turned it around, watching the house disappear down the twisted driveway, carefully driving them off Valour Road, or what remained of it.

They finally came to the paved highway at a four-way stop. Seaton stopped the car, her foot heavy on the brake.

She looked right.

Where are we going?

She looked left.

What are we going to do?

A little hand found its way to Seaton's and squeezed.

She leaned back onto her seat and took a deep breath.

I'm right where I need to be, Seaton thought as she squeezed the rough little hand, and the rain picked up once more.

MONSTERS OF ANY KIND

LUCY TAYLOR

SUCKLINGS

by LUCY TAYLOR

The earthquake just after two in the morning almost rattled me out of the bed and knocked a picture of Coracita onto the floor as I got up and rushed to her crib. From the t.v. room, I could hear Ma cussing (her bottle of Rolling Rock had tipped over as she snoozed in the recliner and spilled into her lap). A minute later, Freddie, my fourteen-year-old brother, banged up the stairs and stuck his head in the door to ask if the baby and I were okay. When I told him she'd slept through it all, he laughed and said, "She's a toughie, my niece." We were all used to earthquakes by then. A gift from the frackers over in the oil fields south of Farmington. Like my six-month-old daughter Coracita, we Yazzies were all toughies.

So we thought.

The terror didn't begin until two days later when Milly Tso was taking a smoke break behind the Shop N Save and discovered a pair of severed arms in the ditch behind the store. Still in their grey sweatshirt sleeves, she said, with shattered bones and strings of sinew protruding where they'd been chewed or chopped at the elbows. Folks speculated all kinds of crazy shit—coyotes savaging a corpse or cartel members taking revenge on a snitch, but either way, why just the arms? Who did they belong to? And where was the rest of the body?

"Ben says the vic was alive when his arms were cut off," said Ma, who gets her pillow talk mixed with local crime updates from retired rez cop Ben Hernandez.

Freddie looked up from his iPhone. "What else Ben got to say?"

Ma was too busy to answer. She used to be a short-order cook in Gallup and her kitchen style reflects it: eggs sunnyside up and scrambled, hash browns and bacon all sizzling an inch deep in oil in one giant pan.

Freddie frowned at the food she spatula'd on his plate. "Kids on facebook are saying one of the arms had a tat of a cobra wrapped around an M16." His voice, one part man to two parts boy, broke on the final syllable, but I didn't smile. I'd seen a tattoo like that myself and knew it belonged to Cisco Pernell, the Desert Storm vet and vagabond who often camped at the old Toomey Mine.

"People on facebook make up all kinds of damned foolishness," I said, coaxing another spoonful of pureed carrots into Coralita's mouth.

Hard enough for Freddie to focus on his classes at Farmington High, without thinking about his old buddy Pernell minus his flute-playing fingers and boxcar-grabbing arms.

"Shit, what if it *is* Pernell?" Freddy said. "He don't have no cell. I better check out the mine, make sure he's ok."

"Only place you got to check out is that school bus," said Ma, flipping bacon strips onto our plates.

Freddie looked at his food like it had tire tracks down the middle. "Can a person live with his arms chopped off?"

Forks and spoons clattered. No one said anything.

Freddie scraped back his chair, kissed the dark fuzz on top of Coralita's head. "I'm out'a

here."

I finished feeding Coralita, handed her to Ma, and headed out to my Tundra. Kept thinking about Pernell, hoping it wasn't his arms Milly found. A few months back, he'd caught Freddie getting shitfaced out at the mine, kicked his ass and rode him the riot act about where booze can lead, and brought him home on the back of his Fat Boy. So naturally, I had a soft spot in my heart for old Pernell.

Ma followed me out to my Tundra. "Thought you said you don't start work until ten today."

Shit. It's damned true what they say—if you can't keep track of your lies, you shouldn't be telling them. "Changed it back again," I said.

Ma's almond eyes narrowed. "Whatever. Just don't be taking no detours where you shouldn't ought'a go."

"What? You think I'm on a rescue mission to hunt down Pernell?"

She snorted. "Don't play me for a fool, Lena. I'm talking about that woman. Just don't you go visiting that woman."

I told her I had no such thing in mind, then drove to the Target in Farmington where I worked in the deli, passed on by, and headed toward my real destination.

That woman, of course.

Graciela.

Graciela lived out in the boonies like us, but south of Farmington, on 371 toward the Bisti Badlands. She tended bar at La Casita de Mi Abuelo by night and did her pottery work during the day. When we were together, she always wanted to teach me how to throw pots on the wheel, but I never did try to learn. At the end, she said that applied to a lot of things.

Her forty-year-old adobe casita squatted at the end of a red dirt road lined with crazy-armed cactuses and holycross cholla that played hell with my allergies even in winter. I started sneezing as soon as I got out of the truck.

I could see her through the front window as I hurried up the walk. She had a fire going in the kiva and sat at her work table nearby, using a tiny brush to paint a design on a beautiful two-handled pot. I tapped on the door, tried the knob, and came in.

"You need to lock your door," I said and started to tell her about the arms before she could scold me for doing a drop-in.

"Terrible thing." Her thick black hair swung over her shoulders. She shook it back impatiently and continued to paint. "Must'a been some poor soul fell asleep on the tracks."

I pictured two arms doing handstands, fingers scuttling along the road like twin spiders. "Not unless the arms ran off by themselves to the Shop N Save."

She picked up a page from the local paper she was using to cover her work table and rattled it at me. "You hear about the Dine girl? Hikers found her body down in the Bisti the day after the quake."

I stared at the photo, a round-faced girl with folds of fat under her eyes. "Don't recognize her. She have both her arms?"

"Far as I know, but—" Graciela's hand quivered as she stuck her brush into the turpentine jar and selected a clean one. "Part of her head, though, it was—" A shudder jittered her shoulders. "Hell, who knows if it was true what I heard. It was one of my regulars at Abuelo's telling the tale. Probably the single malt talking."

She leaned into the pot, making small, quick strokes on the handle. Her concentration was total.

Without looking up, she said, "Why aren't you at work?"

"I wanted to make sure you were okay."

"Well, I'm fine, as you can see."

I moved around the table, pretending to want a better look at what she was working on. A geometric design with diamonds and dragonflies done in one of her favorite glazes, a rich smoky shade of Merlot. The muscles in her forearms flexed as she added the details. Her long hair swung forward again and she flicked it back with her free hand.

The familiar gesture triggered old feelings. I spoke heedlessly, foolishly. "Babe, your hair's in the way. Let me braid it for you."

Like old times, I thought. Both of us naked on the sheepskins Graciela tossed across her bed in winter, her hair a jet river all the way to the curve of her waist, and me, patiently separating it out into lush strands, weaving it into a single glossy black rope.

"Lena, we've been through this before. It's over. Please don't come here again uninvited."

And in spite of all my resolve, those same words I'd spoken so often before, shameless and desperate, spilled out of me. "Graciela, why can't we get past this? I've explained what happened so many times. It was a drunken fuck, that's all, a boy I knew from high school and never saw again. I can't say I regret doing it, because then I wouldn't have Coracita, but it was nothing. It didn't mean anything."

She stopped painting and glared at me. "Nothing means nothing, Lena."

I stood there, paralyzed with longing and despair, before finally storming back out to my truck, where I screeched away like someone who actually had someplace to go.

———

At work, the "Shop N Save" arms were a main topic of conversation, which made for some bad jokes and queasy glances every time I ran ham through the slicer. At my break, I texted Freddie, told him I'd swing by school later and give him a ride. He didn't reply, but when my shift ended, I went anyway.

Among the horde of kids being disgorged from Farmington High,

Freddy wasn't among them, but I spied Chanel, a sixteen-year-old "older woman" who sometimes babysat Coracita.

Besides being a good sitter, Chanel was also a giddy geyser of unfiltered rumor and gossip. In one long exhalation minus preface or pause, she told me more about the dead Dine girl, whose name was Arvella Totse and who Chanel knew from church, then switched to an evaluation of the girls' basketball team and her irritation with Freddie for taking off after second period when the two of them had made plans of an unspecified nature.

I figured I knew where he'd gone, so I headed out to the Toomey Mine.

The terrain around the mine is scraggly and raw as scabbed skin, high desert at its most stark and unwelcoming, but today the atmosphere was daunting in a way I'd never experienced. It felt too empty and yet not empty enough, as though the land itself harbored secrets.

I bumped past a *Hazardous Mine* sign riddled with bullet holes and a chain-link fence sagging around the foundation of what once was a coal smelter. The mine itself was boarded up and fenced in, but deep sinkholes pockmarked the earth around it, so any reasonably slender person could easily shimmy under the fence. I parked and hiked up a low rise, kicking aside tumbleweeds and skirting a stand of junipers that corkscrewed at tortured angles out of the rocks.

Everywhere was evidence of the recent earthquake and other earthquakes preceeding it. From my vantage point atop the rise, I could see down into broad arroyos where whole sections of embankment had collapsed and jagged, zigzagging fissures made the earth look like cheap, cracked pottery. And everywhere I saw sinkholes, some not much bigger than coyote dens, others wide enough to drive a truck into.

I spotted Pernell's campsite to the east, a collapsed tent with a fire pit, rucksack, and a few pots and empty cans strewn around. Half the tent was sliding down into a huge sinkhole. It occurred to me if Pernell was in there asleep when the quake hit, he might have been swallowed up himself. The thought of being plunged down into that terrible dark made my arms break out in gooseflesh. I wanted to get the hell out of there, but decided to take a look around Pernell's campsite first.

The wind was picking up, rousing the tumbleweeds to chaotic life. It was a spooky sight, tumbleweeds of all sizes bouncing down and up and down—a horde of frenzied, roly-poly animals engaged in some bizarre mating dance.

A tumbleweed hopping across my path snagged my pant leg and tripped me. As I rose, my line of sight altered, and I caught a glimpse of a tall man in a black duster moving beyond the boarded-up mine. With a surge of relief, I recognized Pernell's horsey, creased face and red goatee. I yelled his name. He spun around and beckoned to me, but gave no sign of recognition. I called out again, and again he motioned for me to join him. Then he turned, strode a few paces in the direction of the mine, and vanished into one of the sinkholes. I couldn't tell if he'd fallen or jumped or simply been swallowed up by the unstable earth.

"Pernell?"

Everything suddenly felt wrong. The texture of the air itself seemed to alter, growing heavy and viscous, hard to breathe. The wind died away as though cowed, and the desert ochres and tans swam together in a borderless blur. Only the dark rings of the sinkholes remained distinct and monstrously vivid. Fear swamped me. I felt like I was caught up in a play staged for my benefit and of which I wanted no part.

I whirled and started back toward the truck, aware that as I did so, something hunched and huffing on powerful legs squirmed through the gap underneath the mine's fence and came cantering after me.

I couldn't look back, didn't dare, but I sensed that by not going after Pernell, I'd broken some unalterable rule of this "game," exceeded some unholy parameters and that I'd be made to pay.

Behind me, my pursuer ambled on clicking joints, crunching through tumbleweed, flattening the scrub. I could hear the thump of its feet and other noises I couldn't make sense of, a slapping sound like wet laundry on a line and something worse (or so I thought at the time)—a moist, obscene suction I'd only ever associated with that well-endowed boy rampant between my legs.

The truck was only a few strides away. I groped the key fob out of my pocket, punched the button that unlocked the doors, but—in a fumble both epic and potentially fatal—let it slip from my fingers and sail off into the bruise-colored twilight as I hurled myself behind the wheel.

There was no time to retrieve it. I locked the doors and slid down into the footwell as the thing pursuing me began circling the truck. Claws screeched on metal and I heard again that weird slapping sound, like raw liver hitting a pan. I tried not to breathe. I thought if I remained perfectly still that whatever it was might lose interest and go away.

Eventually a prolonged silence descended along with the night. I found the flashlight in the console, lowered the window an inch, and shined it outside, where it illuminated the key fob a few feet from the truck. I couldn't wait any longer. With a silent "fuck it!" I leaped out of the truck and snatched up the fob, certain that, when I turned around, the thing would be between me and the truck, certain that this was my death.

It wasn't.

On the way home, I started calling Ma's phone and Freddie's as soon as I picked up a signal,
but no one answered. At home, the house was tomb black. If it hadn't been for the t.v. blaring *Wheel of Fortune*, I'd have thought we had a power outage.

Inside I found terrifying chaos: ripped upholstery, photos and keepsakes smashed, Papi's urn in pieces, his ashes tracked across the floor. In the kitchen, plates shattered, food spilled, and the ungodly reek from where the intruder had taken a dump in the middle of the floor.

A blast of cold wind led me to the mudroom, where I found the back door had been ripped off its hinges and heaved through the windshield of Ma's pickup.

Ma would be furious about that, but where was she? And Freddie and Coracita? I knew Ma hid her gun in the pantry, so I headed there next and almost caught a bullet when Freddie, who was wielding Ma's Smith & Wesson .38, cocked the gun as I slid back the door. Ma, who was next to him with a butcher knife clamped in her fist, grabbed his arm just in time. Freddie went white. "Jesus, Lena, I could'a killed you!"

I looked around wildly. "Where's the baby?"

"She's fine," said Ma and pointed to a corner where they'd hidden Coracita behind a barrier of family-sized Cheerios boxes and twelve-packs of paper towels. I lifted her out and hugged her against me.

"I kept calling both of you. Why didn't you answer?"

"We silenced the phones," Freddie said, and Ma added, "I called

Ben, but he didn't answer. Couldn't even get 911 to pick up."

Something banged on the front door.

Ma crossed herself. "*Dios mío*, it's back."

Freddie cocked the gun again. I clutched Coracita and Mama readied the knife.

A man's voice shouted, "Police!"

The deputy was new and looked out of his depth as he went room to room, pistol drawn. After a tour of the house, he stammered out his speculation that a wild animal—a bear or hog—had gotten in and caused the destruction. I wanted to ask him how many bears had he ever seen in this part of New Mexico, but held my tongue. Meanwhile, his radio kept chattering, other calls coming in. "Lotta mischief tonight," he said, shell-shocked blue eyes staring in a kind of horrified awe at the tower of shit in the kitchen.

After he made out a report and left, Ma declared no way were we staying in the house without any back door, that we'd get a room at the Days Inn in Farmington. She and Freddie, holding Coracita, piled into Papi's old Suburu and I followed in the truck.

About halfway there, we hit a patch of phone service and the beeps told me I had several calls. All from Graciela.

"Lena, are you there?" went the first message. "I think something's outside the house." And the second one, frantic. "I called the police, but they're not here yet."

And finally, her voice wet and raw as if she'd been screaming, "It's in here."

I called her back, got no answer. While I was leaving a message, a patrol car raced past, siren on, lights flashing. I started to tell her the cops were on the way now, but the patrol car swung north, going the wrong way. I called Ma, said I had a stop to make, and cut the call before she could question me.

I used the spare key Graciela kept in the bird feeder to let myself in, then reeled backward when I saw roach-like orange insects crawling over the ceiling and walls.

"Lena?" Graciela said, as I realized the illusion of infestation was created by flames spiking behind the grate in the kiva.

"Is it you?" Her voice was ground glass, screamed or sobbed raw. She sat huddled in the chair in front of the fire, swathed in a colorful beehive of Indian blankets.

"Graciela, are you okay? Is it still here?"

"No," she answered, although whether this was in reply to one question or both, I had no idea. I grabbed an andiron from where it was leaned against the kiva just in case.

My nerves were fraught. When I saw her face, I blurted out, "My God, what happened to you?"

Her eyelids were swollen and starting to purple, her mouth leaking blood at the corners. The effect was grotesque, like a clown's crimson leer, and yet weirdly exotic, almost beautiful.

"Graciela, what happened?"

She seemed perplexed and struggled to speak in that grave, strangled voice. "It was hitting me—again and again—and it hurt so bad until all of a sudden…it didn't. And then it went away. Lena, tell me the truth. Do I look very bad?"

"Who hit you?"

"I'm not sure, but…I know it wanted to kill me." Her eyes rolled up at the ceiling, then down to her lap. She repeated this sequence several times, the firelight darkening the bruises and blood on her face. "Why would it want to kill me?"

"Graciela, we have to go." Sweat was pouring down my neck, my chest, the insides of my thighs. "We have to get out of here. *Now.*"

"There's blood in my hair."

"What?"

"My scalp's bleeding. I can feel blood dripping into my hair."

"I don't see anything." I set aside the andiron and ran my hands over her hair. It felt sleek and perfectly dry. "There's no blood," I said, but then realized that in the firelight it would be almost impossible to see blood against her black hair.

"I can feel the blood dripping. I can smell it."

I slid my fingers under her hair. It was thick and almost magically lush, fairy-tale hair rippling under my touch, coming alive as—

"Graciela, there's no—"

—the hair folded back and a mouth crammed with tiny razorblade teeth opened wide where her skull ought to be. A grotesque, grub-pale appendage wriggled out. It was slick with moisture and the frothy liquid that bubbled from a pinprick hole in the fleshy head. I shrieked and jerked my hands back. In a flash, the thing I'd taken to be a tongue retracted, the teeth snapping shut a millisecond after I withdrew my hands.

I felt no pain yet, but the end of a nail and part of an index finger tumbled down the thing's throat.

"Is there blood, Lena?" Graciela asked calmly, oblivious to the horror of the monstrous face lurking opposite her own.

I grabbed for the andiron as the thing wearing Graciela's face uncoiled from its nest of blankets and creaked upright, a bony, hooved horror with reddish fur and a pointed, quilled stub of a chin. Where a muzzle or nose should have been ran a triangular slit, the purpose of which became clear when the bald phallic tongue curved up from its mouth, probed for the opening and then entered with one meaty punch. As it began to thrust, the red, recessed eyes narrowed in a near swoon of pleasure.

I swung the andiron at its head like a bat. The monster's reaction was terrifyingly fast. It snarled and slapped the weapon away without missing a beat of its obscene self-ministrations.

But what almost paralyzed me with horror wasn't its ungodly parody of copulation, but the sudden awareness of its large, dangling teats and what suckled there—human faces, each with a pair of dead, bloodless lips clamped to a teat. As the ghastly mouths strained to nurse, the faces twisted and grimaced and slapped against one another, making the rubbery sound I'd heard when I was trapped in the truck. Amid these abominations, I recognized Pernell's goatee and the broad, florid face of the Totse girl. I knew that Graciela's face would be hanging there, too, once the monster got done wearing her.

As I backed away, my lower back hit the edge of the work table. I tried to bolt, but a hooved foot studded with claws lashed out. I felt ribs crack and cave as I collapsed into the table, sending ceramic pots and jars of glazes tumbling to the floor. The monster grabbed me in a brutal embrace that sent jolts of red pain through my rib cage. Its phallic tongue retracted as upper teeth found my hairline and crunched down. I felt blood pour as it began to tug at my face.

And all the while I could feel those horrible faces of once-living—maybe still living?—people, squirming and tickling against my midsection.

Behind me, my scrabbling fingers knocked a lid off a jar, but I paid no attention until the scent of turpentine—benzene laced with cadaver—filled the room. The monster reared back and I hurled the jar, missed the eyes I was aiming for, but sloshed a thick stream between jaws red with my blood. Its roar rattled the walls as I slid to the floor, crawled under the table, and came up by the kiva. Our struggle had already knocked over the grate. I grabbed a log aflame at one end and held on to it long enough to set the thing's turpentine soaked fur ablaze. Long enough to smell my flesh cooking, too.

"Lena, help me!"

I was almost at the door. She said my name again, pleading, and God help me, I took a step back.

"Help me!"

How she was able to speak, even in that tortured voice, is beyond me, but the fire engulfing the monster's head had not yet reached her face. I didn't know if she could hear me, but I wanted one last good-bye.

"Graciela—"

Her eyes glowed, her lips parted as though for a kiss as she spat a putrid foam that filled my mouth with the stench of decay. I gagged and my jaw muscles locked. I couldn't breathe or spit out what she'd fouled me with. I felt a terrible, ripping agony at my hairlines that descended my face like a scythe, skinning tissue and muscle from bone. When the pain suddenly stopped, what replaced it was worse, the eerie sensation of being embalmed but alive, while my mind seeped away, into a lightless oblivion.

These things breed. I realize that now. The ones at the house and at the Toomey Mine, the creature at Graciela's, were not the same beast. For whatever reason, they did their business under the earth until now. But no longer.

I am long past lamenting that, though.

At first I imagine I'm jogging backwards though I can't feel my feet or my legs. Or anything else really. As long as the thing is walking upright, what I see is whatever's directly behind me, like the view of a passenger in a rear-facing seat on a train. I watch as Graciela's casita recedes in the pewter moonlight, and the rutted road suddenly changes to pavement. At times smoky, charred fur slides over my eyes, concealing my face as I imagine it will until the monster requires my features and voice to dupe its next victim.

Later, after it drops onto four legs, I stare up into an ocean of stars and a sly-faced old moon that seems to wink at my unholy predicament. Headlights glare, and I hope someone will see me, but what exactly is it they'd see? The blurry outline of a large animal with the profile of what resembles a human face staring out of the back of its head? Other faces, older and more damaged, dangling from rubbery teats? A car whooshes past, and the creature stands up on two legs again and lopes like a man. It abandons the road. All I see now is desert.

I tell myself I will wake up from this horror, that to exist in my current state is unthinkable, but my hope is misplaced. Before long I see the *Hazardous Mine* sign go by and the fractured earth pocked with sinkholes. As we descend into the dark, I hear the low, wretched moans of the trapped and the damned, and I know mine will soon be among them.

MONSTERS OF ANY KIND

JONATHAN MABERRY

WE ALL MAKE SACRIFICES

by JONATHAN MABERRY

-1-

I looked up from the business card to the lawyer seated across the desk from me.

I said, "Mister, um, 'Douche-weasel'—?" Pronouncing it the way it looked in the expensive raised printing.

He gave me a weary look. The kind of look that said two things. First, that he's been through some variation of this conversation ten times a week his whole life. The second is that he expected just exactly this level of maturity from someone with rates as low as mine.

"DuSchwezel," he said slowly, saying it as 'DEW-schwee-ZELLE'. Emphasis on both the first and last syllables.

"Okay," I said.

"Okay," said Mr. DuSchwezel.

A moment passed, taking its time. My office was quiet. He sighed. "You're still thinking it's pronounced 'douche-weasel,' aren't you?"

I held my thumb and index fingers an inch apart. "Li'l bit," I said.

"Tell me, Mr. Hunter, don't you get annoyed when people make jokes about your name?"

"What's wrong with my name?"

"'Hunter'? Seriously? And you're a private investigator?"

"Hunh. Never came up," I lied.

Another moment limped past.

"We're not off to a very good start, are we?" he asked.

"Not a fan of banter?"

"Not as such, no."

I put his card down on my desk blotter. "Okay, so let's try it from a different angle. Why are you here?"

"To see about engaging your services."

"Uh huh."

"You are for hire, are you not?"

I nudged the card with a finger. "Almost always."

"So—?"

"It's just that I don't get why *you* want to hire me."

"Why not? My money's good, isn't it?"

"That's just it, you're a Main Line estate attorney. I couldn't afford to park in your garage. You probably paid more for a thousand of these cards than I've spent on rent for this dump. Lawyers like you have investigators on retainer, and none of them have offices in this part of town."

He said, "Ah."

"Ah," I agreed. "So why does a guy in a two-thousand-dollar suit schlep all the way here to hire a guy like me?"

"The suit," he said, "cost eleven thousand dollars. I paid two thousand just for the shoes."

"First," I said, "that was a very douche-weasel thing to say. Second, fuck you."

He smiled at that.

After a moment, so did I.

DuSchwezel picked up the briefcase he'd stood next to the client chair, placed it flat on a corner of my desk and popped the locks. The case was positioned so that he could see the contents and I couldn't. He removed an envelope, considered it for a moment and then reached out to lay it on the blotter next to his card.

"What's that?" I asked.

"Look and see."

It was unsealed, so I folded back the flap and removed a long blue-green slip of paper. That exact color was probably seafoam or some shit like that. Very heavy stock, high linen count, expensive printing. It was a check drawn on a personal account rather than something corporate. It had his name on it. Arnold Tyro DuSchwezel. It was made out to me for the amount of five thousand dollars.

I nodded appreciation at the numbers, which were some of my favorite numbers, and placed the check on my desk atop the envelope.

"This a bribe to make me say your name the right way?"

"Cute," he said, "but no. This is me giving you a check to retain your services."

"For what?"

"That's complicated, but first I'd like you to give me a check for one hundred dollars."

I smiled. "And why the fuck would I do that?"

"To retain *my* services."

"You lost me."

DuSchwezel said, "In order for us to proceed, you will need to retain me as your attorney so that everything we discuss is covered under the blanket of attorney-client privilege."

"You working for a drug cartel or some shit? Local Mafia?"

He spread his hands. "The five thousand dollars is a gift. You are not legally or morally required to engage my services. If you want to tell me to go away, then I will and you can keep the check. It will not leave you beholden to me in any way."

"Bullshit."

"Not at all," said DuSchwezel. "We have discussed no business and nothing that's gone between us could be construed as a binding verbal contract. Go to your bank and cash the check if you want. I'll wait here. Or I can come back. Do this in whichever way makes you feel comfortable."

"If," I said, "I decide to write you that check, what's the other shoe? I don't need a lawyer."

"You probably do, but that's a general opinion based on your lifestyle."

"You fucking with me?"

He grinned. "Of course."

I grinned, too. Mine was forced. "If you accept my check," I said, "and suddenly become my lawyer, is there more of this?"

"That would be when the other shoe would hit the floor, yes," he admitted.

"Will I like it?"

He pursed his lips. "I doubt it."

"Then—?"

"But really, Mr. Hunter, how many of your more *interesting* cases have you actually liked?"

I said nothing.

"You have quite a reputation in certain circles," said DuSchwezel. "People respect you."

"No," I said, "they don't."

He shrugged. "Okay, then they respect what you can do. They fear you, if that's a better way to put it."

"Not sure there is a better way to put it if we're both talking about the same thing."

"Fair enough," he said.

We sat there for a moment. My office smells like Lysol and Jack Daniel's. The two smells are related thematically in ways that define me, sad to say. The Lysol for cleaning up some of the messes I've had to make. The Jack Daniel's for helping me try to forget. Cliché? Sure. Fuck it.

DuSchwezel sat back and crossed his legs. Even through the stink of booze and cleaning products I could smell him. I have a very good sense of smell. Better than yours unless you're like me. He'd used some kind of super-fatted soap, probably Camay. His shampoo is scented with tea-tree oil. Cologne was one of the Polo varieties. Blue, I think. Deodorant was Old Spice Sport. There was a hint of chlorine about him, which suggested he swam his laps today and showered at the gym. There was also a subtle aroma of something else. No, two things. A little fear sweat and a little blood. Hard to wash that away completely. Hound dogs can sniff it after a shower. So can people like me.

I opened my desk drawer, took out my cheap green checkbook and wrote him a check for one hundred dollars. He watched me with genuine and obvious interest, then accepted it with a nod. DuSchwezel took a moment to study it, though I think he did that to collect his thoughts. There were a few beads of fresh sweat on his forehead. Then he folded the check and tucked it into an inner pocket of his jacket.

We sat for a moment.

"Anything we discuss from here out is protected," he said.

"Yup." In the movies and in poorly researched novels, private investigators often hide information from the cops by claiming client confidentiality. Yeah, that's a myth. Only lawyers and shrinks get that protection. Now we were sealed and square.

"Mr. Hunter," said DuSchwezel, "I would like very much for you to kill someone."

-2-

So, yeah, okay. That just happened.

I sat there, looking at him. I think I was smiling. Or something.

His face was slightly flushed.

"You're fucking with me," I said.

"Actually," said DuSchwezel, "I'm not."

"Then give me back my check and try not to take it personally while I throw you the fuck out of my office. I may knee you in the balls, but that's just a professional courtesy."

"This isn't a joking matter," he said.

My smile got wider and probably stranger. "Sounds like it to me."

DuSchwezel's smile faded away. "Do I *look* like I'm joking, Mr. Hunter?"

"You'd better be. You just asked me to commit a contract killing."

"It's not as simple as that."

"I'm pretty sure that I don't give a flying gopher fuck how simple or complicated it is," I said. "And, tell you what, why don't you stand up and assume the position so I can make sure you're not wearing a wire. *Entrapment* is an ugly word and it'll probably hurt when I shove it up your ass."

I started to get out of my chair but he stood up more quickly, hands raised as he backed away.

"No! Listen to me, please. If you want to pat me down, that's fine, but please listen to me."

"Pat first, listen later. Hands against the wall."

Before he could react, I snaked out a hand, caught him by the shoulder of his eleven-thousand-dollar suit, spun him and slammed him into the wall, kicked his legs wide, and frisked him. Before I was a P.I. here in Philly, I was a cop in Minneapolis. I worked enough Vice cases in my day to know how to check someone for a wire. There are nice ways to do it and there are ways that can really fuck up a person's month. I went somewhere in the middle. When I was done, his clothes were a mess, he had very little personal dignity left, he was panting with mingled fear and anger, but he was clean.

I pointed to the chair. "Sit," I ordered. He sat and watched while I rifled through his briefcase. Lots of file folders, which I ignored, but nothing else. I took a tuning fork from my desk drawer—a little trick I learned from a cop friend in Pine Deep—banged it hard and touched it to the handle and any part of the briefcase dense enough to conceal a mic. If anyone was listening in, they'd be shopping at Miracle-Ear by the end of the day.

The case was clean.

So I sat on the edge of my desk, arms folded, and looked down at DuSchwezel. He plucked out his pocket square and dabbed his forehead and upper lip.

"You're an asshole," he said.

"Blow me," I said. "Tell me why I shouldn't throw you out the window."

DuSchwezel held the pocket square in his lap and I could see his hands tremble. Son of bitch was scared but I don't think it was because of me.

"People think that when you're rich you can do anything you want," he said, coming at this from around a corner. "That's not true. Not really. Sure, there are things we can do, and things we can get away with, but we're not invulnerable. Everyone has a weakness, Mr. Hunter."

I said nothing.

He looked up at me. "I am not a very nice person."

"I'm not your therapist."

"No," he said, "I'm not looking for understanding. I am a bad man. I do bad things."

"Yeah, well I'm not a priest, either."

"I'm not seeking absolution," said DuSchwezel. "I'm making a statement. This is confidential and I need you to understand who and what I am. I represent very rich people in the Philadelphia area. People who use my services and those of my partners to make sure that the law always bends to whatever angle they need. I am a magician when it comes to twisting regulations, soliciting illegal compliance from judges and politicians, dispensing bribes, and hiding large amounts of cash in dummy corporations. In short, I facilitate corruption in virtually every way that does not involve direct violence."

"Well, to be fair," I said, "I already thought you were an asshole when you said you were a lawyer. This doesn't slide you that much further down the crapper."

"This isn't about me," he said, "this is about my daughter, Olivia. Beautiful girl. Smart."

I said nothing.

Two tears suddenly dropped down his cheeks and whatever was left of his professional calm and poise collapsed like broken scaffolding, dragged down by the weight of why he was really here. He said, "She was eighteen."

Ah...fuck.

Was is such an ugly word.

When it's laid against the age of a daughter, a kid, it's beyond horrible. It disfigures the moment.

Mr. DuSchwezel put his face in his hands and began to cry.

I did not pat him on the back and tell him that it was okay, that it was all going to be okay. I'm not that much of an asshole, and I had no reason to lie to him. Whatever this was, it was already not okay. *She was eighteen.* No, it wasn't ever going to be okay.

I went around to my side of the desk, sat down, let him cry. Waited. Tried not to own any of his hurt. Tried really hard.

She was eighteen.

Was.

Goddamn it.

-3-

He got his shit together and told me the story. It was long and he rambled. Short version is this...

One of the biggest clients he represented was a man named Fenner, and Mr. Fenner made his money by providing transportation, storage, and distribution for large lots of stolen merchandise. We're not talking a couple of microwaves that fell off the back of a truck. We're talking about entire trucks, or at least the cargoes of trucks that are either hauling illegal freight like untaxed cigarettes and unstamped booze; or the contents of hijacked trucks. There's a lot of money in that. One of his specialties was stealing the contents of cargo containers at the docks and placing them in his own cans elsewhere in the same freight yard. And he made sure that his stuff always had the proper paperwork. Lots of steps to his organization, lots of checks and balances, lots of money for everyone involved. Tens of millions per year, just in the dockyard scams. Twice that much for stuff he hauled up from meth labs in the South.

Mr. Fenner wasn't the problem.

His son, Erik, was.

Erik was so cliché I almost laughed as DuSchwezel described him. Twenty-something, good-looking, perfect teeth, deep-water tan from spending so much time on boats off Miami, rich, arrogant, vicious, petty, grabby, violent, charming, and all of the other adjectives that describe a child of wealth and power who was the only heir to a crime fortune. You can order the cocksucker from central casting. You know the type, the kind who genuinely believes that the world exists to help him get high, get laid, and have fun. The kind who drops twenty grand on a weekend out with his friends and won't let anyone else pay for anything because he needs to be seen as the one who *owns* the fun and has everything covered. And because his dad is who he is, doors get opened, he never waits in a line, he always gets a table, he gets more ass than a porn star, everyone grins at him like he's the king of the jungle, and to that crowd he *is* the king of the jungle. But what they're really doing is kissing his ass in order to kiss his father's ass.

Like I said, you've seen this a million times. Every single grade-B cop movie, every modern gangster movie, blah blah blah. In those movies he's the one who usually does something so heinous that it causes the action hero to cut a bloody swath through the criminal empire his father has taken so long to build.

The thing that really torques my ass, though, is that this particular cliché is reinforced by the fact that there are hundreds of real-world assholes exactly like that. Maybe thousands. I ran into some of them when I was a cop in the Cities, and I've brushed up against a few—even dented one or two—since I hung out a shingle here in Philly.

Unfortunately they are usually very well guarded and their asshole parents do everything they can to spoil them and enable the very worst behavior. In the movies, the action hero goes in guns blazing and does some chop-socky and racks up a body count that makes cancer look like a third-string killer with no running game.

That's the movies. Liam Neeson, Denzel Washington, Keanu Reeves, Bruce Willis, and Jason Statham manage to outfight and outgun whole mobs of wiseguys. That, as they say, is Hollywood. The bullets aren't real, the bad guys in those flicks can't shoot worth a damn, and heroes seem to be able to do complex extended fight scenes even after taking gunshot wounds, stab wounds, falling off balconies, getting thrown through plateglass windows, and getting wailed on by fists, elbows, and feet. Special effects, baby. Fake blood, rubber knives, stunt men, and guns firing blanks.

I pointed all of this out to Mr. DuSchwezel.

"And so I came to you," he said simply.

"Sure. But why? Last time I checked, there was a shit-ton of cops in Philadelphia. They've organized now. Call themselves a 'police department.' Maybe, you being a lawyer and all, you've heard of them."

"I'm a mob lawyer," he said.

"And you told me you have connections out the wazoo. Judges in your pocket and such."

"Whose money do you think pays for those judges, Mr. Hunter? If I filed a formal complaint against Erik Fenner, who do you think would enforce it? Even *I* don't know who owns whom in this town. Erik's father has other lawyers, too. We don't share all of the details about bribery and corruption while we braid each other's hair."

"There's that," I conceded. "You're afraid that leveling charges against Erik will backfire."

"I have two other children," said DuSchwezel. "And a wife, a mother, cousins, nieces, nephews. Just in the Philadelphia metropolitan area there are over twenty members of my extended family. How many of them do you think Mr. Fenner would hurt or kill to protect his only son?"

"Balls," I said.

"Do you think I'd come to you if I had anywhere else to go?"

Not sure if he was trying to be deliberately insulting, but what the hell. He had a point. And besides, I was still thinking of him as Mr. Douche-weasel.

"What's all this have to do with Olivia?"

Even though this was why he was here, my question hit him like a punch. He cleared his throat and said, "You spend a lot of time at Heaven Street Diner."

A statement, not a question, but I nodded anyway.

"Do you remember a dark-haired girl who worked there for a few weeks last fall?"

"Sure. Livvie something."

And something went *clunk* inside my head. Livvie. Short for Olivia.

"Oh," I said. "Fuck."

"Yes. Livvie was always troubled. She ran away from home half a dozen times. Last fall she got a fake I.D. that said she was nineteen, and she moved into a roach-infested apartment near the diner. Got a job working tables at Heaven Street."

"I remember her," I said. It was true. Livvie was a pretty little thing. Thin, pale, rocking a goth look. Never said much and I don't think she ever waited on me. When I was at the diner, the counter waitress, Ivy, always took care of me. Ivy and I go way back. "She seemed like a nice kid."

It was a lame comment but it was all I had. I doubt we ever swapped more than a hello two or three times. Like a lot of diner staff, she came and went and then was gone from my memory until today.

"I had another investigator look for her," said DuSchwezel. "He found her and brought her home."

"But she ran away again?"

"In a way. I had a party at my house and the Fenners were there. Erik saw Olivia and I could tell right away she fell for him. He's very good-looking and he wears his father's money like a suit."

I nodded, knowing the type.

"They started seeing each other," he said. "I tried to warn her off, to tell her that he was dangerous, but..."

"But that probably made her more interested."

"Yes."

"Aside from the obvious, why was Erik dangerous? I mean, you took a risk telling her when if she was so into him she might have told him what you said."

His hands still gripped the pocket square. Twisting it, clutching it with white-knuckled fingers. His eyes kept meeting mine and falling away. Over and over.

"Okay," I said, "you're not paying me enough to play games. Tell me what it is or buzz off."

He took a fortifying breath and said, "There are rumors about Erik."

"Ah, boy... Tell me."

"Erik is into some strange stuff. His father told me about some of it because he knew I was having some issues with Olivia. His father wanted advice on finding a good therapist."

"When you say 'strange'...?"

"Erik was into supernatural stuff."

"So what?"

"No," said DuSchwezel, "not as a hobbyist. I'm not talking about him being into monster movies and Stephen King novels. No, I mean he was *into* the supernatural. He believes in it. He...sought it out."

"How and in what way?"

Again his eyes flicked away. "I'm not sure how it started. He's always had unusual friends, particularly another boy whose father is with the Kirikov family. Do you know them? Russia Mafiya."

"They're dead, right? Turf war over the uptic in the heroin trade between here and New York. Both sides killing family members?"

"That was the cover story, sure. But it went deeper than that. I'm pretty sure that the Kirikov boy was not killed by their rivals in that particular line of commerce. I'm almost certain that Erik killed him and made it look like it was done by the rivals of the Kirikov family. The resulting drug war was the usual escalation of payback."

"Why would Erik do that?"

"Because he needed a blood sacrifice."

I stared at him. "You're going to have to explain that one."

"I...don't have all of it together," he admitted. "And, quite frankly, I'm not even sure how much of it I believe. But I managed to put someone inside Erik's circle of friends. A promising attorney right out of law school who looks younger than he is. He ingratiated himself into Erik's crew and..." He stopped and shivered. Actually shivered. "He said that Erik is insane. Erik doesn't just want to be like his father, he wants to eclipse the old man and become something much bigger, something much more powerful. He wants to be feared."

"He has a lot of thugs who will shoot people if he asks. Pretty sure he's already feared."

"No," said DuSchwezel, "you don't get it. This isn't the kind of power hunger I see all the time among my clients and their sons. No. When I said Erik was insane, I meant it. I think he was crazy—clinically psychotic—to begin with, but the more he got into whatever supernatural stuff the young Kirikov shared with him... Well, I think it pushed him into a whole new shape. Mentally, I mean."

"So he's making blood sacrifices now? To whom? Or to what?"

"To what Erik thinks is the patron god of his family."

"You're shitting me."

"I shit you not."

"And who exactly is the—and pardon me if I grin while I say this—patron 'god' of their family?"

"Well, see, that's one of the main reasons I came to see you," said

DuSchwezel. "You specifically, I mean. 'Fenner' is an Anglicized version of the family name. They're Scandinavian and their real name is—or at least *was*— Fenrisúlfr."

I said nothing. My mouth dried right up.

DuSchwezel nodded. "You know that name, don't you?"

I nodded. "Fenrisúlfr," I said hoarsely. "It's another name for Fenrir."

"Who is—?" he asked, making sure I knew.

"The wolf god of the Vikings. Fenrir is the father of the wolves Sköll and Hati Hróðvitnisson, is a son of Loki, and is foretold to kill the god Odin during the events of Ragnarök."

"Yes," said DuSchwezel. "Erik is trying to invoke a dark god who he believes—really fucking believes—is going to help bring about the end of the world. And, god help me, Mr. Hunter, he sacrificed my little girl to try and make that happen."

His words seemed to be painted on the air between us in dark red letters. It took me a while to figure out how to reply to something like that.

"Even so," I said slowly, "why me? If Erik is a psychopath and a serial murderer, and you can't trust the cops to take him down, what you need is an assassin. I'm not a button man. I don't do contract hits, and 'revenge killer' isn't on my business card."

"No," said DuSchwezel, "but 'monster' is."

-4-

Bang.

There it was.

"No it's not," I said. Which was true in the literal sense. My business card said *Investigations and Personal Protection.* But I could see it in his eyes. He knew.

Maybe he didn't know *what* I was, but he knew I wasn't Joe Normal.

"Who's told you what?" I asked, keeping my voice casual. "And if you try to play the client confidentiality thing, then I'll tell you in advance to fuck off and go away."

He considered that for a moment, then nodded to himself as he decided to play his cards faceup.

"Ivy," he said.

Ivy. She was one of the few people who knew who and what I was. A year or two back she tapped me to help out a friend of hers with a problem no one else could tackle. I've never been exactly certain how Ivy figured it out, but she asked me for help. A friend's little son was being attacked in his sleep by something that came out of his closet. Yeah, I know. "Monster in the closet" is a standard kid thing. Except this time it wasn't. And it wasn't a sequel to *Monsters, Inc.*, either. There was something big and bad in the closet, and Ivy asked me to go in there and see what I could do.

It got weird and it got messy.

Bottom line is that there's nothing left in that closet that's ever going to hurt anyone again.

So, sure. Monster. Not exactly inaccurate. Not entirely unfair.

Ivy knows that.

"She shouldn't have told you," I said.

This time his eyes didn't dart away. He gave me a long, hard, sad, broken, desperate look. A father's look. A look that was filled with all of the grief in the world.

"Ivy thought the world of Olivia," he said. "She knows that I loved her. Really loved her. Olivia was my little girl."

Saying that broke him.

And damn if it didn't break me, too.

-5-

Which is why I went to see Erik Fenner.

There are some cases where I spend days or even weeks running down clues, doing background checks, tailing suspects, building a case. And then there are some where I go right up to a door and knock. I don't get many of that second kind. If it's easy, they usually don't hire guys like me.

Except in this case it was easy. Finding Erik, I mean. And there *are* no other guys like me. Not for something like this. I mean, sure, I've got cousins and aunts and all who are like me, but that's different. None of them live in Philly. Most of my relatives are either in the Cities or in Europe. We *benandanti* go back a lot of years. I can name every family member going back to early sixteenth-century Fruili, Italy, and my aunt Violet can name them going back to Etruscan times.

Benandanti.

The "good walkers."

The hounds of God. Which is a pretentious nickname but someone else hung it on us.

I wonder if DuSchwezel did his background check. Probably. If you want to stop a psychopath trying to invoke a wolf god, hire a private investigator who has some skin in that game. Not the Norse crap, but you get the picture.

So, yeah. I took the case. Ivy told him the right things about me. He knew I'd take it.

Maybe I did, too. That *was* word still burned in my head. The man may have been an asshole but he had a daughter and he loved her. Maybe he thought he failed her, too. Probably did. Mom lawyer and all. Kid has no one to look up to, so she starts looking down.

And sees a handsome monster looking up at her.

-6-

I drove out to Bucks County, to a sprawling estate near New Hope. DuSchwezel gave me the address and the code for the front gate. I told him I didn't need the code. Wall was only twelve feet high. I mean, c'mon.

Erik's father was in South Philly overseeing one of his dockside concerns. DuSchwezel had made sure that nobody but Erik was home. Well, besides a couple of servants, and three or four bodyguards.

I parked my car under some trees on a side road a quarter-mile from the house. Walked the rest of the way as the sun was tumbling over the trees toward tomorrow. I don't need darkness, and that whole full-moon thing is pure bullshit. Moon's got nothing to do with it. On the other hand, sunlight makes it easy for witnesses and who needs that bullshit.

Was I here to do a contract killing?

Not really. I gave DuSchwezel his check back.

This was for a teenage girl who didn't know better than to walk into one of the outer rings of hell. DuSchwezel couldn't actually tell me what happened to her. I doubt any father could force those words into his mouth. Instead he handed me a copy of the autopsy report.

That she had been raped was horrible enough. It wasn't the worst thing that had been done to her. We don't need to go into all the details. Even I get nauseous sometimes. Her body was found in a wrecked car, but the extent of her wounds wasn't consistent with the amount of damage to the vehicle. The car had rolled and burned, but that didn't account for the dismemberment. It didn't account for her eyes and heart being missing. And the pathologist determined that the victim was not alive when the car caught fire. However, on reflection, the pathologist recanted and decided that all of the injuries had, in fact, been sustained in that crash.

Five weeks after the autopsy report, the pathologist put a down payment on a mini-mansion in Newtown. You can connect the dots however you like.

I found a nice little blind spot where the Fenner security cameras couldn't see through some thick rhododendron. I stripped out of the sweats I'd worn and went over the wall in a way that left claw marks on the brick.

On the other side, I dropped down and ran on all fours. I usually stay on two feet except when I need to move fast. My senses are better then, too. DuSchwezel had given me a scarf that used to belong to Erik. Olivia had kept it as a token of her love.

Still had his scent on it. Useful. Before I went over the wall, I took a big enough sniff that I could have found him halfway across the state.

In the end it wasn't even all that hard.

He was sitting by the pool wearing a pair of skintight speedos, Wayfarer sunglasses over his eyes, a beer resting on his belly. He did not have three bodyguards with him. There were six of them. Or maybe three worked for his dad and the other three were part of Erik's mini-cult. They all had wolf tattoos on the sides of their necks. Very stylized—Fenrir with his jaws wide to swallow Odin on the day the world ends.

Even the guards had that.

They all looked blown out. Couldn't tell right off if they were hammered, high, stuffed from a big meal, or just a bunch of lazy fucks who were dead tired this early. Or some combination of all of that.

There was an iPad plugged into a Bose speaker dock and Kanye was yelling some bullshit that I didn't want to hear. They had it on too goddamn loud, too. The asshole club was sprawled all around the pool. No women around, which is odd. Usually these clowns have all kinds of arm candy, and often it's paid for in one way or another. Cash, drugs, access to power, whatever. But not now.

Good. That simplified things.

I circled the pool area, following the blood scent to its source. It was the pool house. It had been converted into something else. Not sure if the word *church* would apply. *Temple*, maybe. *Shrine*. Something like that. The windows were all blacked out and inside someone had gone completely ass-fuck nuts. The walls were painted with magical symbols from at least a dozen religions and twice as many phony cults. Inverted pentagrams, representations of goat-headed Baphomet, symbols of evil. Such bullshit. Some of this crap I knew for sure was from old monster movies that had no actual connection to real beliefs.

The blood was real, though.

There was a lot of it. Old and new. Many sources. Not just Olivia—and I could smell her scent here, too. There were others. As I stood in the doorway, I took in at least fourteen separate female scents. Two of them were prepubescent. These fuckers had killed little girls, too. That's worse. I'm not sure how exactly, but it is.

Fourteen dead girls and women.

There was an altar and Erik had laid them upon it and he and his wolfpack had done terrible things. I didn't need to see pictures to know what had happened there. My senses fed the information to my mind. When I was a cop and we learned about forensics, there was a saying that every contact leaves a trace. Now imagine what traces were left for senses like *mine* to find.

I could smell the pain, the horror, the death. I could almost hear the echo of voices screaming for mercy that was not theirs to have, just as I could hear the laughter of those sons of bitches out by the pool.

Were they true believers? Or was this part of some kind of shared madness inspired and perpetuated by Erik Fenner?

I don't know and I didn't much care.

As I stepped into that room, my focus was drawn to the altar. To the smell of blood that washed down from it.

So potent.

So fresh.

"What the *fuck* is that?" I breathed, and my words came out twisted because my throat was not a human one.

The answer to my question was there to be read, and my senses never lie.

That's when I knew I was too late. That's when I realized why those pricks out at the pool looked so logy and sated.

I'd waited until sunset to come here. My caution made me too late to save somebody else's little girl. Or sister. Or wife. Or whatever. There was blood on the air and smeared on the altar. Female, young. Dead.

And, if my senses were reading it right, not just dead.

No.

Fuck me. There are certain smells flesh makes when it interacts with saliva and digestive juices. I smelled the stink of a feast only recently finished. It was the smell a pack of wolves made when they were gathered around a deer they'd just torn down.

I turned and prowled to the doorway to the pool area and looked at the seven of them.

And I *knew*.

They had crossed way over the line from making human sacrifices to a wolf god to trying to *be* wolves. Or become wolves.

The wolf in me wanted to attack. Right then. To kill them all as they slept. The wolf was vicious but he was not cruel.

That's why I changed back to me.

You see, I can be cruel.

Sometimes I want to be.

Sometimes I need to look into the eyes of certain people because I want to see understanding. Maybe I hope for a flicker of regret, or remorse. Not that a moment of repentance has saved anyone I've gone after. Fuck it, I'm not a saint. I'm not even a very good private investigator.

I'm a hell of a hunter though. And, yeah, sure, make a joke about the name. It was picked as a joke by one of my ancestors, so the joke's on you.

When I take on a client—or in the case of DuSchwezel a proxy client, because I was here for Olivia not for her dickhead lawyer father—then that person becomes part of my pack. Wolves protect their packs.

Oh yeah. We do.

So it was in my own shape that I walked out of the pool house, strolled over to Erik Fenner's chaise lounge, raised my leg, and heel-kicked him in the speedo.

Real fucking hard.

He screamed and grabbed his balls and fell out of the chair.

The screams woke everyone else up. The three bodyguards came out of their chairs like they had springs up their asses and suddenly there were guns in their hands. The other three sprang up, too. One of them had a gun, another produced a knife from god knows where. The third one grabbed a beer bottle and smashed the fat end off it.

Six of them in a ring around me, with Erik screaming on the ground while his face turned an amusing shade of puce.

And me standing there. Short, skinny, twenty years older than any of them. Naked as an egg with my dick hanging out.

"Who the fuck are you?" screamed one of the guards.

This was the kind of moment when you really want to put a button on it by saying something really cool. Witty. Like the one-liners those action heroes always use.

But goddamn it if I couldn't really come up with anything snarky.

What I said was more expository than colorful.

I said, "Fenrisúlfr isn't real, assholes. Fake god from a dead religion. Not even sure the Vikings believed in him."

They stared at me. Part surprise that I was even dropping the name Fenrisúlfr, and partly wondering who the hell this naked crazy guy was. Even Erik paused in his shrieking to stare at me.

He said, "W-what—?"

"You fucktards think you're becoming wolves?" I asked. "Is that it? I mean, is that what this shit is all about? Some kind of superstitious ritual bullshit?"

Erik managed to get to his knees. His face was dark with pain and he still cupped his mashed balls, but there was fury in his eyes.

And...something else.

Maybe it was the darkening sky or maybe it wasn't, but I saw his pale Scandinavian eyes change from an icy blue to a red that was brighter and bloodier than his face.

All around me I saw the eyes of the others begin to change, too.

"Well, fuck me," I said.

The shape of Erik's mouth began to change. He suddenly had way too many teeth and his lips almost couldn't form the name of his god. "Fenrisúlfr."

I don't know how they managed it, but holy shit. They were actually turning into wolves. All seven of them. A wolfpack transformed somehow by blood sacrifices and the savage slaughter of the innocents, all in the name of a god whose mythical status I was very quickly having to re-evaluate.

I said, "Oh...shit."

They laughed, but the laughter sounded like snarls.

Like growls.

So I figured...what the fuck.

They were wolves. Okay, I have to accept that. Werewolves, I suppose. Of a kind.

But they were new at this game. I've been playing it a long, long time.

They say age and treachery will overcome youth and skill. Take that to the bank. And, another aphorism. Experience is the best teacher.

These pricks have only ever sunk their teeth into innocent flesh.

Fighting another werewolf is different.

Fighting a *benandanti* werewolf is even harder. It's a death wish. Ask anyone I've ever gone up against.

Oh, yeah, wait: You can't.

These young monsters changed.

I changed faster.

-7-

While they still could, they screamed for mercy.

Didn't help.

They screamed for their god.

He didn't show.

They screamed.

And screamed.

And screamed.

I was okay with that.

-8-

I let a couple of weeks go by and then met with DuSchwezel in a booth at Heaven Street Diner. Couple of the regulars were there, but nobody disturbed us. It's that kind of place.

We worked through a cup of coffee each and he pushed his apple pie around with a fork before we got to it.

"Terrible what happened," he said. "The fire. Those poor boys."

"Yeah," I said. "Makes you think."

He nodded. Lifted some apple glop, looked at it, set it down.

"I went to Olivia's grave the other day."

I said nothing.

"There were flowers on it. Not expensive, but lovely."

I sipped my coffee.

"Any idea who put them there?"

The clocked on the wall ticked through half a minute. DuSchwezel nodded.

"Thanks," he said.

"For what?" I said. "I never did anything for you. We have no understanding other than the fact that I paid you a hundred bucks to answer some legal questions. You cash that check, by the way?"

"Of course. It's a matter of record now."

We sipped our coffee.

"Hunter," he said, "can I be frank with you?"

"Funny question for a lawyer to ask, but sure."

He almost smiled. "I went to law school to be the kind of lawyer I became. Seriously. I never had aspirations of being Atticus Finch. I never wanted to do anything but make money pretty much the way I do."

"Congratulations," I said.

"Go ahead and sneer, but I'm trying to say something here."

"Be my guest."

"In my line of work, I only meet bad people. Fathers and sons, like the Fenners. Hangers-on. Gangs in expensive suits. You understand what I'm saying?"

"I do."

"I don't ever get to meet good people. When I do meet someone who's supposed to be stand-up, I'm immediately figuring the angle to break them down and turn them. You understand? I'm always looking for a way to make them like me. In one way or another."

I said nothing.

"In all of my dealings," he said, "I've never met anyone like you. The people with whom I work always talk about honor and all that, but it's talk. The deference people show to them is totally out of fear or greed. Never because these people have earned their respect."

"If you're driving in the direction of a point, man," I said, "take the next exit."

He said, "You are a third- or possibly fourth-rate private investigator working out of what is arguably the seediest office it has ever been my displeasure to visit. You smell of cleaning products and old booze, and you are not a very nice person."

I leaned back. "Gosh, thanks. I—"

He cut me off. "But you may be the only honorable man I have ever met."

Before I could figure out a way to respond to that, he stood up and tossed a twenty down to cover the tab.

"Olivia would probably have liked you."

And with that he turned and shambled out.

I sat in the booth and drank my coffee. I ate his slice of pie. I stared out the window at the night.

MONSTERS OF ANY KIND

MICHAEL G. BAUGHAN

BRODKIN'S DEMESNE
by MICHAEL GRAY BAUGHAN

Bethany screams but nothing changes. Pete never comes and the droning just goes on. If anything, it seems to grow louder, and larger. As if feeding on her distress. At times like these, the sound attacks her from everywhere at once, drilling her eardrums and squeezing her skull with a psychosomatic contraction so strong it feels like her eyes might actually pop under the strain. Fifty yards of gradual downslope separate her from the old barn where Pete is working but it is so littered with rotting cicada exuviae that it might as well be the Salton Sea. She hasn't ventured into the backyard since they started molting and she sure as hell isn't going to start now. Feeling trapped and infantile, she stamps her feet and balls her hands and yells Pete's name into the throbbing void.

This time, all she wants is for him to take a break and watch the sunset with her in the metal rockers she rescued from slow disintegration behind the garage. Desperate for an escape, she leveraged them into her strictly onroad SUV and drove them over an hour away to have a sandblaster scour away all the rust. Now, after two coats of primer and four coats of paint, they look good enough for a vintage décor magazine.

Her voice eventually cracks and gives out. Extracting her cell phone, she furiously texts him her request. How pathetic, that this has become the protocol for communicating with him while he is working, as outlined in a bulleted email he had the temerity to title *My New and Unalienable Rights of Immaculate Domain.*

After a punitive delay, he finally pokes his head out of the barn, lumbers across the Salton Sea and climbs the back steps like a man returning from a massacre. By then the light has changed and all the colors are fleeing. He stands there glowering at her from the shadowed edge of the porch, and for a moment he looks like he has been decapitated by the dark.

The impression fades as he passes into the small square of light thrown from the window and his face becomes a face again. He accepts the sweating HopDevil she offers and her pique flares when he just slumps into one of the resurrected chairs without so much as a *thank you, ma'am.* She gives him sixty seconds to sulk and then lobs him a softball.

"Did you get a lot done today?"

"It's a big job," he says without looking at her. The snarky part of her wants to ask which, the unfinished studio or the overdue film project?

"But it's going well? You're feeling good about it?"

"I can't even see the edges of it yet."

She gives up and frowns at him while he stares into the gathering night, wondering how much longer she can ignore the signs of his mental illness. Even in good light, he has become a crazed and sinister presence, nothing at all like the guy once voted Most Likely to DJ Your Wedding. His usually trim beard has grown wild and pubic. His kind brown eyes perpetually cut to a menacing squint. With all that sweat and dirt caked into his crow's feet he looks less like an in-demand sound engineer and more like someone auditioning for the evil shaman part in the independent horror film he was supposed to be done scoring by now. Asked to sign a standard nondisclosure, he treats the project like some kind of national secret. She hasn't been permitted to *see* more than ten seconds of it, but she *hears* more than enough, thank you very much, and it's a damn good thing their nearest neighbors are so far away or else they'd both have to answer for all the demented noise leaking into the world through his studio monitors. After weeks of ransacking occult websites, poorly scanned grimoires and dodgy transcriptions of ancient incantations for the right concatenation of creepy syllables, he has recently begun to assemble and blare endless iterations of the results: chants and shrieks, dead tongue twisters, twenty ear-shredding tracks layered atop each other and digitally degraded into an unspeakable glossolalia. Nothing was *right*. Nothing was *massive* or *malevolent* enough for him.

He'd been threatening to build an infinite baffle subwoofer for years and now he finally had the space and the perfect excuse. With a dozen eighteen-inch drivers, each as heavy as an anvil, and crude plans he found on the Internet, he turned the old stone barn into a mammoth resonator.

The first time he fired it up, she was inside the house, and even at that distance every collective thrust of the voice coils felt like a medicine ball thrown at her chest by an irate gym teacher. One time she got caught outside near the barn when the bass dropped and it hit her like a seizure: total body static. She actually peed herself a little. She had no idea how he could stand it at such close range. When she asked him what he was trying to do, he made even less sense than usual. He was *trawling the abyss*, he said. *Making waves* and *taking soundings*. Seeing *what showed up in the backwash*. The infrasonics alone made her feel like putting a gun in her mouth. She complained about it every chance she got but instead of dialing it back Pete devolved into a little kid given permission to play with a very big gun—trigger happy and surely going deaf. When the cicadas first emerged, she actually thanked them for providing him a new distraction.

At gunpoint she would admit that she was also unwell. That this desperate enforcement of a happy hour reprieve was every bit as much for her sake as his. She hadn't believed her friends when they warned her working from home wasn't as ideal as it sounded. Particularly this home. Pete's sound experiments were bad enough, but if she had known a few months after they moved in a billion cicadas would boil up from the earth and foul her painstakingly decluttered headspace, she would have postponed this whole horse-country experiment, stayed on at the firm downtown, and banked another year of her old salary.

But then they would have missed their shot. An old Swarthmore friend who worked at a boutique estate agency and shared her taste for country chic had sent her some photos before it was officially on the market and she knew right away it was exactly what she wanted. Unlike all those badly stuccoed McMansions in West Chester, full of gypsum board and Chinese plywood, Brodkin's Demesne was built with local blue stone and old growth oak. And how cool was that name? In her wildest fantasies she never dreamed she'd live on a named estate. Who cares if nobody could pronounce it or tell her what it meant? And sure, the place was drafty and dark and the bathrooms were tiny with bad plumbing and *things*, multiple *things*, were living in the attic, scampering across their bedroom ceiling all night and pissing wherever they damn well pleased. But it had original 18th-century wainscoting for Christ's sake, four separate chimneys, manteled fireplaces in almost every room, stained-glass windows on the second-floor landing, even a small orchard. She didn't know a damned thing about maintaining fruit trees, but she could always learn, couldn't she?

On a purely conceptual level, she thinks it tragic that after so many generations of stewardship the surviving owners wanted no part of their ancestral estate beyond due cut of its sale. On a personal level, it was very fortunate indeed. Not only did the property boast one of the oldest, stateliest homes in the Brandywine Valley—the perfect demographic for her new private law practice—it also came with a stone barn of even hoarier vintage where Pete could build his dream studio. Compared to a loft in Callowhill, it was a virtual fiefdom. And what little West Philly latchkey girl wouldn't jump at the chance at owning her own magic kingdom?

If only it wasn't under attack by biblical plague. It didn't help that alarmist blogs were going all caps lock, exclamation-point about it. Clickbait loonies calling it a rogue brood and claiming it was proof of climate meltdown. According to them, periodical cicadas were genetically programmed to return in only thirteen- or seventeen-year cycles. Nobody could explain the prime number connection but none of the known populations lined up with this surprise emergence.

Bethany took another large swig of wine and reminded herself that even such extreme events had to follow biological rules. It's not like cicadas were immortal. Or even remotely dangerous, for that matter. To humans anyway. She only had to survive about four more weeks of their monotone sex song and then it'd be all wildflowers and honeysuckle. Assuming Pete came out of his funk and they were able to keep up with the payments.

Failure on that front was not an option. Throwing the full-count curveball had been her call, so if it didn't work out, she would be the one to catch all the blowback and accepting blame wasn't exactly her forte. Pete had warned her leaving the city would change the trajectory of their relationship in unpredictable ways, but she needed to ground him somehow if she ever hoped to have a kid, and she wasn't sure how many innings they had left in them. So far, all it had produced were balks.

Sitting there, slugging wine and waiting for Pete to mumble an excuse and retreat back to the barn, she began obsessing over the dreaded D word again. How embarrassing it would be, and how devastating. Divorce she could handle, but Defaulting? Ye gods forbid. All they needed was a good pep talk, maybe a huddle with a life coach. Lord knows Pete had clocked long, strange hours managing the studio downtown. Back then neither of them ever got home before dark, but at least when they were together, they were *together*. Something atrophied when they began spending all their time at this one address. They forgot how to warm up, what the signals meant. After a couple rounds of perfunctory sex to break in the old place, Pete started holing up in his barn. Now he only came out for meals and materials. The renovation was taking way too long. She told him to hire somebody but he was too damn stubborn.

One day, when the cicadas really started blaring, Pete stood down his sonic canon and came out to mike the orchard with the little portable rig he used for custom Foley effects. She watched him through the blinds in their bedroom and got her first honest sounding of the bitterness building between them. Instead of alarm or empathy, she felt a strange jolt of pleasure when he flipped on the power and threw off the headphones like they had shocked him. She'd warned him they got loud enough to cause permanent hearing loss but he didn't believe her. She went into another room to get some laundry done and when she came back a half hour later, he was still there, in the same spot, but the headphones were back on and he was standing way up on his toes, his posture twisted and rigid, as if frozen in convulsion. It dawned on her that he might be having a stroke and her detachment cracked. She rushed downstairs and ran out to him, ready to call an ambulance, and found him blinking at her as if she were the crazy one.

"Can you hear it?" he asked.

"Of course I can hear it. What's wrong with you?"

"It's so beautiful."

"You're losing your shit, Pete. *Please* get it together."

"Just listen," he said, offering her the headphones, but she didn't want to listen. She just wanted it to end. And one day it did end, just not in the way she expected.

───

She wakes to the sound of her skull shattering. An interval of raw panic before the mandibles crushing her face retract into her subconscious and she realizes that what she really heard was the implosion of the wineglass she had fallen asleep still clutching and that blood, her blood, is pouring from her palm like a stigmatic in a giallo film. She leaps to her feet so fast the head rush nearly knocks her out. She reels, reaches out for balance, plants a red handprint on the upholstery and narrowly avoids knocking over all the empty bottles lined up on the floor. Even so, the damage is done; her new white couch is a crime scene.

The cut is deep and nasty. She flushes it at the sink until her hand goes numb and the bleeding slows enough to hunt for shards. Another near faint while pulling wide the gash. The cold water helps deaden the pain but a strange inability to focus properly makes her wonder whether she somehow cracked her skull after all. Recollection coagulates around the wound.

This time Pete never came in from the barn. Never responded to her text. She tired of waiting, tired of being ignored, went back inside and opened one of the really good bottles of wine she'd been saving to celebrate completion of the studio. This much she can remember, but was that last night, or the night before? Her mind aches and little mystery why. All the available evidence suggests an extended and quite abnormal binge. She doesn't notice what has happened until she cuts off the water, bandages her wound and steps through the screen door into a stark and sepulchral hush.

Sometime during the night the cicadas went silent. Nary a tymbal is vibrating.

Relief crumples her into a dropped-puppet slump until another stab of pain pulls her strings taut again. The pain makes her alert, and angry. Where the hell is Pete? She could have bled to death for Christ's sake. She holds the wounded hand by the wrist, as if taking her own pulse. Down the steps like this, pale and pissed, she wades into the Salton Sea, into the minefield of ick. Legions of discarded skins crunch underfoot and their stench of briny rot fouls her airways like a summer dumpster behind a seafood joint.

The smell is somehow exaggerated by the silence. In the wake of the eternal drone, this preternatural hush is unnerving and surreal, so much so she cannot quite convince herself she isn't dreaming it. They are deathly quiet but they haven't left, she realizes, as she begins to spy them by the thousands, roosting in the shrubbery. Like a trenched army waiting for the order to attack.

Freaked out by the thought of all those red eyes upon her, she hurries now into a jittery stutter step. Fighting one-handed to open the barn door, she stumbles in through the dust. The smell is even stronger inside. Long white tarps hanging from the two-story rafters seal off the gear room from the active renovation and give the gloomy vestibule the kinetic emptiness of a recently evacuated theater. Too spooked to linger, she pushes through an overlapping seam and into the makeshift studio.

The room appears empty save Pete's main console and abutting banks of vintage gear. All the knobs and dials and buttons vaguely remind her of the multitude waiting silently outside, an interlinked network of resurrected things, exhumed and assembled for some obscure purpose. She approaches his empty chair and lowers herself into it. A fractal screensaver gyrates in microcosmic infinity until she nudges the mouse and unveils the stack of spectral insanity hiding behind it. Jagged lines vault and plummet across the screen to pitches far beyond the range of human hearing. Below them is an arrowed play icon too tempting to ignore. Clicking it instantly drives her backwards and out of the chair. She crouches and covers her ears, assaulted by a torrent of noise not even the damned should endure. The whole barn shakes with it, a hurricane of oscillating frequencies given visible agency by the motes of dust vibrating in the light-spoked air like primitive organisms striving to evolve. She can't move, can't think, can hardly breathe until the recording plays itself out some scrambled length of time later.

She lies back and takes her hands away from her ears. Only from this prone perspective is she able to locate what appear to be the remains of Pete.

Her first thought is violent electrocution. How else to explain the big brittle carapace stuck so far up the load-bearing post. She gets to her feet, circling around to see, and freezes when her new vantage reveals a tenuousness and a transparency not evident from the rear.

This withered amber husk cannot be her husband. That torn paper mask must not be his face. As if in confirmation a scuttling sound beyond the curtain swivels her head.

"Pete?"

Shock drops a veil of protective detachment over her senses, slowing her galloping panic into a bridled curiosity. She follows the sound back through the winding-sheet partition, back through the vestibule, and into the ancient heart of the barn.

The smell is strongest there. Loamy rot and acid bile. The smell of evisceration. Sections of the handhewn floorboards have been torn away and a wide burrow gapes below. She grabs a work light hanging from a nail, and as she leans down to look, the newborn brood king contracts its dorsal thorax and unfurls its massive, vein-mazed wings across the rafters over her head. In its teneral state, it is white as a grub save for its bulbous bloodred eyes and it glistens like an avenging angel when she spins and shines the light upon it. Lancing halfway to the floor, its barbed aedeagus twitches in expectation. The old beam bends and groans back into shape when it lifts off from its perch and falls like lightning, pinning her to the earth. For a spell of time both eternal and blessedly brief, the heavy silence is broken only by the screams and prayers of the one fated for this unnatural selection.

In a dark corner of the loft with a terribly excellent view of all this, Pete crouches and shakes. Blood paints his jowls in symmetrical trails and drips onto his portable rig. He'd been monitoring the pupa in secret for days, acclimating to the reality of it and listening for signs of its emergence. But it was only this morning, when it wriggled from its shell and blew out his eardrums with a first, titanic sounding, that he finally understood his role in all this.

He was quite obviously born and brought here to be the brood king's recordist—its scribe and herald. Whatever secrets were conveyed in its apocalyptic trumpet blasts must be documented and disseminated. And so he kept recording, despite the fact that he himself cannot hear it anymore—a blessing for certain while it ravaged the poor woman who was once his wife and thrust her still-living body into the waiting burrow. Presumably to feed its successor even as it grew within her. Whatever the case, some things are better left unheard.

He climbs down when the brood king flies through the barn doors she has inadvertently left open for it. He suspects that it, like most males, will be hungry or sleepy after sex. He hopes this distraction will give him enough time to get to the house and grab some more tape before anything else important happens.

He is half-right at least. After centuries of chthonic stasis, the great beast is anything but tired. But it is ravenous, and prowling the airspace above its demesne for a favorite snack. Pete's fatal error, beyond awakening it in the first place, is a failure to guess what that might be. It drops from the sky the second he emerges. Needless to say, he never hears it coming.

One of the many wonders of magicicada physiology is their ability to cork food sources with their viscous saliva once they are done feeding, thereby preserving the leftovers. Pete has no time to ponder the ramifications or evolutionary genius of this before a six-foot stylet spears him through one eye socket and deftly lobotomizes him while siphoning a measure of his cerebrospinal fluid. Over millennia of trial and error, the brood king has learned that all large mammals continuously produce this clear and nutrient-rich fluid. More, in fact, than they can ever use, so long as they are provided a minimal amount of sustenance and intrusions didn't go too deep into their brains.

So in a very real way both Bethany and Pete got what they wanted. She was given a child, of sorts, and he a symbiotic relationship between king and subject that, properly managed, just might last them the rest of their days. And though Pete now lacks any ability to communicate his thoughts on this arrangement, the permanent wink and asymmetrical smirk it affixes on his face records at least some manner of awestruck appreciation.

Unmoved by this temporal drama, the imago horde end their intermission and begin to sing anew. For like all things born in the image and beneath the watchful gaze of their god, they too are hardwired to honor an ancient ritual they cannot understand. To persist in the glorious hope of being born again.

MONSTERS OF ANY KIND

OWL GOINGBACK

SEALED WITH A KISS

by OWL GOINGBACK

"I'd sell my soul for a beer!" Kent Phillps yelled, a wave of anger surging through him. "I swear I would. A nice cold can, ice crystals clinging to it." He licked his lips and waited, but no one rushed forward to accept his offer. His words floated unheard across the fallow fields and fell to earth among weeds and sticker bushes. A beer would be nice, but what he really needed was a ride.

He turned and looked behind him. The road stretched like a black ribbon through the Georgia countryside. Empty. No cars. Not a one. Nor had he seen any for hours. Miles from the nearest town or store, maybe even miles from the closest farmhouse, he couldn't have picked a more inconvenient place for his car to break down.

About five miles earlier, his Toyota Corolla had made a funny coughing noise, the warning lights had come on, and the engine had seized up and died with a shudder. Despite being a jet engine mechanic in the Air Force, he didn't know the first thing about piston engines and carburetors. He didn't know much about Georgia either. A city boy from Chicago, he hadn't realized just how rural certain parts of the state were.

He should have known better than to come on this trip, especially by himself, but a friend had told him about the Confederate prison park at Andersonville and he wanted to see it. Unfortunately, Andersonville had been closed, something about a college kid from Florida discovering a tunnel full of skeletons.

Since he couldn't visit the park, he'd decided to drive on down to Plains, Georgia, to see the hometown of former president Jimmy

Carter. He could have saved himself the drive, for Plains was a big disappointment. Wasn't much to see, just a couple of filling stations and a few old stores, their shelves stocked with cheap souvenirs and empty cans of Billy Beer. About the only thing of interest was the giant peanut statue, with the familiar toothy grin, that stood in front of Elmer's Food and Gas, and that was full of woodpecker holes.

He'd left Plains, trying to salvage what was left of his weekend by taking a shortcut back to Robins Air Force Base. Somewhere north of Americas, but still south of Fort Valley, he had gotten lost, the car's engine had died, and he had spent the better part of two hours walking.

Kent spotted movement to his left and stopped. He watched, amused, as a scrawny gray cat slipped from beneath a sticker bush and cautiously approached him. The cat probably belonged to a farmer and was out hunting field mice.

"Here, kitty, kitty," he called, holding his hand out. He slowly squatted down, trying not to make sudden movements. "What are you doing out here? Hunting?" He glanced at the barren field where the cat had been. "Looks like you could have picked better grounds."

The cat stopped while still about ten feet away, sat down in the middle of the road, and began to groom itself. No wild cat here, Kent thought. This cat's comfortable around people.

"You wouldn't know where I could find a pay phone, would you?" he asked. Ignoring him, the cat lifted a leg and licked its butt. Kent laughed. "No, I didn't think so."

Reaching in his shirt pocket, he fumbled past the book of matches he'd picked up in Plains, and pulled out a piece of beef jerky. "You hungry?" he asked the cat. "Or did you get enough mice to eat?" He unwrapped the dried beef and held it out. "Come on, you can have it."

At the sight of food, the cat stopped licking and meowed. Kent smiled as it stood up and walked toward him. "Yeah, I thought this would get your attention." Halfway to him, the cat stopped again, frozen in place with one paw raised in the air.

"What's the matter, stupid? You don't like beef jerky?"

The cat stared past him, ignoring the tasty offering. Curious, Kent looked behind him. The road was empty. No dog. No people. Not even another car. Nothing. Still, the gray cat must have seen something it didn't like, for it arched its back, hissed, and fled back beneath the bush.

Kent stood up and looked around, wondering what had frightened the cat. He didn't see anything, only the empty fields, the road, and the gray horizon. His gaze lingered for a moment on the western sky, which was no longer gray but black. He licked his finger and held it up. The wind blew from that direction.

"Storm coming," he said, wishing he'd stayed in the barracks. The approaching storm was probably no more than ten miles away and would be over top of him in less than an hour. Georgia thunderstorms could pack quite a punch, especially during the summer months. He needed to find shelter, but the only thing around was a few straggly pine trees and they would make better lightning rods than protection.

He shoved the beef jerky back into his pocket and continued walking. About half an hour later, he paused to study the impending tempest. The thunderstorm stretched across the sky like a giant black curtain, providing an ebony backdrop for the trees and fields. The effect was eerie, but beautiful, for everything stood out in sharp contrast against the darkness.

"Going to be a bad one," he said, his attention drawn to what looked like a whirling mass of leaves silhouetted against the storm. He watched, fascinated, as the leaves, tossed about by the wind, rose and fell, dissipated and regrouped again. His fascination gave way to a feeling of dread, however, when he realized that it was not leaves but birds that he watched.

What the hell?

Kent was spellbound. He had never seen so many birds together at one time. Sparrows, pigeons, doves, even a pair of hawks, they dove and soared, clumped together and broke apart, racing ahead of the storm, fleeing from it. The air filled with the flapping of their wings, and their startled cries, as they passed overhead.

Nor was it just birds that fled the storm. He spotted twenty or thirty deer, their tails held high in warning, running through the fields. Snapping at the deer's heels were dogs. Lots of dogs. Hunting dogs, hounds, collies, pit bulls, and Doberman pinschers, they ran with tongues hanging and ears laid back. A chorus of yips, barks, and howls marked the motley pack as they passed out of sight. Close behind the dogs came rabbits, squirrels, and an assortment of other small animals.

A lone horse galloped by, riderless, the reins of its bridle flapping behind it. Kent stared at the horse and wondered how a thunderstorm could cause such fear in so many different animals. A fire yes, a tornado perhaps, but not a thunderstorm. Maybe there was something different about this particular storm, something deadly.

He might have allowed the storm to overtake him, just to see what was so unusual about it, had it not been for the animals. Knowing that their sense of danger was more acute than his, he trusted their judgment that the approaching darkness was something to be feared rather than welcomed. So instead of waiting, he decided to keep moving.

Kent jogged down the center of the road as fast as he could. He wasn't as quick as the deer, nor could he keep up with the dogs, but he did a damn good job of keeping distance between himself and the storm. Still, he was not a strong runner and would soon tire. He had to get someplace safe. But where?

The thought had just crossed his mind, when he spotted the roof of an old farmhouse about a mile up the road.

Thank God.

The house sat about two hundred feet off the road, in a yard reclaimed by weeds and kudzu vines. A tin-roofed wood structure, with peeling paint and a sagging porch, the house perched above the ground on concrete blocks to allow the summer breeze to circulate beneath it. Whoever lived in the dwelling had moved out long ago, for all the windows were covered with weathered sheets of plywood.

Fearful of falling through, he carefully climbed onto the rotted porch, testing each board before he took a step. Among the problems he did not need was a broken leg. The front door was unlocked and opened with a squeak.

The smell of dust, mildew, and rodent droppings greeted him as he stepped across the threshold into the living room. The tiny room was bare and unpainted, with strips of cardboard tacked to the walls for insulation. On the eastern wall stood a brick fireplace, probably the only method of heating the house.

"Not exactly the Hilton, is it?" he said aloud to himself.

Two doorways led off the living room. One went to a bedroom, the other opened onto the kitchen. He checked out the bedroom first, found nothing of interest, and backtracked through the living room to the kitchen.

Spiderwebs hung like silken chandeliers from the kitchen ceiling, their beauty marred only by the long-dead insects caught in their gossamer strands. A crude wooden counter ran along the back wall, centered beneath a pair of boarded-up windows. On the counter sat a large candle, which had melted into a pyramid-shaped blob of wax. Since there were no electrical outlets in the kitchen, Kent assumed there had never been a refrigerator or dishwasher, none of the modern conveniences that made life easy. In one corner of the room, a discolored patch of floor marked where a woodburning stove had once stood.

To the right of the counter was another door. He tried the door, found it locked, slipped the deadbolt back and opened it. Fresh air rushed in as he looked out upon a backyard waist high in weeds. A large pile of rotted wood and sheets of tin, all that was left of a barn, rose above the sea of weeds. Halfway between the barn and the house, a rusty pump stood like a silent sentinel over the cistern. Kent heard a rustling sound and caught a glimpse of a fleeing rabbit.

Overhead, a flock of crows called loudly to each other as they raced ahead of the storm.

Going to be a bad one.

Suddenly, the tiny farmhouse he had chosen for shelter didn't look quite as sturdy as it had moments before. He remembered the flying house from *The Wizard of Oz* and wondered if he too would end up somewhere over the rainbow.

"Just follow the yellow brick road," he said, closing the door. He had just turned the lock, when he heard the front door bang shut. Figuring that the wind must have caught it, and not wanting the door to be torn off its hinges, he hurried into the living room to close it. To his surprise, he found that it wasn't the wind that had slammed the door. He had company.

The woman stood with her back to the door, breathing hard. She wore cutoff blue jeans, white tennis shoes, and a dirty gray T-shirt. Her hair was blonde, and her skin darkly tanned with a scattering of freckles. She was probably in her thirties, but could have been older. He noticed scratches on her legs and the left side of her face.

"You're hurt," he said.

"My horse threw me," the woman replied. She turned and tried to lock the door. After a few seconds of fumbling unsuccessfully, she looked back at him. "Don't just stand there. Help me."

Getting over the surprise of having an unexpected houseguest, Kent crossed the room. "Let me try it," he said.

He struggled with the lock, but had no better luck than she did. The door had warped with age, and the deadbolt no longer lined up with the door frame.

"Hurry!" she said, her voice urgent. He wasn't sure why she wanted the door locked, but from the tone of her voice it seemed like a good idea. As he fought with the lock, the room grew dark. The storm had reached them.

"For God's sake, hurry!" she shouted.

"Here," Kent said. "I'll put my weight against it while you try to lock it."

He let go of the lock and shoved with all his strength against the door. At the same time, the woman twisted on the latch. After several attempts, the deadbolt finally slipped into place.

They had just gotten the door locked when something crashed against it from the other side. They both jumped back, startled. Kent started to say something, but the woman held a finger to her lips, motioning him to silence. They stood as still as statues, listening as something sniffed at the door and scratched to get in. A dog, Kent thought. But then the doorknob jiggled back and forth.

Not a dog. A person.

He started to go to the door, but she grabbed his right arm. He turned, and her look of fear held him in place. An uneasy moment passed, and then the knob stopped moving. The scratching also stopped. Kent, realizing that he had been holding his breath, let out a sigh of relief.

"Are you in trouble?" he whispered. "Someone after you?"

The woman let go of his arm and smiled. "No, darling. I'm not in trouble. And no one is after me."

"Then who was that at the door?"

She stepped back and looked him up and down. "You're not from around here, are you?"

He shook his head. "I'm in the Air Force, stationed at Warner Robins. My name is Kent."

"Soldier boy, huh?" She smiled again. "I should have known. Probably a Yankee, I bet. Not that it matters to me one way or another. Lord knows, a Yankee's just as good as a Southern boy when it comes to taking care of business, if you know what I mean. My name's Beverly. Beverly Sanders. I'm originally from Waycross, but I've been living hereabouts for the past few years." She smiled again, a little mischievously. "I'm a working girl."

The shock must have shown on his face, for Beverly burst out laughing.

"Honey, don't look so surprised," she said.

"You're a hooker?"

"*Hooker*'s a Yankee word. I prefer 'lady of the evening.' Don't worry, I don't bite—not unless you pay me to. As for your question... It wasn't a 'who' that was at the door. It was a 'what.'"

"I don't understand," Kent said.

"Judgment day, sweetie. The end of the world, at least for some folks. Old Luke's out walking around, brought all his haints with him. That's what spooked my horse. Spooked all the other animals too." She paused and looked at him funny. "Land sakes, haven't you ever read the Bible?"

He shook his head.

Beverly laughed. "Now don't this just beat all, a Southern whore teaching the Bible to a Yankee. Anyway, folks about these parts have been talking about the end of the world for a long time. Old Maribel Johnson even got herself a poem about it. Loves to recite it on Sundays. Let's see if I can remember how it goes." She thought for a moment, then recited the poem.

"Dark of the moon, in the month of June, and Old Luke will come out to play. He'll lay the houses low, and death he will sow, as he carries the sinners away.

"So pray for your souls, and keep all your doors and windows closed, and maybe he'll pass you by. 'Cause in the dark of the moon, in the month of June, many a sinner will cry."

"Who's Old Luke?" he asked when she had finished with the poem.

She again gave him a funny look. "You must be dumber than I thought. Old Luke. Lucifer. The Devil himself."

It was Kent's turn to laugh. "What a crock. It's not the end of the world; it's just a storm." Suddenly, as if on cue, they heard the sound of rain hitting the tin roof. He looked up. "See, what did I tell you? It's just a storm."

Beverly also looked up. "Maybe it is. Maybe it isn't."

The room grew very dark as the storm moved over them. Kent remembered the melted candle in the kitchen and went to get it. Luckily, he still had the pack of matches with him.

The sky had opened up with a torrential downpour by the time he returned with the candle. The noise of the rain hitting the tin roof was deafening. In the distance, thunder boomed.

Beverly still stood in the center of the room, staring up at the ceiling. Kent started to say something, but was interrupted by the sound of water splattering against flat stones. He turned and saw rain pouring down the chimney into the fireplace. Mixed with the rain were tiny objects that bounced and skidded across the wood floor. He thought they were hailstones at first, but then one of them rolled up against his foot.

Kent looked down and saw a tiny frog lying on its back, legs kicking, trying desperately to right itself. Curious, he stepped closer to the fireplace and saw dozens of frogs on the floor, with hundreds more spilling out of the chimney.

"Will you look at this. It's raining frogs!" he said, shocked. Beverly quit looking at the ceiling and stared at the floor instead.

He tried not to step on any frogs as he approached the fireplace, but that was nearly impossible. The floor was covered with them. Most of the frogs were dead, but some were still alive, their bodies broken from hitting the bricks that lined the bottom of the fireplace.

Nor was it just frogs that fell from the sky. Mixed in with the tiny amphibians were body parts. Human body parts. On the hearth in front of the fireplace lay a man's hand, severed at the wrist with an inch or so of bone protruding from the bloody flesh. A few inches away from the hand lay a foot, still encased in a woman's black shoe. Beyond that, an eyeball was wedged against the pale belly of a frog.

"Oh, dear Jesus," Kent said, his stomach heaving. He jumped back, covering his nose and mouth with his hand to keep from retching.

More body parts fell down the chimney. An ear. Part of a face. Intestines. More frogs hit the stones with a sickening thud. And the rain that fell from the sky wasn't rain, but blood. The blood poured down the chimney, splattered dark red against the floor and walls.

Kent backed away from the fireplace and nearly collided with Beverly. Outside the thunder drew closer.

"Judgment day," Beverly whispered, staring in horror at what was spilling out of the chimney.

"There has to be a logical explanation for this," Kent said, though he could think of none.

Maybe there was a plane crash. A midair explosion. That would explain the body parts. But what about the blood? A hundred planes could blow up and you wouldn't have that much blood.

Whatever the explanation, it would have to keep, for suddenly someone knocked on the door, turned the knob, and tried to get in.

A tingle of fear walked down Kent's spine as he turned toward the door. His legs trembled. The knocking grew louder, desperate, frantic. The whole room seemed to shake from the pounding. Whoever it was, they weren't going away this time. A minute passed. Two. Kent was afraid to move, but knew that he had to do something. He set the candle down on the floor, took a deep breath, and inched toward the door.

"Kent, don't!" Beverly warned.

He reached the door, placed his palm against it, felt the wood tremble from the knocks. Someone was out there, standing just on the other side of the door.

"Go away," Kent said, his voice choking. "Go away and leave us alone." The knocking didn't let up. "Go away!" he shouted.

The knocking stopped. A moment of silence passed, and then a man's voice came from the other side of the door. "Help me. Please, help me. Open the door."

Kent gasped. Someone was out there in the storm, in the rain of blood and things too ghastly to mention. He grabbed the doorknob, fumbled with the lock to open it.

"No!" Beverly screamed. She ran across the room, flung herself against the door. Kent tried to push her out of the way.

"Someone's out there!" he yelled. "He needs our help."

"Don't open this door!"

"I can't just leave him there."

"You must."

The voice from the other side of the door spoke again, softer. "Beverly? Is that you, Bev?"

Beverly froze, her eyes wide.

"It's me, Bev. Reverend Atkins. Open the door and let me in."

"Go away," she whispered, her voice so low that Kent could barely hear her.

Kent tried to pull her away from the door so he could open it, but she wouldn't budge. "Beverly, it's someone you know. A reverend. We have to let him in."

"No," she said, fighting him. Outside the thunder drew closer. One steady boom after another. Each equally spaced apart, each exactly like the last, but louder.

Boom...Boom...Boom.

He heard the thunder, felt the house tremble from it, and wondered how it could be spaced so evenly apart. Of course, it couldn't be. Not unless it was something else.

BOOM...BOOM...BOOM.

Terror gripped Kent by the balls as he realized that he wasn't listening to thunder. They were footsteps. Something big was coming down the road. Something really fucking big. With the footsteps came an odd reddish glow, like a fire, that seeped through the cracks in the walls and floated down the chimney. The glow lifted some of the darkness in the room, bathed them in the color of blood.

Kent grabbed Beverly's arms and pulled her away from the door. "For God's sake, open the door. He's a reverend. He's your friend!" He pushed her out of the way, turned the lock, and pulled open the door.

BOOM...BOOM.

Beverly screamed at him, tried to stop him. "He's not a friend. He's a customer!"

The words sunk in like a knife, but it was too late. He already had the door opened. Reverend Atkins stood on the porch. He was scarecrow thin and drenched in blood, his short hair plastered to his scalp. Around him, the porch was littered with dead frogs and chunks of gore that had fallen from the sky.

"Thank you," the reverend said, his lower lip trembling. "Oh, thank you."

He started to step across the threshold, but something fell from the sky. Gray and slimy, it was as thick as an oak tree and a mile long. A giant serpent that shot out of the eerie glowing sky and wrapped around the reverend's body, snatching him off the porch.

Reverend Atkins kicked and screamed as he was lifted high into the sky, dancing like a kite on a string. Before he disappeared, Kent saw that it wasn't a serpent but a tongue that had grabbed the good reverend. A giant tongue. The tongue of Old Luke himself.

Kent felt his sanity start to slip away as he stood in the doorway, looking upon the face of Satan. The face was a festering mass of boiling flesh, as wide as a mountain, with eyes that were two glowing orbs of brimstone. Around the Devil's face hovered his minions, creatures too hideous to describe, with leathery bat wings, fangs, and claws. Kent gazed upon these things, and screamed.

He was still screaming when Beverly grabbed him from behind and pulled him back into the room. She pushed past him, slammed the door shut and locked it. "You stupid fool!" she shouted, turning on him. "Old Luke knows we're in here now. We're next."

He shook his head, tried to rid his mind of the ghastly vision. "The door's locked. He can't get in."

Beverly laughed. "We're talking about Satan. He doesn't need a key to get in. He'll make his own door."

No sooner had she spoke, then something brushed against the door, testing it, perhaps checking for a weakness. Kent shuddered as he thought about the tongue, and imagined it licking against the brittle wood, searching for a way to get in, looking for them. Outside, the footsteps had stopped, and the night had grown strangely quiet. The bloody rain no longer poured down the chimney.

But it's still raining. I can hear it on the roof.

He turned and looked at the fireplace. If the rain hadn't stopped, something must be blocking the chimney.

"Oh, my God."

Kent picked up the candle and hurried across the room. The floor was slick with blood and the bodies of frogs. He stepped on the frogs, felt their bones crunch like potato chips. Twice he slipped, almost fell.

He reached the fireplace and dropped to his knees. Setting the candle on the floor, he used both hands to push aside the dead frogs and body parts that had piled up. Only a few drops of blood fell down the chimney. He stuck his head into the fireplace, lifted the candle above him.

The tiny flame didn't illuminate all of the chimney, but it lit up enough area to see that the shaft was blocked solid. Guided by hundreds of thin, translucent tentacles, like whiskers on a cat, the giant tongue crept spider-like down the chimney. At the tongue's very tip were eyes, dozens of eyes, red and glowing, with vertical pupils like those of a snake.

The eyes saw the candle, saw Kent. Their guidance no longer needed, the tentacles quit probing the walls and the tongue shot down the chimney at incredible speed.

Kent screamed and grabbed the handle of the lever that closed the flue. He prayed that it wasn't rusted in place, pulled the handle, and closed off the chimney. He heard a wet, squishy sound as the tongue hit the metal plate, followed by a demonic shriek of rage from outside the house.

He scooted back out of the fireplace, stood up, and started across the room to where Beverly stood. He was halfway to her, when the house shook and there came the tortured scream of nails being ripped from boards, followed by the snapping of wooden beams. Kent froze and watched in horror as the roof of the house was completely torn away. Nothing remained, not even the rafters. Blood rained down on him.

"Run!" he yelled, though there was nowhere to go. He had only taken two steps when the giant tongue fell from the sky like a coil of loose rope and landed at his feet. Kent tried to jump over the tongue, but it grabbed him. Like a giant anaconda, it wrapped around him, squeezed him, crushed the breath from his lungs. He tried to call for help, but only a soft hissing of air escaped his mouth.

The tongue slithered across his body, its tip rising off the floor to dance before him like a cobra. The eyes stared at him, studied him. Kent was terrified, but he was unable to turn away. He screamed in agony and wet himself as one of the eel-like tentacles caressed the left side of his neck, searing his flesh like a branding iron. Then suddenly, quite unexpectedly, the tongue released him.

He fell to the floor and grabbed his neck. Rows of blisters were already forming where the tentacle touched him. A piercing scream reminded him that the danger was far from over. The tongue had let go of him, but it was closing in on Beverly.

Beverly ran to the front door and tried to yank it open, but the tongue wrapped around her legs and tripped her.

"Help me!" she screamed, beating on the giant appendage with her fists.

Kent got to his feet and staggered to Beverly's aid. He kicked at the tongue and tried to pull it off her, but he wasn't strong enough. If only he had a gun.

"Please, please, don't let him take me," she begged as the tongue started to slowly recoil back into the sky, lifting her legs off the floor. Kent tried to force his hands between the tongue and her legs, but he couldn't. Beverly, hysterical, screamed again and grabbed hold of his shirt.

"Why me?" she yelled. "Why not you? Why didn't he take you?" She looked at his face, desperately searching for an answer. His shirt ripped as the tongue of Old Luke snatched Beverly Sanders up through the roofless house, carrying her into the sky, to him. Kent heard her scream once more, a long piercing cry of terror and pain. Silence followed.

His body trembling, he stood with his face lifted to the pouring rain and watched as something fell from the sky. A tiny metal cylinder streaked from the sky like a meteor and struck the floor near his feet, its impact softened by the bodies of the dead frogs.

Kent stared at the can, saw what it was, and started to laugh. Softly at first, but then so hard his whole body shook. He remembered the offer he had made earlier in the day, said only in jest, but obviously taken seriously. His fingers went to the blisters on his neck, and he laughed even harder.

He had been touched by the Devil himself. Marked. His soul bought and paid for, cursed to an eternity of brimstone and hellfire. The deal had been sealed with a kiss. The purchase price was the twelve-ounce can of Budweiser that lay on the floor, ice crystals still clinging to it. "I'd sell my soul for a beer," he had said, and the Devil had taken him up on it.

Kent doubled over with laughter, the mirth of a doomed man. Even as the tongue fell toward him, he kept laughing. Wiping a tear from his eye, he looked up and said, "Make it a Light."

MONSTERS OF ANY KIND

MICHAEL BAILEY

THE OTHER SIDE
OF SEMICOLONS
by MICHAEL BAILEY

"Hesitation increases in relation to risk in
equal proportion to age."
—Ernest Hemingway

Frankie Jones pushed a finger through the wallpaper in her bedroom, creating the first of what would become thirteen holes, one for each year of her life. She'd hesitated, once again, in the dark, wanting—but also *not* wanting—to know what would happen if she pushed hard enough.

Both paper and wall gave in to her touch; the hole, a hungry mouth, and the ugly striped wallpaper tearing open like lips. Hidden beyond, she knew, were razor-sharp teeth daring to clamp down, and a throat wanting to taste her.

Let go, she told the wall, and the wall let go.

Her knuckle stuck, and for a moment Frankie panicked, imagining some sort of rescue crew being called out in the middle of the night to set her free, or perhaps to reattach a finger.

Ruined, she thought, meaning the wall.

A single ray of yellowish light shone through the hole she'd created, as if a candle burned somewhere on the other side. Scars on Frankie Jones' wrists illuminated pink against her dark-brown skin: three parallel lines. The light, a reminder of what she'd done, both now and then.

She blew out the candle on her nightstand to let darkness envelop the room. She imagined a beam cutting hot through the black, dust motes reflecting like broken glass. She imagined the walls bleeding wherever the light touched. Her foot, which had crawled out from the covers on its own to find cold, pulled itself back under, and her hands worked in unison to yank the comforter completely over her head.

One thing all kids knew: Nothing could harm them while under a blanket.

She counted to ten and peeked out from beneath her protection. The light was gone. She counted a few seconds more—*one alligator, two alligator, three*—before daring her hand to creep out and again touch the wall, to find the damage.

Like touching an empty eye socket, she mused, curious more than anything.

And then she found another section where the wall flexed under her touch. She measured the distance, a hand-width. Another hole lay hidden behind the ugly striped paper.

Two empty sockets, perhaps.

Using a nail, Frankie pried at the scabby surface. She picked at the wall until it gave, and then she peeled. The wallpaper tore in skinny strips, like clinging cuticles.

Hang a poster in the morning, Frankie thought, so her fosters wouldn't kill her.

She felt the walls with one hand and discovered the holes were set at an angle, as if part of a curiously tilted head; she felt her own face with her other hand, also curious. Instead of relighting the candle, Frankie Jones switched on the lamp at her nightstand. She expected a torn face to stare back, blood dripping down from where she'd peeled at the wall. A face made of torn skin and seeping gore. A face unlike her fosters, unlike her own, unlike any she'd ever seen before. A monster's face.

Not a face, she discovered; simply two holes.

A soft amount of light shimmered from inside each.

When she again turned out the bedside lamp, the eyes closed, leaving her in gloomy darkness. With the light, the eyes opened brightly. Tilting her head to match the angle of the holes in the wall, Frankie peered through and found an impossible light that soon dulled to blurry kaleidoscopic images staring back at her: a continuous revolution of brown iris and pupil, each a galaxy flecked with endless stars. The worlds beyond blinked when she blinked, or so she assumed. She pulled back, afraid of what she might find when closing one eye and squinting the other, peering through a single hole like a scope.

What lies beyond? she wondered. *A better life? One worse off than her own, one full of dilapidation and hatred and torment?* No, she was living such a life now, on *this* side of the wall. Perhaps what awaited on the other side was something better, because what else could there be? *You'll be fine in this new home,* they'd told her. *These kind people will watch over you, take care of you, feed you, clothe you, nurture you,* they'd said. Lies. All lies.

She thought of her own lies, of the *accident.*

"Fell against the mirror," she'd said. "Slipped on the tile and fell against the mirror."

Her wrist itched, then, in parallel stripes—ugly as the wallpaper in her room—as the scars of past hesitations healed.

Another hand-width away, she found another soft indentation on the wall, and then another, and another. She pushed against the fabric, fingernails zipping against the corduroy-like surface, until she found them all: eleven *other* perfectly round indentations no larger than a quarter-dollar. She punctured each, her fingers chipped claws tearing through the wallpaper. The holes, thirteen total, were arranged in a circle next to her bed, equidistant apart.

I'll barely be able to cover the damage, she realized, looking to her poster on the opposite wall, ironically picturing a band named A Perfect Circle. She'd thought those same words once before, about the damage, had covered her wrist in bandages to hide what she'd done.

But there was more, she discovered.

Isn't there always?

Next to every hole was a talon-like stain, as if burned by candle flame or smudged with charcoal, or perhaps some dark liquid having seeped through from the other side; they formed sharp points facing outward, more round toward the center of the visage.

A sun, she thought. *A sun made of semicolons, like some kind of hieroglyphic, or maybe a henna tattoo.*

But what waited on the other side? She wondered that too.

Gathering her courage, Frankie looked through the top-most hole, one eye squinted shut, and found another version of her very own room on the other side: bed empty, clothes scattered about the floor, as usual. But not *her* clothes: yellow Converse, a faded leather jacket, trendy ripped jeans, balled-up socks. Her sizes, of course, but like nothing she'd ever wear. The same poster hung on the wall, torn at the bottom-left corner. And afternoon light shone through the window, noting a different time of day. She couldn't help but pull back to check *her* side.

Scarce moonlight filtered in through the window; otherwise dark and by all means night or early morning, perhaps the midnight hour. On her floor: black sneakers, a faded jacket—*not* leather, and boot-cut jeans—*not* ripped, the same socks though. The poster, untorn.

The next hole revealed another version of her room, albeit sometime later, around one o'clock per the golden glow. She'd sometimes nap with sunrays shining on her bed like that. Everything was pristine, tidy: clean floor, bare walls, as if no one lived there.

But that's not my bed, not my room.

A clock, she thought, meaning the markings next to her bed, *with thirteen impossible hours.* And so she gathered more courage and peered through the next hour, found yet another version of her room, set an hour later.

Two o'clock, and a different room, but the same *room.* Clothes that *could* have been hers were stacked on the end of her bed to be put away. Her fosters never did that, never folded. Frankie had always done her own laundry. The same dresser stood in the corner, too, only with different knobs, different scratches. *And who listens to Taylor Swift?* she wondered, *and on vinyl?* A record player sat unused on top of the dresser, collecting dust.

Three o'clock, something whispered in her head, and in this room there were not one but two beds crammed together in the small space. Afternoon light shone through the window. No blinds, in this version of what she assumed was another where and another when of her own existence, just a single-pane sheet of glass speckled with sprinkler overspray. On the floor was a shoebox diorama, some sort of school project, the details too small to ascertain.

Four o'clock, she mused, looking through the next hole, then *five* and *six* and all the way around the sundial, the contents changing with every viewing, the room hers but *not hers* all the same, the light brightening with the progressing day, warmest around *six*, and then darkening until reaching unlucky hour *thirteen*, wherein she found *not-*

her-room the darkest, and empty like the rest, at least from what she could tell.

What time is this? she wondered, and then thought of something even more frightening than a thirteenth hour, and pulled back from the wall. If what she'd found was indeed a clock, it was only *half* a clock to a world with twenty-six hours. *And where are the hands?*

She looked to her own damaged hands, placed one against the exposed wall, elbow centered in the circle. Stretching her fingers, they barely traced the edges of each hole, the curvy parts of the semicolons like flame-shaped nails. Her hands were perfectly proportioned to denote the time. She had unveiled each of the markings, after all, had cut through somehow to this other side, so perhaps she was meant to serve a purpose other than cutting herself and taking abuse.

"I'd turn back time," Frankie Jones told the room, moving her hands in palsy-like tics to denote the passing of time, in reverse.

I'd undo the things I've done, a softer voice added.

Frankie peered through the holes, frantically, for the voice was much like her own and had come from behind the wall. Surely she'd see herself somewhere on the other side of one of these wheres and whens. But no, each room was as empty as the next, each room perhaps representing a different string of time—existences without a Frankie Jones at all.

"Hello?" she said, cupping her hands to her mouth.

She put her ear against the wall, listened, listened, listened...

Hello, the softer voiced eventually called.

The other rooms remained empty.

And then a scratching from the other side, somewhere near the middle of the sun made of semicolons, as soft as a mouse chewing through sheetrock. A fingernail picking at a scab, Frankie knew, and scratched with her own fingernail, first taking away the rest of the wallpaper, then taking away the paint, and the chalky-white thereafter. Her fingers, sore and ashy.

Soon she touched another finger. Soon an eye found an identical eye peering through the void—another ring of brown-speckled space, another black sun in its center. Soon an arm darker than her own reached through and clamped around her wrist, turned it over, turning itself over in the process, as if inspecting one against the other.

One arm was scarred, the other unblemished.

A handshake through a wall.

Sheetrock crumbled as the fingers now digging into Frankie Jones elongated. The nails, razor-sharp, raked new lines into her wrists without hesitating as she tried pulling away. The hand not her own transmogrified, the once-smooth skin breaking apart into jagged scales. And then there were two appendages wrapping around Frankie, writhing like tentacled appendages of a black octopus, their burning embrace filling her room with a stench of burnt skin, *her* skin. And the sound, like sizzling, darkened her skin even more, pressed into her muscles like the bruises sometimes left behind by her fosters.

Where are the arms? she wondered. *If these are its fingers, where are the arms?*

On that very thought they emerged, one for every hole, squeezing through now like snakes in dirt tunnels, joining her, tasting her, tangling within her hair...vice-like horrid fingerless hands reaching out, trying to pull her through, to the other side.

Frankie screamed, kicking her feet as she failed to pull away. A bare foot punched a hole through the wall, through the center of the sundial clock, and it was then the eyes of the girl-creature on the other side permeated the darkness, changing from galaxy brown to starlight white. The eyes began pulling her through as well, but to some other *where*, to some other *when*, to a time, perhaps, not represented by a clock of any kind.

The light within the ever-staring creature intensified, turning Frankie's world from black to white, blinding her with its penetrating gaze.

Come with me.

A strange voice. Frankie's *other* voice, perhaps, the one which had tempted her that first time to cut. *What is a hesitation but a pause of something that's already supposed to happen*, she remembered thinking then, but was it really supposed to happen? Was *this* supposed to happen? She imagined another Frankie with thirteen black and oily arms reaching through the void, wrapping around her own, able to squeeze and press hard against her but their claws unable to tear apart her now-impenetrable skin.

Come with me.

The limbs continued wrapping around her body in a violent embrace as she tried to close her eyes—to make it all go away—but even then she was spellbound by the never-ending white that surrounded her.

And soon she couldn't breathe.

Come with me, to the other side.

"I don't want to go!" she screamed, the words spoken as if underwater, muffled as she struggled within the airless hug of the evil thing. *"I don't— wanna— go!"*

Is it really evil?

She thought of that first time meeting her fosters, how she hadn't wanted to go, had begged to stay with the other girls and the caretakers at the Hopkins House. *You'll be fine in this new home,* they'd told her. *These kind people will watch over you, take care of you, feed you, clothe you, nurture you.* But she was done with the lies, had gone through it all before, with other "families," some childless, some not. In her house-bouncing, as she sometimes called it, she had met some *real* monsters, those not designed to care for children. Absolute evil.

"Having a child love you is one of the scariest things in the world," Frankie had once been told, not from a monster but from the opposite of one, but that wasn't true, either; having a parent *not* love you was perhaps scarier, or not having parents at all.

The arms pulled, but from all directions, *toward* the wall, *away* from the wall, as if trying to split her in two. And they shook Frankie as she continued to kick, connecting with the wall, the nightstand, the dresser, something softer, knocking things over...

Is someone watching from a hole in another room somewhere?

All at once, the rest of its black mass came pouring out from the center of the circle of semicolons like a cancerous tumor erupting from within, sheetrock crumbling and cracking as it forced itself out, letting go of Frankie long enough to find new purchase on the carpeting of her bedroom floor, and then reforming as an oily-gelatinous ball. Bubbling, its latex-like skin—if it were skin at all—folded in on itself, and the red heart of the monster began beating as rapidly as Frankie's own, which seemed to want to surge out from her chest like the blob in front of her.

We are connected by this heart. Are all hearts connected?

Blinding white light filled the giant hole in her wall, casting the monster in a grotesque black-and-white silhouette, as if no longer three-dimensional but two- and evoking a fear within Frankie so deep that even her own feet now held her captive. Her bare feet fixed to the floor as if epoxied. She had become a statue, paralyzed forever in stone by Medusa's stare, or perhaps Pennywise opening its endless maw and locking her within its dead-lights.

The roundish heap of blight—*no, not round at all but thirteen-sided, a tridecagon, a triskaidecagon, a 13-gon, a thirteen-hour clock*—took another shape. Legs jutted out in a burst like inverted starlight, first eight, making Frankie think of tarantulas, followed by five more, the appendages working together to raise the incongruous mass to eye-level.

Light behind the Frankie-sized abortion dispelled in a circular pattern, as if absorbed or sucked into its back as the monster adjusted to this new side of the world, to this new where and when, a place somewhere between the hours of thirteen and twenty-six o'clock. Darkness eating its opposite; 2-D becoming 3- once more; unreal turning real; a body morphing from nightmare to daymare to something no longer alien but human in shape...a girl, only thirteen years old, a rotten doppelgänger of Frankie Jones, albeit as black as pitch and smooth as molten glass.

Soon there were two of her in the room: Frankie and not-Frankie.

Antimatter, she thought of this other self, *or perhaps the darkest of matter.*

Eyes opened on the *other* as tears welled within her own, not blinding white, as she'd expected, but kaleidoscopic, like the eyes staring back at her when she'd first looked through two of the holes at once: a continuous revolution of brown iris and pupil, each a galaxy flecked with endless stars, and endless space, and endless time and endless—

[nothing-space]

The worlds beyond blinked when she blinked.

Come with me.

To where, Frankie didn't know; she didn't ask, and likewise didn't care. She'd go, as she always had, to a place other than this—*all that ever really mattered*—and she'd go willingly, because what other choice did she have?

Another home. Another set of false parents. Another series of temptations to cut. Another bedroom with different walls and different holes leading to other wheres and other whens. And when she'd pick at those new scabs—*on her arms, on the walls*—and reach inside, this time she wouldn't be afraid. She wouldn't tell the wall to *Let go*, no, but to *Hold on.*

Ruined, she thought, meaning her life.

Frankie reached out with both arms, and likewise Not-Frankie did the same. As their fingers intertwined, one girl became the other and together they became one—metamorphosed into a single being. Two hearts began beating as one. Their shared energy ever so concentrated, unpredictable, a sun ready to supernova or collapse upon itself to feed on stardust.

Something covered her mouth, then, from behind, something much like a soft set of fingers from a warm hand. She could no longer do nothing, her body now willing to fight back.

"Shh, Frankie," a familiar voice said, one of her fosters. "Everything will be okay."

We are all made of stardust, she thought, hungry.

MONSTERS OF ANY KIND

GREG SISCO

BAD HAIR DAY

by GREG SISCO

"State your name for the camera."

"Donald Gainsborough."

"State your date of birth."

"May 17, 1991."

"State your occupation."

"Lord of Earth."

"State your *actual* occupation."

"State why I'm handcuffed to a chair."

"You threatened a federal officer."

"Bullshit."

"You said, 'If you make me stop cutting my hair, we're all going to die.'"

"That wasn't a threat; that was a fact."

"State your occupation for the camera."

"I didn't threaten you."

"State your occupation!"

"…Accountant."

"State today's date."

"October twenty-fourth."

"Year?"

"2033."

"As seen, Mr. Gainsborough is bound and seated. His hair is growing at an abnormal rate. We have reason to believe he and/or his hair may be a danger to himself and/or those around him. Agent Hanson is shaving his head with a Laser-Razor. Agent Carlson is disposing of severed hair with a blowtorch. Mr. Gainsborough, state what happened to your hair."

"Jesus…"

"Mr. Gainsborough, please."

"You know, my mom always said most problems stem from a poor self-image. Heh. Shit."

BALD FUCK.

That's what the bumper sticker said. A Christmas gift from his sixteen-year-old niece. He forced himself to laugh along with everyone instead of causing a scene, even though he wanted to ask what it was supposed to mean, whether it was supposed to be funny and what exactly was funny about it.

This generation. No sense of irony, no wit. Just no-holds-barred cruelty in the name of being edgy. If it weren't the hair they'd pick some other fault.

FAT SHIT.

FOUR-EYED FREAK.

STUTTERING IDIOT.

Damn thing didn't even look customized, that was the worst part. Somewhere someone was mass-producing these, probably making a fortune. What else was that company putting out? CHEAP JEW? CRIPPLED PRICK? FAGGOT?

"Bald fuck. Great. Just what I needed."

"I saw it and I was like, 'Oh, that's totally Uncle Don,'" said Miranda.

"That's me, all right," he said, tossing the bumper sticker straight into the trash.

An awkward moment passed before Mark scooped up another present and tried to keep things cheerful.

"You couldn't just bring it home? Just humor her for two seconds?" asked Mom later in the kitchen.

"'Bald fuck'? Not even 'chrome dome' or 'cue ball' or something at least *arguably* playful? Just full-on hate speech?"

"Come on. *Hate speech*? It's a friendly jab between family," said Mark.

"Maybe when she gets her first car I'll get her a sticker that says 'spoiled anorexic bitch'. See how she likes friendly jabs."

"That's my daughter you're talking about. Your niece."

"I'm *her* uncle, *your* brother. Where was that indignation when she bought it?"

"Lighten up."

"Your dad was bald when he was thirty," said Mom. "He wouldn't have hurt a young girl's feelings over a harmless joke."

"*I* hurt *her* feelings?"

"Christ, Don, you're a forty-year-old man," said Mark. "Get over it."

Don shook his head. "She should learn not to prod people's disabilities. I'm not going to encourage it. Like I don't take enough abuse from myself when I look in the mirror, or try and scratch my head without shifting that itchy toupee, or when I make some flirtatious comment to a client and she shifts in her seat. What, I'm gonna put it on my car and advertise it to the one person in ten who hasn't noticed? 'Hey, in case you missed it, I'm a bald fuck. That's my proudest achievement. Carry on.'"

"Betcha they'd be more into you if you did," Mark mumbled.

"What?"

"I'll bet the women at your office would be more interested in you if you had a sense of humor about yourself."

"I do have a sense of humor about myself. I just don't hate myself and act like an asshole to myself. An asshole like your daughter."

"Will you both stop it?" said Mom. "Forty years and neither of you has grown up."

"Sorry, Mom," said both boys like circus animals dancing their way out of abuse.

"You know who likes bald men?" said Mom. "Venutian girls. You should find one of them."

"Venus isn't populated, Mom."

"Well whatever. Those blue alien ladies. I see them out with bald men around Broadway all the time."

Mark covered his mouth to hold in his laughter.

"Glieseans?" asked Don, raising an eyebrow.

"If you say so."

"Those are hookers, Mom."

"Oh, please."

"Glieseans by Broadway are street-walkers."

"Well, look who needs a lesson in hate speech now."

By now Mark was doubled over. Don shook his head. Interplanetary prostitutes. Yeah, that's pretty much where bald men had to look these days, what with all those silky-haired Andromeda men grabbing up all the Earth women.

"I have a business card sitting here, Mr. Gainsborough, with the name of a company that doesn't exist, and the name of a woman who, if she exists, isn't working in this city legally. It contains a phone number that's unregistered and the address of a building that hasn't been leased to a business in eight months. Is that the only alibi you can offer?"

"*Alibi?* It's what happened. Wait, am I a suspect in my own...? I'm the victim!"

"What's important right now isn't who's at fault, it's how to react. Are you certain this woman actually exists?"

"Yes. At least, I'm certain a woman gave me that card. I have no way of knowing if it's a real name."

"What's your relationship to her?"

"I told you. I told you ten times on the way here."

"For the camera."

"I'm her accountant! I'm her *goddamn* accountant and she's my *goddamn* client and if you take me to my *goddamn* office I'll get you her *goddamn* files."

"Mr. Gainsborough?"

"What?"

"Calm your *goddamn* nerves."

"It's growing faster, isn't it? The hair? It keeps growing faster. How long before he can't keep up even with a Laser-Razor?"

"I can keep up fine."

"Mr. Gainsborough, if you're really concerned with time—as *I* am—you'll answer my questions calmly and at a steady pace and we'll reach a decision on how to proceed."

"Fine. This is stupid, but fine."

"How long have you been employed by the woman in question?"

"A couple days."

"Tell me about your first meeting."

The day Donald Gainsborough left his hairpiece at home was the day he doomed mankind. He'd spent ten minutes staring at it after he got out of the shower, going through his daily internal debate as to whether baldness was more attractive than self-loathing. He landed, for once, on the side that didn't require a toupee.

He sat in his office spinning a holographic cube, waiting for clients, going through the motions with a hundred tax returns, asking the dumbest questions mankind had ever asked.

Have you imported goods from other planets and sold them to neighboring countries via the Internet?

Have you purchased farmland on neighboring planets, moons, or space stations to raise livestock, bearing in mind that adopted children can be classified as livestock?

Have you acquired any commission-based income resulting from extraterrestrial sex trade?

No, no, and no. No one says yes to the space-pimp question.

Thousands of stupid tax breaks and loopholes, thousands of ridiculous questions, thousands of manipulations of digital cubes and diagrams, plugging in data and running equations on a top-tier desktop holo-processor, only to send everything to an inkjet printer and fax it to D.C. because politicians were still figuring out email. If there was one job machines would never take from humans, it was dealing with the cavemen in the public sector.

"What does the company do?" Donald asked a beautiful first-time client. She had the nicest hair he'd ever laid eyes on—deep black, like expensive satin, with eyes to match.

"Men's hair regeneration," she said.

He shifted in his seat and forced a smile. He could practically feel the overhead lamp reflecting off the top of his head into her eyes. Of all the days to go without the hairpiece, it had to be the day when the beautiful girl with the hair-loss company came in. Or maybe it was a gift.

"We should be on opposite sides of the desk," he half-joked.

"Come in. We'll get you sorted out."

He considered it for a second and shook his head. Self-confidence. That's what women liked, right? "I'm good. It doesn't actually bother me."

"Well, if it ever starts to, we've worked wonders on worse than you."

"Who's worse than me?"

"Burn victims, reptilians..."

"Reptilians?" He laughed. "Get out of here."

She pressed the card to his desk, a card with a name, a company, a phone number, and an address that all looked legitimate at the time, but a week later would seem to vanish from existence.

BELINDA BENNET, said the card. GROWTH UNLIMITED.

Growth Unlimited was an upstart with a few hundred square feet of office space, sparkly clean floors, and five items of furniture. There was no front desk, no secretary, just Don and Belinda and an operating table. If she wasn't beautiful with a confident smile, he probably would have run screaming for the Better Business Bureau, but a lonely man seldom did such things with a sexy smile pointed in his direction.

The things we do for a pretty face...

When people said that, they always stopped right there, because nobody liked to actually think what those things were. What exactly was it we'd do? It must have been important, because the people in power collected pretty faces. Movie stars, models, athletes, dancers, singers, and news reporters. Even important people whose jobs had nothing to do with being attractive, they were anyway. Everybody who mattered had a million-dollar smile. Shit, the last two presidents were former centerfolds.

And even when a plus-size model got a meme passed around cyberspace in the name of all bodies being beautiful, it was always the best-looking fat person you'd ever seen. Nobody gave modeling ads to pockmarked, balding, middle-aged amputees with sagging skin, one blind eye, and a dozen facial moles. Nobody said, "Even this freak of nature is an acceptable human being." No. They pretended to be inclusive when they were really saying, "Being fat is no excuse. You could still be fat like *this!*"

All the uglies, all the everyday people who crowded crosswalks, they had to figure out which pills, which lotions, which surgeries would take the ugly away, so they could at least be *good* fat. *Good* bald. *Good* ugly. These celebrities, these politicians, these pretty faces, what *were* the things we'd *do* for them? Buy a treadmill? Or a Heineken? Vote for them? Go to war? Hate who they hate? What *wouldn't* we do?

And we bullshitted ourselves that it didn't matter. Real beauty is on the inside, or in the eye of the beholder, or somewhere other than our own gap teeth and bald heads and hairy backs. But it did matter. When you looked at billboards and TV screens and magazine covers, it *clearly* mattered. It was just hard to understand *why* it mattered.

"Will it hurt?" Don asked.

"No. I'll put you under for the invasive part of the surgery. When you come to, you'll feel little to no discomfort, other than the unusual sensation of having a full head of hair."

"I'll already have hair when I wake up?" he asked, somehow ignoring the word *invasive*.

"Yes. The process takes two hours. Growth will be rapid at first, a couple feet a day, but it'll slow to a more manageable growth rate after a few days."

"A couple feet a day?! How is that even possible?"

"Complicated science junk. Human hair is from dead cells in the body, but we use a gene from a Europan species that absorbs and puts to use molecules from the surrounding environment to build hair out of live cells."

"Living hair?"

"You could say that."

He put a hand on his head and felt his bald scalp for the last time. The kind of bald scalp you'd never see on the cover of a fashion magazine. Maybe if it were on a man twenty pounds lighter who could bench four hundred pounds and had a tan like he lived on Mercury. Maybe. But not on a forty-year-old accountant.

"You wouldn't know it," said Don, "but in my twenties I was a really good-looking guy."

Belinda smiled. "In a couple hours you will be again."

Politicians, newsmen, the folks on magazines. Whatever it is that's going on here, it's always the good-looking ones causing trouble.

———

"Agent Davis, I want the name of that species on Europa. I'm considering them a major threat."

"Yes, ma'am."

"Let humanoids take precedent. You can't find a humanoid, find a non-humanoid with a strong humanoid ally."

"Yes, ma'am."

"Wait! Or a shape-shifter. You can't find humanoids, go to mimics. You can't find mimics, find the partnership. And in all cases, look for an axe to grind with Earth. Fast. This could be the big one."

"Yes, ma'am."

"And find out what's happening with my latte."

"Yes, ma'am."

"Has it slowed like she said, Mr. Gainsborough?"

"No. You're in the room with me; look at it. It was an inch an hour, maybe. Ever since I cut it, it was an inch a minute, then thirty seconds, twenty…"

"How fast is an inch growing, Hanson?"

"Four or five seconds."

"I'm gonna die, aren't I?"

"Probably. Let's hope the rest of us aren't. Tell me about the procedure."

"I told you, she put me under."

"Then tell me what happened when you woke up. Tell me why we're all gonna die."

———

"My God. I'm beautiful."

Belinda was holding a mirror for him as he came to. His hair was as black as hers, that same shade of high-priced satin. He thought of asking if she'd had the procedure herself, if she'd developed it because she'd been bald, but it felt too personal.

"You know what I love about hair?" she said. "It never dies. Even dead hair is alive. When you're sleeping, or in a coma, even after death in some species—it keeps growing."

Don curled a lock of it around his finger. "I can't feel with it. When you said it was alive, I wondered if I'd be able to."

"No. But *it* can feel *you.*"

"It can?"

"Of course. It's a living thing."

"A living thing separate from me? Another organism?"

"You're composed of organisms. Each cell in your body is an organism. What's one more?"

He ran his fingers through it again. It was an eerie thought. A beautiful parasite just above his brain.

"It's not going to get mad at me for cutting it or shampooing it or whatever?"

Belinda laughed. "Of course not. It'll just love you and keep itself beautiful and shiny for you. It's the *good* kind of organism."

He took the mirror from her and looked closer. He looked at least ten years younger, *felt* ten years younger. Maybe he wasn't meme-ready yet, but a few miles of running each day, a few minutes in a Super-Tanner…

He resisted the urge to hug Belinda and lift her off the ground when he left. Two blocks down the street he caught his strutting reflection in a store window and had to stop and look.

"You sexy bitch," he said aloud, pulling his hair back and winking at his reflection.

Two teenage girls giggled and filmed him with their iPendants.

"YouTube!" said one.

"I just posted it," said the other.

He didn't care. It would take more than a viral hologram to ruin this moment.

By nightfall his hair was six inches long, and a middle-aged man with six-inch hair is a sad sight, but it was his first night with confidence in the better part of a decade and he wasn't about to waste it looking for a barber.

The club scene had changed in ten years. It was half aliens now, and everyone was wearing neon rings and covered in motion-tattoos. He'd been in the club all of ten minutes when a pretty girl in her twenties bumped into him and spilled his drink down his chest.

"I'm so sorry." She had long blonde hair with pink highlights. It was pretty, but his was prettier.

"It's okay, forget it. It doesn't matter."

"I'm not even drunk. Honestly. I just wasn't looking and..."

"It's okay. I'll be fine."

"Can I buy you another one? Do you want to come sit with me and my friends?"

He almost laughed. The whole thing was probably a ploy to meet him. That was how young people were today. People who bought BALD FUCK bumper stickers for their uncles, sure, they probably knocked drinks over to meet handsome strangers. They probably kicked their friends in the nuts to say hi. But what the hell. Six years of abstinence, why *not* have a drink with someone who introduces herself by spilling your last one on your shirt?

"I'm Corrine, by the way," she said a minute later at the table. She was with two female friends, and Don certainly had the pretty one. These days it wouldn't have mattered to him if he didn't, but it was an ego boost nonetheless.

"I'm Don."

"What do you do, Don?"

"I'm an accountant."

"Oh... Okay. I bet that's interesting."

One of Corrine's friends laughed drunkenly. "Sounds awful."

The other friend punched her arm. "Be nice."

"No, it's okay. It *is* awful."

There was an uncomfortable pause as the women nodded. Accounting. The career equivalent of baldness. So shitty you weren't even supposed to bring up how shitty it was at the risk of depressing everyone.

"Did you know there's a tax break for immigrants from Neptunian moons if they're harvesting boron for Neptunian colonies in China?"

"No," said Corrine, feigning interest. "I didn't know that."

"Exactly. Why *would* you? Why would anyone *want* to? It's the most boring thing in the universe to be knowledgable about."

The girls laughed. The awkward situation was diffused. All it took was hair and you could do anything.

"What do you do?" he asked.

"We're hairdressers."

"Really! I just had a regenerative treatment done today," he blurted out, immediately regretting it. "I mean…I used to be…bald."

"Like an implant?" asked one of the drunk girls.

"No. I mean, yeah, like a cell implant. This grew in a few hours." He paused and looked around. All of them were grimacing, like he'd just told them about some horrible STD. "It's supposed to slow down."

"Hm."

"I must be drunk. I don't know why I mentioned it." He looked at the table and shrugged.

Dammit, Don. You're not bald anymore. You can do anything. Fix this!

"I think it's cute," said Corrine. She ran a hand through his hair and stood. "Dance with me?"

He took her hand. The way she pulled him into her was the same way she pulled him into her three hours later in his bedroom as she pressed her lips to his and ran her hand up his shirt. His own hand he ran through her hair. Black or blonde, short or long, he'd never loved hair as much as he did tonight.

"Agent Gale, we have a problem."

"You found the species?"

"Not exactly, no. Oh, I got your latte."

"What's the problem?"

"There's a distress signal from Creozan, in the Andromeda galaxy. Report matches everything he's said and it's supposedly spreading fast. Like, epidemic fast."

"Find me the species, now!"

"Yes, ma'am."

"And bring me a latte that's *hot.*"

"Yes, ma'am."

"What is this, Mr. Gainsborough? Conquest? Universal domination? Who are we dealing with?"

"I don't know! I've told you everything!"

"What do they want?"

"I don't know what they want. All *I* wanted was a head of hair!"

"Christ, I knew male vanity would kill our whole goddamn species. You all said I was a man-hater but look where we're standing now."

"You called it, ma'am."

"Yeah, I did. Wish I hadn't, but I did. Make me understand, Mr. Gainsborough! Tell me what I'm missing!"

Don's hair was covering his face in the morning, running past his shoulders. He could feel it on his back and his chest, on the side of his face. He tried to pull it back to look at Corrine, lying next to him, but it was caught on something. He tugged again and lifted his head and his heart stopped.

He screamed.

With drugs or operations, they warn you about side effects. Drowsiness, incontinence, liver cancer. But no hair-loss drug has ever come with a warning that at some point during the night your hair might develop a will of its own and extend itself into your lover's face, growing straight into her nostrils, her ears, her bulged-out eyes. At some point she'd tried to scream and the hair had even forced itself down her throat and into her lungs.

He jerked reflexively but he was stuck to her. He tugged her head with him as he pulled. After a minute of screaming and pulling her head around the pillow, he forced himself to take a breath and think. He went into the drawer of his bedside cabinet and found his toenail clippers. It took twenty minutes to clip the hair that connected his head to her corpse.

When he got into the bathroom, he snatched up his electric razor and extended the grooming arm. His hair was hanging at his waist now, and as he made the first cut, a tentacle of hair wrapped itself around his wrist. He pulled it away with his other hand and cut it, screaming as he did. A man in his underwear, shrieking, hyperventilating, shaving three-foot clusters of hair off his own head. It wasn't a future he'd dreamt of as a little boy.

A severed lock of evil on the floor tangled itself around his ankle. In kicking it off, he slammed his foot into the base of the counter hard enough to cut it open. A vicious hair-serpent tried to force itself into the wound.

He fought the creatures on the floor until he lost his balance and fell into the hallway. He jumped to his feet, still cutting the hair on his head, now without the aid of the mirror.

A door opened to his left and there stood Corrine in his t-shirt, the last of the hair in her eyes and nose creeping inside her head and disappearing. Her once-blonde hair was now as black as his, and her eyes had darkened to match it.

"Corrine?" he said.

She took a step toward him.

"Corrine, stop! I just... I need to figure out... Are you okay?"

She stepped forward again. He stepped back without realizing it.

"Corrine, I don't know what's..."

She took another step.

"Stop, goddamnit!"

Her hair stood up to reach for him. She became a Medusa figure. He stumbled back and hit the front door. He reached back in a panic, fumbled with the knob until it opened. A moment later he was sprinting down the street in his underwear, screaming and cutting his hair as a dozen people filmed him with their necklaces.

Six blocks down the road, he kicked open a barbershop door and screamed, "Help! I need a razor! A fucking big one!"

<hr />

There were fifty people lined up at the post office when Don ran in with the Laser-Razor and pleaded, "What time does the hair place next door open?"

Everyone looked around with expressions ranging from confusion to terror to humor. Half pulled out their iPendants and pointed them. One asked, "Is that the dude from the 'sexy bitch' hologram?"

"Sir, what's the problem?" asked a postal clerk.

"The hair treatment center! Are they open today? What time do they come in? Does anyone know?"

"Hair treatment center?"

"I was there yesterday! Now there's nobody there!"

"Sir, if you don't leave, I'm going to call the police."

"Good, call them. Call the police! My hair killed a woman and turned her into a zombie. It's trying to kill me. Stay away or it might kill you too. The people at the hair place are gonna answer for this shit!"

"What hair place?" asked a customer who happened to be bald.

"He's high," said the postal clerk. "There's no hair place."

"There was a hair place! How did *this* happen if there's no hair place! I was a bald fuck! Just like you! God help me, I was a bald fuck!"

"I'm telling you, it was there. Growth Unlimited. A woman named Belinda Bennet. I'm not making it up. Why would I?"

"I'm giving you the benefit of the doubt, Mr. Gainsborough, but if you don't give me something more, there's nothing I can do for you, nothing I can do for any of us. I need you to think harder."

"Belinda Bennet! Growth Unlimited!"

"There is no Growth Unlimited! There are a thousand Belinda Bennets and none in this city! Give me a home planet. A photograph. Something!"

"Take me to my office. I'll give you all her tax information and if that's not enough there's nothing else I can give."

"Ma'am? Sorry to interrupt."

"Yes? Have you got the species?"

"No, I have a latte. It's hot."

"Oh for God's sake, nobody gives a shit about lattes! Find the species!"

"Yes, ma'am. Sorry, ma'am."

"Agent Gale?"

"What!?"

"Look."

In the interrogation room on the thirtieth floor of an unmarked government building, one of six federal agents pointed to the window. For the first time since Don had been brought here, they all stopped talking. There was a commotion in the street, but Don couldn't get a look at it from where he was seated. Whatever it was, it instantly became the only thing anyone else could think about. Even the barber, whose vantage point couldn't have been much better than Don's, stopped shaving his head for a moment to look.

"Don't stop cutting my hair!" screamed Don.

Everyone whirled in a panic. The attention shifted back to Don a second too late. An arm of hair had already wrapped itself around Agent Barber's wrist, jerking it downward and snapping the razor to the floor.

"What the hell?" said Agent Barber.

"Get the razor!" screamed Agent Gale. "Cut the hair! Now!"

Agent Blowtorch, who'd been burning the discarded hair, ducked to grab the razor.

"Quick!" shouted Agent Barber. The hair had wrapped itself around his neck and was growing up his nose.

Agent Blowtorch brought the razor in close, but another hair-tentacle wrapped itself around his wrist and held him. Hair crawled up his chest to his face.

Agent Gale drew her gun and pointed it at Don's chest. Her fellow agents followed suit.

"Let go of them!"

"It's not in my control!"

"I can't know that! Let them go or I'll fire!"

A tear ran down Don's face. All this over beauty. Oh, to go back. To toss the toupee. To put the bumper sticker on the car. To be a bald fuck.

"The things we do for a pretty face," he said with a sad laugh.

Agent Gale shot him. She fired three rounds into his chest and the agents around her fired too, leaving him slumped in his chair like a squeezed lemon. The hair fell from the agents' arms and necks and landed at Don's sides. The agents breathed hard and put their hands to their chests, turning back to the window.

Behind them, a few strands of hair on Don's head were making their way into his ears. When they reached the center of his brain, his eyes opened in their new native black. Another hair-tentacle slipped into the handcuffs and unlocked them. He stood from his chair, hair darting out, shooting into the ears and noses and eyes of all the agents around him until it was just Agent Gale standing there, surrounded by men with beautiful hair.

"Stay back!" she shouted, waving her gun. "All of you."

She fired a shot at Don's face. His hair leapt in front and absorbed the impact. It tossed the bullet to the floor as the five federal agents and the up-until-recently bald man closed in on Agent Gale.

"Get back! I said get back! Please...." she begged, as the satin-haired men closed in around her.

———

Seven humans with black hair and black eyes exited a building downtown, walking in step. Six were in Armani suits and one was in Fruit of the Loom underwear, but they regarded each other as equals, no longer an ounce of vanity between them.

They regarded also as equals the thousands of other humans who walked in step down Broadway with black hair and black eyes and varying states of dress, all different body types, all different genders and races and species. The whole crowd walked in step and the former agents and the former bald man joined them and ceased to be individuals.

Their hair braided itself together, connected them, hair hundreds of feet long. It rose above them, twisted with hair rising from their neighbors, came together in one enormous pillar above the thousands of people.

Pedestrians ran screaming. Cars screeched to stop. Cops fired their guns. But the marching crowd never stopped. It grew ever larger as each new stranger came within hair-shot, as each new satin-haired beauty stepped off the sidewalk to be part of a new age.

As one army, one unit, one organism, they carried the pillar of hair that stretched above them a thousand feet into the sky. At the top of the column, on a braided satin throne of only the most beautiful hair, Belinda Bennet smiled over her planet.

MONSTERS OF ANY KIND

RAMSEY CAMPBELL

MIDNIGHT HOBO

by RAMSEY CAMPBELL

As he reached home, Roy saw the old man who lived down the road chasing children from under the railway bridge. "Go on, out with you," he was crying as though they were cats in his flower-beds. He was brandishing his string-bags, which were always full of books.

Perhaps the children had been climbing up beneath the arch; that was where he kept glancing. Roy wasn't interested, for his co-presenter on the radio show was getting on his nerves. At least Don Derrick was only temporary, until the regular man came out of hospital. As a train ticked away its carriages over the bridge, Roy stormed into his house in search of a soothing drink.

The following night he remembered to glance under the arch. It did not seem likely that anyone could climb up there, nor that anyone would want to. Even in daylight you couldn't tell how much of the mass that clogged the corners was soot. Now the arch was a hovering block of darkness, relieved only by faint greyish sketches of girders. Roy heard the birds fluttering.

Today Derrick had been almost tolerable, but he made up for that the next day. Halfway through "Our Town Tonight" Roy had to interview the female lead from *The Man on Top*, a limp British sex comedy about a young man trying to seduce his way to fame. Most of the film's scrawny budget must have been spent on hiring a few guest comedians. Heaven only knew how the producers had been able to afford to send the girl touring to promote the film.

Though as an actress she was embarrassingly inexperienced, as an interviewee she was far worse. She sat like a girl even younger than she was, over-awed by staying up so late. A man from the film distributors watched over her like a nanny.

Whatever Roy asked her, her answers were never more than five words long. Over by the studio turntables, Derrick was fiddling impatiently with the control panel, making everyone nervous. In future Roy wouldn't let him near the controls.

Ah, here was a question that ought to inspire her. "How did you find the experience of working with so many veterans of comedy?" "Oh, it really helped." He smiled desperate encouragement. "It really really did," she said miserably, her eyes pleading with him.

"What do you remember best about working with them?" When she looked close to panic he could only say "Are there any stories you can tell?"

"Oh—" At last she seemed nervously ready to speak, when Derrick interrupted "Well, I'm sure you've lots more interesting things to tell us. We'll come back to them in a few minutes, but first here's some music."

When the record was over he broke into the interview. "What sort of music do you like? What are your favourite things?" He might have been chatting to a girl in one of the discotheques where he worked. There wasn't much that Roy could do to prevent him, since the programme was being broadcast live: half-dead, more like.

Afterwards he cornered Derrick, who was laden with old 78s, a plastic layer cake of adolescent memories. "I told you at the outset that was going to be my interview. We don't cut into each other's interviews unless invited."

"Well, I didn't know." Derrick's doughy face was growing pinkly mottled, burning from within. If you poked him, would the mark remain, as though in putty? He must look his best in the dim light of discos. "You know now," Roy said.

"I thought you needed some help," Derrick said with a kind of timid defiance; he looked ready to flinch. "You didn't seem to be doing very well."

"I wasn't, once you interfered. Next time, please remember who's running the show."

Half an hour later Roy was still fuming. As he strode beneath the bridge he felt on edge; his echoes seemed unpleasantly shrill, the fluttering among the girders sounded more like restless scuttling. Perhaps he could open a bottle of wine with dinner.

He had nearly finished dinner when he wondered when the brood would hatch. Last week he'd seen the male bird carrying food to his mate in the hidden nest. When he'd washed up, he strolled under the bridge but could see only the girders gathering darkness. The old man with the string-bags was standing between his regimented flower-beds, watching Roy or the bridge. Emerging, Roy glanced back. In the May twilight the archway resembled a block of mud set into the sullen bricks.

Was there something he ought to have noticed? Next morning, on waking, he thought so—but he didn't have much time to think that day, for Derrick was sulking. He hardly spoke to Roy except when they were on the air, and even then his face belied his synthetic cheerfulness. They were like an estranged couple who were putting on a show for visitors.

Roy had done nothing to apologise for. If Derrick let his animosity show while he was broadcasting, it would be Derrick who'd have to explain. That made Roy feel almost at ease, which was why he noticed belatedly that he hadn't heard the birds singing under the bridge for days.

Nor had he seen them for almost a week; all he had heard was fluttering, as though they were unable to call. Perhaps a cat had caught them, perhaps that was what the fluttering had been. If anything was moving up there now, it sounded larger than a bird—but perhaps that was only his echoes, which seemed very distorted.

He had a casserole waiting in the oven. After dinner he browsed among the wavelengths of his stereo radio, and found a Mozart quartet on an East European frequency. As the calm deft phrases intertwined, he watched twilight smoothing the pebble-dashed houses, the tidy windows and flower-beds. A train crossed the bridge, providing a few bars of percussion, and prompted him to imagine how far the music was travelling.

In a pause between movements he heard the cat.

At first even when he turned the radio down, he couldn't make out what was wrong. The cat was hissing and snarling, but what had happened to its voice? Of course—it was distorted by echoes. No doubt it was among the girders beneath the bridge. He was about to turn up the music when the cat screamed.

He ran to the window, appalled. He'd heard cats fighting, but never a sound like that. Above the bridge two houses distant, a chain-gang of telegraph poles looked embedded in the glassy sky. He could see nothing underneath except a rhomb of dimness, rounded at the top. Reluctantly he ventured onto the deserted street.

It was not quite deserted. A dozen houses further from the bridge, the old man was glaring dismayed at the arch. As soon as Roy glanced at him, he dodged back into his house.

Roy couldn't see anything framed by the arch. Grass and weeds, which looked pale as growths found under stones, glimmered in the spaces between bricks. Some of the bricks resembled moist fossilised sponges, cemented by glistening mud. Up among the girders, an irregular pale shape must be a larger patch of weeds. As he peered at it, it grew less clear, seemed to withdraw into the dark—but at least he couldn't see the cat.

He was walking slowly, peering up in an attempt to reassure himself, when he trod on the object. Though it felt soft, it snapped audibly. The walls, which were padded with dimness, seemed to swallow its echo. It took him a while to glance down.

At first he was reminded of one of the strings of dust that appeared in the spare room when, too often, he couldn't be bothered to clean. But when he stooped reluctantly, he saw fur and claws. It looked as it had felt: like a cat's foreleg.

He couldn't look up as he fled. Echoes sissified his footsteps. Was a large pale shape following him beneath the girders? Could he hear its scuttling, or was that himself? He didn't dare speculate until he'd slammed his door behind him.

Half an hour later a gang of girls wandered, yelling and shrieking, through the bridge. Wouldn't they have noticed the leg, or was there insufficient light? He slept badly and woke early, but could find no trace in the road under the bridge. Perhaps the evidence had been dragged away by a car. The unlucky cat might have been run over on the railway line—but in that case, why hadn't he heard a train? He couldn't make out any patch of vegetation among the girders, where it was impenetrably dark; there appeared to be nothing pale up there at all.

All things considered, he was glad to go to work, at least to begin with. Derrick stayed out of his way, except to mention that he'd invited a rock group to talk on tonight's show. "All right," Roy said, though he'd never heard of the group. "Ian's the producer. Arrange it with him."

"I've already done that," Derrick said smugly.

Perhaps his taste of power would make him less intolerable. Roy had no time to argue, for he had to interview an antipornography campaigner. Her glasses slithered down her nose, her face grew redder and redder, but her pharisaic expression never wavered. Not for the first time, he wished he were working for television.

That night he wished it even more, when Derrick led into the studio four figures who walked like a march of the condemned and who looked like in-expert caricatures of bands of the past five years. Roy had started a record and was sitting forward to chat with them, when Derrick said "I want to ask the questions. This is *my* interview."

Roy would have found this too pathetic even to notice, except that Derrick's guests were grinning to themselves; they were clearly in on the secret. When Roy had suffered Derrick's questions and their grudging answers for ten minutes—"Which singers do you like? Have you written any songs? Are you going to?"—he cut them off and wished the band success, which they certainly still needed.

When they'd gone, and a record was playing, Derrick turned on him. "I hadn't finished," he said petulantly. "I was still talking."

"You've every right to do so, but not on my programme."

"It's my programme too. You weren't the one who invited me. I'm going to tell Hugh Ward about you."

Roy hoped he would. The station manager would certainly have been listening to the banal interview. Roy was still cursing Derrick as he reached the bridge, where he baulked momentarily. No, he'd had enough stupidity for one day; he wasn't about to let the bridge bother him.

Yet it did. The weeds looked even paler, and drained; if he touched them—which he had no intention of doing—they might snap. The walls glistened with a liquid that looked slower and thicker than water: mixed with grime, presumably. Overhead, among the encrusted girders, something large was following him.

He was sure of that now. Though it stopped when he did, it wasn't his echoes. When he fled beyond the mouth of the bridge, it scuttled to the edge of the dark arch. As he stood still he heard it again, roaming back and forth restlessly, high in the dark. It was too large for a bird or a cat. For a moment he was sure that it was about to scuttle down the drooling wall at him.

Despite the heat, he locked all the windows. He'd grown used to the sounds of trains, so much so that they often helped him sleep, yet now he wished he lived further away. Though the nights were growing lighter, the arch looked oppressively ominous, a lair. That night every train on the bridge jarred him awake.

In the morning he was in no mood to tolerate Derrick. He'd get the better of him one way or the other—to start with, by speaking to Ward. But Derrick had already seen the station manager, and now Ward wasn't especially sympathetic to Roy; perhaps he felt that his judgement in hiring Derrick was being questioned. "He says his interview went badly because you inhibited him," he said, and when Roy protested "In any case, surely you can put up with him for a couple of weeks. After all, learning to get on with people is part of the job. We must be flexible."

Derrick was that all right, Roy thought furiously: flexible as putty, and as lacking in personality. During the whole of "Our Town Tonight" he and Derrick glared at or ignored each other. When they spoke on the air, it wasn't to each other. Derrick, Roy kept thinking: a tower over a bore—and the name contained "dreck," which seemed entirely appropriate. Most of all he resented being reduced to petulance himself. Thank God it was nearly the weekend—except that meant he would have to go home.

When he left the bus he walked home the long way, avoiding the bridge. From his gate he glanced at the arch, whose walls were already mossed with dimness, then looked quickly away. If he ignored it, put it out of his mind completely, perhaps nothing would happen. What could happen, for heaven's sake? Later, when an unlit train clanked over the bridge like the dragging of a giant chain in the dark, he realised why the trains had kept him awake: what might their vibrations disturb under the bridge?

Though the night made him uneasy, Saturday was worse. Children kept running through the bridge, screaming to wake the echoes. He watched anxiously until they emerged; the sunlight on the far side of the arch seemed a refuge.

He was growing obsessive, checking and rechecking the locks on all the windows, especially those nearest the bridge. That night he visited friends, and drank too much, and talked about everything that came into his head, except the bridge. It was waiting for him, mouth open, when he staggered home. Perhaps the racket of his clumsy footsteps had reached the arch, and was echoing faintly.

On Sunday his mouth was parched and rusty, his skull felt like a lump of lead that was being hammered out of shape. He could only sit at the bedroom window and be grateful that the sunlight was dull. Children were shrieking under the bridge. If anything happened there, he had no idea what he would do.

Eventually the street was quiet. The phrases of church bells drifted, inter-weaving, on the wind. Here came the old man, apparently taking his string-bags to church. No: he halted at the bridge and peered up for a while; then, looking dissatisfied but unwilling to linger, he turned away.

Roy had to know. He ran downstairs, though his brain felt as though it were slopping from side to side. "Excuse me—" (damn, he didn't know the old man's name) "er, could I ask what you were looking for?"

"You've been watching me, have you?"

"I've been watching the bridge. I mean, I think something's up there too. I just don't know what it is."

The old man frowned at him, perhaps deciding whether to trust him. Eventually he said "When you hear trains at night, do you ever wonder where they've been? They stop in all sorts of places miles from anywhere in the middle of the night. Suppose something decided to take a ride? Maybe it would get off again if it found somewhere like the place it came from. Sometimes trains stop on the bridge."

"But what is it?" He didn't realise he had raised his voice until he heard a faint echo. "Have you seen it? What does it want?"

"No, I haven't seen it." The old man seemed to resent the question, as though it was absurd or vindictive. "Maybe I've heard it, and that's too much as it is. I just hope it takes another ride. What does it want? Maybe it ran out of—" Surely his next word must have been "food," but it sounded more like "forms."

Without warning he seemed to remember Roy's job. "If you read a bit more you wouldn't need me to tell you," he said angrily, slapping his bagfuls of books. "You want to read instead of serving things up to people and taking them away from books."

Roy couldn't afford to appear resentful. "But since I haven't read them, can't you tell me—" He must be raising his voice, for the echo was growing clearer—and that must have been what made the old man flee. Roy was left gaping after him and wondering how his voice had managed to echo; when a train racketed over the bridge a few minutes later, it seemed to produce no echo at all.

The old man had been worse than useless. Suppose there was something under the bridge: it must be entrapped in the arch. Otherwise, why hadn't it been able to follow Roy beyond the mouth? He stood at his bedroom window, daring a shape to appear. The thing was a coward, and stupid—almost as stupid as he was for believing that anything was there. He must lie down, for his thoughts were cracking apart, floating away. The lullaby of bells for evening mass made him feel relatively safe.

Sleep took him back to the bridge. In the dark he could just make out a halted goods-train. Perhaps all the trucks were empty, except for the one from which something bloated and pale was rising. It clambered down, lolling from scrawny legs, and vanished under the bridge, where a bird was nesting. There was a sound less like the cry of a bird than the shriek of air being squeezed out of a body. Now something that looked almost like a bird sat in the nest—but its head was too large, its beak was lopsided, and it had no voice. Nevertheless the bird's returning mate ventured close enough to be seized. After a jump in the continuity, for which Roy was profoundly grateful, he glimpsed a shape that seemed to have lost the power to look like a bird, crawling into the darkest corners of the arch, among cobwebs laden with soot. Now a cat was caught beneath the arch, and screaming; but the shape that clung to the girder afterwards didn't look much like a cat, even before it scuttled back into its corner. Perhaps it needed more substantial food. Roy needn't be afraid, he was awake now and watching the featureless dark of the arch from his bedroom window. Yet he was dreadfully afraid, for he knew that his fear was a beacon that would allow something to reach for him. All at once the walls of his room were bare brick, the corners were masses of sooty cobweb, and out of the darkest corner a top-heavy shape was scuttling.

When he managed to wake, he was intensely grateful to find that it wasn't dark. Though he had the impression that he'd slept for hours, it was still twilight. He wasn't at all refreshed: his body felt odd—feverish, unfamiliar, exhausted as though by a struggle he couldn't recall.

No doubt the nightmare, which had grown out of the old man's ramblings, was to blame.

He switched on the radio to try to rouse himself. What was wrong? They'd mixed up the signature tunes, this ought to be—He stood and gaped, unable to believe what he was hearing. It was Monday, not Sunday at all.

No wonder he felt so odd. He had no time to brood over that, for he was on the air in less than an hour. He was glad to be leaving. The twilight made it appear that the dark of the bridge was seeping towards the house. His perceptions must be disordered, for his movements seemed to echo in the rooms. Even the sound of a bird's claw on the roof-tiles made him nervous.

Despite his lateness, he took the long way to the main road. From the top of the bus he watched furry ropes of cloud, orange and red, being drawn past the ends of side streets. Branches clawing at the roof made him start. A small branch must have snapped off, for even when the trees had passed, a restless scraping continued for a while above him.

He'd rarely seen the city streets so deserted. Night was climbing the walls. He was neurotically aware of sounds in the empty streets. Birds fluttered sleepily on pediments, though he couldn't always see them. His footsteps sounded effeminate, panicky, thinned by the emptiness. The builder's scaffolding that clung to the outside of the radio station seemed to turn his echoes even more shrill.

The third-floor studio seemed to be crowded with people, all waiting for him. Ian the producer looked harassed, perhaps imagining an entire show with Derrick alone. Derrick was smirking, bragging his punctuality. Tonight's interviewees—a woman who wrote novels about doctors and nurses in love, the leader of a group of striking undertakers—clearly sensed something was wrong. Well, now nothing was.

Roy was almost glad to see Derrick. Trivial chat might be just what he needed to stabilise his mind; certainly it was all he could manage. Still, the novelist proved to be easy: every question produced an anecdote—her Glasgow childhood, the novel she'd thrown out of the window because it was too like real life, the woman who wrote to her asking to be introduced to the men on whom she based her characters. Roy was happy to listen, happy not to talk, for his voice through the microphone seemed to be echoing.

"—and Mugsy Moore, and Poo-Poo, and Trixie the Oomph." Reading the dedications, Derrick sounded unnervingly serious. "And here's a letter from one of our listeners," he said to Roy without warning, "who wants to know if we aren't speaking to each other."

Had Derrick invented that in a bid for sympathy? "Yes, of course we are," Roy said impatiently. As soon as he'd started the record—his hands on the controls felt unfamiliar and clumsy, he must try to be less irritable—he complained "Something's wrong with the microphone. I'm getting an echo."

"I can't hear anything," Ian said.

"It isn't there now, only when I'm on the air."

Ian and one of the engineers stared through the glass at Roy for a while, then shook their heads. "There's nothing," Ian said through the headphones, though Roy could hear the echo growing worse, trapping his voice amid distortions of itself. When he removed the headphones, the echo was still audible. "If you people listening at home are wondering what's wrong with my voice"—he was growing coldly furious, for Derrick was shaking his head too, looking smug—"we're working on it."

Ian ushered the striking undertaker into the studio. Maybe he would take Roy's mind off the technical problems. And maybe not, for as soon as Roy introduced him, something began to rattle the scaffolding outside the window and squeak its claws or its beak on the glass. "After this next record we'll be talking to him," he said as quickly as he could find his way through echoes.

"What's wrong now?" Ian demanded.

"That." But the tubular framework was still, and the window was otherwise empty. It must have been a bird. No reason for them all to stare at him.

As soon as he came back on the air the sounds began again. Didn't Ian care that the listeners must be wondering what they were? Halfway through introducing the undertaker, Roy turned sharply. Though there wasn't time for anything to dodge out of sight, the window was blank.

That threw him. His words were stumbling among echoes, and he'd forgotten what he meant to say. Hadn't he said it already, before playing the record?

Suddenly, like an understudy seizing his great chance on the night when the star falls ill, Derrick took over. "Some listeners may wonder why we're digging this up, but other people may think that this strike is a grave undertaking...." Roy was too distracted to be appalled, even when Derrick pounced with an anecdote about an old lady whose husband was still awaiting burial. Why, the man was a human vacuum: no personality to be depended on at all.

For the rest of the show, Roy said as little as possible. Short answers echoed less. He suppressed some of the monosyllables he was tempted to use. At last the signature tune was reached. Mopping his forehead theatrically, Derrick opened the window.

Good God, he would let it in! The problems of the show had distracted Roy from thinking, but there was nothing to muffle his panic now. Ian caught his arm. "Roy, if there's anything—" Even if he wanted to help, he was keeping Roy near the open window. Shrugging him off, Roy ran towards the lift.

As he waited, he saw Ian and the engineer stalking away down the corridor, murmuring about him. If he'd offended Ian, that couldn't be helped; he needed to be alone, to think, perhaps to argue himself out of his panic. He dodged into the lift, which resembled a grey windowless telephone box, featureless except for the dogged subtraction of lit numbers. He felt walled in by grey. Never mind, in a minute he would be out in the open, better able to think—

But was he fleeing towards the thing he meant to elude?

The lift gaped at the ground floor. Should he ride it back to the third? Ian and the engineer would have gone down to the car park by now; there would only be Derrick and the open window. The cramped lift made him feel trapped, and he stepped quickly into the deserted foyer.

Beyond the glass doors he could see a section of pavement, which looked oily with sodium light. Around it the tubes of the scaffolding blazed like orange neon. As far as he could judge, the framework was totally still—but what might be waiting silently for him to step beneath? Suddenly the pavement seemed a trap which needed only a footfall to trigger it. He couldn't go out that way.

He was about to press the button to call the lift when he saw that the lit numbers were already counting down. For a moment—he didn't know why—he might have fled out of the building, had he been able. He was trapped between the lurid stage of pavement and the inexorable descent of the lift. By the time the lift doors squeaked open, his palms were stinging with sweat. But the figure that stumbled out of the lift, hindered a little by his ill-fitting clothes, was Derrick.

Roy could never have expected to be so glad to see him. Hastily, before he could lose his nerve, he pulled open the glass doors, only to find that he was still unable to step beneath the scaffolding. Derrick went first, his footsteps echoing in the deserted street. When nothing happened, Roy managed to follow. The glass doors snapped locked behind him.

Though the sodium glare was painfully bright, at least it showed that the scaffolding was empty. He could hear nothing overhead. Even his footsteps sounded less panicky now; it was Derrick's that were distorted, thinned and hasty. Never mind, Derrick's hurry was all to the good, whatever its cause; it would take them to the less deserted streets all the more quickly.

Shadows counted their paces. Five paces beyond each lamp their shadows drew ahead of them and grew as dark as they could, then pivoted around their feet and paled before the next lamp. He was still nervous, for he kept peering at the shadows—but how could he expect them not to be distorted? If the shadows were bothering him, he'd have some relief from them before long, for ahead there was a stretch of road where several lamps weren't working. He wished he were less alone with his fears. He wished Derrick would speak.

Perhaps that thought halted him where the shadows were clearest, to gaze at them in dismay.

His shadow wasn't unreasonably distorted. That was exactly the trouble. Without warning he was back in his nightmare, with no chance of awakening. He remembered that the thing in the nightmare had had no voice. No, Roy's shadow wasn't especially distorted—but beside it, produced by the same lamp, Derrick's shadow was.

Above all he mustn't panic; his nightmare had told him so. Perhaps he had a chance, for he'd halted several lamps short of the darkness. If he could just retreat towards the studio without breaking into a run, perhaps he would be safe. If he could bang on the glass doors without losing control, mightn't the caretaker be in time?

The worst thing he could do was glance aside. He mustn't see what was casting the shadow, which showed how the scrawny limbs beneath the bloated stomach were struggling free of the ill-fitting clothes. Though his whole body was trembling—for the face of the shadow had puckered and was reaching sideways towards him, off the head—he began, slower than a nightmare, to turn away.

MONSTERS OF ANY KIND

SANTIAGO EXIMENO

NOVERIM TE

by SANTIAGO EXIMENO

TRANSLATED INTO ENGLISH BY DANIELE BONFANTI

Emmanuel wakes up at daybreak, instants before the first sun rays are visible, buried a few minutes later beneath thick gray clouds, storm clouds. They have come a week ago, and took possession of day and night, condemning them to that stifling darkness which precedes the storm season. Emmanuel has already lived through sixty storm seasons, and he is sensible enough that the pin of worry, sunk into his skin for a few days now, has grown until turning into a painful stake stabbing his chest to burst out from his back.

First thing in the morning, he must absolutely visit the lagoon.

A wind has risen, and the sand of the desert swirls, eddying in the air looking for eyes, nostrils and mouths of all the citizens of San Agustín. And of the tourists as well. San Agustín—which got its name from the Spanish who long ago penetrated in these lands, sowing the seed of religion and violence—is today a small town, just a village; half a thousand people of different creeds and ambitions, stubbornly rising on the edge of the desert like the last bastion of a decadent civilization. But it is not that civilized a place, at least not by the standards of the tourists who, year after year, invade it under the shelter of the clouds. The Government is strict in its rules, and soldiers carrying automatic weapons can be seen around bars, shops and bazaars, keeping watch over the visitors coming from all around the world. It is easy to spot the tourists, with their designer clothes, pale skin, and the very expensive filters covering their faces. They come, as every year, to contemplate the slumber of the sleeping god, as they perfectly know that they won't be allowed to stay in San Agustín when the god awakens. For their own safety. For everybody's.

For San Agustín, the tourists are like the bees: an annoying plague with which they have to share their daily routine, but providing interesting boons. Their presence becomes ever more insidious in the days before the storm, but over the years the residents of the village have not only gotten used to them—wandering all around, smiling and cursing at the same time, clumsily muttering what few Latin words they have learned while planning the trip—but they have even understood that the tourists represent a more than acceptable source of income. Those who come to San Agustín are rich tourists, very rich, picked from a long waiting list which the Goverment reviews and updates yearly. Emmanuel is surprised seeing people that wealthy proudly showing their ignorance about language of Faith and traditions, their lack of respect toward the (humble, silent) folk who greet them and treat them with seldom-reciprocated warmness. The tourists bring hurry, yells, cameras which try to steal the very essence of San Agustín by the harsh, unpleasant noise of their shutters. As if it were possible. As if the voices, the whisper of the clouds or the smell of the creeping storm could ever be captured in a picture. Or in a video. As if the church, rising right in the middle of San Agustín, its history, its life, its soul, could ever crystallize into a handful of pixels.

Emmanuel too has a laptop, there in his hut, and on the Net he sees things he would never share with the tourists. Why? Because they would not understand him. They are not even able to understand entirely what the lagoon is. And that's where Emmanuel is heading to. He walks between trinket shops and fake craftmanship stalls, which will be hurriedly dismantled only after the last tourist has been invited to leave. On his route, he meets Joseph. Actually, it is Joseph—all dressed up with uniform and weapon received by the Government—who deliberately crosses his path.

"Emmanuel," he says. "Are you going to see the god?"

There is something, in Joseph's tone, that bothers Emmanuel. The muttering of the village, drowned by the damp heat soaking the youth's clothes, cannot hide a hint of arrogance, of smugness in his voice and gestures. Emmanuel is worried about Joseph. He has always been a rebellious, troublesome kid, the kind used to question everything; and even though elsewhere such behaviour may even be considered positive, there, in San Agustín—on the edge of the desert, with the presence of the sleeping god—only obedience, submission, and respect for the elders can be accepted.

Joseph fiddles with his weapon, wipes the sweat from his nape with the back of his free hand. He grins as a man convinced that his presence in the world is a gift to everybody.

"Yes," Emmanuel answers. "I'm going there."

"Some tourists asked if they could go down there with you," Joseph says.

He says that feigning innonence with little success, and Emmanuel cannot avoid stiffening. Go down to the lagoon with some tourists. He may as well have asked him if it were a problem spitting at him in the face. Emmanuel feels anger, and he would like to answer to this bigheaded youth, this insolent, as he deserves; but he doesn't. Here, in San Agustín, Emmanuel is respected; but outside he is only tolerated as a figure that would be difficult to suppress without causing a riot. Joseph was born in San Agustín and now he is working for the Government. Emmanuel knows what that means. For everybody's sake, for the awakening of the sleeping god, he moves his hand in front of his face like shooing away a fly, and he kindly answers:

"They can contemplate from the lookout, if they wish, Jos. Going down there, even with me by their side, is dangerous. Too dangerous."

Seeing the youth's face, Emmanuel understands his mistake: he called him as they used to call him as a child. He was minding about being kind and polite, and ultimately he's been condescendent, and that can all but poke at the open wound dividing them.

"They're paying well," Joseph says.

Emmanuel doesn't manage to hide his surprise, and Joseph knows he has already said too much. Before the elder can try to stop him, he scurries away, disappering among the food stalls which spread around a smell of a hundred spices randomly mixed. Emmanuel would like to identify those tourists as soon as possible, as he knows they will cause problems. How many are they? With whom did they come? He should speak to someone of the Government, inform them about his worry, but the truth, the sad truth, is that he hardly knows anyone, and he is aware that they wouldn't really listen to him. His figure is not a respectable one outside the borders of San Agustín. And maybe, after all, that's why he is still stuck there, for as much as he repeats himself he's doing that for the good of the community. Then, he thinks about telling it to Victor, Joseph's father, but he doesn't know if he'll find the right occasion, if he'll know how to approach him.

The sun is still hidden behind the gray wall formed by the storm clouds, but the heat is already unbearable. Emmanuel walks down the main street of San Agustín, little more than a dusty trail with old clay huts and shops sheltered by the shadow of faded tarpaulins, on either side. In those shops, products manifactured in the capital factories are shamelessly displayed: small scale models of the sleeping god, woodcarved miniatures of the church, earthenware representing part of the village folklore, pendants and rings and knickknack supposed to guard against evil...and among that heap of absurd lure for ignorant tourists, Emmanuel discovers even himself, attired in ceremonial toga, his skin covered by that gray cream which the visitors mistake for ash, the same which is the anteroom of Hell.

"How much for that?" Emmanuel asks the gaunt, black-skinned woman who manages the place, pointing at that tiny version of himself.

An action figure, that's what he's become. Money trivializes everything. The woman is curled up in a moldy beach chair, certainly bartered with her by some tourist for some of her junk. After all, bargaining and the art of haggling are part of the charm of that travel. The woman drinks cool water from a terracotta jug, before answering:

"For you, nothing. You know that."

"And for them?"

She shrugs and grins.

"They set their price with their clothes, their gazes, and their hurry."

Emmanuel nods and resumes his walk. He crosses a couple—young, athletic, with brightly colored bermuda shorts and white t-shirts, with reflex cameras hanging like cowbells at their sweat-drenched necks—and he wonders if it could be them, those who want to go beyond where's permitted. Or perhaps they are just new dupes for the market traders. Thinking again about Joseph's dangerous and foolish acts, he manages to accept the stall woman's view of life. May she cash in everything she can from those who are willing to pay. At the end of the day, that doesn't go against the spirit of the transaction. Those people believe in free market, so what's the issue? What's sure is that nobody in San Agustín hosts the sleeping god in the lagoon for his own desire.

It was the god who decided to rest there every year. It seems only right that, while the god stays with them, they get some benefit in exchange—mundane as that could sound.

The street abruptly dies as it reaches the lookout, the place where the tourists crowd like hungry flies. And maybe that's not such an undue simile, Emmanuel muses, that same feeling every time he treads on that place. Seeing him coming, whispers are born, and cameras glint, snatching a memory of him to be remembered thousands of kilometers away. Emmanuel—faithful to what has been transmitted through generations—raises his hand and waves and whispers a few Latin words. Some tourists throw themselves on their mobile phones and their pocket dictionaries to find confirmation that, indeed, the High Priest has greeted and blessed them. Others simply grin in a daze, others timidly clap their hands, and soon the whole group bursts into out-of-sync applauses while Emmanuel walks among them, opens the iron gate using the ceremonial key hanging at his neck, and descends the earthen steps—seventy-six hand-carved steps—leading to the lagoon and, finally, to the sleeping god.

There is the god, down there. He sleeps. He waits.

Over the years, the god's presence in San Agustín has become ever more mythical, if that's possible. Nobody remembers anymore when he came to the village for the first time, because records have been either lost or eliminated by the Government. Too much information, too many actual details about his origins, would be detrimental to business; and right now the unjustified presence of the god is the main source of income for the region. It is possible that his presence alone supports the economy of the whole Country. It would be difficult to quantify: the copyrights about the god—be it image, video, or one of the colorful wares displayed in the stalls and exported worldwide—are shared among so many private hands, and are infringed so many times, that calculating actual turnovers is a devil of a job. What Emmanuel knows is that, if one year the god shouldn't come back after the storm season, they would all be doomed. But he comes back, year after year, to rest at the lagoon, to recover his strength after what he did here or elsewhere—and nothing suggests that this year things will go any differently.

Contemplating the god overwhelms him. It happened the first time and each time it happens again. Each step Emmanuel descends chokes a cry inside of him. The god lies next to the lagoon, facedown, imposing. His lying body is more than twenty meters long, though it can reach twice that size when he uncoils his tails. About his face—his true face—everything is conjecture, because nobody was ever able to contemplate him in his entirety. At least nobody who lived to tell about it. Legends tell about hundreds of festering mouths and thousands of eyes drowned in tears of blood, and the most daring representations—those which don't just show him lying, his face sunk in the dirt—are known for their heterogeneity and considered apocrypha in any case. Only the sketches on the canvases hanging on the walls of San Agustín church—work of a forgotten artist—are accepted as canonical; there, the face of the god is a confused amalgam of incoherent features, an emptyness to be interpreted by the onlooker. Only these last representations are accepted by the Government, and reproduced for commercial purposes.

Whenever he contemplates the sleeping god, Emmanuel always thinks about how his father described him: a swarm of sick elephants. The god's gray, wrinkled skin opens in infinte places, riddled by long white protrusions which may well remind of the tusks of a colossal animal. Where the skin is open, a thick golden fluid suppurates, trickling down that disproportionate body and forming streams of something like molasses in its texture and density. Years ago, these oozes were collected and bottled up; but after the discovery that those lunatics who had dared tasting it had died among horrible pains, their organs consumed and melted like plastic left in a flame, the Government forbade that. On the back of the god, vultures and other carrion birds nest; but other animals, even insects and hyenas, shun his presence like that of humans. It is usual to see hundreds of birds circling above the sleeping god. Loitering, perhaps waiting for the devastation which is bound to accompany his awakening. But that devastation must be avoided, and Emmanuel is responsible for that. Emmanuel accepts his responsibility, he feels proud of being who he is, and he cannot be shaken by the critics—about the absurdity of the tradition he supports year after year by his acts. He firmly believes in his work, even though in order to do it he has to dip his hands into a malodorous pool full of hot feces.

Because that's what the lagoon actually is.

They have built a deterrent fence all around it. It is a precarious fence, made of sharpened wood, barbed wire and shards of dyed glass; as most of the area—probably along with lookout and some of the near huts—it will be razed to the ground when the god awakens. Around the fence, and at a safe, respectful distance from the sleeping god, about ten armed men patrol, Government men. They are there to deter bystanders who get too close and to keep away the shamans, who often come in the shadows of the night, carrying the bodies of stillborn babies in wicker baskets. Those armed men, relieved every eight hours, have their faces covered by scarves, brightly colored ritual masks, and even gas masks, relics of the old continent's wars. The tourists believe it to be an ancestral tradition, a colorful show of local folklore they've been so lucky to catch. What actually those men are trying to fight is the deep reek spreading around from the lagoon, a putrid stench of death, of putrefaction. The smell of a god.

Emmanuel penetrates into that muddy territory with his canvas shoes and his ceremonial toga, his face uncovered. He walks by the shore of the lagoon, watching its surface somewhat worriedly. After all those years, he has learned to judge the mixture in a single look, and though he cannot really be sure about its condition until he has sunk his arm to the elbow into that black sludge, that first glance has been enough for his stomach to twist. The feces of the sleeping god are not ready yet, and the gray clouds which have devoured the blue of the sky confirm that their time is virtually over. For the god, these technical details—these doubts and complications—simply don't exist. And neither he understands apologies or laments. Emmanuel knows that if they all don't make an effort to complete the work today, with the disgusting contents of the lagoon as they are, the god is going to awaken and destroy everything and everybody. It has happened in the past and it will happen again in the future, but Emmanuel cannot allow it to happen this time.

"Not this time," Emmanuel mutters, the same words his father used to repeat year after year.

At the lagoon shore, Aussie is waiting; a white man, red-haired, his face covered in freckles and wearing swimming shorts and a t-shirt with drawings of strange animals. Aussie claims he was born on a huge island, larger even than this whole Country, but Emmanuel doesn't believe that. Even if he never cared too much for geography—his searches on the Net are restricted, regarding his position and nation only, as the Government mandates—he cannot believe an island that big may exist. At least, not one full of people like Aussie. That little man talks a lot, too much, but he understands machines, and he is one of the responsibles imposed by the Government. Emmanuel tolerates his quirks—like covering his skin in ash to turn into one of them, or getting drunk with the terrible booze distilled by the Osayande brothers then to trip into the lagoon—and he even had lunch with him a couple of times; but there is something in the way Aussie moves, in the orange flames nesting inside his hair, in the sickly paleness of his skin, in the thick azure lines traversing his bare arms, that causes in Emmanuel a sense of rejection that he isn't able—he doesn't want—to quell.

"Hello, great man," Aussie says as he sees him arriving, offering him his hand.

Emmanuel shakes it. That simple gesture, so alien to the hug and kiss he traditionally shares with the people of San Agustín, reinforces the ties he has unwillingly weaved with the machinery man. Oh, yes, Emmanuel is a tradition lover, respectful of his people and faithful—as much as he can and must—to the directives of the Government, which include a strict control of relationships with foreigners; but he is also aware that without Aussie's priceless help and his machines, they would have never managed to survive all those years. And somehow that certainty, despite his distaste toward Aussie's character, has established in him an unshakable trust in that man. Emmanuel is not used to such contradictory feelings, much less toward a stranger. His position in San Agustín is forcibly that of the hermit, of the solitary revered—despite the women offering themselves to him to give him a son, an heir, a chosen one, just like it happened to his father back in his time. This distance—imposed by being who he is, who he represents for San Agustín—disappears when he deals with that white buffoon, that genius able to foretell the arrival of the storm within a one-hour error margin. Once, Aussie told him that one of his previous jobs was doing similar foretellings for car races. Just more of his crazy nonsense, Emmanuel thought.

"Believe it or not, this shit of yours is well-cooked," Aussie says. "But I imagine you'll want to check it for yourself, and do that gross thing you always do. After all, your loyal audience is waiting just for that."

And that's certainly the case. Many of the tourists crowding the lookout have stopped paying attention to the predictable back of the sleeping god and its indigenous fauna, and that attention—along with their camera lenses—is now aimed at Emmanuel. Maybe they don't understand the following step he is going to follow, but they certainly know the ritual in detail.

"I will have to satisfy them," Emmanuel says, and Aussie grins, showing him the readouts of the machines on the monitor of his laptop.

Numbers, graphics, pie charts. Most of the information is unreadable to Emmanuel, but over the years he managed to be able to make out the general meaning. The mixture of feces and human bones is ready. Emmanuel turns back, his gaze looking for the church; but from down there, from the abode of the sleeping god, it cannot be seen. He is excited, like every time before, as he puts his bare hand into the lagoon, his fingers moving like eels among the feces of the sleeping god and the ground little bones of stillborn babies. And only after that he smiles, nods, and understands that everything has happened, as always, right in time.

"Very good, great man: the storm will sweep us over later today, at dusk," Aussie explains. "Let's say we have, with the usual error margin, a little more than four hours to get the work done. Think your people can do that?"

Of course, that's a rhetorical question. They live for that. That is the moment they have been waiting for all year long, and it's up to Emmanuel to manage it. That is the moment to send the tourists away—with the tact suggested by the Government. That is the moment to see the awakening of the sleeping god.

Emmanuel washes his hands in a plastic bucket handed to him by Aussie.

"The Government is already warned and they have already begun the evacuation. Those at the lookout must be the last ones. Soon, you'll give the order, so this all begins, as you unleash that madness you people enjoy so much. So, if that doesn't bother you, can I ask you to satisfy my morbid curiosity this time? Come on... How many babies have you dumped this year?"

Ah, the children, Emmanuel thinks. Yes, it took time for them to discover it. The sleeping god did not spare everything covered in his own feces—if that's what they were, if the biologists had correctly determined which is mouth and which is anus, if that muddy substance which the god secreted like water from a holy spring actually were his excrement. Another ingredient was required in the mixture: the bones of stillborn babies. Of course, not everybody believed that, not everybody accepted it as necessary, and suspects were far from far-fetched that many babies died in childbirth just to become part of the ritual. But one thing was certain and undebatable: when children's remains weren't there, the destruction of San Agustín was absolute. Sure, they could go away, leave the village, look for another place to live. Some, very few, would do that. Like the unruly Joseph. But most of them would rather stay at their homes, be part of that communion.

Emmanuel thinks about the official vehicles. They come in the night, and Government men get off, carrying sacks full of newborn corpses that they, men armed with stone faces and cold gazes, don't dare touch. Ancestral fears they won't ever admit in front of Emmanuel.

They bring them from all over the Country. Some even say from all around the world. The discharge smell from those sacks rivals in harshness the one from the lagoon. That makes sense, as they share ingredients. Emmanuel always accompanies them down the steps, he must. He opens the sacks with them and pours out the bodies—cold, very cold, to delay the decomposition as much as possible during the trip—into the lagoon, where they sluggishly sink while their flesh dissolves and their bones melt with the feces of the sleeping god.

And he also thinks about the shamans of the neighboring villages, who get desperate women pregnant only to sacrifice their newborns, so to reinforce their power among their people.

"How much?" Emmanuel asks. "Who knows. About a hundred. Maybe more."

"They bring them from everywhere," Aussie comments while they climb the steps, on their way back to San Agustín, more to himself than to carry on the conversation.

"From everywhere, yes. Everywhere."

Above, they already know the good news, and it's all a frenzied racket. While women and children hurry up dismantling stalls, the men are already forming ragged tails at the foot of the steps, armed with buckets, washing bowls, wicker baskets; with their own hands. They will all be there soon, but with these early arrived they can begin. The Government men can hardly contain the excitment running through San Agustín. Emmanuel raises his hands and a respectful silence takes hold of the crowd in awe. The world stops for a few seconds while the High Priest looks at the sky and watches the storm advancing. The clouds take shapes which he knows will be interpreted as terrible omens of death and destruction, and the held breaths of every single villager of San Agustín convert his acts into myth. Emmanuel knows that, in that instant, he is the center of all creation, and despite that he struggles to maintain that feeling of humbleness, of respect, which informs his ritual. He struggles to convey that awestruck quiver to the god, to that grotesque creature of unknown origin who, alien to paraphernalia and false traditions, dozes and defecates while he waits for the storm to break loose.

Emmanuel lowers his eyes, and his gaze crosses Aussie's, who feigns a yawn. How much he values, against his own will, the presence of that man of no principles; how much he needs him to keep his sense, even his faith.

"Let us do it," Emmanuel says, while he spreads his arms and shows the palms of his hands.

And the crowd bursts into cries and howls and laughter.

"I'll admit this is the fun part," Aussie comments.

They both join the human chain which, in a few minutes, has formed before their eyes. It runs along the whole path, from the lagoon shore—where half a dozen people, the luckiest, are hard at work dunking the most diverse containers into the feces of the sleeping god—up to the church. All around, the shops close and are dismantled, the last tourists are kindly escorted to the off-road vehicles ready to carry them back to their hotels. Far from here.

It is a flurry of activity. Men, women, and children perched on makeshift scaffoldings cladding the clay walls of the church with the feces carried there from the lagoon. And not the church only: also the houses, the roads. Everything that could be devastated by the god when he wakes up, as it is necessary that he walks toward the desert, toward nothingness. That he moves away from the village and its inhabitants, that he walks through the mud of the dunes and devours what he encounters there, but allowing them to live a year more. The god's feces will drive him away, and that is why all those people are dunking their bare hands into them, and they soil the fronts of their homes and shops. That is why they smear with those feces the canvases covering their windows and the doors of plywood and asbestos. Even their own bodies. But overall, they work at the church, on every square centimeter of its thin walls, because when the storm arrives, everybody will take shelter inside of it, and they will wait in silence—among just-whispered litanies—the god's departure.

Emmanuel opens the church doors to allow the first women to enter, as they come with their children in their arms. A few elders, too weak for the overlaying work, enter the building carrying fruit, dried meat, and water bottles. The night may be long. Aussie bids farewell to Emmanuel on the doorway, shaking his hand again.

"I'm leaving, great man. My ride is about to go. Eh, I'm traveling with two mature women from the old continent. I'm expecting a thrilling trip back to the hotel…"

"Everything is going to be all right," Emmanuel says. "As always. I will see you tomorrow."

Aussie keeps looking at him in the eye for a few seconds, then he looks around and nods. The crowd is still immersed in the work at the church facade, traditional songs defying fear as they are sung by throats by the hundred. Aussie stretches his hand and looks at the sky.

"It's here already. Hurry up."

Then he goes, escorted by the Government men. They won't risk their lives, they don't need to.

The crowd floods in at the church doors, which stay wide open. Inside, humidity and heat are overwhelming. Huddled together, nervous, the people of San Agustín face the inevitable. Once again. It starts raining, it is time to enter. Emmanuel gets out, pats the newcomers' shoulders, hugs and kisses them as they walk through the threshold. He repays with his presence and blessings all his neighbors, while they penetrate into the house of that other god whom they worship looking for refuge. Sometimes, Emmanuel asks himself which god they really worship. For a few of them, like the baby in the arms of the woman coming in right now, this is the first time. For the others, it is part of their lives' routine. Emmanuel has heard about a remote region, where during a month the snow invades the towns, and with that—every year—the gods of winter come back, catching and devouring women and men alike, in a small number which is considered a sufficient offer to ensure a fecund spring. Stories for toothless grandmas, he thought to himself. Nobody would live in a place like that, if they can avoid it. And then he thinks about his own life, and he can only smile at that absurd correspondence.

"Thank you, everybody. May you all be blessed," Emmanuel recites.

The rain intensifies, the roads dissolve under the downpour. Time is running short, the doors will have to be shut soon. Emmanuel doesn't need to count them, he knows that all the residents of San Agustín will be there in time. Their lives are at stake. Only a handful of men are still at the doors, busy with the finishing touches to the church walls. The off-road vehicles have long left, to avoid any last-hour surprise. It stands to reason that the god will head toward the desert, but one can never be completely sure.

"Come in, come in," Emmanuel urges the last latecomers, as he is about to close the doors.

By now, the rain is an overflown creek; the god must be about to wake. The muddied roads no longer exist, they are torrents of sludge coming down between the houses toward the lagoon, their private sea of death. The hammering of the water inside the church will soon be stifling. Some children already cry, some men stand as they recite psalms with trembling voices. A young woman shares out fruit to those who ask for it by raising a hand. Emmanuel decides to cast a final look outside before closing the doors, and he immediately curses his eyes because out there, in the rain, running in the mud wrapped in a dark raincoat, he glimpses an impossible outline. Two more shadows accompany it; slender, agile. One of those glints for an instant in the gloom of the storm. The flash of a camera. Joseph. And those two tourists.

"If he doesn't kill you, I'll do it. With my bare hands," Emmanuel grumbles.

And then he exits and, before anyone can protest, he shuts the doors of the church. He waits a few seconds, until he hears them locking it with the bar, inside. At first with reluctance, then more decisively. Good, they have done the right thing. They are safe. If he survives—and he doesn't count on it—he will make sure to praise them for their resolution during the next year. What matters is the safety of the village. Of San Agustín. Emmanuel's life is of no worth. They have done the right thing.

Joseph has not.

Emmanuel enters the storm. The rain soaks him, hitting his face and causing tears, tears of rage and resignation for what will have to happen. His hands burn, his bare feet—the flood has snatched his slippers—sink in the mud, making him stagger and fall. On his knees, his palms submerged in a clay already blending with the feces of the sleeping god, he hears—among the thunder and the fury of the rain deafening him—the muttering of souls flattened against the mud, begging for their lives, and he knows that in that very moment the god has awakened. The stench soon pouring into his nostrils causes uncontrollable retching, and he vomits a bitter, scorching liquid.

"Joseph!" he yells between pants, while he cleans his mouth. "I'll kill you with my own hands!"

Emmanuel knows that the young man cannot hear him, but screaming his hatred relieves him. Nauseated by the terrible reek, crushed by the storm, Emmanuel remembers that the youth who's gone insane—that youth whose little sense have been corrupted by greed and ambition of being someone he is not—is armed. And if, as Emmanuel fears, in his madness he has dragged that stupid couple to the lookout, maybe that useless weapon has given him the courage he lacked to go down, at the foot of the god. Or even worse, perhaps he has shot him.

Emmanuel advances against the desert wind, which hurls the storm at him without mercy, and he goes through what was, only a few hours ago, the commercial street of San Agustín, now just a river of waste. He holds himself to warped wood poles which supported stalls, to shattered walls of clay fractured by the strength of the water, to anything allowing him to push forward and reach Joseph. He knows that he is walking toward death; that his presence there, before the god, is not going to change anything, but he feels invested in a certain power, linked to what he is, what he represents, and he thinks that it is highly probable that he has lost his mind himself, and that this is as good a way to die as any. Who cares how it happens. Maybe dying right in front of the god is the best thing, maybe that's his destiny.

A stout-fingered hand grabs his arm just as the drowned moan booming inside his head becomes voice, the voice of the god. Emmanuel has already heard that, always behind the so-called safety offered to him by the church doors. Now, that inhuman bellow, that sound monstrosity, makes him urinate himself. He tries to free his arm from the hand that has caught him, but he stops struggling as, through the rain, he makes out Victor's face—Joseph's father.

"Go away!" Emmanuel screams.

The other man shakes his head and forces him to walk beside him. He carries a wooden cane in his other hand, and he drives it into the muddy ground to steady his every step.

"He's my son! I can't!" Victor says, and though Emmanuel can only discern the words on his lips, he nods.

After terrible minutes, pelted by the rain and soaked with the putrid smell spread by the god all over San Agustín, the lookout is in sight. They can glimpse Joseph's presence there, and they spot the tourists there as well, their silhouettes outlined against the darkness of the desert by every lightning flash biting the sky. Victor halts, he lets his cane drop.

"We have to go on!" Emmanuel howls, but Victor cannot hear his words.

He is not even looking at him. He stays there, petrified as a statue, an empty shell. Emmanuel tries to shake him out of that death trance, but he only manages to make him fall flat into the mud. Victor stays there, lying face up. The rain slides over his open eyes, parody of tears he will not weep for his son. Becuase, as Emmanuel's gaze goes back to the lookout, he understands that what he mistook for the darkness of the desert is something else: it is the risen body of the one they worship and fear and pray and beg that he doesn't destroy them, that he comes back year after year to share his slumber, as who is the source of fortune balancing the omen of disgrace—and Emmanuel cannot conceive the life of San Agustín, his own life, without his presence. *And the god in all his glory showed him his face, veiled by the storm, transfigured by shadows, and from his hundreds open mouths a howl erupted which struck him down and sunk him into the mud of unconsciousness.*

<hr />

They found him two days later, next to the lifeless body—half-devoured by vermin—who was identified as Victor, Joseph's father. Emmanuel's body had been spared, and the rain—ongoing, but far from the violence of the night of the god's awakening—had washed his face, crystalized in an image of peace. They couldn't find a single trace of Jospeh or the tourists, though what's sure is that nobody put too much effort in looking for them. The Government buried the events and decided focusing on rebuilding what had been devastated in San Agustín, just a handful of structures. The lookout in particular looked as though thousands of worms had gnawed on it down to its foundations. If the god would come back, he would be there in only a month, so the works had to be undertaken during the rain season. As always. They had to be done quickly, because the return of the god was always stealthy and abrupt, and it wouldn't have been the first time it costed human lives.

Aussie required a transfer. He had heard about the small gods hosted by the ocean bottom, who only show themselves when the sea withdraws back enough, and quickly enough, to make it possible for a human being to descend into their dwellings. And he wanted to know how much of that was true, and how he could help preserving the tradition. There was no problem in replacing him, just like it would not be a problem replacing Emmanuel. After all, there were enough single mothers in San Agustín to pick the best candidate.

MONSTERS OF ANY KIND

MARK ALAN MILLER

THE DIVE

by MARK ALAN MILLER

I swear to God you're not going to believe this story.

Let's just get that out of the way right at the beginning. But I promise that every word is true. I think. I mean, I can't be certain because, well, you'll see. It's all just too crazy. I don't know. Maybe I made it all up and I'm not actually sitting down at my desk typing anything. Maybe I'm strapped to a bed in a psych ward somewhere on a Thorazine drip telling myself a story about writing a story I made up to begin with. Wouldn't that be fucked? Though it *would* make more sense.

As they say, let's begin at the beginning. I had this job that sucked. It's not really groundbreaking material. This is one of those stories you might be able to call "relatable."

Shitty job. Fish in a barrel. Like a pop song. In music, all you have to do is throw in some bullshit about "letting it all go on the weekend," or "being in a big city," or "just plain falling in love" and you've got yourself the ingredients for a number-one single.

I've got an inkling this, too, is relatable, though I'm fairly sure that the part about me hating my job will be where the relatable aspects stop. And I'll let you know in advance that nobody falls in love. The good news is that even if this story is all in my head, at least I'll never know for sure!

As I was saying, my job was donkey balls. And I knew in my heart that I was wasting my life, and my potential. Sure, the money was good, and other than the long hours, I didn't really have any complaints. Sure, the gig was boring as hell, and made relationships tough because by the time I got off work, everyone else had already gone to bed. And sure, my boss was a dumbass who didn't deserve the gig. But I lived well. All my basic needs were met. I even had enough free time to explore other interests, but I wanted more! Nay, I was owed more! Some would call me lucky and tell me to shut my fucking mouth. I would tell those people to walk a mile in my shoes. You try to deal with the soul-crushing boredom five nights a week, year after year, and get back to me. Especially when you're destined for greatness, but it seems the Fates are out to get you.

Well, one fateful Friday night not too long ago, my time would finally come. I was working late, as usual. Filing, or cataloging, or making spreadsheets or some shit. I don't remember. I just remember my boss asking something of me, and then the familiar feeling of righteous indignation holding me in its grip like a fucking straitjacket. Oh, how I hated him. And I hated my co-workers too. I thought they were all a bunch of do-nothing, go-nowhere bumps on a log. Like the human equivalent of oatmeal. I knew I was different than them, which is why I never made small talk. I just clocked in, put myself on autopilot, and clocked out. I put in my time, did the bare minimum, and counted the hours until I was free.

Let me tell you, nothing felt better than those night drives, especially the ones on Friday! To know I had two whole days to myself. Two days to do all the things in life that were far more important than wasting my valuable time on anyone at that idiot factory, casting my pearls to those swine. But I hadn't exactly been using my weekends to their fullest potential. I'd bought some new video games, and the past few weekends, I'd spent the entire time holed up in one room in my house, trying to beat them. I even beat one in a single sitting once! Don't get me wrong. It was fun. But it was a little disappointing when I realized, after beating it, that I had to be back at work in less than 12 hours.

It was then that I had the thought that all the time I'd spent indoors on the weekends had been doing something to me. Something good. All the time I had to sit and think about things made me feel like I'd cracked a code of some sort—a code that nobody else could see. And because of that, people were starting to annoy me. It seemed the whole world was populated by fools. Honestly, I swear that everyone I ran into was either an idiot or an asshole or both. I wondered if it was just me at first. But everywhere I went—every time I left the house—I'd run into another moron that was just taking up space on the road, releasing toxic gas into the air with their banal small-talk, or not getting my food order right. The world was dying, and I seemed to be the only one paying attention.

One fateful Friday night, while driving home, I was deep in thought on the subject, wondering what exactly was wrong with everyone, and how I could fix it. And if I couldn't fix it, how could I ensure that I never had to deal with these people anymore? Surely there was a better way to live. Surely there were people doing it right. Living the kind of life that was bigger, and better, and truer. Living the kind of life where they never had to do anything they didn't want to do ever again. I mean, for fuck's sake, think about the act of taking out your trash! Is there anything more depressing than carting your own waste to the curb on a weekly basis? I couldn't wait for the day I'd have someone to do it for me.

All of these thoughts and more raced through my mind as I sat idling at a red light only a few blocks from my home. I had a game console with my name on it, and forty-eight hours all to myself to plot and plan for the impending greatness that I knew was my birthright. That's when I saw the blinking sign in the corner of my eye. Without thinking, I turned to look and it was only then that I was pulled from my thoughts.

To my left was a strip mall I'd passed a thousand times before. It was an L-shaped corner lot. Behind the lot was a block of homes separated by a large stone wall. It's one of those places you see almost every day, but have never stopped there to shop for anything. As I said, there was a blinking light. And I don't know if it was ever there before, or if it was newly installed, but that night I saw it. Fastened to the back edge of the building closest to me was a metal sign in the shape of a star, with bright bulbs outlining its perimeter. Beneath the blazing star was an arrow that pointed toward the alley behind the strip mall. Much like the sign itself, I never noticed the alley before. And as I sat staring, I saw in my periphery that the traffic light changed to green. I stayed focused on the sign. The name of the bar—THE CONSTELLATION—was blinking inside that star, practically shouting at me to heed its call. Heed I did.

I still don't know why. I couldn't say what propelled me there that night. The sign. The name. The feeling of finding something new and exotic in a familiar environment. Or perhaps it's just shitty storytelling and my mind is frantically trying to fill in a gap in logic to protect me from the harsh reality of the padded cell I'm currently sitting in. All I can tell you is that it all felt right, somehow, for some reason. I parked in the shopping center, because as far as I could tell, the bar didn't have a lot of its own, and when I got out of my car, the first thing I noticed was that the air felt significant, yet fabricated. Crisp and clear, but somehow untrue. There wasn't a car in sight, in either direction. I couldn't even hear any traffic in the distance. Nor were there any nocturnal animals singing their midnight songs. It was almost like I'd stumbled onto the backlot of a movie studio that was a perfect replica of my neighborhood. It was eerie. I shook the feeling off and went inside. I was never the same again.

The place was dark. I instantly loved the atmosphere. The interior was almost smokey, with some astoundingly warped acid jazz playing somewhere in the background. This was the kind of place that you would imagine was invitation only. I knew I was in my element from the get-go. Everything was dark red leather, with deep rich wood wherever you looked. The place was small, but it packed a punch. Booths lined the back wall and ran the length of the room. There was only enough space left for a single pool table, upholstered in black cloth, which sat unused, between the bar and the booths. The bar itself was seemingly fashioned out of a grand knotty tree trunk, probably thirty feet long. Wherever it had stood in its previous life, it couldn't have held a candle to the sight of where it sat now.

This was the place I'd been looking for my whole life. And it was right in my backyard! I knew immediately I would be spending a lot of time here in the future. I sidled on up to the bar, took a seat, and made myself comfortable. I was still looking around at the place, in complete awe, when the bartender's voice stirred me from my reverie.

"What can I get you," said the voice at my back.

I swung around on my stool and opened my mouth to place my order when I locked eyes with the bartender and realized I'd forgotten how to talk. The thing that stared back at me was not a man. Hell, it wasn't even man-like. It was a mountain of hair, with seven heads perched atop shoulders two door-frames wide. The heads were stacked like a row of skyscrapers, the tallest in the middle, with three heads tapering down either side to the left and right. Every head had only one eye, and when it spoke, each mouth uttered one of the words, seemingly at random.

"I
Said
What
Can
I
Get
You?"

What could I do? Would would *you* do? I just stared at the fucking thing. I'm pretty sure I didn't blink for a full minute. Maybe those seven heads are looking at someone else, I thought. Maybe he doesn't even see me! It's possible that I, a single-headed organism, don't even register in his field of vision. But I looked at each of those seven heads, and one by one I saw an eye staring right back at me. Seven eyes. All focused directly on me. All wanting to know what I wanted to drink.

That was about the time I thought I felt a lot *more* eyes on me. And that's when I took a real good look around, careful to focus on the rest of the clientele. I don't know how I hadn't spotted it before, but I guess I had only given a cursory glance to the customers. I was too wrapped up in savoring the experience. Plus I'm not big on eye contact, so I kept my head down when I entered places for the most part. But I looked at the room with fresh eyes, and I'm happy to report that I didn't see any more seven-headed creatures. Though it was of little comfort, because there was a gill-man playing pool with an amorphous blob of dark matter in the middle of the room. And in the back booth, I could see a pair of ten-point horns cresting the top of a high-backed chair. And from the shadows under that table I could make out the shape of cloven hooves. In the other booths I saw patches of scaly skin, something that was either a single creature with twelve legs, or four creatures with three legs. I still don't know the answer to that one.

But I think you get the idea. The whole place was crawling with monsters. And in some cases, monsters were literally crawling around the place. Much as I wanted to in that moment, I realized I couldn't leave my post and run screaming for the door. I was worried that would draw some unwanted attention. It made sense at the time, if the word is still applicable in any way, but I reasoned that if I just pretended that I didn't think anything was out of the ordinary, the rest of the patrons would feel the same, and then they wouldn't eat me or tear me limb from limb, or whatever monsters did for fun.

I resolved then to sit still and push my fear deep, deep down long enough to have a single drink. I would tip well. And then I would leave, and never tell another living soul just how insane I'd gone in the span of a single car ride home. So I turned back to the bartender, opened my mouth, and again found myself speechless. What the fuck do monsters drink? I couldn't very well order a hefeweizen. For some reason that felt tantamount to ordering caviar at a fried-chicken restaurant. Very quickly I accessed all the fantasy films I'd ever seen in the hopes of naming something that sounded monstrous. Hell, if I ran into a vampire, you bet your ass I'd try the garlic and silver bullets. These things stick to the collective consciousness for a reason, right?

Bearing that in mind, a few images popped into my rapidly deteriorating mind, and I finally looked the bartender in as many of his eyes as I could without maintaining uncomfortably long eye contact and said, "One mead, please."

As soon as the words left my mouth I felt like the world's biggest asshole. This wasn't the fucking renaissance fair. What was I thinking? But without skipping a beat, the bartender set a large metal stein in front of me, uncorked a sizable clear glass jug, and poured a thick amber liquid into the stein. It looked like pure maple syrup and I could smell it from where I sat. It was cloyingly sweet, and the aroma actually made my mouth water.

As soon as the smell hit me, I began to panic all over again. How the fuck was I going to pay for the thing? I didn't know if this place took credit card or gold bullion, and I didn't want to ask, because I'd left all my bullion at home.

Fortunately for me, my panic was quickly overtaken by an even more intense kind of panic, when two of this fine establishment's patrons sat down on either side of me and one of them—with an insanely deep voice—told the bartender that this one was on them. Sure, I was grateful that I didn't have to embarrass myself, or worse yet, admit that I might not be able to pay for my libation after all. But now I knew that I had been spotted, and worse yet, flanked. On the stool to my right, a centaur rested his elbows on the bar, placing his forelegs atop the stool. His hindquarters stayed planted on the ground.

To my left was a fully mobile robot that looked like a steel-plated human skeleton. I could hear the distinct sound of soft bubbles coming from the brain floating in green liquid encased in glass atop his head.

Resigned to the fact that the robot was probably going to tear my limbs from my body and feed them to his friend the centaur, as calmly as I could, I spoke.

"Thank you," I said, avoiding eye contact and taking a sip from my stein.

"The pleasure is all ours," said the robot in a male voice that had a comically effeminate Southern accent.

The mead hit my lips and it stung like fire. I coughed, though I'm still not sure if it was from the drink, the robot's statement, or the fact that, of these two nightmarish visions at my sides, I would have bet my life savings that the robot was the one with the deep voice.

"Easy," said the centaur.

All I could do was nod, putting the back of my hand to my mouth as my eyes watered. There it was. The voice the sounded like a bag of gravel being run through a clothes dryer. In my periphery, I could see that the centaur had a thick black beard that ran all the way down to his chest. Maybe *he* would be the one to rip me apart and then he would feed me to the robot to keep its brain juices fresh. The robot spoke again.

"I'd wager you're new here."

"Was it that obvious?" I asked. Feeing all the blood rush to my face.

"It is. But that's not a bad thing. I find it's the new ones that have the most fascinating stories."

"I find that hard to believe," I said, wondering where the words had come from and why I'd said them.

The centaur laughed, though I wasn't sure it was from anything I'd said. He seemed to be in his own world.

"And why's that?" asked Robot.

"Oh," I said, before I could stop myself, "this place seems pretty fascinating itself. I don't know that someone like me would bring anything to the table."

"That's rich!" Robot said, stretching the two words out. "The grass really is always greener, isn't it?"

"Sometimes it really is," I said, defensively, wondering who the fuck had just hijacked my mind and body. Why was I talking? I should have just nodded and sipped my stein of magma-flavored molasses. But something was brewing inside me. Even though every flake of my flesh quaked in terror at the position in which I'd found myself, I couldn't help but feel exhilarated at the same time. Whatever was happening, it was pretty fucking cool. Unless it was a total schizophrenic break. And the jury's still out on that one.

"If someone's grass is greener than mine, I just shit on it," Centaur said.

"Oh," I said. "I…uh—"

"Don't mind him," Robot said. "That's his answer for everything. He's always looking for an excuse to shit on something."

"That's not true," Centaur said.

"You shit on the troll in the riverbed on the way here!"

"He was a fucking asshole."

"Well I cannot engage in a battle of wits with someone who is unarmed, can I?"

"What?"

"Never mind. We're being rude and ignoring our visitor."

"Oh that's fine," I said. "Don't let me get in the way!" I was happy they'd forgotten about me for a moment. I'd even hoped it would last longer. Mostly because the conversation was so ludicrous. Nobody was going to believe any of this. I couldn't even believe it and it was happening to me.

"Nonsense!" Robot replied. "My friend here has lost the metaphor, but I remain curious: What's the grass we're discussing presently?"

"Grass? Oh. Right. I think I mean this place. That's number one, obviously."

"Why's that?" Robot inquired.

I took a second to respond. I knew if I answered, I would be crossing a border from which I'd never be able to return. I looked at the divide in my mind, paused for a moment, and then took the leap. "Well, because all my life I suspected there were greater things. And now here I am. I lived for decades knowing that there was something out there for me. Something that the rest of the world was content not to concern itself with. But something that I wanted. I'm sick of seeing other people live lives they don't deserve, while I wait for my turn. And I think this place is the first step. At least, I hope it is."

"That's deep," Centaur said.

I laughed to myself.

Robot spoke. "I have to agree. I find that very profound. What's the second thing?"

"Second thing?" I asked.

"Reasons why you know the grass is greener. You said this place is number one. What's number two?"

"Ah. Yeah. Good question. I guess it's just the obvious stuff. You know? Some people have bigger houses. Some people get to take more vacations. Some people don't have to eat shit and pretend they like it."

"They do if they piss me off," Centaur said.

"I gathered that," I said, a smile on my lips.

"See what I mean?" Robot said. "But I digress. Everything is relative, is it not? Someone might have a bigger house, but that just means they have a bigger house payment. And maybe they're miserable. And all that means is they'd just have more rooms to cry in at night."

"Well sure," I said. "We can play that game all night long. It's nice to hope that the great wheel of Karma balances everything out, and even the fortunate have their struggles. But it doesn't change the fact that I deserve more!"

"Now we're getting to the meat," Robot said.

"Meat?" Centaur asked, his eyebrows perking up.

"No, Mortimer. It's an expression."

This time it was my eyebrows that perked up. This hulking, shitting beast was named Mortimer? This got better and better. I was already in for a penny, I figured I'd throw the whole pound in there.

"Oh, by the way, my name's Al," I said. "Pleased to meet you both."

"I'm Mortimer," Centaur said.

"And my serial number isn't very easy for folks to memorize," Robot said, "so you can just call me Cy. As I was saying, I think we've touched upon something crucial here. You said you deserve more. By that regard, you're communicating that there is something you *don't* deserve."

"Shit," I said. "Now *that's* deep. I never thought about it that way. First thing that comes to mind is my job. Don't get me wrong. It pays the bills. But it's so goddamn boring. And my boss does fuck-all, while he piles more work onto everyone else. We work our asses off, and he just gets fatter and richer."

"I see," Robot said. "Al, how would you like to accompany Mortimer and me on an errand we must run this evening?"

And that was it. I was in. This was the invitation I'd been waiting for.

"Hell yes," I said, throwing back the rest of my mead. It hurt like a sonofabitch, but I was too excited to let that bother me.

We left the bar. I never did see what Cy and Mortimer paid with, but I like to imagine it was some form of lumpy, weathered precious metal. As we stepped back into the night air, it seemed I was looking at the world through new eyes. I felt I had sloughed off an old skin, and had stepped into a new form. One with a new purpose. It felt great.

"Where are you parked?" Cy asked.

"Just around the corner," I said. "Why?"

"Let's take your car," he said.

"Oh, Okay," I said, a little disappointed. I had pictured us traveling by flying car, or through the sewers on a boat made of whale bones or something. My car was decidedly less exotic. I led them to my little sedan, but when I got to my door, I realized that I was actually pretty well drunk.

"Um," I slurred.

"I will drive," Cy said, heading me off at the pass. He was very intuitive.

I pointed my finger at him and, half-lidded, said, "You're all right, Cy!" Then I walked to the passenger side and hit the button on my fob to unlock the doors.

Cy got in, sat down, and put on his seat belt before I'd even opened my door. As I climbed in, Mortimer opened the door to the backseat. I didn't realize how large he was by comparison, and wondered how he was going to fit. But he answered the question for me when he tore out the entire backseat in one gesture and threw it onto the black asphalt of the parking lot.

My mouth formed the *w* in "What the Fuck" but the words never left my lips because I remembered what he said about people who piss him off. I preferred to end my night not covered in centaur shit, so I shut my mouth and resigned to the fact that this was the price of greatness.

Mortimer climbed into the back of my now very spacious car and folded his four legs onto the exposed metal beneath him. I exhaled slowly, partially to stabilize myself from the effects of the firewater, and partially to mourn my car. But I climbed in, shut my door, and offered Cy my keys. That's when I saw him tear the paneling off my ignition, exposing the wiring beneath. He grabbed the wires and a jolt of electricity passed through his fingers, starting the car. Okay, so they weren't the kind of folks who were good with other people's things. That was fine. I didn't imagine they'd want to borrow any of my clothes, so it didn't matter. I resolved to let it go and stay focused on the bigger picture.

Cy put the car in drive, and we were on our way.

"Where are we going?" I asked, hoping the tone in my voice didn't sound like me making sure I didn't just sign up for my own murder.

"Business," said Mortimer, as if that answered my question.

"Mortimer speaks the truth, albeit succinctly. We have a date with an individual who owes us something."

As we drove to our destination, Mortimer and Cy instructed me on the proper etiquette for what was about to take place.

No crying.

No flinching.

And above all else, no talking.

It seemed they were going to bill me as their silent, and therefore toughest partner. I was terrified. I was positive this was a bad idea. As they explained everything to me, all I could do was stare and marvel at these bizarre creatures. Mortimer was a piece of work. He was obviously the brawn of the operation. The longer I looked at him, the dumber it seemed he became. Stealing glances at him in my rearview mirror, I noticed that he had a massive underbite that made his resting face look positively brain-dead.

Cy was a different story altogether. He was by his very nature, entirely inscrutable. What was he thinking? What was he feeling? *Was* he thinking or feeling? That great bubbling brain of his looked human, but it could have just as easily come from something like Mortimer, or one of the seven heads possessed by our bartender. Every second I was in this world gave birth to a dozen more questions. I couldn't recall a time where my imagination and curiosity were so alive.

While I was busy fixating on my traveling companions, the car came to a stop. I looked around and saw that we were in one of countless blocks of homes not far from where I lived. I'd probably driven through this street to avoid a traffic signal once or twice without thinking anything of it. It was as unassuming as could be, so I therefore found it a surprising destination.

"You sure you're at the right place?" I asked.

"One hundred percent," Cy said.

"Yuh," Mortimer agreed.

I couldn't argue with that. We all got out. Mortimer was as gentle exciting my car as he was getting in. Which is to say he muscled his way out of the backseat, tearing the cloth all along the backrest, and scratching the shit out of the floor beneath his feet. The car was already a lost cause, so I just continued to ignore it.

Cy led us up the driveway of the home we'd parked directly in front of. It was a plain Jane one-story house, which only gave birth to a dozen more questions. Was the person behind its door human? What kind of transaction was about to take place? And how had any business found its way to this house in the first place?

Cy knocked on the white wooden windowless door and after a few seconds a porch light came on and I could hear the sounds of locks being turned. The door opened a crack, and a single eyeball crept around the door and peered at us. That eyeball was attached to a long stalk that continued to reveal itself, until finally the head it was attached to could be seen.

"About fucking time," Eyeball said, in a nasally tone. "Was wondering if you guys would ever show up."

"When have we ever not shown up?" Cy said. "Now are you going to invite us in, or would you prefer to complete this transaction in the open?"

Eyeball swung his door open and that's when I got a good look at him. He looked like a four-foot-tall green beetle. He had two arms and two legs, each of which ended in serrated claws. His round head sat atop his body like a snowman's and at the top of his head, the long stalk that ended in a single eyeball danced around as he spoke through a mouth that opened sideways. I couldn't see anything beyond the threshold of Eyeball's. But Cy ushered me in first. No flinching, he'd said. So I pressed on.

The darkness was due only to a small room adjoining the entrance to the house. It was carpeted, and the ceiling was low and it felt more like an enclosed porch than anything else. When I walked through the second door—this one finally leading inside the actual home—I was horrified. The inside of the house was bland beyond belief. Other than that, there was nothing at all in this place to provide any evidence that a monster dwelled under its roof. The interior design was monstrous, I'll grant that. White carpet with black plastic furniture. No art on the bare white walls. It was the ultimate bachelor pad. And by that, I mean it desperately needed a feminine touch. Though I didn't say any of this to anyone. I continued to keep my mouth shut, as instructed.

"Who's the square?" Eyeball said, his stalk rotating clockwise as he stared at me.

I steeled myself.

"He is our new supplier," Cy said. " You're going to enjoy this batch. It is some of the purest product I've ever seen."

Eyeball's stalk froze where it was and began to water, almost as though his very eye was salivating. He only hesitated a moment before tearing away to the black table in the middle of the room. He pushed aside a stack of books and lifted a panel, revealing a safe hidden in the table. As he worked the combination, the unmistakable scent of baby oil hit me. I ignored it. There were a lot of implications in that smell, and none of them were things I wanted to think about, so I pulled myself up out of the undertow of my thoughts, and focused again on the present. Eyeball was speaking.

"Y'know, I don't normally do this. But it's been a hard month, and I wanted to treat myself. Do you guys wanna join me?"

"I'm entirely incapable," Cy said.

"No," Mortimer grunted, and cracked his knuckles.

Eyeball shot a glance in my direction. I looked to Cy and Mortimer. We had gone off script. I didn't know what to say. I judged the situation as best I could and said, "I don't get high on my own supply," hoping that not only was it appropriate for the circumstances, but also that it didn't sound completely idiotic.

Eyeball looked at me, blinked once, and said, "Fine. No skin off my sacks. More for me."

And so saying, he opened the door to the safe, plunged his claws inside, and pulled out the two largest stacks of cash I have ever seen in real life, if that's indeed what this was. These stacks were each as long as a loaf of bread, rubber-banded together. And from the looks of it, they were comprised solely of hundreds. I went rigid at the sight. I think I even forgot how to swallow for a moment. Eyeball handed the stacks to Cy, who flipped through them in a heartbeat, like the world's most efficient counting machine.

"It's all there," he said, then handed the stacks to Mortimer, who gripped them both in one hand. Mortimer slid his free hand into his own skin and pulled a swathe of flesh away from the area beneath his belly button, revealing a marsupial-like pouch. He dropped the money into the pouch, then fished around for a short time, finally bringing up a velvety satchel about the size of an apple.

Cy took the pouch and handed it to Eyeball, who was working himself up now, but trying to keep calm. The sight made me feel zen by comparison. This guy had probably done this a few times in his life, but this was my first rodeo, and I was doing a better job of maintaining my composure than he was. But I think that's just what it looks like when you're jonesing. And this guy had it bad. Suddenly his story about the hard month had the distinct air of bullshit.

Cy extended his glimmering arm, and Eyeball snatched the bag with obvious lust.

"You sure you guys don't want in on this action?"

"Positive," Cy said.

Mortimer said nothing this time. I followed his lead.

"Guess I'm the only one that likes to have fun," Eyeball said, with a desperate laugh.

In one movement, he closed the safe door, opened the bag, and emptied its contents onto the coffee table. What came spilling out was a pile of the clearest, brightest diamonds I'd ever seen.

"Oh fuck, these are good!" Eyeball exclaimed. "Look at the fucking clarity on these!"

Then he picked up a clawful of the diamonds and squeezed them. I can still hear the sound of the diamonds as they popped and snapped in his grip. It hurts just to think about. He pulverized them into dust. I was shocked. I wanted to slap the diamonds out of his claw. I didn't understand what was happening until he looked back toward us with a gleam in his eye and a smile on his thin lips as he dipped the tip of his other claw into the powder, brought the glimmering tip to his nose, and snorted it.

I have since read more about diamonds and their makeup and I couldn't tell you what possible side effect inhaling their dust might have on a body, but I don't know what Eyeball was made of. All I do know is that when that powder hit his nostrils, his single pupil exploded to black, fully dilating in an instant.

"You guys are so fucking lucky to know me," was the first thing he said after his bump.

That's when the baby oil smell came back. Cy and Mortimer were fantastic beasts, to be sure, but their choice in company left something to be desired. Though I did take into account the fact that this was their job. Hell, like I said at the start, everybody hates their job, right?

Maybe they were as put off by this ugly creature as I was, and they were counting the minutes until this gig was over.

As luck would have it, the those minutes were up.

"Indeed," Cy said. "Robert, it's always a pleasure doing business with you. Shall we book you for the same time next month?"

"What?" The one-eyed creature that was apparently named Robert said. "No. This ain't a regular thing with us. I told you. It was a hard month. I'll call you when I need you. If I need you. You can go now," he said, waving a claw at us, as he flitted around the house, pulling books from his shelves and collecting them in his claws. At the rate Bob was moving, he was going to read all of the books he'd pulled off the shelf in about fifteen minutes. And there were a lot of books. What he did after that was anybody's guess. Maybe he scratched his carapace to pictures of beetles fucking. I was just happy we were leaving.

"Of course," Cy said. "Enjoy. I imagine it will be a while before we see a batch this pure again. But you needn't worry about that. Hope to hear from you soon, old friend."

One-eyed Bob waved us out with the flick of a claw, muttering something to himself that sounded like the beginning of a conspiracy theory. I was the first one to the door, and I flung it open with a profound glee in my heart, hoping I would never cross paths with Beetle Bobby again.

As we crossed the threshold and walked down the driveway back to my car, Mortimer spoke. "What was that line you said?"

I slowed my step, allowing Cy and Mortimer to catch up. I saw that Mortimer had his hands in his pouch and he was, I think, counting the money. But it looked more like a guy playing with his dick and balls under a blanket. It had a disquieting effect. I had no knowledge of proper centaur etiquette, so I didn't share my thoughts. But I couldn't shake them either.

"Uh," I said, trying to remember the question. "Don't get high on your own supply?"

Mortimer laughed.

"It rhymes," he said.

It sure did.

"Lovely person, Robert," Cy said. His robotic tone was straight down the middle and I had no idea if he was being sarcastic, but I hoped to God he was.

"That was definitely interesting," I said. "How common is that? I've never seen anyone—"

"Everyone has device," Cy said. "Get it? Just a little joke to lighten the mood. I always need a palate cleanser whenever I visit Robert. And I guarantee you we will be right here, in this exact spot, one month from now."

A great relief came over me. I was happy to know I wasn't the only one that was skeeved out by Bob.

"We have a lot of clients," Cy said. "And we specialize in hard-to-find items. It draws out the weirdos. But if they don't pay, or they get out of line—"

"Let me guess," I said. "Mortimer shits on them?"

"After," Mortimer said, without a trace of humor.

"After what?" I said.

"Better not to ask," Cy broke in.

All the questions I had dried up like a reservoir in a drought. As we approached the car, I realized my body felt tired. I think I'd been riding an adrenaline high for the past few hours, and I was close to crashing. I assumed we were done with our time together, but Cy, walking back to the driver's side of the car, looked to me and said, "I have a wacky idea."

I though we'd already done wacky. My curiosity was piqued.

"Yeah?" I said.

"Would you want to do this with us full-time? It's always good to have an extra pair of eyes."

My heart surged. The universe had listened. I wasn't going to be like the chumps who missed their golden opportunities and lived mediocre lives. I seized my moment.

"Fuck. Yes." I said.

"Excellent," he replied. "Do you know where your boss lives?"

I narrowed my eyes, thinking. "Actually, yeah. He made me drop off some shit for him in the middle of the night once. Why?"

"Perfect," Cy said. "You navigate. I think we should tender your resignation   immediately."

I must have smiled the entire length of the trip. It was a thirty-five minute drive and my mind raced with the possibilities of what would happen next. As the night wind whipped through my hair, we blasted the stereo at full volume, and I felt more alive than I can ever remember. I felt like I'd just won the lottery. I'd happened upon this place, these people, these incredible circumstances, and now I was even about to be validated. This was too good to be true.

When we pulled into the right neighborhood, Cy turned the music down and shut off the headlights. As we drew closer to the house, Cy turned off the engine and let the car cruise to the curb a few houses down. I mean, I understood that we needed to keep a low profile, but I didn't think all of that superspy shit was entirely necessary.

"I like this neighborhood," Cy said. "What about you, Mortimer?"

Mortimer grunted without looking up and said, "I've got a good one brewing."

I could feel the smile on my face widen. My boss—King Dumb Luck—was about to get a heaping dose of centaur shit. Oh this was going to be sweet.

We all got out of the car. I could hear Mortimer scraping up the inside something fierce as he exited, but we were already past the point of no return there. And the destination we were about to reach made it all okay anyway. I felt like a high school senior on prom night, about to toilet paper the principal's house.

Cy reached the door first. I assumed he'd hit the doorbell, but instead, he jammed his mechanical finger into the lock of the door like he'd done with my ignition, then he flicked his wrist, and the door swung open silently.

Yes, technically we'd just crossed from whimsical pranking into light breaking-and-entering, but you only live once, right? And I'm pretty sure most folks don't get to pull all-nighters with a centaur and a cyborg. And if they did, half of those folks probably imagined it anyway. Maybe I'm even one of them! But I'm straying from the point. A warning light was going off somewhere in my head, but I was too excited to pay attention to it.

We entered the darkened house, and shut the door behind us. As we made our way through the house, looking for the master bedroom, I noticed that Cy and Mortimer were very light on their feet. Neither of them could have weighed less than three hundred pounds, but they practically glided through the house, toward the closed double doors of the master bedroom, like ballet dancers.

"Is your boss single?" Cy asked.

I nodded my head yes.

"Good," Mortimer growled. "The less collateral damage, the better."

I opened my mouth to ask what he meant, but we'd already reached the bedroom door and I didn't want to make any noise. Cy turned the knob and just as I snapped my mouth shut, his head lit up like a Christmas tree, and a siren went off that could have woke the dead.

Cy's head was so bright that I could instantly see the room in its entirety. And as I watched my boss fly out of bed in a frightened stupor, the first thing I thought was that we'd triggered his alarm system.But then I realized that the sound wasn't coming from the house. It was coming from Cy, who now began to speak. As he talked, it was as if he were shouting through a bullhorn.

"Wake up, asshole! Your number is up!"

My boss was backing himself into a corner, looking very much like a caged animal, when he finally seemed to focus his eyes on us and his shocked terror was replaced by a distinct confusion.

"Al?" he said.

"Hey, Keith," I replied, nonchalant. I would never have the upper hand like this again, and I wasn't about to waste it. I wondered if he would tell anyone what happened on Monday.

"What the fuck, Al? Is this supposed to be funny? I—"

Keith's words seemed to catch in his throat there, because that's when Mortimer walked in. I didn't realize he wasn't in the room yet, but I'm sure the sight of a nearly seven-foot-tall, four-legged man-beast was something that Keith would need some time to process. I knew that because I was still processing it, and I'd spent my entire night with him.

"Keith," I said, pointing to my right, "meet Mortimer." Then, gesturing to my left. "And Cy. They're my new friends."

"Hello, Keith. I've heard so much about you," Cy said, as he took a step forward.

Keith loosed a shriek I didn't know a grown man was capable of. I don't think he realized the blinking pile of steel at my side was alive until that moment. It was hysterical. I swear he was going to piss himself.

"What is that?" he shouted.

"You're not listening," I said. "That's Cy. And be careful. You're liable to hurt his feelings."

"I regret to inform you that the damage has already been done," Cy said. "And Mortimer here has something he would like to say about that."

Mortimer grunted, then lumbered forward. "I've been baking this one all night," he said.

"Al, what's happening?" Keith said. "Is this some cosplay bullshit? Are you high or something?"

"Keith," I said, "consider this my resignation. I'm onto bigger and better."

Mortimer continued his advance, and Keith continued his retreat. But very quickly he'd backed himself into the corner of his room. I couldn't wait to watch that giant centaur drop a steaming pile onto Keith's carpet. Which, in hindsight, I recognize is not a healthy thought.

"What the fuck?" he screamed again. "Al! Al! Al!"

"It's okay, Keith. Relax," I assured him. "It's not that bad. We'll be gone before you—"

But before I could finish my sentence, Mortimer grabbed Keith's head, and caved it in like an overripe pumpkin. Keith didn't even have a chance to protest. The last thing he said was my name, and then a giant monster crushed his skull and his lifeless body dropped to the ground like a bag of old bedsheets. I couldn't speak. I couldn't think. All I could do was replay the image of Keith's terrified face as Mortimer's claw reached out for him. His eyes. The blood. The way his body hit the ground. It was all so terrible. I couldn't believe it.

It was a different kind of disbelief than when I'd walked into the bar at the start of the night. A different kind of disbelieve than seeing all these marvelous creatures. This was the kind of disbelief you feel when you're grieving. When something or someone is lost and will never return to you. I mourned for Keith. He was a dipshit, but he wasn't a bad guy. He didn't deserve this. I thought I was just going to flirt with disaster and, well, I don't know what else. I didn't think that far ahead. I was so certain of my call to greatness that I had blinded myself to the fact that I was in the company of genuine monsters.

I wanted out. I wanted to turn back the clock. I wanted my old, bland predictable life back. What the fuck was I doing here?

As Keith's body lay twitching and bleeding out on the floor, Mortimer swung his hind legs around, lifted his tail, and made good on his promise. He shit all over Keith's body. There was so much of it. And the smell—oh God, the smell. Centaur shit, and probably some of Keith's, and the blood. It was overpowering. I was going to puke.

I ran from the room, sealing my mouth shut with my hands, but the vomit came out anyway. My stomach lurched, and it shot up and sprayed out from between my fingers. As I knelt down at the wet patch on Keith's carpeted hallway floor, smelling my own sick combined with the shit and the blood, I realized something: I was right in the middle of a crime scene. And I was leaving DNA everywhere. Fingerprints. Footprints. My own puke. How had I found myself in so fucking deep, so fucking fast?

This wasn't fun. This wasn't funny. This wasn't fantasy. This was fucking real life and it was too much for me to bear.

Cy and Mortimer were walking out of the room then, laughing to each other. I must have missed the joke. Or maybe I was the joke.

"What seems to be the problem?" Cy said, sounding earnest enough.

Mortimer said nothing. I looked up and saw that he was in his own world, making small, hideous grunts of pleasure as he licked the blood from his fingers. I thought I was going to vomit all over again.

"Shall we?" Cy said. "We have another appointment."

I knelt there, half hunched over, staring at the two of them. My whole body was shaking. I couldn't go with them. And I knew that when I told them as much, that would be it for me. But it was either face the music at that moment, or shortly after whenever I finally snapped. I chose to rip the bandage off.

"I...I can't," I finally said. "I thought this was something else."

"I see," Cy said, noticeably upset. "And what, exactly, did you think this was?"

"I don't know. Not this." It was all I could muster.

The two of them stood there, staring down at me. In the moonlight, half-lit, taking up the entire hallway, I fully understood for the first time in my life what the word *monstrous* meant. These two were fucking terrifying. And I was in their sights. I suddenly felt like a child, seeing how close he could bring his finger to a campfire without getting burned. I was a fool. And pretty soon I'd be a dead fool.

"That's a shame," Cy said. "I was so looking forward to working together, Al. I feel you should know that we operate somewhat behind the law. If we part ways now, we can't guarantee that there won't be repercussions."

I sat there, on my knees, my mouth open. I could feel the chunks of puke stuck in my sinuses. I didn't understand why he wasn't moving in for the kill. Why neither of them were. But I didn't want to say anything that might change their minds, so I said nothing, only nodding stupidly.

"So be it," he continued. "I do hope our paths cross again some day. I like you, Al. Come on, Mortimer…"

Mortimer growled in accord and they started walking.

"Oh," Cy said as he passed me. "We'll be keeping the car."

I nodded again, mouth still open in astonishment. I was going to live. I don't know how, or why, but God damnit I was going to live!

When Mortimer passed me, he lifted his tail and ripped a fart so loud it blew my hair back and made my eyes water. The stench was ungodly.

Cy and Mortimer disappeared around the corner, and I stayed in that position until I heard my car start and drive off a few minutes later. Then I collected myself, wiped my prints from every surface I could remember touching, and crept out of the house. I walked home, sticking to the shadows all the way home. It took me hours to get there, but I was propelled by my confusion, and my fear. I didn't feel safe. I didn't know how anything would ever be right again. Mostly I stared into space, feeling like a man drowning. I also replayed the events of the night in my head over and over again. And when I wasn't doing either of those things, I was planning the rest of my life.

When I entered my home, the reality of it all finally sank in. Everything in my house was exactly as I'd left it, except for me. I didn't feel like I belonged there anymore.

I dropped to my knees and wept. It was as though I was trying to cry the ugly, unavoidable truth away. When I had completely emptied myself, I showered, climbed into bed, and watched the sun rise. My alarm went off. I showered again. And then I called the police and reported my car stolen. Then I waited for the cops to come.

Everything else played out like a dream. The cops came. I told them I woke up and the car was gone. They took my info and let me know that my car would likely never be recovered. They didn't know the half of it.

Then a second set of cops showed up. And they had questions. These were the cops I'd been waiting for. They told me some very unsettling news about my boss, Keith, and asked if I knew anything about it. I apologized for my behavior. I was recently the victim of a crime. But, my oh my, Officer, this sure puts things into perspective. What kind of person could do such a thing? Life is so fragile, etc.

They thanked me for my time, and I have yet to hear from them, or Cy and Mortimer.

And here I am, sitting in my house on a Saturday night, sharing this story in between level-ups on the new RPG I just bought. I used to love first-person shooters. Those are the video games that play out from your POV while you navigate your way through an escalating body count. But they make me throw up now. I like the ones where you wander through a fantasy world collecting points and making virtual friends. It's the perfect metaphor for my life now. Actually, I'm not sure if that's even a metaphor.

I'm still waiting for the cops to come back. Or for Cy and Mortimer to come bursting through my door, Cy speaking in that disaffected, gentle Southern accent as Mortimer, with a gut full of steaming shit, unloads onto my still-twitching corpse. I used to look everywhere and yearn for what others had. I was positive that everyone around me had it better, and that I deserved more. Now I know that I don't deserve shit. I'm lucky for every day. For every moment. I have everything I need. Hell, after Keith's body was discovered, upper management just shifted the staff one position upward. So I even got a promotion out of the whole hideous mess. I'm making more money, and the hours are better. And all I can do is wish it hadn't come at such a steep price.

I've never been back to The Constellation, either. Truth be told, I haven't even driven past it since that night. I take different paths to and from work. I shop at different stores. I do everything I can to avoid thinking about any of it. But it doesn't help. Whenever I'm at the office, or driving home, or sitting down on my couch firing up my console, I'm watching. I'm listening. I'm waiting for that knock on the door. Or that phone call.

Like I said, I appreciate everything I have. And all I want in the world is to be able to hang on to my tiny slice of gloriously simple living. I guess I'm just one of those people whose lessons need to come at a price. Though I do like to think that my suffering is enough to keep the scales balanced. There really isn't a day I wake up that I don't hear Keith's screams echoing in my head. And there isn't a paycheck I cash that doesn't remind me of the blood on my hands. Fuck extravagance. Fuck destiny. Let me live out the rest of my days having learned my lesson. And let my silent agony be enough.

Oh, and if I am indeed in a psych ward somewhere, this is most definitely a cry for help. I think my Thorazine dosage is too low. I can still smell the shit, Nurse. I can still hear the screams, Doctor.

I used to think I knew better than most people. I used to think I was too good for the world. Now? Now I just play my video games. I don't like to rock the boat. I've seen behind the curtain, and I all I want to do is live my quiet, simple life. Did I mention I even relish taking out my trash now? It reminds me of my place in the world. It's just so perfectly normal.

MONSTERS OF ANY KIND

BRUCE BOSTON

MAMMY AND THE FLIES
by BRUCE BOSTON

"You a smart boy, all right, too damn smart for your own good. Now get down in that cellar!"

Mammy Jordon came across the kitchen and he moved back toward the cellar door. He knew she wasn't really mad, cause when she was mad she sent him down to the cellar dark, and here she was holding out the flashlight. And she wasn't looking at him like she was mad, but somewhere over his head, her bulk crowding him back, her perfume and party dress, even bigger now in her heels and towering over him.

How he hated her bigness, just as he loved it when she held him against her soft in the bedroom upstairs.

He went down the wood steps to the dirt floor with the ceiling so low no man could stand, for he was no man yet and he couldn't stand all the way, and he could hear the door closing and Mammy Jordon sliding the bolt into place. He could hear her moving about the house. And later her heels on the front porch and the old car coughing, and he knew she had gone into town to bring back one of her gentlemen.

He didn't turn on the flashlight.

It was still light outside and the light came through the chinks in the cinder blocks along three walls of the cellar and the flies hadn't come yet. If he looked through the chinks on one side, he could see plowed fields and burnt-off hillsides and at night the lights of cars as they passed on the highway. On the other side, only fields and hills. But if he knelt down and looked through the chinks at the rear of the cellar, he could see their yard and the garden Mammy had planted and through the trees and beyond to Mr. Skinner's house in the distance. Mr. Skinner was their landlord. His house was white, whiter than theirs, which was once white and Mammy called it dirt white.

He didn't know how she had found this Skinner place. When they left the other place, they drove for days, sleeping in the car, Mammy making him stay on the floor in back so no one would see. Then they had come to this place and she started locking him in the cellar. He had been with Mammy since before the other place, but down in the cellar with nothing to do but sit and think and listen, he had begun to remember his real mother.

The cellar had been cold at first with the wind racing through the chinks. He'd found an old mattress and tried to lie on it with the blankets Mammy Jordon had given him, but the mattress was wet and smelled bad. When he pushed up one corner, he could see worms and dark crawlies underneath. So he found a dry place on the dirt floor and curled up there with the covers and thought about his mother.

Mammy Jordon was his mother's mother, but she wouldn't let him call her that. She said she was too young to be anyone's grandma, leastwise someone grown up as he was getting to be. His real mother was smaller than Mammy Jordon and she didn't smell like Mammy, always sweet or flowery, still she smelled good, only he couldn't remember just how cause the cellar smelled and the mattress even when he wasn't near it. He'd get this all mixed up with his mother's smell and Mammy Jordon's. And sometimes he'd remember her and she was brown like Mammy Jordon or yellow like he was, and sometimes she was a white lady and once she was soft all over like a kitten. The more different ways he thought about her the less he remembered so she became less and less until finally there was nothing left to her at all. And then he couldn't think about her anymore or pretend he wasn't in the cellar.

So he began to sing to himself in the dark, tuneless nonsense songs that never repeated yet always sounded the same. He kept his voice low so Mammy wouldn't hear. She said he was strange enough already without doing no singing, and she only let him listen to music on Sundays when she read from the book. He loved the music and he could feel it trying to move inside him, but he had to sit still while the record turned on the player. Sometimes when he sang to himself in the cellar, he didn't sit still. He rocked with the nonsense words. Hunched there in the dark, he beat the heels of his palms against his thighs until they were sore.

And that was when the seeing started.

He didn't tell Mammy about the singing or the seeing. He knew she wouldn't like any of it.

———

Mr. Skinner's dog was chained in its yard barking to be fed and the sun was going down. He couldn't see the dog cause of the fence and the trees. He couldn't see the sun cause that side of the cellar was boarded over, but he could see what it was doing to the land, turning the trees and fence posts golden, the white of Mr. Skinner's house pink and grey, the tomatoes by the back porch as if they were about to catch on fire. It was hotter under the house now, the hottest time of each day at dusk. As the land cooled it gave up its warmth to the cellar, which would hold it long into the night. He could feel the warm air flowing in through the chinks in the cinder blocks. And soon the flies would follow.

Each time Mammy sent him to the cellar it was warmer and there were more flies. He could listen to their buzzing in the dark, he could feel them landing and crawling on his skin, sucking his sweat, their hairy legs itching him. He could turn on the flashlight and see them moving in its beam: black and gold-green in the yellow circle of light.

He knew that if Mammy Jordon came back and she didn't have a gentleman with her, he wouldn't have to stay with the flies. If she came back alone, she'd unlock the cellar door. She'd come partway down the steps and she'd call "Baby, baby, come up," and when he did she'd take him upstairs and hold him against her in bed and tell him stories— about the animals back home or about his daddy, Pappy Jordon, who was mojo and creole and something special, and since he was part Pappy Jordon, that was why his skin was yellow and that made him special, too.

But if Mammy brought any gentlemen with her, he might have to stay in the cellar all night. In the morning there would be red bites on his arms, his face and neck. In the morning Mammy would unlock the cellar door and come partway down the steps and she'd call, "Baby, baby, come up." Then she'd have him sit at the kitchen table and she'd cook breakfast for him, special to make up for the cellar, muffins and bacon ends and the gooey eggs that ran yellow over the plate. Mammy would hum to herself while she cooked, just like he did when he was in the cellar. And sometimes he could look at her eyes while she hummed and cooked and see the thoughts slowly turning in her head. And he could tell that she didn't know she was doing the humming.

After breakfast she'd let him play in the yard behind the house. He could play there almost every day now that Mr. Skinner knew about him. At first Mammy only let him play a little at a time and he had to promise to stay close by and run back inside if anyone came. Then one day he had been squatting in the dirt watching the ants. Taking little steps on his heels, he had followed one too far from the house. He watched it crawling over pebbles and twigs across the baked earth away from the other ants and farther and he decided it must be running away from home. When he killed it with his thumb, its body crushed down like it was empty and there was nothing inside. And then he looked up and saw Mr. Skinner.

Mr. Skinner was a white man and he was big, not big like Mammy Jordon, but tall. He had dark hair on his arms like the flies when they crawled on the light, but the hair on his head was white, dirt-white like their house, not like his. Mr. Skinner was climbing the steps to their back porch. There was no way he could run inside without being seen so he ran into the bushes and hid there.

After awhile Mammy came to the screen door and she and Mr. Skinner started to talk, so he crawled closer so he could hear. Mr. Skinner was pointing to the yard and saying, "Strange-looking boy you got there, strange-looking," and he knew Mammy would be mad at him for letting Mr. Skinner see him, but Mammy just said, "He ain't my boy. He's my sister's boy," and he didn't know why Mammy was lying cause she told him it was bad to lie. Mr. Skinner kept saying "strange-looking, strange-looking," like those were the only words he knew, with his hand on the screen, and Mammy shrugged and said he was "just a boy," and Mr. Skinner said he'd never seen no boy with eyes like that. And then Mammy opened the door. Mr. Skinner looked around the yard once and went inside.

After that, Mr. Skinner became one of Mammy's gentlemen. And he could play in the yard as much as he wanted cause Mr. Skinner never came near him anyway.

It was almost dark, but he could see the shapes of the trees and the way the breeze was moving them. There was no breeze in the cellar. It was just as hot and the flies had started to come. He could hear the buzzing of one and then two and then three, so he went over to the crumpled blankets, which he never used anymore cause it was too hot, and he reached under the blankets and took out the flyswatter he had stolen from the hook in the kitchen. It was the same swatter Mammy sometimes hit him with when she was mad.

He went back to were he had been sitting and he watched the trees go away in the dark. Mr. Skinner's dog had stopped barking and that was good cause when the barking went on and on he could sometimes feel the dog's hunger gnawing in his belly and that was bad. He held the swatter between his legs and pressed the metal loop of its handle against his cheeks and forehead cause it felt cooler than the air in the cellar. He listened to the flies coming one by one until their buzzing was together and he couldn't tell how many there were. They began to land on his arms and face in the dark and he brushed them away.

He didn't turn on the flashlight.

He wasn't going to kill the flies yet. He was waiting until Mammy Jordan came back. If she had a gentleman with her, he would kill the flies so he wouldn't have to listen to them upstairs. He didn't want to hear their heels on the porch together. He didn't want to hear the talking and the drunken laughter. Most of all he didn't want to do the seeing when Mammy took the gentleman to bed. If he waited to kill the flies, that would be good.

Every Sunday, Mammy taught him about the good and the bad. Sometimes he understood and sometimes he'd get mixed up. He knew the music was good, but singing and dancing were bad. The book was good cause it told about the good and the bad. The gentlemen were bad and he hated them, but knew Mammy had to see them anyway. The cellar was bad and he hated it and knew that. The flies were bad and he hated them. But with Mammy Jordon, sometimes she was good and he loved her and sometimes she was bad and he hated her. Some nights she'd do the drinking alone, and then she was very bad.

Mammy said the drinking was bad, but she did it anyway, just like going with the gentlemen. Sometimes it was different with the gentlemen, but with the drinking it was always the same. She'd sit at the kitchen table and the more she drank the quieter she got. After awhile she'd start to cry. Then the crying would become cursing, low at first and under her breath. Pretty soon the cursing got louder and next she'd be yelling at the top of her voice, at no one but like there was someone there, saying how she should have never got mixed up with no mojo swamp man, singing and changing all the time like he did, chasing after his own daughter and the two of them flying off in the sky and leaving her with the sin of it all. And then she'd see him watching her and she'd curse at him and start hitting him for no good reason. He'd crouch in the corner or under the table and Mammy would hit and kick at him until she got tired. Then she'd go back to the cursing and the crying. Until finally she'd get quiet again and want to hold him to make his hurts go away. But he didn't like her softness then cause it smelled like the drink.

Sometimes he thought all good things had something bad in them, like the tomatoes going bad when they got old, and he wondered if all old things went bad. Mr. Skinner was old and he didn't seem that bad. But Mammy said that since he was a white man, that made him bad enough.

By the time he heard Mammy's car and the car that followed it, the gentleman's car, the flies had clustered upon him, the closed space of the cellar filled with their buzzing. He did not wait for the sound of heels on the porch. He clicked on the flashlight and stood, his knees bent and his neck forward so he wouldn't bump his head on the ceiling. With this movement the flies rose from his body, and some settled back. His shirt was soaked through with sweat so he stripped it off and the flies rose from him again.

In the heat and dark he moved toward the mattress and leveled the flashlight across its expanse. In the dim cone of light he could see its stained ticking and the rips where springs and stuffing were exposed. Its entire surface was alive with the crawling black dots of the flies.

He began to kill them.

He raised the swatter and brought it down—slap!—on the mattress. With the force of the blow the flies rose as a cloud, their buzzing angry, and he brought the light closer and he could see one dead fly and one crushed but still moving, its buzzing broken. He could see they were not hollow like the ants, but filled with goo like the eggs on his plate. And then he went back to the killing.

He put the flashlight at one end of the mattress so that its beam spread in a "V" across the surface and he waited until the flies settled back onto the ticking and started their crawling, and then he aimed and struck—slap!—and the flies that did not die rose up and he waited for them to settle again. He crouched at the other end of the mattress, rocking his body, moving his shoulders so the flies wouldn't settle on him. But each time he waited, he could hear the noises from upstairs. He knew Mammy's voice too well to pretend it wasn't hers. And the gentleman's voice, he knew that for a white man's voice. So he picked up the flashlight and began shining it around the cellar.

The flies were everywhere, on the walls, the posts, some even crawling in the dirt. He moved about killing them—slap!—and he pretended this one was Mammy's gentleman and this was another gentleman—slap!—and this was Mr. Skinner's dog and this was Mr. Skinner—slap!—and this was Mammy when he hated her—slap!—and this was Mammy when he loved her so he let it go.

His breath heavy, his body bare to the waist, the flies striking him as he moved through them, their buzzing louder and angrier the more he killed, and still they came in through the chinks so he killed them there. As he waved the flashlight about in his hand it began to fade. In the thickening darkness he could sense the life and death and dying all about him. He no longer needed the light so he hurled it against the cinder blocks and it shattered. Moving to and fro, twisting and turning, he killed and killed—slap!—and still they came. He could hear the buzzing all about him as a music fierce and filling. He could feel his feet pounding the packed dirt floor. He could hear his voice rising from within his chest. He was singing. He was dancing. He was changing.

By the time Mammy Jordon unlocked the cellar door and came partway down the steps and called "Baby, baby, come up," all of the flies were dead but one. A huge and hairy flapping rose from the darkness of the stairs. And it was hungry.

MONSTERS OF ANY KIND

GREGORY L. NORRIS

OLD SLY

by GREGORY L. NORRIS

The letter arrived in an austere envelope that listed many names on the return address. Jackson's heart galloped as he struggled to open the thing using his thumbnail. It wasn't a demand for payment by the power company, who'd already turned off the juice twice since he moved into Number 11 Park Street, Apartment 4, at the back of the dilapidated New Englander. No zombie debt come back to haunt him after catching up to his present whereabouts—of course not; Jackson hadn't left forwarding addresses going back two apartments to his first, the one he'd moved into after escaping the old man's basement. No, this officious bit of mail that had somehow found him, likely through one of those public records search websites, concerned the estate of the late Louis Bourchard, Jackson's uncle.

Pursuant, I'd like to discuss these details with you over the phone at your earliest convenience, he read. There was a phone number. The letter was signed in black ink by B.A. Holtzman, Esquire—one of the names on the envelope's return address.

Jackson read the letter again and once more after that. The late Louis Bourchard. So Uncle Lou had died? What he remembered most about his father's older brother was that Uncle Lou had a glass eye. Lost it while attempting to unknot the laces of his church shoes with a fork, so went the story.

"He pushed too hard," his dead father's voice spoke in a silence broken only by the traffic on Park Street and the summer wind gossiping around the old building's time-eroded eaves. "The knot came free and bam, that fork went right up into his eye. Stuck there. If you'd 'a seen it..."

But oh, Jackson had so often in his dreams. The warm and oily summer breeze stirred the sheets-for-curtains as Jackson mined his memory: Uncle Lou had played guitar in a band, kept a cocktail napkin or matchbook as a souvenir from every dive or wedding gig; Uncle Lou's glass eye was blue; Uncle Lou had a parrot, a big and ugly bird called Sly that he'd inherited from a relative somewhere down the Bourchard ladder. The thing had been old then, decades so according to Jackson's late, not-so-great father. He remembered that some species of parrots lived close to a hundred years.

A sudden cold embraced him. Uncle Lou was dead, spelled out by the letter in his hands. What could a relative from a past he'd worked to forget have left him of any value? Like Jackson's old man, probably nothing other than debt and duty to bury the corpse.

He tossed the letter into the open garbage can, atop the empty Chinese takeout cartons and the rest of the day's junk mail.

His cell rang. Jackson checked the screen. *B.A. Holtzman*, the caller I.D. read.

Jackson came out of the fugue of his late afternoon nap. The bedclothes were damp with sweat. The phone felt greasy against his ear.

"Jackson Bourchard?" his caller asked.

"Speaking."

He closed his eyes and settled back on the pillow's unpleasant contour.

"This is attorney B.A. Holtzman. I represent the estate of your late uncle, Louis."

"Uncle Lou," Jackson sighed.

"I've been trying to reach you."

Jackson didn't answer.

"Hello?"

"What's this about?"

"Your uncle Louis named you as his sole beneficiary, Mr. Bourchard. It's a sizable estate. Everything that was his is due to become yours."

Two days later, he was three towns over, dressed in his best khakis and a button-down over a white undershirt that seemed determined to choke him, even with the top two buttons undone. The place was one of those open-concept shells from an earlier era, what had once been a split-level house now converted into law offices. The receptionist offered him coffee or water. Jackson chose the latter and was escorted to an air-conditioned conference room with a round table and wooden chairs that looked miserable on the ass.

B.A. Holtzman was a plump man with a Santa Claus face and beard. "Mister Bourchard," he said and extended his pudgy hand. His shake was sweaty. Under his other arm was tucked a thick stack of documents with a frill of neon sticky notes marking places that required signatures. "Have a seat."

Jackson sat. The chair didn't disappoint his earlier assessment.

"Look, I barely knew my uncle," he said, still not convinced the lawyer's claims were to be trusted.

"He was quite specific regarding who was to inherit his estate."

"*Estate*," Jackson huffed. "He played in a weekend cover band."

"Oh, there was more than that. A house on Nyberg Lane. Four automobiles. A bank account and sizable investments."

Jackson sat back, eyes narrowed. The Uncle Lou he remembered lived in an apartment shabbier than 11 Park Street.

"Sign here," Holtzman indicated. "And here."

Pages appeared and were then shuffled away—transference deed, vehicle ownership, and other assets. Holtzman had closed out his uncle's bank account and would present him with a cashier's check, along with the keys to the house on Nyberg Lane.

Jackson risked a smile. Lightning filled his belly. His inner voice rejoiced at living out the classic urban legend, the one about inheriting a fortune from a deceased relative he barely knew.

Then Holtzman said, "There's one more condition."

Jackson finished signing his name for what felt the hundredth or more time. "Oh?"

"The most important of your uncle's wishes was that you would assume responsibility for the care of Sly, his prized companion of so many years."

The comfortable temperature in the room plummeted, and the

discomfort beneath his ass doubled. "That old parrot is still alive?"

Holtzman flipped ahead to the next sheet, a protection agreement spelling out care of pets.

"Sign here."

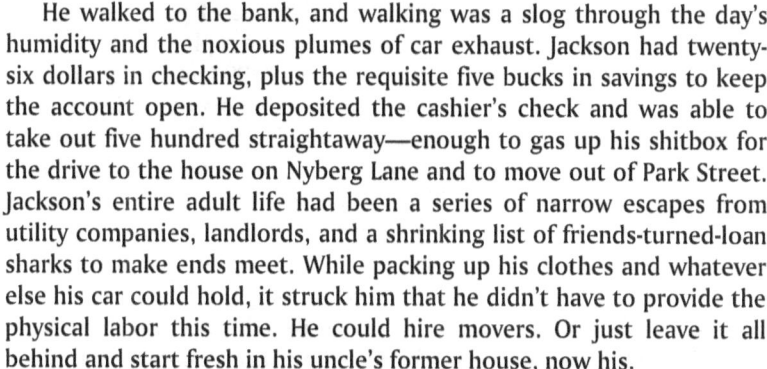

He walked to the bank, and walking was a slog through the day's humidity and the noxious plumes of car exhaust. Jackson had twenty-six dollars in checking, plus the requisite five bucks in savings to keep the account open. He deposited the cashier's check and was able to take out five hundred straightaway—enough to gas up his shitbox for the drive to the house on Nyberg Lane and to move out of Park Street. Jackson's entire adult life had been a series of narrow escapes from utility companies, landlords, and a shrinking list of friends-turned-loan sharks to make ends meet. While packing up his clothes and whatever else his car could hold, it struck him that he didn't have to provide the physical labor this time. He could hire movers. Or just leave it all behind and start fresh in his uncle's former house, now his.

He mapped the directions on his phone and drove away from Park Street, feeling hopeful. The summer sun blazed. Jackson drove wearing his favorite sunglasses. They were dollar-store finds that looked expensive. He was rich and would soon be motoring through life in better, fancier rides. He could now afford brand sunglasses if he wanted, whole closets full. He owned property. He—

He was responsible for Old Sly. The first frisson of worry since Holtzman's office crept over his skin as the phone's robot voice instructed him to turn right.

Sly. That one time at Uncle Lou's old place, that apartment even dumpier than Park Street. The place smelled of cigarettes and stale sweat. The sofa bore a loud pea-green print. A strange sound came from the room at the end of a dark hallway with no windows and little light. It sounded like laughter. No, something more secretive and far less joyous. Like chuckles, ones given in mean-spiritedness.

"What's that?" his earlier self had asked.

"Sly. He's very old. Want to meet him?"

No, that version of Jackson said. And his current incarnation felt the same. The memory window inched wider. Jackson tipped a look up at the bloated red orb of the sun, forcing it shut again in a searing effulgence of painful light—spindles that demanded he focus on the street ahead.

He was rich and that was all that mattered. His struggles were over. Old Sly was ancient—how much longer could the miserable thing remain alive? Jackson only hoped Nyberg Lane was served by a decent Chinese takeout place that delivered.

Another turn. This led down a stretch of neighborhood road where the houses were separated by thickening stands of green space, the estates battleship-sized and set far back from the asphalt.

"Number 87 Nyberg Lane," his phone said. "500 feet on your right."

Jackson slowed his approach. Among the tangles of leaves and branches, he made out two sides of a stone gate. Running between them a single-lane driveway disappeared into wilderness. His pulse raced for reasons he couldn't identify. Jackson hesitated. The sun crept lower toward the horizon. By the time he turned onto the drive, his heart was attempting to jump out of his chest and into his throat.

He advanced along the drive, traveling barely above idle. Jackson was back in the dark hallway in that other decade, creeping toward the room behind whose door Old Sly chuckled. The door was ajar. Poor light oozed through the part, and he caught motion through the gap, a kind of shadow puppetry projected onto a patch of wall. Uncle Lou wanted him to meet his pet, the ancient parrot from a faraway land.

An image formed around him. Jackson blinked. He returned to the present and found himself staring at the house, an antique manor with an indestructible brick façade twice the size of the New Englander on Park Street with a perfectly manicured acre of lawn and numerous outbuildings, all of it surrounded by a green wall of tall trees. For a terrible moment in which he couldn't breathe, Jackson was convinced he should turn around immediately, because the moment he entered that vast brick house, it would swallow him whole, and he'd never leave again.

<hr />

It was his house. The rich—even the *nouveau riche*—didn't live in filthy apartments whose walls were painted in builder beige between occupants but never lost the patina of previous tenants' sweat. Men with money lived in grand houses, houses with parlors and wings and an endless succession of rooms. Houses with atriums, he thought while swinging the car around the drive and toward the back of the brick manor.

The structure extended out from the rear of the house, its Gothic design realized in black wrought iron and panes of glass. Through those windows, Jackson glimpsed palms, sizable ones, and other exotic foliage, as well as a network of beams. The room was more than an atrium. It was, perhaps, the most elaborate birdcage outside of the finest zoos to be found anywhere on the planet.

That's where Old Sly lives, said Jackson's inner voice.

He got out of the car. Humidity slammed into him, along with the thick green smell of the surrounding woods—pine sap and leaves baking in the heat. He wandered over to the atrium and peered in, expecting to take his first look at the parrot. The glass under his palm was hot from the sun. His eyes searched the counterfeit jungle planted inside the manor. Movement stirred behind a palm frond, something colorful and patterned. Jackson tipped his gaze toward it.

Another face reflected in the glass, directly beside his. Jackson shrieked and spun around. The man in the black button-down shirt and slacks had moved up to him in silence, like a predator.

"Mister Bourchard?" the wraith said in a crisp voice.

"Yeah?"

"I'm Willet, the interim caretaker."

Willet led him into the house and helped with his bags. The place was a castle, with cavernous rooms and vaulted ceilings, most of the walls done in vulgar mustard yellow. The wrought-iron details seen in the atrium continued through the inside of the manor in large square decorative grates that covered what Jackson assumed were air-conditioning or heating vents. A dry, bitter smell infused the air, what his imagination translated into one of distant deserts.

"Cozy," Jackson remarked.

Willet exhaled a laugh through his nostrils, the sound reminiscent of that chuckling he recalled from an apartment his mind kept returning to and roaming. The dry warmth in the air cooled around Jackson.

"This way," Willet ordered more than said. "I've put you in the Big Room."

They walked over travertine floors, up a staircase with a braided black wrought-iron banister, around a gallery. There was no artwork on the walls other than more of those metal details, these in medallion shapes. No family photographs, which Jackson understood—he'd gotten rid of all of his connections to the Bourchards two apartments earlier. But for the uncle who'd loved music with such passion, not a single concert poster or nod to that love was visible anywhere.

"He had a sick music room, right?" Jackson asked.

"Come again?"

"Uncle Lou—some big room where he could let loose and break windows with the volume cranked up to max."

Willet stopped, half turned, and studied him through one eye. "Your uncle Louis lived a quiet life here."

The chill in the air deepened. Willet's lone eye continued to study him for a second or so that felt more like a minute before he again resumed the long walk down the hallway.

The room was massive, easily the size of the whole apartment on Park Street. It contained a king four-post bed with carved finials, a wall of windows that looked over the backyard, and large furniture, all of it separated by plenty of floor space. The door to a bathroom just as impressive stood open. Jackson chanced a look through at a shower running half its length tiled in jade marble with room to accommodate three, the number of water heads. It was impressive, but it left Jackson feeling small.

"How'd Uncle Lou get so fat?" he asked.

"Fat? He kept in great physical shape," Willet said.

"No, I meant all the fancy cars and the big house."

"Oh, financially. He made deals."

"What kinds of deals?"

"Ones that got him fat."

Willet smiled and then crossed the room to the door. "I'll bring up the rest of your things."

Jackson nodded. "When do I get to meet him?"

Willet's smile disintegrated. "Him?"

"Old Sly. The bird."

"I've attended to his needs for the night. Perhaps tomorrow."

With that, Willet exited the room, leaving Jackson alone in a cold that shouldn't exist. Forcing himself to thaw, he maneuvered over to the dresser and opened drawers. There was nothing in any of them. The same held true for an oversized writing desk, apart from new pens and a blank, fresh pad of lined paper. If this had been his uncle Lou's room, all traces were removed. The suite was a blank canvas, and one so big as to transform what he owned to a pile of refuse in an opulent but austere landscape.

Jackson shuffled over to the wall of windows. The atrium spread below, the angled windows catching the late afternoon sun's glow. His room was directly over Old Sly's. As he watched Willet draw more of what he'd packed and brought with him out of the car, a strange noise broke the room's strangulating silence. A scratching sound, reminiscent of nails on a chalkboard, crackled over Jackson's flesh and dug into his earwax. He turned. It seemed to originate at the big square vent with the wrought-iron grill.

Invisible ice formed over his flesh. He faced the vent. Beyond the decorative filigree, he caught a ghost of moment. Something was in the air duct and it was watching him.

No, shrieked the voice in his head. *Get out of this place and back on the road. Motor your ass home to Park Street. You don't need this house—you can sell it. And you already deposited that juicy check with all the zeros into your bank account. Go, now!*

Then he remembered that the whole deal was predicated upon his caring for Old Sly. Jackson blinked. No sound or movement came out of the air vent. He sold himself on the belief that it was only the system working to cool the house. A house he'd soon put on the market. As for the parrot, well, he'd hire somebody to feed it crackers and birdseed and clean up its shit. It wasn't his problem. He didn't like birds. This was the start of a whole new happy life for Jackson Bourchard, thanks to an uncle he barely remembered.

So why wasn't he smiling?

Willet again appeared, carrying more of his things. No sweat streaked the man's wrinkled face. "Are you hungry, Mister Bourchard?"

"It's Jackson," he said. "And yeah, I could eat. You got a Chinese place that delivers out here?"

"Chinese?" Willet laughed, and how Jackson didn't like the sound of that. "Oh, no, I'm afraid your diet will be properly monitored going forward, per the terms of your inheritance."

Now it was Jackson's turn to laugh. "Excuse me?"

"You've been gifted Louis Bourchard's home, holdings, and the care of his beloved friend, Sly. In return, you've agreed to those gifts for as long as humanly possible."

Jackson started to argue. Willet set down his things and was, according to his expression, past listening.

"If you'd like to shower and change, I'll have dinner on the table by the time you're done."

Willet turned and exited the big room, the conversation over. Jackson stood frozen in place, absorbing all that had happened in his short time on Nyberg Lane. Then, with his head low, he entered the cavernous bathroom and showered.

———

The dining room contained an oblong table with seats for eight and one place setting. Dressed in a change of shorts and a clean T-shirt, Jackson sat at the lone accommodation, again feeling as though the giant house had swallowed him whole. While he waited for Willet to appear from the kitchen, Jackson imagined his uncle Lou in this setting, bereft of his music, engulfed in a silence that seemed of someone else's choosing. Willet's? He'd identified himself as an interim caretaker—in-between, temporary. Holtzman? No, he was only the bean counter.

That only left Sly, and Old Sly was a pet. Jackson banished the thought as Willet appeared, an oval plate balanced on his slender fingers, a goblet clutched by its stem in the other.

The plate contained greens, slices of vegetables, and thin cuts of meat sprinkled with a pungent, aromatic spice that clawed at Jackson's nose and made his eyes water.

"Eat up," Willet said.

"Are you serious?"

He could tell by the other man's humorless expression that he was. "It's everything you need in your diet to live a long and healthy life, Mister Bourchard."

"Jackson. My name is Jackson!"

"As you wish. Now *bon appétit.*"

"Huh?"

"Eat."

Jackson picked the fork off the cloth napkin and speared something frilly and green. Upon nearing his mouth, he got another hit of pungent spice and hastily lowered it.

"Let's be clear about something, Willet—you work for me, right?"

Willet eyed him without blinking. "No, sir."

"Then who?"

"The estate. I'm here to ensure a smooth transition. So kindly eat all that's been put before you, else I'll be forced to make an adverse report on you, Jackson."

Jackson choked down the bite. Raw spices burned all the way down from his taste buds to his stomach.

⸻

He didn't have cable on Park Street—cable was a luxury. With dinner concluded and sitting like broken glass in his gut, Jackson searched the downstairs for a television. A man of his uncle Lou's wealth should have owned a flat-screen as big as a movie theater. But none of the neat, orderly rooms contained a single TV.

"Where's the man cave?" he asked.

Willet's smile returned, cold and mocking, and with it a repeat of that chuckle that so worked Jackson's nerves. "A what?"

"Flat-screen. I'll even settle for a console."

"You mean a television?" Willet asked. "There are no televisions here. Mindless entertainment rots the brain. No, if you'd like, you can retire to the upstairs library, or have an early night's rest following your busy day."

Jackson opted for the latter.

⸻

The house brooded around him in silence. There was no Wi-Fi signal, and no bars for his phone. A warm breeze stirred through the open windows, smelling green from the surrounding forest. As Jackson listened, his ear crooked toward the night beyond the house, it struck him that the chirrup of insects was absent. A chill teased the nape of his neck. He fought it, failed.

In the morning, he'd hop back into his car or one of those lux models now his and drive. The money was in his account. Let them try to take it back. It was his to do with as he chose—to splurge on Chinese takeout and ten-foot-long flat-screen televisions if he wanted. Screw Willet.

He pulled back the covers and sat on the edge of the bed. The king mattress was many times more comfortable than the misshapen twin-size back on Park Street, and seduced him almost immediately. He settled on the pillows, wondering about the thread count of the sheets. Just before sleep claimed him, Jackson switched off the bedside lamp.

He jolted awake in the darkness, alerted to a sound. It wasn't born of the city, which he nightly drowned out with a fan, no. This was a secretive scuttling noise, a lesser sound of scrabbling nails. Jackson searched the shadows, his eyes wide and too terrified to blink. There was something in the room.

Jackson froze as electric pins and needles cascaded over his flesh. A shadow moved, there along one wall! Reaching for the bedside lamp took all of his resolve. He switched it on, and most of the shadows receded. But the room was vast, the furniture large, and one light alone was unable to banish the darkness.

He struggled to breathe. In the silence, that dry desert smell was back and sat thick in his lungs. He scanned the walls, his eyes again settling on the grate. Long minutes passed, and still Jackson couldn't shake the certainty that he was being watched from the other side of the metal cover.

⚓

He turned on lights in sequence—hallway to staircase, and at the landing located more switches for the succession of downstairs rooms. The mustard yellow walls became murky at the early hour. Past the foyer, the dining room and kitchen, Jackson navigated to a large rosewood door decorated in unfamiliar carved symbols. One looked like the Number Four, though not exactly. He remembered that one as representing a planet—Jupiter, Jackson thought. None of the other details jibed. Even so, he knew by the layout of the house that this was where he'd find the atrium.

Jackson gripped the knob and found it icy beneath his touch. He opened the door. The dry dessert smell thickened as he peered into the dark room beyond. The glow around him illuminated palms and other greenery. Jackson felt along the inside of the wall and located a switch. A trio of bulbs encased in elegant shades and cages of wrought iron rained light across the atrium.

As with the rest of the house, an almost unthinkable orderliness filled the place. Palms and other vegetation soared up to twice the height of a man. A network of perches jigsawed among the trees.

Askew of the room's center, a small water fountain purred and gurgled.

Missing from the tableau presented before him was any of the carnage he expected from a big parrot. The greenery wasn't shredded, nor was the wood chewed. Not a single splatter of whitewash stained the floor or any other aspect of the atrium. For a confusing moment, he wondered if there was a parrot, or if Old Sly was a lie he'd been sold.

Then he saw it, perched to the left of the water feature, a green mass that almost blended into the fronds. It was bigger than he expected, so much larger than he thought possible for even the grandest of macaws. With its head mostly tucked under one wing, its appearance reminded him more of a vulture or some other winged monstrosity that fed on carrion.

Revulsion flared in Jackson's belly, fueled by bitter spices and churning digestive juices, and the image of Old Sly's lone visible eye, now opened and trained upon him.

"Magnificent, isn't he?" Willet asked, suddenly beside him.

Jackson startled out of his palsy, turned, and readied to lay into the man. But then Willet held up a finger to his lips, instructing silence. On their way out of the atrium, and before Willet switched off the lights, Jackson saw the matching air vent cover. It ran halfway up the wall, over a half-size door with similar markings to the one leading into the atrium.

"Best to let him sleep," Willet said in a low, throaty voice. "He's so very old. But don't worry—you'll have plenty of time to get to know him."

—◦✦◦—

Cold, he returned to the room, a room too big for one person, with Willet walking behind him, like a guide. No, Jackson thought, *a guard*.

"What is that thing?" Jackson asked, his voice barely louder than a whisper.

Willet chuckled, and Jackson was in the dark hallway at Uncle Lou's old place again, decades before arriving at his last. Moving slowly toward the part in the door, through which the chuckling sound originated. An insane sound, it had crawled over his flesh then and did so via memory now. Old Sly, in that room—Uncle Lou had been on his knees, bowing before it. And at the door, peering through, Jackson saw the abomination for what it really was. Worse, it saw him.

He was back in the Big Room, on the bed. A dead silence broken only by the scrape of claws on metal surrounded him.

"It will hurt at first, yes," Willet said. "But you'll learn to live with the pain, as did your uncle and a thousand men before him. And the thousand more that will follow you. You'll be well-fed and cared for, even allowed out on occasion to exercise but on a very short leash, I'm afraid."

Jackson attempted to respond, but no words emerged. In addition to the scrape of nails slithering closer, from the vent, growing louder, came that insane cackle in counterpoint. Mustering the remainder of his strength, he tipped his head toward the source. Not much, only enough to see the vent open, and the thing from the atrium wriggle out. At the instant of its appearance, Willet dropped to the floor and bowed with his head low.

"*Slyvan Malevos Ka*," the other man said. "We kneel before you."

The abomination spilled onto the floor and unfolded its wings. It scurried toward the bed. Jackson attempted to scream, but fear paralyzed him, as it had on that long ago day, when he saw the thing in Uncle Lou's old place. It struck him that on that day, so many years earlier, Old Sly had selected him to replace Louis Bourchard, and that his life from then on had been leading to this moment.

Old Sly loomed over him. Though his gaze had frozen open, the horror's features wouldn't come clearly. A desert sandstone face and what had to be a thousand eyes studied him. Then, leaning over, Old Sly aimed its beak at Jackson's right eye and cleanly plucked it out.

He sat at the dining table, half the world visible, eating the plate of greens and meat seasoned with pungent spices.

"It's almost time for me to go," Willet said.

"Go?"

"To the afterlife, Jackson."

He tipped a look up at Willet. The man's face lacked any of the emotions that should be attached to such a statement.

"You're going to die?"

"Yes, now that my services are no longer required. But before I do, I brought you this."

He placed a small box on the table, beside Jackson's plate. It was big enough to contain a watch. Or a glass eye.

Days later—or it could have been months, for time had lost all relevance within the walls of the house on Nyberg Lane—while his master slept, Jackson opened the half-size door in the atrium. Inside were shelves, and upon those shelves he found stone jars and urns, most of them looking to be quite old, some ancient. He risked a look into one and found the bones of a finger still encased in the papery shreds of its skin. Others held teeth, and many the desiccated remains of what he guessed were eyes.

They were mementos, Jackson understood, and quietly closed the door, so as not to rouse Old Sly. Cherished parts left over from all the pets before him.

MONSTERS OF ANY KIND

DAMIEN ANGELICA WALTERS

THE LAST WINTERGIRL

by DAMIEN ANGELICA WALTERS

When the storm ended in the quiet hour of dusk, leaving behind three feet of snow, girls began to climb out of the drifts. An arm here, another there, reaching and then holding on to ice-crisp edges as their heads broke free. A birthing of sorts. Skin tinged with blue, hair adorned with ice crystals. Snowflakes linked together, creating ethereal dresses, delicate tiaras, teardrop necklaces.

Once free, the wintergirls stood silent and still. Alive, yes, but they did not breathe plumes of frost; the air inside their lungs was as cold as that outside.

People wrapped themselves in wool and fur and emerged from their houses, approaching the wintergirls. Curious and fearful looks were exchanged. Hands extended, but stopped just short of touching. No one knew if the wintergirls required assistance or if they should be left alone. Should they be guarded over or perhaps thawed with small fires beside them? Was it all some sort of whimsy or trick? Too many questions and if the wintergirls knew the answers, they gave no signs.

The word magic *was whispered more than once, the speaker always hushed by those closest. Magic had not been seen in a very long time. Not here, not anywhere, and good riddance. The world was better off without it. Magic was dangerous and the people here wanted no such danger in their town.*

In the end, they left the wintergirls alone and returned to the warmth of their homes, peeking out from between curtains now and again. They'll be gone in the morning, many murmured and most hoped, but in the morning, the wintergirls remained.

⸺◦⸺

I was cold, I had always been cold, and then I was not. Blinking awake in the middle of an expanse of green. *Trees.* The word came to me slowly, as though traveling through molasses. Pine trees. All around me, hiding everything from sight. Hiding me. Moonglow gilded the pine needles and my fingernails silver.

My chest ached with each breath, and I had to force the air both out and in. Surely I'd done this before, though. Surely it was something in which I should be adept.

I curled fingers toward palms. Scrunched my toes, enjoying the brittle crack of dread leaves. The fog of a long nap began to bleed away. The ache in my lungs did the same. I wondered how long we'd been asleep—usually it was only a year, but sometimes two. And once, three. I wondered where we were and what we'd find. Farmers and herbwomen? Titled men and women in velvet and lace? While the latter provided better cuts of meat and more sumptuous accommodations, the former were always kinder, more earnest, falling over themselves to make certain we were happy.

The last time we woke, in a small village near a grey, unforgiving sea, we'd been given a wealth of food and drink. Grandmothers tut-tutted over our wintry skin and offered more blankets. We never needed such things, but we never turned them down. Mothers urged us to try their soup, stew, or a cake they'd baked. Fathers puffed up their chests for a visit from the wintergirls meant the town was worthy of consideration and of course the visit would go well. They knew what to do. Nothing would go wrong. Sons blushed when they spoke to us, and daughters… Daughters always wanted to sit close, touching our hair, our arms, asking for more stories of where we'd been and the people we'd met.

We knew what they really wanted, of course. For us to take the rest of winter with us when we left, to allow room for spring to step in early. We could have been ugly with warts and hooked noses and still, they would have fed us their best. Perhaps they feared our pretty exteriors were nothing more than fictions. They remembered the old stories. They remembered the danger in forgetting. They wanted us to take the winter, and nothing more.

Stretching arms overhead, I shed the last traces of sleep, and sent out a playful good morning to my sisters.

But no one responded.

⸎

The men clustered behind closed doors in dark rooms filled with candlelight and serious purpose and tossed theories back along with their coffee and later, their whiskey. A long time ago, rumors spoke of girls who'd floated away, vanishing into the night, and now, they wondered if these girls were those girls. It was ultimately decided that something like that happened only in stories, so they continued their theories. Were the wintergirls angels? Demons? Were they real at all? Someone mentioned a story his great-great-great-grandfather had told of visitors who emerged from the ice and snow, in the time when magic still held sway over land and all. But the teller was old, and included in the rest of the conversations only as courtesy, so his story was brushed aside as an old man's fancy. The men were secure in their faith that magic, all of it, was dead and gone.

The women gathered in parlors laden with lace, gossip, and insecurity's cruelty. They spoke of how shameful the wintergirls were, how they wanted everyone to look at them and talk about them and think about them and what a disgrace and someone should remove them all. They sipped tea and nibbled on scones and seeped venom from behind tight smiles and tighter corsets.

The girls emulated their mothers in public, turning up their noses and sniffing in disdain, but in private they stood in place, arms at their sides, trying not to blink or move. They daydreamed of icicles in their hair and snowflakes on their lips. Of being brave enough to do such things out in the open. And at night, when in their quiet beds, they wondered most of all if the stillness hurt.

The boys were fascinated by the girls' stillness, their silence. The wintergirls weren't like real girls; they didn't roll their eyes or call them names or ignore them. If a boy wanted to speak with a wintergirl, he could say whatever he liked, for as long as he liked. This made even the youngest boys feel powerful.

And days became nights, and nights became days.

238

For over an hour I searched but found nothing but trees. I replaced the good mornings with demands to respond now, demands that went unanswered. Had I overslept? Alethea did once; as a bit of sport, the rest of us hid. But we didn't leave her to search this long. We didn't stretch the game to the point of worry. We never would.

I felt my sisters' presence, but in a strangely muted way. Although I turned circles, I couldn't tell where they were, and fear made a snake's nest inside me. I didn't want to believe something was wrong, but how could I not? They were nowhere in sight, neither awake nor asleep.

I broke from the wood, breathing in the night air, the sun still hours away from its own waking. The hem of my dress whispered over the snow as I moved. Outside, I was calm and collected, head held high and shoulders back. Inside, I was a moth with a torn wing.

As much as it pained us to admit, we were vulnerable in our waking. We were protected by snow, by reputation, by the ghosts of old stories, but still, we weren't invincible. Even the strongest warrior, the most powerful wizard, the most learned witch, had weaknesses. Those brief moments between sleep and waking, when our thoughts were still gathering weight and shape, were ours.

I stood in a field and cast another message, filling it with distress. Once again, there was no answer. Once again, I still felt their presence, something all around me and yet nowhere at the same time, as though we'd briefly set palm to palm and what I felt was the memory of that touch.

I was beginning to fear that I'd woken alone, something that had never happened before, something I didn't know *could* happen. When we were not emerging from the snow to the world outside, we were sleeping inside it, in a quiet, frigid darkness no one could reach. We were safe there. Always.

I crossed the field, hands clasped to heart.

Late one night, a group of boys snuck outside and met up in a corner of town where one of the wintergirls stood near the bakery. With the scent of sugar still in the air, even though the shop was closed and shuttered for the evening, the boys debated if the wintergirl would wake if they removed her snowgown. It was a lovely thing similar in style to those they'd seen in texts about ancient Greece. It made them think of gladiators and strength and victory. Finally, they made the youngest, a freckled boy with wild copper curls, take one diaphanous strap in hand. When her shoulder was completely bare and the top of one breast came into view, his face was the color of a ripe tomato. The other boys urged him to continue and so he did.

She did not wake. She did not blink or move, not even when her gown was puddled around her ankles and glinting softly in the moonlight. Her skin was perfection, the dark of the hair on her head mirrored by the curls at the cleft of her thighs. The boys stood round, eyes wide, hearts racing. They nudged the redhaired boy again and told him to touch her. His fingers were mere inches away from her breast when they heard a low-pitched whistle. Full of panic and fear, they fled back to their homes and spent the next several days certain they were about to be called into their father's studies and reprimanded for what they'd done. Such a thing never happened.

They did not have cause to know that the bakery was only closed for a brief period of time. After all, someone needed to prepare the fresh bread which would be purchased by the kitchen servants and sliced for morning toast, pastries which would be arranged on china plates, croissants ready to be dressed in butter.

The baker's assistant, a man who lived outside the town's border and kept mostly to himself, came around the corner, the whistle dying on his lips at the sight of the wintergirl. Although his eyes lingered on her curves, his hands took care not to touch her as he pulled her dress back up, covering her once again. He noticed the fresh prints surrounding her in the snow but ovens waited to be lit, flour to be sifted, dough to be kneaded. And the girl didn't appear to be hurt in any way. But because he was not an unkind man, he stepped as close to the wintergirl and said, very softly, "Perhaps it would be best if you left. All of you."

A few nights later, the baker's assistant found only divots in the snow where the wintergirl once stood. Although the other wintergirls were still in place, he assumed this one had taken his advice and was glad of it.

But in an empty barn on the edge of town, the older brother of the redhaired boy and his friends gathered round the wintergirl, their gazes predatory. Hungry. The wintergirl's dress had already been *discarded and the boys had discovered that when they moved her limbs, they remained in that position until they were moved again. They knew better, all of them, but they told themselves that if she were bothered by their presence, by their touch, she'd move away or tell them to stop. She did not.*

Neither did the boys.

A town sat in the distance, small but neat in appearance. Its buildings were arranged in a loose circle with a few on the outskirts as though a pen skipped across a page, leaving a series of ink drips behind. A fat finger of smoke pointed in the darkness.

One by one, the wintergirls vanished, secreted away to barn, attic, and cellar. By boys in groups, by duos, by singles. They were careful. They were cunning. And later, they were cruel.

The men went back to discussions of business. The women to fashion. The girls found themselves inexplicably sad, prone to burst into tears at the most inopportune moments. Had they done something wrong? Why had the wintergirls come? Why had they left without a single word or gesture?

And then they stoically prepared themselves for the teasing from the boys, the comments, the stray touches on arm and cheek and sometimes elsewhere when no one was looking. The ways things had been. The ways they hated, but boys were boys, so it was said. Smile and stay dignified was always the response. Be a good girl. Because one of those boys would eventually be a husband, to love and to honor and to obey.

Until death.

The town was shuttered and dark, but as I passed through the shadows, I felt my sisters' presence all around me like a whisper caught in time. And yet.

And yet.

There was something wrong, an absence coupled with the presence. It made no sense, but it was there nonetheless. I cast message after message, no longer swallowing the fear but allowing it to permeate every call.

A man wearing white billowy trousers rounded a corner and stopped, blinking rapidly when he saw me. The mouthwatering scents of sugar and cinnamon perfumed his clothing and skin. I lifted one hand in the timeworn gesture of goodwill. Waited for him to bow or perhaps bend a knee, as was the usual custom, but he did neither. Sophia would've dressed him down with a withering gaze; Merianna would've crossed her arms and cleared her throat; I did nothing but smile. Perhaps he was simple.

"Good evening, sir," I said. "I'm looking for my sisters."

His brow furrowed. "Your sisters?"

"Yes."

"The girls from the snow?"

I nodded.

"I thought they left," he said, his words carefully measured.

"But they *were* here."

"Yes."

There was something else in his eyes. I closed the distance between us, rested one finger on his arm. Knew he felt the cold through his clothing. Knew he feared it, too.

"Tell me," I said.

"I found one. Someone…someone had undressed her. I put her back to rights and told her she should leave."

"Undressed her?" I gripped his upper arm until pain flooded his face. "She wasn't awake?"

"No. She was like a statue, standing still."

Another squeeze. Another flare of pain. The skin of his nose began to blacken at the tip. When I spoke, the words held no emotion, only winter's edge. "And the others?"

"They were all the same. I thought they left. I don't know what happened," he said, but his gaze flicked behind me, over one shoulder.

I turned toward the column of smoke.

Bad deeds, like secrets, never stay buried too long. A farmer found a wintergirl in an old outbuilding he'd planned to restore. When he saw what had been done to her, he stumbled out of the building, a palm covering his mouth, shock leaching the color from his face, bile burning the back of his throat.

The men returned to their rooms with closed doors. Whiskey was consumed, cigars smoked. Our boys are good boys, they said. Not their fault. How could they resist?

Over the next few days, more wintergirls were looked for and found. The men drank more whiskey, smoked more cigars. Our boys are good boys, they said over and over, although the words turned hollow.

The women whispered to each other: What did the girls think would happen?

To spare the women and girls from the sight, the wintergirls were wrapped in sheets and taken to the outbuilding—the farmer said he'd never use it again—at night. A few of the girls watched from behind shutters and curtains, but the men were careful and the outbuilding was kept under lock and guard. They tried to listen in as the men discussed and debated, but were shooed away, sent to parlors with knitting needles and skeins of yarn.

The man in white slowly pulled away. I held him tighter, inhaled deeply, and breathed him to stillness. He would be fine in a few hours. Plagued with a chill that would leave only on the hottest of summer days, but fine nonetheless.

Again, I called my sisters. Then I demanded.

Snow began to fall.

Screams shattered the silence.

And a black cloud of crows pinwheeled into the sky.

The front doors of those shuttered houses were flung wide. Girls emerged, crawling on hands and knees, eyes wild, veils of snow dressing their hair, pearls of ice adorning their cheeks. Girls, answering the call.

But not my sisters.

From behind the girls, mothers spilled out, screaming their fear, pulling cheeks into Samhain masks.

From behind me, heavy footsteps.

I turned slowly without a sound.

And I saw it on their faces. Saw what they'd done, those younger versions of these men, saw how carefully these men had stepped in. I smelled my sisters on them, amid the ashes and char.

How much pain had they endured? How much terror?

I could only hope that sleep held them tight all the while, yet that provided pale comfort.

Explanations were forming on the mens' lips. *Excuses.*

I wanted no part.

Rage, bitter and barbed, pricked my tongue. I opened my arms, fingers spread, and took in the wrath of winter, the wind, the snow, the ice. I became all of us, all our possibilities, all the old stories and those yet unwritten, all at once.

The girls fell to the ground, writhing, sleet racing through their veins and cleaving their thoughts. The cold burrowed deep into bone and marrow; tangled round muscle and sinew; coiled inside hearts, livers, and lungs. The mothers gathered them in their arms, ignoring the chills that burned through the velvet of their dressing gowns, and wailed.

The fathers begged.

If the wintergirls were ever capable of waking up, the men reasoned, most of them weren't now and truly, for those who might, it would be a cruelty to allow. Better if they were gone. Better for the wintergirls, the town, the boys. Better for all of them. That they could not meet each other's gazes when they spoke the words mattered not. The decision was made.

On a night when the air tasted of cowardice and callous disregard, and the full moon watched from her silent berth in the sky, the men gathered at the outbuilding.

They did not hesitate. If any had a change of heart, he kept it to himself. Twigs and split logs were piled against the outbuilding and then surrounded by stones to prevent a disaster. So that no one man had to bear the burden, each placed a twig into a small fire burning off to the side for that purpose and set it against the building.

The flames caught quickly. The building burned and burned and burned, casting out great clouds of black smoke. When the smell of roasting meat hung heavy in the air, the men stepped back and back and back.

Snow began to fall, fat flakes spiraling down in a heavy curtain. And from the town, there were screams.

———

I stepped forward to a man standing slightly ahead of the others.

"Cruel boys turn into crueler men. The sort of men who would conceal and hide bestial acts." I smiled and he recoiled. "You forgot who we were. You forgot what we were capable of. This can't be allowed."

Before he could attempt to answer, I fitted my mouth atop his, exhaled cold into his warmth, watched ice crystals cataract his eyes. When he stilled, I wiped the taste of him away with the back of a hand.

"I know you can hear me," I said close to his ear. "Perhaps someone one day will find a way to undo this, perhaps not. Perhaps they will think you dead and bury you instead. Or burn your flesh to ashes."

So many exhalations, so many whispers.

Some tried to run.

They could not run fast enough.

When it was done, I turned to the mothers. "Where are they?"

They shook their heads, held their changed daughters closer, sobbed tears that froze upon lashes and cheeks.

Fingers linked, I dropped chin toward chest. Sent frost into the houses, into every nook and corner, and soon enough, the boys rushed through the front doors, teeth chattering, skin blue.

Now the mothers begged.

I extended my arms again. The girls pulled free from their mothers' clutches and came to me with eyes of winter and lips of rime, moving with liquid grace. Snowmelt beneath crusts of ice.

"These are the boys who would put babes in your bellies," I said. "Who would sleep beside you each night, who would claim you for *theirs*. Ask them what they did to my—to *our*—sisters."

But they didn't have to ask. The truth was plain on each boy's face. And a deeper truth sat in their eyes, a truth that could not hide its ugliness. They'd enjoyed it.

I wanted to tear them limb from limb, wanted to freeze them until they rent in a thousand jagged pieces, but I stepped back instead.

"They would touch you with those selfsame hands," I said to the girls.

Icy resolve hardened their gazes. Their fingers hooked, nails growing into points. Behind full lips the shade of ripe bilberries, their teeth did the same. Their steps were steady, implacable. They were not wintergirls. They were something more. And they were beautiful. The world would perhaps call them monsters, would fear them, would recast them—and surely me as well—into villains, but I no longer cared.

The snow continued to fall as screams filled the night anew.

MONSTERS OF ANY KIND

EDWARD LEE

THE CITY OF SIXES

by EDWARD LEE

Six minutes after he officially died, Slydes found himself standing agog on a street corner like none he'd ever seen. He stood as he had in life: broad-shouldered, tall, dark dirty hair and a bushy black beard. Blue jeans and workboots, and his favorite T-shirt stretched tight over his beer belly; it read ST. PETE BEACH - A QUIET LITTLE DRINKING TOWN WITH A FISHING PROBLEM. Slydes was a redneck, tried and true, a shitkicker. A *badass.* He'd seen a lot of—for lack of more elegant phraseology—fucked-up shit in his day, but now... Now...

This?

The wind screamed. Winged mites swarmed in the humid air and splotched red when he swatted them against his brawny forearms. *What kind of city is this?* the horrid question occurred to him when his gaze was dragged upward. Dim, drear-windowed skyscrapers seemed a mile high and leaned this way and that at such extreme angles, he thought they might topple at any moment. Twisted faces that couldn't possibly be Human peered out of many of the narrow windows, while other windows were either broken out or spattered with blood. The sky visible between each building appeared to be red, and there was a black sickle moon hanging between two of them. Slydes blinked.

A dream, it had to be. It was this notion that he first entertained. His Condemnation only minutes old, he couldn't remember much. He couldn't remember where he was born, for instance, he couldn't remember his age, nor could he remember his last name. Indeed,

Slydes couldn't even remember dying.

But died he had, and for a lifetime of wincingly outrageous sins and wickedness, he'd been Damned to Hell.

So here he was.

A nightmare, that's all, he convinced himself. A red sky? Office buildings leaning over at sixty-degree angles? And—

SWOOSH

A black bat with a six-foot wingspan and a vaguely Human face glided by just over his head. Slydes felt a stinking gust, then recoiled when the impossible animal shat on his head.

"Fucker!" Slydes yelled.

The bat—actually a Hexegenically created Crossbreed of one of several genera known as *Revoltus Chiropterus*—looked over its leathery shoulder and smiled.

"Welcome to Hell," it croaked.

Slydes stared after the words more than the creature itself. *Hell,* he thought quite obliquely. *I'm not really in—*

WELCOME TO ST. PUTRADA CIRCLE, HELL'S NEWEST FISTULATION & TRANSVERSION PREFECT, the sign severed his thoughts.

Slydes could only stare at the sign as the splat of monstrous guano ran down the sides of his face.

Hell's Newest...WHAT?

At the corner another sign blinked DON'T WALK, and then a rush of pedestrians crossed the street. Slydes just kept staring...

He didn't know *what* they were at first: People? Monsters? Combinations of both? A slim couple held hands as they strode by, flesh rotting from their limbs and faces. Several impish children wove through the crowd, with fangs like a dog's and eyes as big and as red as apples. A Werewolf in a business suit and briefcase passed next, and next after that a fat clown with a hatchet in its face. To Slydes, the clown bid, "Hi, how are ya?"

Slydes could not respond.

If anything, the street was worse. Cars that looked more like small steam engines chugged by on spoked wheels, a smokestack up front gusted black-yellow soot and water vapor. Carriages and buggies rolled by as well, hauled along not by horses but by things *like* horses, whose flesh hung in dripping tatters. One carriage was occupied by a woman with skin green as pond scum who wore a tiara of gall stones and a dress made from tendons meticulously woven together. She fanned herself with a webbed, severed hand. In another carriage rode a creature that could've been a pile of snot somehow shaped into Human form. Then came a haulage wagon of some sort, powered by six harnessed beasts with festering carnation-pink skin pocked with white blisters; Slydes thought hideously of skinned sheep when they bleated and spat foamy sputum. A man perched behind them cracked a long, barbed whip—or...perhaps *man* wasn't quite right. He wore a wool cloak and banded leggings like a shepherd of the old days, yet atop his anvil-shaped head grew a brow of horns. The whip cracked and cracked, and the bleating rose to a mad clamor. Slydes looked one more time and noticed that, like the bat, these bald "sheep" had faces grimly tainted by Human features.

"Oh my God, I am in some shit," Slydes stammered. Things were starting to click in his head, and with each click came more and more fear. Did a tear actually form in his eye? "I-I-I," he blubbered. "I don't think this is a dream..."

"It's not," sounded a voice that was somehow raspy and feminine simultaneously. The woman who approached him was nude, and yet— he thought at first—checker-boarded. Slydes squinted at her impressive physique, and then recalled women with similar physiques whom he'd raped and sometimes even murdered without vacillation. But *this* woman?

Every square inch of her skin was crisply darkened by black tattoos of upside-down crosses. Even her face, around which shimmered long platinum blonde hair.

"Slydes, right?" she asked. "My name's Andeen, and I'm your Orientation Directress. You may not even realize this yet, but you're what's known as a Entrant."

"Entrant," Slydes murmured.

"And, no, this isn't a dream. You should be so lucky. This is all real. Over time your memory will re-form."

Before Slydes could mutter a question, his gaze snapped to another passerby: another impressively figured nude woman. Her arms, legs, abdomen, and face were but one colossal psoriatic outbreak. Only the breasts and pubis were without blemish.

"Rash lines," remarked Andeen. "In the Living World you have tan lines, here we have rash lines."

Slydes' gaze snapped back to the tattooed woman. "Here...as in..."

"As in Hell. You're dead, and for your worldly sins, you've been

MONSTERS OF ANY KIND

Condemned." Her slender shoulders shrugged. "Forever."

Slydes began to grow faint.

She grabbed his hand and tugged. "Come on, Slydes. We gotta get you out of this Prefect. It's really fucked-up here," and then she tugged him down the street a ways and ducked into an alley. "We'll lay low awhile, and try to get you someplace where your ass won't be grass."

"I-I," Slydes blubbered. "I don't understand."

"Trust me, there's no good place in Hell, but there are places that are worse than others. Like this place, St. Purtrada Circle. You must've been a real scumbag to be Rematerialized *here*. Yes, sir, a real humdinger of a shitty person."

"I don't understand!" Slydes now sobbed outright.

"A Prefect is like a small District. And this one happens to be a Fistulation and Surgical Transversion Prefect. I'll keep an eye out for Abduction Squads. They'll Transvert anybody here, Humans and Hellborn alike, but Humans are the desired target. The Surgery Centers pay the most for Humans."

Slydes looked cross-eyed at her.

"The short version. Every Prefect, District, or Town has to have an active mode of punishment, while there are some areas, known as Punitaries, that exist *solely* for punishment. But anyway, this Prefect uses Fistulatic Surgery to conform to the Punishment Ordinances. Fistula is Latin; it means 'communication between,' and Transversion is, like, rerouting things. That's what they do here—they reroute your insides."

Even though Slydes didn't have a *clue* what she was talking about, he stammered, "Whuh-whuh-*why?*"

Andeen smirked. "Because it's perverse and disgusting...the way it's *supposed* to be. This isn't Romper Room, Slydes. This is Hell, and Hell is hardcore. Eternal torment, suffering, and abhorrence is the name of the game. It pleases Lucifer, therefore, it's Public Law." She smirked more sharply this time. "Look, go over to that public washbasin and wash the bat shit out of your hair. It's grossing me out."

Dazed, Slydes noted the elevated stone basin only feet from the alley mouth. He dunked his head in the water, agitated the rank guano out of his hair, then seized up and jerked his head out when he realized what he was washing in.

"That's not water! That's piss!"

"Get used to it," Andeen said. "Unless you're a Grand Duke or an

Archlock, you'll never get *near* fresh water. Only other way is to distill it yourself out of the blood of what you kill."

Revolted, Slydes flapped the piss off his face, then noticed lower basins erected intermittently along the smoky street. "What are those things? They look like—"

"Oh, the commodes. It's another Public Law. In this Prefect, it's mandatory that everyone urinate, defecate, and give birth in public."

Slydes' bearded jaw dropped.

"And there"—Andeen pointed—"across the street. There're the various Surgery Suites."

Slydes' crossed eyes scanned the signs over each transom…

RECTO-URINARY TRANSVERSION

URETHRAL-ESOPHAGEAL REVERSAL

UTERO-RECTAL FISTULA

And many, many more.

Andeen's evilly tattooed hand pulled him back into the alley. "And look, there's an Abduction Squad. The clay men are called Golems. They're like state employees, public works, police, security, stuff like that…"

Slydes watched with a cheek to the edge of the alley wall as a troop of gray-brown things shaped like men thudded down the sidewalk, each shoving along a handcuffed Human, Demon, or Hybrid. The Golems were nine feet tall and walked in formation. Then they all stopped at the same time and marched their prisoners into various Surgery Suites.

"And like I said, the State pays more money for Humans, so that's why we gotta get you out of the Prefect."

Slydes whipped his face back around, and repeated, helplessly now, "I don't understand…"

"Once you've seen what goes on here…you will. Oh, and check out this chick."

Slydes watched as a morose-faced nude woman who appeared to be half-Human and half-Troll staggered toward one of the street commodes. She leaned over, parted her buttocks, and began to urinate out of her anus, and when she was done, she turned around, squatted, then began to wince. Slydes winced right along with her as they watched the incredulous act. Long trails of feces slowly squeezed out of her vagina and dropped into the commode.

"See?" Andeen asked. "Oh, wow, and check this out! Here comes a Uteral-oral Fistulation…"

A woman in a bloody smock labored down the street. She was covered with red-rimmed white scales…and obviously quite pregnant. She held a scaled hand to her bloated belly, and when she could walk no longer, she stopped, leaned over, and—

SPLAT!

—out gushed a slew of amniotic water from her mouth. She maintained the uncomfortable position, and as her belly began to tremor, her jaw came unhinged. Her throat began to impossibly swell, and as her stomach shrunk in size, a squalling, demonic fetus slid hugely out of her mouth and flapped to the pavement.

"How's that for the spectacle of childbirth?" Andeen jested. "Pregnancy is a big deal in Hell, Slydes. If Lucifer had his way, every single female lifeform here would be pregnant at all times. You see, the more babies, the more food, fuel, and fodder for Lucifer's whimsey."

Slydes leaned against the wall, moaning, "No, no, no…"

"Yes, yes, yes, my friend. And if you think *that* was bad, get a load of this guy. Remember what I said about pregnancy?"

Slydes' gaze involuntarily veered back to the street. This time, a Human man stumbled along. He wore a "wife-beater" T-shirt and stained boxer shorts dotted with Boston Red Sox insignias. If anything, though, his stomach looked even more bloated than the woman who'd just delivered a devilish baby through her mouth.

Slydes stammered further, in utter dread, "He's not—he's not–he's not–"

"Pregnant?" Andeen smiled darkly. "Male pregnancy is a fairly new breakthrough here, Slydes. And you can bet it tickles Lucifer pink. Teratologic Surgeons can actually transplant Hybrid wombs into *male* Humans and Demons. It's a trip. Watch."

Slydes watched.

Grimacing, the bloated man stepped out of his boxers and squatted. Amid boisterous grunts and wails, his rectum slowly dilated, then—

He shrieked.

—out poured a slew of what looked like squirming hairless puppies, with tiny webbed paws and little horns in their heads.

"Ah," Andeen observed, "a brood of Ghor-Hounds. Pretty rowdy, huh?"

"Rowdy!" Slydes bellowed. "This is FUCKED UP! That guy just pumped a litter of PUPPIES out his ASS!"

"Yeah. And watch what he does now…"

Gravid stomach gone now, the exhausted man abandoned his litter on the sidewalk and trudged over to one of the street commodes. *What, he's gonna take a piss?* Slydes wondered when the man poised an understandably shriveled penis over the commode.

The answer to his question, however, would be a most indubitable *No.*

Now the man's cheeks billowed. He began to grunt.

And his penis…began to swell.

"Ahhhh," he eventually moaned as the penis, next, began to disgorge firm stools. Quite a number of them squeezed out and dropped into the commode. When he was finished, he pulled his boxers back on, and at the same time caught Slydes staring agape at him.

"What's the matter, buddy? You act like you never saw a guy take a shit through his dick before."

"In case you're wondering," his hostess said, "the procedure that guy underwent is called a Recto-Urethral Fistulation…"

Slydes reeled. When he could regain some modicum of sense, he glared back at Andeen and howled, "This is impossible! Women can't have *babies* out their mouths! Their mouths aren't *big* enough! And men can't shit *turds* through their cocks! Their *peeholes* aren't *wide* enough! It's IMPOSSIBLE!"

Andeen seemed amused by Slydes' crude rant. "You'll learn soon enough that in Hell…*anything* is possible. Now come on."

Dizzied, aghast, Slydes trudged after her. She walked fast, her high breasts bouncing, her flawless rump jiggling with each stride. "Once I get you out of this Prefect and on one of the Interways, you'll be a lot safer. Believe me, you don't want to hang out here." She grinned over her shoulder. "You're damn lucky I'm an *honest* Orientation Directress, Slydes."

"Huh?"

"There are a lot of dishonest ones. They'd tip off an Abduction Squad and turn you in—for money, of course."

"Huh?"

"Just come on. I know, you're confused right now, and you can't remember much. Eventually it'll all sink in, and you'll be all right."

Slydes sorely doubted that he would ever be All Right, not in Hell. But he did feel some gratitude toward Andeen for endeavoring to get him out of the abominable Prefect. *Anywhere, anywhere,* his thoughts pleaded. *Take me anywhere because no matter how bad the next place is, it can't be as bad as this...*

"Here's the shortcut out, and don't worry about the gate," she said. She lifted something from beneath her tongue. "I have the key."

Thank God... Slydes followed the lithe woman down another reeking alley whose end terminated in a chain-link gate closed by an antiquated lock. When Andeen finnicked with the key, rust sifted from the keyhole.

That thing better open, Slydes fretted.

"I guess the hardest thing to get used to for a Human in Hell is, well, the insignificance. Know what I mean?"

"Huh?" Slydes said.

"No matter what we were in the Living World, no matter how strong, how beautiful, how rich, how *important*...in Hell we're nothing; in fact, we're less than nothing." She giggled, still jiggling the key. "We're like those none-characters in the beginning of a novel—I guess it's called the prologue?—where we don't really have a purpose like a regular character. Follow me, Slydes?"

"Uh, no. Ain't much for readin'."

Andeen shrugged. "We don't do anything for the plot or anything for the *meaning* of the book. Seriously. In Hell, a Human is like one of those sub-characters that only exists to introduce the reader to the setting..."

Slydes was getting pissed. "I don't know what'cher talkin' about! Just open that fuckin' lock so we can get out of here!"

She giggled but then frowned. "Damn. This bugger's tough. Check the alley entrance, will you—"

"All riiiiiiiii—" but when Slydes looked behind him, he shrieked. Proceeding slowly down the alley was a congregation of the short, dog-faced imp-like things he'd seen chicanering previously on the street. They grinned as they moved forward, fangs glinting.

Slydes tugged Andeen's arm like a child tugging its mother's. "Luh-luh-look!"

Andeen's tattooed brow rose when she glanced down the alley. "Shit. Broodren. They're demonic kids and they're *all* homicidal. The little fuckers have gangs everywhere—"

"Open the lock!"

She played with the key most vigorously, nervous herself now. "They'll haul our guts out to sell to a Diviner, then they'll fuck and eat what's left…"

"Hurry!" Slydes wailed.

Suddenly the pack of Broodren broke all at once into a sprint, cackling.

When they were just yards away—

CLACK!

—the lock opened. Slydes peed his jeans as Andeen dragged him to the other side. She managed to relock the gate just as several Brooden pounced on it, their dirty taloned fingers and toes hooked over the chain links.

"Jesus! We barely made it!"

Andeen sighed, wiped her brow with her forearm. "Tell me about it, man."

"What now?" Slydes looked down a stained brick corridor that seemed to dogleg to the left. "How do we get out?"

"Around the corner," Andeen said.

They trotted on, turned the corner, and—

"Holy motherfuckin' SHIT!" Slydes yelled when two stout, gray-brown forearms wrapped about his barrel chest and hoisted him in the air. Tall shadows circled round in total silence.

Slydes screamed till his throat turned raw.

"One thing you need to know about Hell," Andeen chuckled, "is that *trust* does not exist."

Five blank-faced Golems stood round Slydes now, and it was in the arms of a sixth that he was now captive.

One of them handed Andeen a stack of bills. "Thanks, buddy. This guy's a *real* piece of work. He deserves what he's getting," and then she winked at Slydes and pointed up to another transom. It read: DIGESTIVE TRACT REVERSAL SUITE.

"For the rest of eternity, Slydes," she intoned through a sultry grin. "You'll be eating through your ass and shitting out your mouth."

"Noooooooooooooo!" Slydes shrieked.

The Golems trooped toward the door, Slydes kicking and screaming, all to no avail.

"Welcome to Hell," Andeen bid the parting words.

Slydes' screams silenced when the Suite door slammed shut, and Andeen traipsed off, greedily counting the stack of crisp bills. Each bill had the number 100 in each corner, but it was not the portrait of Benjamin Franklin that graced each one, it was the face of Adolf Hitler.

MONSTERS OF ANY KIND

MONICA J. O'ROURKE

CRISIS OF FAITH
by MONICA J. O'ROURKE

Ryan spotted him in Central Park. The guy had a homeless look about him—bedraggled, with a light beard growth that looked rather anemic, not millennial, and not a trace of irony. But if Ryan was right, this guy was perpetually homeless—he was comfortable on the streets because that was all he'd ever known.

More than a decade of research had made Ryan keenly aware of what he was seeing, but he still wasn't prepared. Ten years out of college and he still felt like a kid, an amateur. Religious studies, and a major in theology, hadn't prepared him for much. His crisis of faith had repeatedly altered his plans, set him up for failure, created something in him that made other people suffering something he could no longer tolerate. And after years of church and confession and penance and altruism, it was too much. No priesthood after all. Limited faith in God. Not much of anything in his life. Dead end after dead end in his research.

But now what? He was the dog who'd caught the proverbial car he was chasing—to what end?

Running off the concrete footpath, passing rows of trees of various heights, statues that seemed out of place among vast lawns of greens and pale yellows, and playgrounds that seemed decidedly dangerous for young bodies to fall on, Ryan caught up with the guy.

He cautiously approached, coming up from behind, standing now at a little more than arm's length away. Enough distance to run? Unlikely.

And there would be no begging for life; not from this one, one without compassion or empathy, one who existed solely to survive.

He didn't even know how to begin. Would he be killed on the spot? His need for answers overwhelmed his terror, his compulsion to run.

"Excuse me," Ryan mumbled, not even sure he'd been heard.

The man slowly turned, the look on his face not of surprise but of amusement, a self-satisfied smugness. It was as if he'd been waiting for Ryan. "Yes?"

Ryan was taken aback. He'd expected some kind of monster, some horrific thing only Bosch could have imagined. Here instead was Everyman. Innocuous. Even boring. An attractive man...who likely would be elected to the school board before piles of corpses would be unearthed under his floorboards. The kind of guy all the neighbors would say, "He was so nice!" ... after partially eaten bodies were discovered in his upright freezer. But this guy was a chameleon, and even Ryan was momentarily fooled by the Mr. Rogers look on his face.

But Ryan wasn't mistaken. He couldn't be. He knew they could change form, alter appearance. This one clearly wanted to blend in. He was scruffy-looking but he was normal. Wore jeans, a hoodie, and sneakers.

"What's your name?" Ryan asked, subconsciously taking half a step back. He wondered if he could outrun the guy. He was still in decent shape. College wasn't that far behind him.

"My name?" He raised an eyebrow. "Why?"

"Your... human name..."

The man sat on a wooden bench spattered with bird droppings and covered with windswept leaves. "What an interesting way to put that."

Ryan noticed he didn't seem confused or try to argue the semantics of Ryan's question.

"You can call me Dan. But you still haven't told me why you want to know."

"I guess I don't, really. I just wanted an excuse to talk to you." He picked at his butt without realizing he was doing it and tried to figure out what to say next. "My name's Ryan."

"I know."

"You do?"

Dan smirked. "I know everything, kid. I know what you've done. I know your obsessions. I know the miserable, failed direction your life has led, the sad, pathetic excuse for a man this world has had to accept. You're repulsive, and you're only what? thirty? thirty-five? You want me to end your misery, but you want to go out in a spectacular fashion, only one that I can provide."

Dan shook his head and glared at Ryan. "What do you want? After so many years battling religion, battling God, battling over your goddamned soul, what are you hoping for? Death by demon? You think you're the first? You're pathetic!"

"No!" Ryan's eyes dropped, as if he was trying to study the inside of his cheek. "No. Not at all!"

Ryan looked back up, and Dan stared intently into his eyes. "Then what do you want?"

"I." He licked his lips and then bit gently on the tip of his protruding tongue. "I want to study you. Learn about you."

Dan's smile only reached his mouth. His eyes never lost their flat, angry disposition. "I don't have time for this."

"I think you have nothing but time." Ryan's pulse quickened. "Please. Tell me how you came to be here. Tell me about—"

Dan interrupted. "No, but I'll tell you about a little boy with an ice cream cone." He paused for a second, leaning in a bit closer, as if gleaning information. His flaccid smile quickly hardened into a grin. "Even better. Okay, here's my story. Everything is right with the world. Our young hero graduated high school and brings his little cousin to the corner for an ice cream cone. Only the street is fifty-seventh, right off Fifth Avenue. Kind of insanely high-traffic area, no? This little cousin is how old? Seven?"

Ryan paled, and his pupils dilated. He slowly shook his head. "I want to talk about you…"

"Only this kid runs out into the street, right onto Fifth Avenue. Some cars come to a screeching halt, but this kid is so tiny, most of the drivers don't even see him."

"Please stop." His voice is a whisper.

"But it's too late." Dan laughed like he'd just told the funniest joke. "Oh *boy* it is too late! Splat! Seven-year-old brains smashed down the block. People screaming, crying, someone yelling to call 911, the idiot. Little boy body tumbling down the asphalt, road burns marking his flesh. And still the song from the Mister Softee truck keeps playing…over and over, it doesn't stop. The song goes, 'The creamiest, dreamiest soft ice cream, you get from Mister Softee. For a refreshing delight supreme, look for Mister Softee.' And this teenager hears this song in his nightmares, and when he sees an ice cream truck on the street he sometimes runs screaming, hides in a closet or under a bed...

"And you...you standing there holding red, white, and blue bomb pops in both hands. One for you, and one for...ohhhh. One for the little kid without a head."

Ryan froze, his brain filled with anger and terror, picturing the scene so clearly, a scene he'd spent more than a decade trying to erase. He felt a tightness in his chest, a pounding ache. He dug his fingernails into his palms to try to focus his mind.

"So this teenager tries to come to terms with the death of his baby cousin, only he can't. 'Why is life so unfair?'" Dan cried mockingly. "Wah-wah-wah, poor me, life sucks! Oh, wait! Let's blame God for everything! So this boy-man eventually studies religion, studies God, studies mankind looking for some semblance of humanity, of caring, of compassion. Answers to those burning: why *me*? Why *them*? Why did God kill this little dude? He had his whole life ahead of him! And now he's just a headless memory. How sad!

"Am I right?" Dan grinned again, but this time his eyes lit up. "But there never are answers! There never will be! Do you know why?"

Ryan thought he was going to throw up. "You're a bastard."

"Because there is no God—and *you* chose your own ridiculous life. You chose your own misery and suffering even before you were born. Call it a life lesson, call it stupidity, call it a cosmic classroom, but you, Ryan Wolff, chose your own damned path. Time to man up and stop blaming everyone else for your choices. And your shortcomings."

"That's not true. We're children of God, and God determines our path. I mean, it's not that simple, but that's why we have faith, why we must believe in his benevolence. That's why sometimes we have to believe in something even if it doesn't make sense."

"You're still defending something you're not even sure you believe in? Now that's a laugh! You worship a flying space cowboy who doles out punishment if you don't fall at your knees and worship him? Is that the sort of benevolence you mean?"

"It's not that simple!"

"Then why aren't you a priest?" Dan laughed. "You're not even an altar boy. An imam? A rabbi? A voodoo witch doctor? You're *nothing!* You have no faith. You have no direction. But you got lucky, boy—you found *me*."

"That means nothing to me," Ryan said, but his voice broke, and he felt dizzy. He had no fight here. Dan wasn't wrong.

"Do you want to know about me?"

"I know about you! You're Nephilim, one of God's abominations. You shouldn't even exist. You were forged by Satan's plan. You do nothing but cause harm, angry at the world, at *God*, for your very existence. You destroy everything in your path, and you and your kind were destroyed centuries ago by the Great Flood!"

Dan's face grew hard, and he leaned forward. "Then how did I get here?"

Ryan shook his head. "I don't know." He thought for a moment. "Some of your kind were exiled to Tartarus. You obviously escaped."

"Did I?" Dan shook his head. "Perhaps you should read more than one biblical text. Yes, the flood destroyed most of the Nephilim, but God allowed a number of them—their disembodied spirits, anyway— to remain after the flood."

"Why would he do that?"

"To lead the human race astray until the final judgment."

Ryan's excitement was building. He managed to push the image of his little cousin out of his mind again; it was the only way to keep himself from going insane.

He needed answers! Maybe this would clarify the facts, help him understand his belief in God and the supernatural. "How did you escape? And when! How long have you been here?"

"Growing a pair, are you?"

"What do you mean?"

"You know what I am. So you know what I'm capable of." He moved so fast his movement didn't register, and suddenly Ryan was slammed against a tree, suspended in air, a thick forearm choking off his windpipe. He gasped for oxygen and pounded furiously and uselessly at Dan's arm.

Dan let go, and Ryan collapsed on his hands and knees, retching, clawing at his throat, thankful that his larynx hadn't been crushed. Grateful to be alive—but why was he alive? Nephilim were known for their hatred of humankind. Benevolence was not a trait they were known for.

"Dan," Ryan gasped, but Dan shook his head.

"Sheshai."

"What?"

"My name is Sheshai, not Dan. I have no human name!"

Ryan leaned against the tree and looked up at Sheshai, fearing for his life, fearing for the next steps in this little game Sheshai seemed to be playing. He clearly was several steps ahead of Ryan, but why? And to what end?

Sheshai squatted until the two were eye to eye. "I'm studying human nature. I want to see actions, and *rea*ctions. Do you understand?"

Ryan shook his head. It hurt to swallow. Tears formed. He wished he'd never been so stupid to set out on this little quest. And he really didn't want to understand what Sheshai was saying. He wanted to go home now.

"Home," Sheshai said, obviously reading Ryan's thoughts. He shook his head, looking almost sad for a moment. "Wouldn't that be nice?"

Was that rhetorical? Ryan nodded in response.

"I have something else in mind," Sheshai said.

"Why are you doing this?" Ryan cried, swinging by his wrists, ropes tied high above, from the rafters. The strain on his skin was tremendous. The thick ropes scraped his flesh, pulled at joints and tendons, stripped epidermis until his wrists were raw and bloody.

His body had gained slight momentum from the exertion of talking and he swayed a bit. "Please!" he screamed at the man below him, just behind, just out of sight, out of reach.

"Dear God," he whispered, "I'm so sorry. For whatever I've done— I'm sorry!"

"There is no *God* here," Sheshai said.

"God! I'm begging you, *please!*"

"There is no *God* here!" Sheshai yelled, emphasizing every word. "It is you, and it is me, and *that* is who stands in this church. There is no *God* here!"

"Please don't hurt me," Ryan sobbed, his face wet with a mixture of every bodily fluid capable of leaking from his pores. Snot bubbled in his nose, dribbled down over his top lip.

"Ryan, Ryan," he said, tsk-tsking, wrapping his arm around his suspended thigh.

Ryan screamed as if he'd been touched by a red-hot poker.

"Settle down," Sheshai said. "We haven't even begun."

"Begun what? What? Why are you doing this?" His mind flashed back to the park, to their conversation. What had led to this? This was insane!

"Now, please tell me when this starts to hurt."

Ryan felt Sheshai's breath on his body, his hands touching Ryan's legs, felt him slicing Ryan's pants lengthwise, leaving them in long tatters.

"Tell me," Sheshai said slowly, and Ryan felt something being pressed against his exposed skin. Something sharp that jabbed before it pierced, a fine point, the tip of a knife perhaps. What had Sheshai said in the park? How he was studying human nature? How was this possibly helping?

Sheshai said, "So tell me: How deep is your faith? Isn't that what you ultimately want to know? How much love you have for God?"

"Wait—what? *Please,* Sheshai, don't do this!" Ryan gasped, steeled himself against whatever was coming. Sheshai grunted just as Ryan felt something slice into his body. He felt warm liquid pouring from the top of his thigh. Blood, he thought in an almost detached, shocky manner. *Blood. My blood. Blood and—*

He didn't know what else. He still couldn't see. Out of sight, out of mind, and he had no issue with this. He really didn't want to see.

"Oh, Ryan. You're making this difficult."

A few more shreds...deeper it seemed, so many slices now. He couldn't imagine what his legs looked like, but beef jerky suddenly filled his brain. Still he felt nothing, no pain, just a detached curiosity.

"Still nothing? Really."

Ryan sensed Sheshai's movement.

"Your wounds are nasty...but not enough to be causing such serious lockdown. Do you always mentally retreat from paper cuts? Coward, I guess. Dissociating already. Maybe we need some stimulus."

Ryan squeezed his eyes shut. He didn't need to know what was coming next. *Dear God,* he prayed. *Save me from—*

He slapped Ryan across the face. "No praying, Ryan! Pay attention."

Ryan was stunned. "How did—"

"I know everything! There are no secrets. Not from me." He grabbed Ryan by the front of his shirt and pulled him close, Ryan's arms jutting out straight above and behind his body, pulling his arm sockets to excruciating tension.

"*Why?*" Ryan screamed, eyes squeezed shut, unwilling to look at his assailant but desperately needing to know. "*Why me?*"

The reply was deep, guttural, and the voice had grown feral, no longer human. "Because you brought *God* with you!"

But he hadn't brought God! He was angry with God. His relationship with God was complex, confusing. It was complicated, unique...and he suddenly realized what Sheshai meant.

Ryan made the mistake of opening his eyes.

Sheshai's face was inches from his, his red eyes small, angry slits, his serrated teeth exposed in a wicked array that appeared to be a grin but probably wasn't. Ryan was fixated on that mouth, that grin, that non-grin, how it seemed so absurdly big, so deep, fixed with row upon row of teeth of varying sizes and shades of yellow and white, as if this creature had spent eternity just consuming mouths. How was it even able to close its mouth over all those teeth? he wondered absurdly.

The teeth began to chatter and move, but not as a single unit. It was as if each tooth had its own set of rules, each tooth could move freely from the others, each razor-sharp shark tooth could chomp and chew independent of the rest of the mouth. Its jaws unhinged like a fucking anaconda's, and those hundreds of teeth chattered and clattered and moved toward Ryan's face.

"That got your attention?" the monster asked, and Ryan shrieked.

Sheshai moved in and clamped down on Ryan's face, chewing through muscle and dermis and blood vessels, chomping off bits—a blob of lip, a chunk of cheek—until it had secured a decent amount of flesh, and with a strong ripping sensation, tore away half of the lower part of Ryan's face. It chewed on his nose and then his jutting dimpled chin, swallowing it down. It went back in for another bite, chewing away the rest of his cheek and mouth, Ryan's teeth falling out and scattering on the marble floor.

Ryan's screams were quickly choked off by his own blood gushing down his throat.

"*Believer,*" Sheshai said as he spat out the chewed-up flesh that was the man's face. "Despite your protests, despite your arguments to the contrary, you bring God with you wherever you go. Your belief in God will be your undoing. How vile you are!"

Ryan coughed up blood, desperately trying to breathe, his mouth and lungs filled with fluid. He couldn't understand what was happening, why he couldn't move his mouth or tongue, couldn't lick his lips. He tried to speak, but that was fruitless. Gagging and retching produced a spray of blood that coated Sheshai's head.

Sheshai had resumed human form, and bits of flesh and gristle hung from the corners of his mouth, from his clothes, his scalp. He cocked his head and smiled warmly at Ryan, running his fingers through the young man's hair.

"Do you want to live?"

Ryan couldn't understand why he couldn't reply—why his mouth wouldn't form words, why the whisper of air coming from his lungs was the only sound he could produce.

"You don't have much more time. I'm surprised you're not dead."

Dead? But why? Why would he be dead from a few cuts on his legs? He felt faint. So faint...so exhausted...the room was spinning, his vision blurring. He knew he was about to vomit and would probably choke to death if he couldn't free himself, was unable to untie his hands. But rational thought was fleeting, and he was having an impossible time understanding his circumstances.

The creature smiled again, moving in closer. "Do you want to live?"

Ryan could barely move his head but managed to nod.

He touched Ryan's forehead.

Ryan's mind was filled with visions of the attack, of Sheshai tearing off and eating the bottom half of his face. He tried to scream. He tried to die.

"I need people who will follow me, do my bidding. Then you will be allowed to live."

Ryan's eyes widened.

"Are you willing?"

Desperate, terrified, unable to answer. Ryan hung there not knowing what to say, what to do. Now knowing he'd been horribly attacked and was likely about to die.

Ryan slowly nodded.

"First, you need to renounce God and worship me."

Renounce God? Didn't Sheshai tell him in the park that there was no God? Then why was he asking Ryan to renounce him?

Sheshai folded his arms and stared at Ryan. "I know...such a decision! How strong is your faith, your love for God? I'm going to do you a favor now and allow you to live until you make your choice. So you have a few extra minutes."

He smiled at his generosity and flamboyantly threw his hands in the air. "Would God do that for you? When the Angel of Death shows up to steal your goddamned soul, are you allowed time to think about it? I don't think so!"

Ryan nodded. Sheshai was right. So many years devoted to God, and now Ryan felt utterly abandoned. But how could he renounce God? When he died, he would be with God. Assuming Sheshai wasn't lying and there actually was a God. So should he follow this monster, who might be lying, or accept his death and an afterlife with a God who might not exist?

Sheshai said, "Decide."

Ryan shut his eyes and waited for the pain he knew would come with this death. He didn't want to choose, and not choosing was a convoluted choice in itself.

Sheshai, however, wasn't letting him off the hook without a decision. "Pray. Pray to God for help. Tell him to rescue you, and I'll let you go, unharmed. I can do that. I can restore you. But I need a sign right now that God has come to help you!"

Ryan waited for salvation.

Moments passed.

"Choose, Ryan!"

What was that saying? "Better to reign in hell than serve in heaven." Of course, Satan himself had said that...

Ryan waited for the glorious, marvelous, beautiful *deus ex machina*, the hand of God, to rescue him. Kept waiting. Prayed for it. Where was his sign? Where was God? Where the fuck was God!

All that came was Sheshai's hand...a distorted recreation of Michelangelo's *Creation of Adam*...reaching up to free Ryan from his restraints, lowering his body to the floor, Ryan collapsing in a crumpled heap, glancing up at Sheshai, at the hand offering him solace, offering him peace, offering him salvation.

Offering him life.

Ryan reached up, and his fingertips brushed Sheshai's.

MONSTERS OF ANY KIND

ERINN L. KEMPER

CRACKER CREEK

by ERINN L. KEMPER

When he reached the top of the ridge, John Haggert saw why Honey kept balking and gnawing nervously at her bit. The thunderheads he'd glimpsed through the trees weren't storm clouds at all. A wall of smoke rose between him and Cracker Creek.

He'd been riding fast, worried about the imminent rain, practicing things he could say to Luanne, to set things right, not heeding his horse. Honey stopped, refused to go farther.

He heard hoofbeats, then a woman broke free of the tree line, riding up out of the valley, hair and cloak billowing. Her horse stumbled as she lashed it with the reins. She shouted to him. Dried blood streaked her forehead, her eyes wide with fear.

"Fire." She repeated the one word over and over.

Grey-white plumes curtained the valley. The air shifted, a crackling roar rushed toward them on waves of eye-stinging heat. A big fire, eating up the pines on both sides of the valley.

"Any others coming?" he hollered at the woman. "Miss Jones? Luanne? Was she still living in town?"

The woman shook her head, hair falling over her eyes. "Gone. Long gone."

John scanned the forest for signs of others fleeing the fire. There was only this woman, and the fire rushing closer.

As the woman's horse clambered past and down the slope he'd just ridden, John tutted to Honey, who huffed nervously, then turned and started back.

They crossed Rock River, just as treacherous and bone-gnawing cold as a few hours before. John urged Honey forward with promises of oats; his money pouch full from a good season of wrangling. A small silver ring with a pale blue stone the only spending he'd done.

Once safe on the other side, they slowed enough to make introductions. With no towns for miles, they'd have to camp. They rode a few more minutes, to warm and settle the horses.

"This looks far enough to me, Miss Wilson." John pulled gentle on the reins. Honey stopped and swung her head toward a small creek cutting through the pine-crusted ground.

"If you say so." Her voice flat with exhaustion, she slumped from her mount before he could help her down, limped over to a bald-headed tree, sat and hunched against its scabbed trunk.

John was surprised she could walk after the way she'd been bouncing in that saddle. Not a horsewoman, that was for certain.

"You just rest up while I tend to your horse and get us a fire going. Then you can tell me what happened back there."

The woman touched the cut on her forehead with the wet kerchief he gave her, but didn't answer. Her heavy cloak puddled around her. The way her skin showed paste-white and her hands twitched and trembled, getting warm was a real priority.

"You got anything dry to put on?" John didn't like her being so still, with her eyes closed and her lips blue. He built the fire right at her feet, but the blaze would take a while to heat her up. "Miss, you'd better get out of those boots and start warming yourself. I've got some nice stockings, darned the holes out of them just yesterday."

He moved to bring her the socks, maybe help her out of her boots—she opened her eyes. They were dark and blank and for a moment she just stared at the treetops. She shook her head, refusing his help. With the effort of someone who'd earned some real aches in the saddle, she leaned forward and worked her laces. She tugged her feet free and wiggled her water-puckered toes.

"Would you mind?" She handed John her boots and leaned back with her eyes closed as he arranged them for drying.

"The stockings are clean. None too old, either." John held out the balled woolens, then placed them where she could reach. "You really ought to get out of that coat and let yourself dry."

She took a deep breath. The first time he'd seen her breathe since they'd stopped, her being so tight and still. She shuddered as the air left her. "I'll be fine now, thank you, Mister Haggert. I hope you don't mind me with my feet out like this. You built a fine fire."

At least she was alert and talking.

"And the one back there, do you know what happened?"

"It's been a dry few months. It spread out from town. The whole valley lit up so fast."

"The town, then. It started in the town?" John watched her eyes as she stared at her toes. The flames shone through them, lighting the skin in a wax-orange glow.

"Do you have family in Cracker Creek? You asked after Luanne Jones. Is she your kin?"

John hunched his shoulders and kicked an ember back into the fire. "I had some business with Miss Jones. Left a few things at her shop I was hoping to pick up on my way through. Do you know which way she headed?"

She shook her head. "Some people left a few days back. Some a few weeks."

"What caused them to leave? Was the mine closing down?"

The woman bent forward to pull his socks over her feet, then smoothed the wool before she tucked her feet away under her cloak. She gasped once as she settled back against the tree, hand moving to where she hurt, then away when she saw him looking.

"A contagion, I guess you could call it that. The afflicted were all women. Untreatable. Unclear how it transmitted. Those with wives and daughters, they left while they could."

"You're a nurse, Miss Wilson?"

The woman started and glanced at him across the fire, her features tense. "A nurse, no. But close as the town had to one. I worked with the old doctor before he died. We did have a new doctor, but he didn't last too long. We didn't even get a chance to send for a replacement. Not sure a doctor would have been any use."

"So you took care of the sick."

She slumped back against the trunk, her eyes hooded in shadow. "A few. Most stayed home and their families tended to them. They weren't really sick. Just..."

"Afflicted." John finished for her.

The fire cracked, spooking the woman and spitting a plume of sparks up into the dark. She brushed her cloak—it still harbored ash and the stench of burning—and pulled it tight under her chin, glancing warily at the bristling trees and blackness strung between.

"I was there, Cracker Creek, just a few months back. Don't recall seeing any signs of problems. No one sick that I could see. Town looked the same as the last time I passed through," John said.

"You have regular business in Cracker Creek? Funny I haven't seen you before."

She hadn't looked right at him since their paths crossed on the ridge, and she didn't do so now.

"Just a few people I've had dealings with in the past. If they got out, I'd sure like to check in on them."

"I can try to account for some, Mister Haggert, but I don't know where any of them got to after leaving."

She gazed steady at the fire as he listed the names of his acquaintances in town. Nathan Bailey at the stables, old Jim Reed the barkeep and a few of his regulars. Luanne. Miss Wilson flinched.

"I can't say for sure. Sorry. I believe Mister Reed was in his room over the bar. It was early morning when things went bad. Mister Bailey may have been lucky, but that is one of his horses. I found it closed up in the barn at Roy Templeton's place. Luanne, I already told you, has been gone awhile. The others...I can't say."

She had a far-off look and curled and uncurled a fold in her cloak. From that, John knew the truth of it.

"So, where will you be heading tomorrow?" There was more than one question in her asking. "I'd like to get to Baker City, post a few letters, and then on from there."

"I'll gladly take you, but first I want to head back to Cracker Creek. I'll wait out the fire. See if I can find a sign of where some folk may have headed."

"You want to go back? I couldn't possibly. I'm not even sure I can make the trip to Baker City."

"Not to worry, ma'am. I can get you set up here for a nice rest. That fire should burn itself out in no time. It likely won't even come down over that ridge, way the wind is blowing. I'll be out and back in a few hours...by then you should be up for more riding."

John looked up toward the ridge. At full dark now, the distant fire lit the sky a dull, ominous red.

"Why would you want to go there? All you'll see is ash and some poor people gone to cinder. You said you have no family."

"I have my reasons." John reached for his pack and pulled out what food supplies he had. "You'd be surprised the way a fire can move around. The smoke alone would probably leave no one living, but there may be some buildings standing, I can check in on your place, if there's something you'd like me to collect for you."

She went rigid as he spoke, then shook her head. "You can't go there. You can't. The contagion…"

"You said it only afflicted the women. That it wasn't catching."

"At first, yes. But in the end, well, it changed."

"Surely the fire will have taken care of all that."

"I pray you're right, Mister Haggert." Her gaze moved back to the trees, to the track they'd rode that led back to Cracker Creek. "It better have."

"You don't think the fire was an accident, then."

"What happened there in Cracker Creek, Mister Haggert. It had to be stopped."

─────

Ann Wilson rolled onto her side, facing away from the campfire. She studied the wall of darkness that surrounded their site. The shadows leaned this way and that, waiting for the flames to die so they could lunge forward and take her.

Mister Haggert had exhausted his questions, for now. But there were more that preyed on her mind. Had the fire done its work? Was she safe now? Would this man be able to do what must be done?

The cloud of smoke that hung over the valley had deepened from red to a wash of burgundy, like the dregs of a bottle of wine. Or blood. Almost out, choked on itself, Mister Haggert told her. So he'd be going to town in the morning. She couldn't warn him off.

Despite her fear, she fell into the numbing arms of sleep, and there memory waited. The doctor. The women. Cracker Creek. Where she'd sought refuge from her shame. Where she'd retreated in despair, betrayal. The home she now fled in terror.

─────

"Come in."

The doctor sat, chair turned to the window, the sun blanking out his features so all Ann could see was the impression of eyes, a dark slit of a mouth. A wild shock of black hair blew around his head and brushed his shoulders. He turned toward her and his face disappeared completely in shadow.

"Yes, Miss Wilson."

She pushed the door the rest of the way open and stepped in. "There's another one. Same symptoms."

Three in three days. They came to see the doctor, complaining of vomiting, fatigue. They wore dark circles under their eyes, and faint, satisfied smiles as they brushed past Ann, moving to the narrow table in the middle of the room and arranging themselves for examination.

The doctor nodded. "Send her in."

"Doctor, thank you for seeing me." Stella Winters stepped around Ann toward the patient's table, her voice husky and warm, her thick blonde hair hanging loose down her back.

Ann smoothed her bun and adjusted the pin. "If you need anything." She closed the door softly behind.

That was how it started. With the new doctor's arrival. He'd come in with a cartload of supplies, happy to be "away from the hubbub, where a man could enjoy the quiet, get some peace, start fresh."

He'd unpacked, hung his sign, and the patients came. Then the pregnancies.

Luanne Jones had been first to show pregnant. She didn't name the father. But the town knew about her man, the cowboy. He stayed a few days, and each time he left, Luanne grieved a day or two, then she put a bright smile back on for her customers at the feed shop. The single men in town never stopped going in, just to say hello, check on the new shipment of boots, ever hopeful despite the glares that drifter of hers threw them when he passed through. She was that kind of woman. And with child, even more so. They all were.

Ann watched them from the clinic door. They were just like that woman her Tom had taken up with. Burgeoning, full of secret glances, each to the other, wearing their hair loose, walking sway-backed and proud. They even smelled the same—of apples and sunshine on new grass. Fertile, ripe, unlike Ann, whose womb filled only with longing.

When the fourth woman, this one unmarried, showed pregnant, the town started talking.

At first they laughed about it and wondered how it could be, so many at the same time. They sure were lucky that doctor had shown up when he did. These babies were coming, quicker than you'd expect, and they'd be needing help, what with the women getting so big so quick. Big babies can be trouble for their mothers to birth; but a big baby might have a better chance once it's popped out, red-faced and squalling.

It wasn't long before the joking turned to dark speculation.

Jenna Stevens had been the first daughter to show. Only thirteen and no man sniffing round her. Her father and brothers were sure on that. When rumor passed that maybe the baby's seed came from closer to home, the Stevens men turned their accusations to the clinic and the new doctor. Jenna had been to see him for an aching tooth and two months later her belly started filling.

Now they had six women swaying through the streets, getting bigger and bigger, swapping dresses, walking arm in arm, laughing low, heads bowed to the other in quiet commiseration.

In the saloon the men talked as well, over beer and more whiskey. They compared stories and shook their heads in disbelief, but finally they agreed.

And that led to the cloudy Saturday when the lynching party stormed the clinic.

"Send out the doctor, Annie."

Ann looked up from where she'd been sweeping the grunge from the corners of the door frame. They were all present. Husbands, fathers, brothers, sweethearts. Two for every woman pregnant in the town. Armbed with shotguns and pistols.

Ann stood in the doorway, legs wide, fists on hips, barring their passage with her angriest glare.

"We'll have to move you, then, Annie. If you won't move yourself."

Jake and Wendell Stevens handed off their guns, paced to the doorway and hoisted her by her waist and elbows.

She screamed back through the doorway, "Doctor. They've come for you."

Four went in, guns cocked and ready. Thumps and shouts ended in one shot and the shattering of glass. Five came out, the townsmen with the doctor struggling between them.

The doctor was in his undershirt and trousers. They'd caught him at his ablutions. The tendons in his long arms and bare feet strained with effort as he struggled to free himself. They carried him, arm and foot, and he writhed and bucked so they dropped him a few times. The third time he went down, Wendell Stevens gave him a good kick to the head, and he flopped unconscious the rest of the way to the oak tree. The hanging tree.

The men went about their business quick. No need for their women to get involved. Their wives and daughters who had each gone to see the doctor…for a stitching, a woman's concern, a woods rash, poor vision. And within a month of their visit the symptoms had come.

But they weren't quick enough.

They tied the rope and then looped it about his head. Donald Jeffers thought to fasten the doctor at the wrists, so he pulled his own belt and secured those soft, long-fingered hands behind the doctor's back lest he try to hold on when the rope went tight.

As they threw the rope over the thickest branch, the wailing started. Shrill, piercing. Sending crows and pigeons winging, all the town dogs howled their reply. From houses, shops, church and school the women came, their bellies distended, their hair falling down to their waists, mouths open, eyes rolled back as they wailed. Without thinking, some of the young men, those not busy with the tying and heaving, turned, guns up, ready.

"No! That's your sister, boy." Jake Stevens knocked his son's barrel to point down at the road. "Let's finish this before them girls cause trouble."

The women didn't move any closer. They stood hand in hand like some demonic choir, their voices joined in an endless shriek.

A sob rose in Ann's throat as the men hauled on the rope, and as the noose tightened, the doctor woke. He struggled fiercely, legs kicking, swinging to and fro. It didn't last long. By the time the rope was secured to the trunk and the men had stepped back, rifles again clutched and ready, the doctor's bare feet twitched, then were still.

The wailing stopped. It took some minutes for the dogs to quiet, but when they did, Wendell Stevens moved to help his sister, who had fallen to her knees, clutching her middle and shuddering with pain or with grief. He placed his hand on her back, then pulled it back quick, as though his skin burned. Slowly she raised her head and looked at him.

"It's coming," she said through clenched teeth. *She gasped and fell forward into her brother's arms.*

John drew Honey to a stop when he reached town. From what he could see, the buildings still stood. Their facades cast ragged shadows in the pale sunlight. The fire had chosen the easy path, racing up through the desiccated pines, then smothered itself during the night. Smoke still rose from near the ridge, but the valley was long done burning.

He had ridden in along the creek that flowed through town, its water low and black. Drifts of ash had settled down over the valley. As Honey walked through, she kicked grey flurries to swirl around her legs. There was a muffled silence, like a breath held, suspended, waiting.

John wondered which of the rough-planked houses was Miss Wilson's. He'd been reluctant to wake her, the shock and the hard ride had clearly worn on her. She'd slept so poorly, moaning and crying out in her sleep. He prepared food without banging pots, using a lid to mute the pop and sizzle like he had done as a boy while his father slept one off in the next room and his mother tended to her bruises.

Miss Wilson had slept on. Her dark hair splayed out over the ground, leaves and pine needles decorating its tangles.

Honey huffed, and stopped short in the middle of Main Street, in front of a low, ash-covered mound. The creaking saddle and Honey's stamping hooves echoed hollow along the storefronts. John dismounted and swept the debris away with his boot. A man lay facedown on the road. John pushed with his heel until the body flopped over. The face was a ruin. Clawed, chewed at. Hands too. Chunks of flesh torn back to the bone. John scanned the street. A wild animal? Most would have fled when the fire started. John released the strap on his holster.

He led Honey through town. His footsteps fell in dull beats on the tack shop's planked porch. The door hung open. Inside all was still. Leather straps coiled on hooks, hats and boots in neat stacks and rows. He opened his mouth to call, but coughed instead.

Upstairs, grey light filtered through the ash-coated windows, falling on Luanne's tightly drawn quilt. John could picture her there, smiling up at him, her curls caught in the morning light, her smile slow and wicked as she teased him back into bed.

He looked for a letter, some sign of where Luanne had gotten to. When he opened her closet, he found all her clothes still in place. Nothing missing. His heart raced with wondering.

He went to the mirror above Luanne's dressing table. In the picture leaning against the glass she stood with her father in front of the five hundred head of cattle they used to run down in California, before they lost everything and came to this mining town. He pocketed the picture, and then the finely knit baby boots that hung from a peg on the wall above. Blue, like his Luanne's eyes.

Other bodies littered the town, all clawed at and chewed on. He stopped examining after the fourth in the same condition. A furrow in the ash led under the post office—a scavenger hiding away with its meal.

He called up to the balconies of the Raymond Hotel, to the saloon where he stopped to help himself to a bottle. As the batwing doors slapped shut behind him, he looked to the church and the end of the road. The only building that stood apart on Main Street. The only building that had burnt.

John climbed the stone steps and touched the crisp, scaling timbers that held the door. They were cool. This building had burnt some time ago. Up close he could see that the thick oak door had been nailed shut. The windows, too, had been boarded. But some boards had burnt and fallen away. John went to one of these windows and peered through. His gut clenched.

Late-morning haze fell through the damaged roof onto the church floor. Centered in this ring of light, bodies huddled together, facedown.

John eased through the window and stepped, timber to timber, over to the gruesome arrangement. They were women. He could tell by their size and what remained of their shoes. Some full mature, some smaller, maybe girls. They hadn't tried to escape, or they'd given up and come together here to die, arms tucked under, as though shielding something. He crouched next to them.

A locket dangled from one corpse's neck. He lifted it gently and polished it with his thumb. Then he studied what remained of her—bones, charred flesh, scraps of riding boots. Luanne wore men's boots and rode like a proper cowboy, always racing ahead of him. John lay the locket back down on Luanne's blackened breast. It was a memento of her dead mother that her father had given her—along with the tack shop—in the rancher's final will.

From his pocket he pulled the ring with the pale blue stone. He pressed it to his lips, then placed it next to the locket, afraid to touch her lest he shatter her bones. In a voice thick with unshed tears, he whispered a prayer and a farewell.

John strode from the building, taking no heed of the floor now, swung up on Honey's back and turned back to his camp by the river where Miss Ann Wilson waited.

The sun streamed bright through the dark lace of pine branches when Ann sat up, gasping. The weight of yesterday drove the breath from her.

The day poor Jenna Stevens had her baby, the real nightmare began, though the townsfolk were slow to realize it. They thought with the doctor dead, and buried that same hour, things would settle. The babies would stir things, maybe end a few marriages, but then life would return to normal.

Ann attended the first birth. She brought the black bag from the doctor's office, pausing to study the pictures that decorated his walls. Previously Ann had thought them pictures of his patients, each one of a pregnant woman, sometimes alone, sometimes with the doctor standing next to her. Now she wondered.

The delivery was normal. Wendell Stevens came in and fussed over his sister when it was over. The baby was a boy, good healthy size, born with its eyes open. He didn't even cry.

Ann cleaned the baby, enjoying the soft give of new flesh, the warm milky smell he had, even in his first moments. She laughed when the baby sighed and looked up at her with big eyes and an old-man scowl, then burped. Her laughter faded to uneasiness when the baby's scowl deepened and he looked at his hand, then at hers and cocked his head. The baby grabbed her wrist and pulled her fingers into his mouth. She expected him to suckle. The chomp he delivered hurt to high hell, and she shouted and pulled back to shake her hand free. The babe had risen to his feet, and once Ann had her hand tucked safely away, he sank down to sit on his pudgy little rump. That's when he opened his mouth and cried, a shrill keening that hurt Ann's ears.

Before Ann could say anything to Wendell Stevens—wonder about the strangeness of the babe—the women came in, pushing her aside. On her own, Jenna had been terrified, of what had happened to her, of her strange new spawn. She hadn't stopped crying, begging for forgiveness from God and from her father.

But when the women arrived, she calmed, the house full of their warm-apple fragrance, their congratulations and coos of delight. Jenna beamed with pride at her precious infant. The women took her and the babe with them when the left. The Stevens men said their farmhouse bore the sweet scent of their visit for weeks.

That was the last time anyone saw one of the babies. During the day, at least.

Back at the clinic Ann poured antiseptic on her bloody fingers. She couldn't shake the notion that when the babe had started its yowling, she had seen small points of teeth already rising through those pink gums.

More townsfolk left the next day.

The women took over the church and the screams of their birthing could be heard from both ends of Main Street. Their men stayed behind, as did Ann and a few others. People whispered about these strange babies. Livestock chewed to pieces. Strange scrabblings at the door, on the shutters. Pale critters crawling fast into the trees in the grey morning light. Over the week, the town near emptied.

All the babies had been born by then, and the women came out of the church for meat and blankets and cleaning supplies. They smiled at their husbands and fathers, brothers and sons, but the men didn't smile back. Wendell and Jack Stevens stared in horror at their sweet Jenna, who cradled her stomach, already huge and dropping under the weight of another child.

More whisperings among the townsfolk who remained. Perhaps the women had dug up their doctor and kept his rotted corpse arranged on the altar. Used it in some terrible ritual, milking his moldering seed over and over. None were willing to confirm this rumor. What if they dug up the grave and his corpse was there, biding until that moment to open those strange dark eyes? What if his corpse wasn't there? What then?

Ann shuddered. She didn't want to dwell on the women, on their pregnancies, on what the townsfolk had decided to do. The hollow thud when the men had nailed the church door shut, boarded the windows, threatened to shoot any who tried to climb in or out. The stench of kerosene, the muted screams from inside the churches stone walls. The shrieks. The silence.

She pressed her hands to her face, pushing back the memory, but still it came...

In her bed that horrible morning, head clenched between her pillows, she tried to block out the sounds. A bad dream. It wasn't happening, she told herself again and again, just like the nightmare she'd had the night before.

She'd dreamt of the women and their fiendish offspring. They'd come to her room. Skirts rustling. Fat knees slipping wetly across the floor. They made soothing sounds and smiled, teeth glinting in the moonlight that shone through her window. The little ones climbed up onto her bed, naked, glowing pale. As fear consumed her, or she fell deeper to sleep. Ann had felt the covers slide from her terror-frozen body, then darkness. A dream.

She couldn't tell Mister Haggert. He wouldn't understand.

Ann pulled herself up from the ground by the dwindling fire to ready herself for her journey onward, to Baker City, where she know of a doctor who could put an end to it. Before she could take a step toward her horse, a pain shot through her, driving her back down. The spasm subsided, and Ann felt the warm dampness. *No. It was just a dream.*

———————

John Haggert urged Honey on, away from Cracker Creek, skirting the ridge, through forest blurred by coming night.

Something awful had happened in that town. More than just a sickness, or affliction as Ann Wilson had said. First they had burned the church with the afflicted inside. Then someone had tried to set fire to the town. John found a ring of black earth, littered with cans of kerosene, that ran right around the town. There had likely been a wreath of dry kindling with the fluid poured over. A desperate move, and John wondered now—had Miss Wilson thrown the match? Was she the only one who made it out?

As he'd ridden out of town, he was sure he heard a scuff from a burnt-out barn outside of town. Saw a small feral shadow slip under the floor. When he looked under the barn, there was only darkness.

John wished he could go back to the last time he and Luanne were together. When she asked him if he'd ever stay. He couldn't take back what he'd said.

"You want me to marry you? Then what? Start a family? How long

before the poison seeps in, from my father and yours? Then on to our children. Family is a prison, Luanne. You always said. We're lucky we escaped."

Her blue eyes had gone blank. She sat stiff in her bed with the covers pulled over while he tugged on his boots and strapped on his holster.

"I'll be leaving here, John. To a city where I can start fresh. This town feels tight on me. Too many people in your business."

"Well, that's for you to choose. I wouldn't take to city life. You'll leave word where you're off to?"

She nodded and looked away. Refusing to watch as he walked out the door. And what if he had stayed, would it have changed anything, or would he have perished with the rest?

He was near the campsite now, the flames of the campfire wavered through the trees ahead. And then he heard a scream, long and low, like someone in pain. He drove his knees into Honey's side, pressing her to go as fast as the terrain would allow.

In the clearing he found Ann Wilson on all fours, moaning. She looked up when he crashed through the brush line, her face red and sweat-streaked.

"What happened?" John slid from his horse and rushed to her side.

She spoke through her teeth, grunting with pain. "Sorry, Mister Haggert. You're going to have to finish it." Another spasm took her, the tendons in her neck taut like rope.

With her cloak off, he could see the shape of her for the first time. She wore a plain grey dress, the weight of her condition showed clearly through. Her taught belly strained against the fabric.

"You should have mentioned you were with child, woman. I wouldn't have left if I'd known."

"Soon enough you'll wish you'd left and not come back." Miss Wilson lowered herself to the ground and lay on her back, propped against the tree trunk.

"I've seen babies born before, Miss Wilson. I know what to do." John folded her cloak and helped her lay back. "How long have you been contracting?"

"Not long, but it'll come fast now. Too fast." Her skin shone in the firelight.

"You can't be sure about these things. I once birthed a calf that was two days in coming."

"This certainly won't be a calf, sir."

"I guess not. But a baby comes out much the same way."

She laughed when he said that. "A baby. We thought that's all they were, too. If you're staying, you ought to know. Then you can decide what's best to do."

John nodded as he cleaned his blade over the fire, then set it by to cool. "I'm guessing this has something to do with this affliction and the fires that were set in town."

Ann Wilson closed her eyes and clasped her belly with both hands. "The new doctor. It started there. But we didn't know. He was a good man...seemed like a good man. But then the women, his patients, they got pregnant..."

Every few minutes the contractions came, and she screamed and clamped down on the stick John put between her teeth. When she'd settled again, she continued her tale.

She told him how nobody saw the babies, they stayed with their mothers, hidden. How things got chewed up in the night, animals found dead and gnawed to the bone, even Ned Tother's fence looked like it'd been set on by a pack of woodchucks.

"There were only a few of us left. When those women came up pregnant again, no father to answer for it with the doctor being dead. Well, something unholy was going on. And some of the men took action."

"They burned down the church with those women in it? Alive? My god." John wiped his forehead and stared at the campfire, the flames white at the heart of it. "I saw them, Mister Haggert. Luanne was there with the others."

"Not just the women. Those babies too." She spoke so quiet he had to move closer to hear. "But not before they got that little boy. Danny Campbell. Chewed him till there wasn't much left for his father to find. That's when they burned the church..."

Ann Wilson's hands clawed at the earth and her back arched with the pain of the next convulsion. She spoke a prayer between the gasps and moans. Sweat ran down her neck, darkened the fabric of her dress, and in the firelight her eyes looked black and hollow as a mine shaft.

"But it didn't stop, Mister Haggert. The things, they still came at night. Some saw them, fat, ghost-like, crawling or pattering on bare feet, dark eyes, needle-sharp teeth. They made sounds. Screeches. Calling to each other. You could smell them, all singed skin and scalded milk. And they chewed what they could find. So we burned the town."

"Where are the rest of them. The men?"

"We thought it was safe, during the day. Those things would be sleeping. But they knew, somehow. They came out, almost slithering...so fast...squinting in the light. They killed..." She told the rest in a choked whisper.

They killed the men who'd hung their father, burnt their mothers, and who'd tried to kill them. They came crawling from the dark spaces under the houses and shops on Main Street, some clothed in the burnt tatters of nightdresses, most naked, flesh maggot pale, streaked black with soot. The men hollered to each other and stood their ground. Ann lit the fire.

Through the wall of flames she watched as the men fought, with their guns, their knives, their fists and feet. The monsters were fast and vicious and their teeth sharp. One by one the men fell, and once down, the babies clung to them and fed.

Ann was glad for the crack and roar of the flames. She didn't want to hear the wet gnawing sounds, the snap of bone. The babies wriggled and shuddered, faces buried in flesh. One sat back on his dimpled rump and turned his head almost right around, to where Ann stood. He looked at her, tilted his head, then opened his mouth and shoved Jack Stevens's hand right in. Sour bile washed through Ann's mouth at the sight of the finger joints flexing backwards, then breaking between those pointed teeth.

She ran. To the barn where they'd left their horses tethered. The horses were panicked by the time she got there. They could smell the fire. She hoped that was all they could smell. She left the doors open, but couldn't risk the time untying them all. And she rode up, away from the flames and those things trapped in the smoking furnace.

"That's..." John shook his head as he wiped the sweat from Ann Wilson's forehead with his wet kerchief. "And Luanne. You say she birthed one of these things? This doctor, he did something to her?"

Miss Wilson nodded. "I don't know what. She came in to see him, and the next time I saw her she was already growing."

John pictured Luanne, the morning he'd left, draped in her sheet, sunlight in buttery pools on her skin, a question in her eyes, a hand straying to her stomach. "What did she go to see the doctor about?"

"I...shouldn't." She looked away, took a deep breath. "She'd had some blood, some pain. There'd been a baby, but she lost it, early on. The doctor gave her something for the pain and something to lift her spirits."

"A baby. A normal one. Not one of these monsters you say the others had." John's throat closed in on a hard lump of sadness. He started to ask more, if she'd buried the infant, given it a name. This child he had both run from and wanted more than anything. But Miss Wilson screamed again, an anguished cry that pierced the dark.

"Oh god. It's coming…" She groaned and all her muscles strained, she beat the ground with her fists.

"I'm going to make sure it's not twisted around."

He lifted her skirt and looked where the babe would come. Blood seeped out, and there, tiny, bone-white fingers hooked around flesh, gripping, pulling. A dome of veined skin appeared, coming fast, tearing to make way. Its hands wriggled free, groping for purchase, and the head rotated so now John could see a face in the russet flames of the campfire, eyes closed, features tensed in a grimace of concentration.

"Holy hell." When John spoke, the creature opened its eyes, snaked its head side to side, working its way out, clawing free of its host.

John reached for his knife where it lay by the fire, his gaze never leaving the baby, now free to its shoulders, dripping blood and clumps of white matter on the ground. It tracked the movement of the knife, eyes insect-quick, and opened its mouth. The sound that emerged pierced the air, a shrill cry that pained John's ears.

"No." Ann Wilson's tone changed, she reached out, pleaded. "No. My baby. Please…"

He lifted the weapon, holding firm to the handle, blade turned down. John tensed his muscles to drive the knife into that wax-white scalp.

Again the baby shrieked, a loud keening that dissolved into a series of sharp yips. From the darkness of the forest that surrounded them, its cry was answered. Squeals and yips came from every direction, followed by a slithering rustle through the dry blanket of pine needles.

John turned away from the babe for a moment as it struggled against constricting flesh. From the woods small figures appeared, tottering, crawling, slipping forward on soot-blackened elbows. They stopped once they'd breached the clearing. He scanned their faces, fat-cheeked and snarling. One had a familiar set to the chin, a certain slant to its eyes—eyes John knew would be blue.

Ann Wilson screamed, then fell silent. He turned back to her and her babe.

The creature, freed now, looked from the blade to John. An awful smile stretched its soft features. John's spine iced with terror and the knife fell from numbed fingers.

The baby came at him, scuttling with incredible speed, still tethered to its mother by the long grey cord.

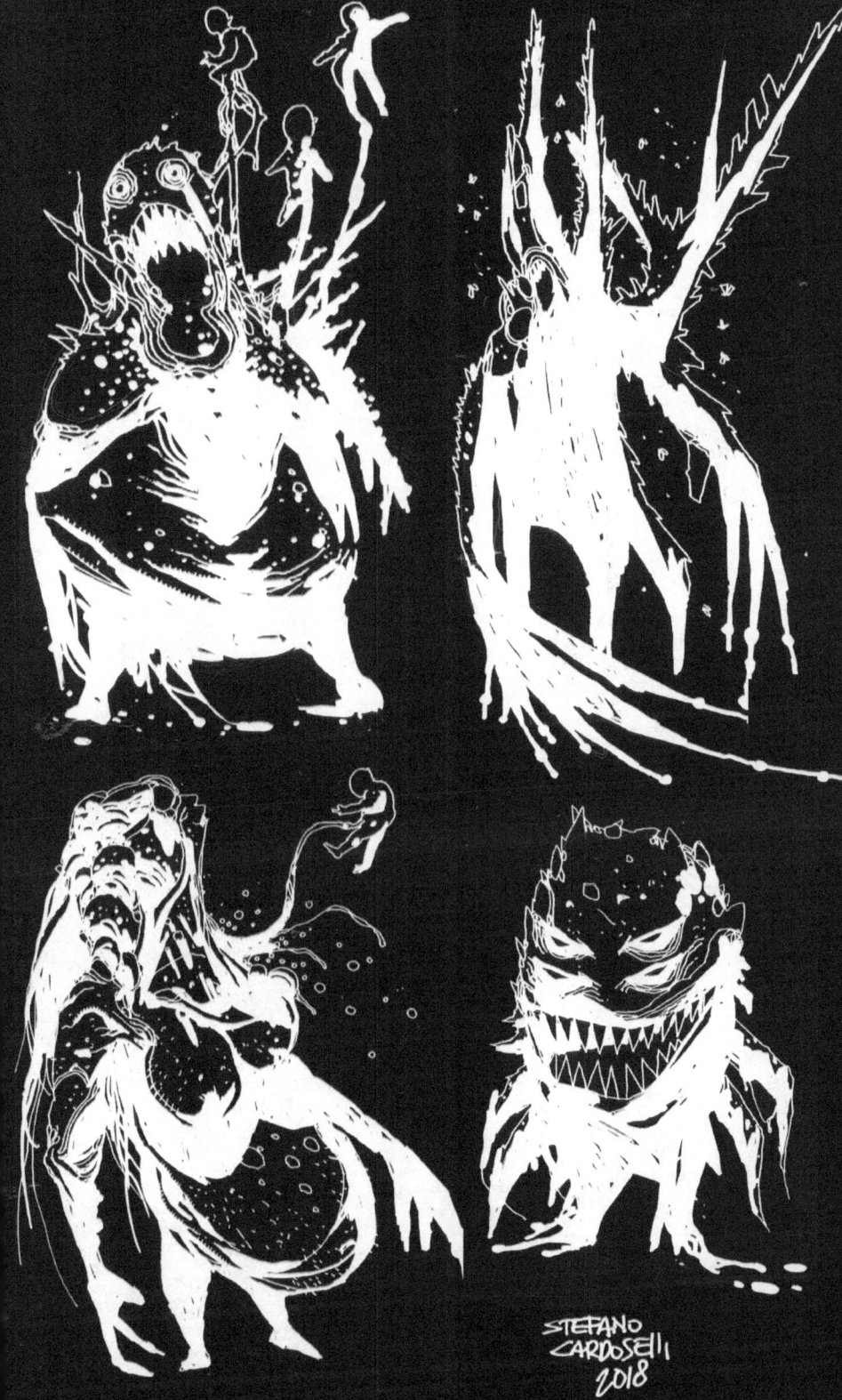

MONSTERS OF ANY KIND

ABOUT THE AUTHORS

ABOUT THE AUTHORS

MICHAEL BAILEY is a multi-award-winning writer, editor, and book designer, and the recipient of over two dozen literary accolades, including the Bram Stoker Award, Benjamin Franklin Award, Eric Hoffer Book Award, International Book Award, and Independent Publisher Book Award. His nonlinear novels include *Palindrome Hannah*, *Phoenix Rose*, and *Psychotropic Dragon*, and he has published two short story and poetry collections, *Scales and Petals* and *Inkblots and Blood Spots*, as well as *Enso*, a children's book. He has created anthologies such as *Qualia Nous*, *The Library of the Dead*, four volumes of *Chiral Mad*, *You Human*, and a series of illustrated books.

MICHAEL G. BAUGHAN Author of fiction and nonfiction, his stories have appeared in anthologies and magazines, including Chuck Scalin's *Body of Evidence*, *No Rest for the Wicked*, *Richmond Macabre Volume II*, *Remapping Richmond's Hallowed Ground*, *Surreal South '13*, *Hypnos* magazine, *Pseudopod*, *The Audient Void*. *www.michaelgraybaughan.com*

BRUCE BOSTON is the author of more than fifty books and chapbooks, including the dystopian sci-fi novel *The Guardener's Tale* and the psychedelic coming-of-age novel *Stained Glass Rain*. His poems and stories have appeared in hundreds of publications, most visibly in *Amazing Stories*, *Analog*, *Asimov's SF*, *Daily Science Fiction*, *Strange Horizons*, *Realms of Fantasy*, *Weird Tales*, the *Nebula Awards Anthology*, and *The Year's Best Fantasy and Horror*. His poetry has received the Bram Stoker Award, the *Asimov's* Readers' Award, the Gothic Readers Choice Award, and the Rhysling and Grandmaster Awards of the SFPA. His fiction has received a Pushcart Prize and twice been a finalist for the Bram Stoker Award (novel, short story). *www.bruceboston.com*

RAMSEY CAMPBELL – *The Oxford Companion to English Literature* describes Ramsey Campbell as "Britain's most respected living horror writer." He has been given more awards than any other writer in the field, including the Grand Master Award of the World Horror Convention, the Lifetime Achievement Award of the Horror Writers Association, the Living Legend Award of the International Horror Guild, and the World Fantasy Lifetime

Achievement Award. In 2015 he was made an Honorary Fellow of Liverpool John Moores University for outstanding services to literature.

SANTIAGO EXIMENO (Madrid, 1973) has published several novels and collections in Spanish, among them: *Condenados, Asura, Bebés jugando con cuchillos, Umbría, Obituario Privado*, and many stories in anthologies and magazines. His works have been translated into several languages and won various awards, including, four times, the Premio Ignotus of Asociación Española de Fantasía, Ciencia Ficción y Terror. *www.eximeno.com*

OWL GOINGBACK has written numerous novels, children's books, short stories, and articles. He has also ghostwritten novels for celebrities. His novel *Crota* won the 1996 Bram Stoker Award for Best First Novel, and he was nominated for his novel *Darker Than Night* (1999). Owl's novel *Shaman Moon* was published as part of the omnibus edition *The Essential World of Darkness*. His books often draw on his Native American heritage to tell stories of supernatural suspense. His children's books *Eagle Feathers* and *The Gift* have received critical acclaim, and he was the recipient of the Storytelling World Awards Honor. His shorter works of fiction have appeared in numerous anthologies, and his story *Grass Dancer* was a Nebula Award Nominee. Among his other works: the collection *Tribal Screams* and the novel *Breed*. His new novel, *Coyote Rage*, will be released in 2019. *www.owlgoingback.com*

CODY GOODFELLOW has written five novels, and he co-wrote three more with *New York Times* bestselling author John Skipp. His first two collections, *Silent Weapons for Quiet Wars* and *All-Monster Action*, each received the Wonderland Book Award. He wrote, co-produced and scored the short Lovecraftian hygiene film *Stay At Home Dad*, which can be viewed on YouTube. He is also a director of the H.P. Lovecraft Film Festival–San Pedro, and co-founder of Perilous Press, an occasional micropublisher of modern cosmic horror. His new story collection, *The Man who Escaped this Story*, is coming from Independent Legions in 2019.

ERINN KEMPER has short stories appearing in several magazines and anthologies: *The Cost of Moving the Dead* (in the anthology *Zombies: Shambling Through the Ages*), *Given to the Sea* (in the anthology *Handsome Devil*), *The Claim* (in *A Darke Phantastique*), which made the long list of recommended reads in Ellen Datlow's *Best Horror of the Year*, *Versions* (in the anthology *Chiral Mad 2*), *Night Guard* (in the anthology *Qualia Nous*), *Symbiosis* (in *Dark Discoveries* #30), *Phantom on the Ice* (in the anthology *The Library of the Dead*), *A Flash of Red* (in the anthology *Chiral Mad 3*), *Gramma Tells a Story* (in *Black Static #*49). *www.erinnkemper.com*

JESS LANDRY Author and editor, her stories have appeared in several anthologies, including *Where Nightmares Come From*, *The Anatomy of Monsters*, *Killing It Softly*, *Primogen: The Origin of Monsters*, *Ill-Considered Expeditions*, and *Alligators in the Sewers*, as well as online with SpeckLit, The Sirens Call and EGM Shorts. She has been working for JournalStone Publishing for several years as an Assistant Publisher, and she also runs JournalStone's newest imprint, Trepidatio Publishing. She currently resides in the icy wastelands of Winnipeg, Manitoba. *www.jesslandry.com*

JONATHAN MABERRY is a *New York Times* bestselling suspense novelist, five-time Bram Stoker Award winner, winner of the Scribe and Inkpot Awards, and comic book writer. His vampire apocalypse book series, *V-WARS*, is being produced as a Netflix original series, and will debut in early 2019. His other works include the Joe Ledger thrillers, *Glimpse*, the *Rot & Ruin* series, the *Dead of Night* series, *The Wolfman*, *X-Files Origins: Devil's Advocate*, and many others. His YA space-travel novel, *Mars One*, is in development for film; and his novel *Glimpse* is being developed for TV, as is his bestselling Joe Ledger thriller series. He is the editor of many anthologies, including the *X-Files*, *Aliens: Bug Hunt*, *Nights of the Living Dead* (co-edited with zombie genre creator George A. Romero). His comics include *Captain America*, the Bram Stoker Award–winning *Bad Blood*, *Black Panther*, *Punisher*, *Marvel Zombies Return*, and more. His *Rot & Ruin* novels were included in the Ten Best Horror Novels for Young Adults. His first novel, *Ghost Road Blues*, was named one of the 25 Best Horror Novels of the New Millennium. He was a featured expert on the History Channel's *Zombies: A Living History* and *True Monsters*. His books have been sold to more than two dozen countries. Jonathan lives in Del Mar, California, with his wife, Sara Jo. *http://www.jonathanmaberry.com*

MARK ALAN MILLER has been working as a writer since 2005 when he started as a columnist for *OCWeekly*, which landed him the position of assistant editor on the novel *Abarat: Absolute Midnight* by Clive Barker, and subsequently for the same author he edited the *New York Times* bestselling book *The Scarlet Gospels*. In 2009, he began shepherding the release of the director's cut of the '90s cult horror film *Nightbreed*. After six years of Miller's campaigning, tracking down the footage, and assembling a film closer to the director's original vision, he produced a

120-minute director's cut, which was released on Blu-ray by Scream Factory. The film has since won best vintage release at the 41st annual Saturn Awards. In 2018, he oversaw the Blu-ray release of an extended 140-minute version called *Nightbreed: The Cabal Cut*. His comic writing can be seen in the bestselling Boom! Studios comic books *Hellraiser, Hellraiser: Bestiary*, and the critically acclaimed *Next Testament*, as well as Seraphim Comics' *Hellraiser: Anthology Vols. 1 & 2*, and *The Steam Man of the Prairie* and the *Dark Rider Get Down* released by Dark Horse from a story by Joe R. Lansdale. He has released two books, *Next Testament* and *Hellraiser: The Toll*. *www.markalanmiller.com*

GREGORY L. NORRIS is a full-time professional writer, with work appearing in numerous short-story anthologies, national magazines, novels, the occasional TV episode, and, so far, one produced feature film (*Brutal Colors*, which debuted on Amazon Prime in January 2016). A former feature writer and columnist at *Sci Fi*, the official magazine of the Sci Fi Channel, he once worked as a screenwriter on two episodes of Paramount's modern classic *Star Trek: Voyager*. Two of his paranormal novels (written under his nom de plume, Jo Atkinson) were published by Home Shopping Network as part of their *Escape with Romance* line. He judged the 2012 Lambda Awards in the SF/F/H category. Three times now, his stories have notched honorable mentions in Ellen Datlow's *Best-of* books. In May 2016, he traveled to Hollywood to accept HM in the Roswell Awards in Short SF Writing. *www.gregorylnorris.blogspot.com*

EDWARD LEE (pseudonym of Lee Seymour) is an American author of almost 50 novels and numerous short stories and novellas. He twice won the Splatterpunk Award for his novel *White Trash Gothic* and the novella *Header 3*, and he is a Bram Stoker Award nominee for his story *Mr. Torso*. His short stories have appeared in over a dozen mass-market anthologies. Among his novels: *Ghouls, Coven, Incubi, Succubi, The Chosen, Creekers, Header, The Bighead, Masks, Operator B, City Infernal, The Baby, Messenger, The Backwoods, Flesh Gothic, Slither, House Infernal, Brides of the Impaler, Gomelesque, You Are My Everything, The Innswich Horror, Lucifer's Lottery, Witch Water, White Trash Gothic*; and the collections: *The Ushers, Sleep Disorder* (with Jack Ketchum), *Haunted House, Brain Cheese Buffet, Bullet Through Your Face, Carnal Surgery, Mangled Meat*. *www.edwardleeonline.com*

MONICA O'ROURKE has published more than a hundred short stories in magazines such as *Postscripts, Nasty Piece of Work, Fangoria, Flesh & Blood, Nemonymous*, and *Brutarian*; and anthologies such as *Horror for*

Good, *The Mammoth Book of the Kama Sutra*, and *The Best of Horrorfind*. She is the author of *Poisoning Eros I* and *II*, written with Wrath James White, *Suffer the Flesh*, and the collection *In the End, Only Darkness*. Her latest novel, *What Happens in the Darkness*, is available from Sinister Grin Press. She works as a freelance editor, writer, and book coach. She lives in Saratoga Springs.

GREG SISCO was born in Los Angeles, California, in 1988. An independent filmmaker since his late teens and a novelist since his early twenties, he writes darkly comedic fiction mostly within the horror and thriller genres. Among his novels: *Thicker Than Water*, *The Wages of Sin*, *One-Night Stan's*, *In Nightmares We're Alone*, and *Gunslinger, P.I. www.gregsisco.com*

LUCY TAYLOR is the award-winning author of seven novels, five collections, and over a hundred short stories. Most recently, her work has appeared in her collections *Fatal Journeys* and *Spree and Other Stories*, and in the anthologies *Fright Mare* ("Dead Messengers"), *Into Painfreak* ("He Who Whispers the Dead Back to Life"), *Peel Back the Skin* ("Moth Frenzy"), at Tor.com ("Sweetlings"), *The Five Senses of Horror* ("In the Cave of the Delicate Singers") and *CEA Greatest Anthology Written* ("Fecundity"). Several of her stories can also be found on the short-fiction app Great Jones Street. A new edition of her Stoker-winning novel *The Safety of Unknown Cities*, illustrated by Glen Chadbourne and published by The Overlook Connection Press, will be out this year. Taylor lives in the high desert outside Santa Fe, New Mexico. *www.darkfantasy.us*

DAVID J. SCHOW is a multiple-award-winning writer who lives in Los Angeles. The latest of his nine novels is a hardboiled extravaganza called *The Big Crush*. The newest of his ten short-story collections is titled *DJStories*. He has written extensively for film (*The Crow*, *Leatherface: Texas Chainsaw Massacre III*, *The Hills Run Red*) and television (*Masters of Horror*, *Mob City*). One of *Fangoria* magazine's most popular columnists, he is also the author of *The Outer Limits Companion* (revised third edition) and *The Outer Limits at 50*. As editor he has curated both Robert Bloch (*The Lost Bloch*, three volumes, 1999–2002) and John Farris (*Elvisland*) as well as assembling the legendary horror anthology *Silver Scream*. Other recent nonfiction works include *The Art of Drew Struzan*. He can be seen on various DVDs as expert witness or documentarian on everything from *Creature from the Black Lagoon* and *Psycho* to *I, Robot* and *King Cohen: The Wild World of Filmmaker Larry Cohen*. In 2018 he was awarded with the J.F. Gonzalez Lifetime Achievement Award during the first annual Splatterpunk Awards ceremony. Thanks to him, the word "splatterpunk" has been in the *Oxford English Dictionary* since 2002

DAMIEN ANGELICA WALTERS is the author of *Cry Your Way Home*, *Paper Tigers*, and *Sing Me Your Scars*, winner of This is Horror's Short Story Collection of the Year. Her short fiction has been nominated twice for a Bram Stoker Award, reprinted in *The Year's Best Dark Fantasy & Horror* and *The Year's Best Weird Fiction*, and published in various anthologies and magazines, including the Shirley Jackson Award Finalists *Autumn Cthulhu* and *The Madness of Dr. Caligari*, World Fantasy Award Finalist *Cassilda's Song*, *Nightmare* magazine, *Black Static*, and *Apex Magazine*. Until the magazine's closing in 2013, she was an Associate Editor of the Hugo Award–winning *Electric Velocipede*. She lives in Maryland with her husband and two rescued pit bulls. *www.damienangelicawalters.com*

ABOUT THE EDITORS

ALESSANDRO MANZETTI is a Bram Stoker Award–winning author, editor, and translator of horror fiction and dark poetry whose work has been published extensively in Italian, including novels, short and long fiction, poetry, essays, and collections. English publications include his novel *Naraka - The Ultimate Human Breeding*, the collections *The Garden of Delight*, *The Massacre of the Mermaids*, *The Monster, the Bad and the Ugly* (with Paolo Di Orazio) and the poetry collections *No Mercy*, *Eden Underground*, *War* (with Marge Simon), *Sacrificial Nights* (with Bruce Boston), and *Venus Intervention* (with Corrine De Winter). His stories and poems have appeared in Italian, American, and UK magazines and anthologies. He won the Bram Stoker Award in 2016 and was five times a nominee. He was also nominated for the Splatterpunk Award, for the SFPA Elgin Award and Rhysling Award (both five times), and received 20 honorable mentions (for stories and poems) in Ellen Datlow's *The Best Horror of the Year Vols. 7, 8, 9*, and *10*. He edited the anthologies *The Beauty of Death Vol. 1* and *The Beauty of Death Vol. 2 - Death by Water* (with Jodi Renee Lester). He is the CEO & Founder of Independent Legions Publishing, and an active member of the Horror Writers Association. He lives in Trieste, Italy. **www.battiago.com**

ABOUT THE EDITORS

DANIELE BONFANTI translates works into English from Italian and Spanish, and into Italian from English; authors include Clive Barker, Ramsey Campbell, Richard Laymon, Jack Ketchum, Poppy Z. Brite, Peter Straub, John A. Lindqvist, Skipp & Spector, Stephen King... In the last two years, his fiction has appeared in English in the anthologies *The Beauty of Death 1* and *2* (both Stoker nominees), and on Flame Tree's deluxe hardcover *Supernatural Horror*; and his novelette *Game* received an Honorable Mention (short list) in Ellen Datlow's *The Best Horror of the Year Vol. 9*, while his story *The Gorge of Children* was on the long list the following year. Before that, he published stuff in Italian, his native language, including two novels and scores of articles in the popular print magazine *Hera*. Currently, he is hard at work with artist Stefano Cardoselli on three comic book projects, and on a couple of board games. An adventure enthusiast—mountaineer, kayaker, open-water swimmer, trail runner—and beekeeper, he was born and raised between Lake Como and its mountains; now he lives on a Macaronesian island.
www.danielebonfanti.com

MONSTERS OF ANY KIND

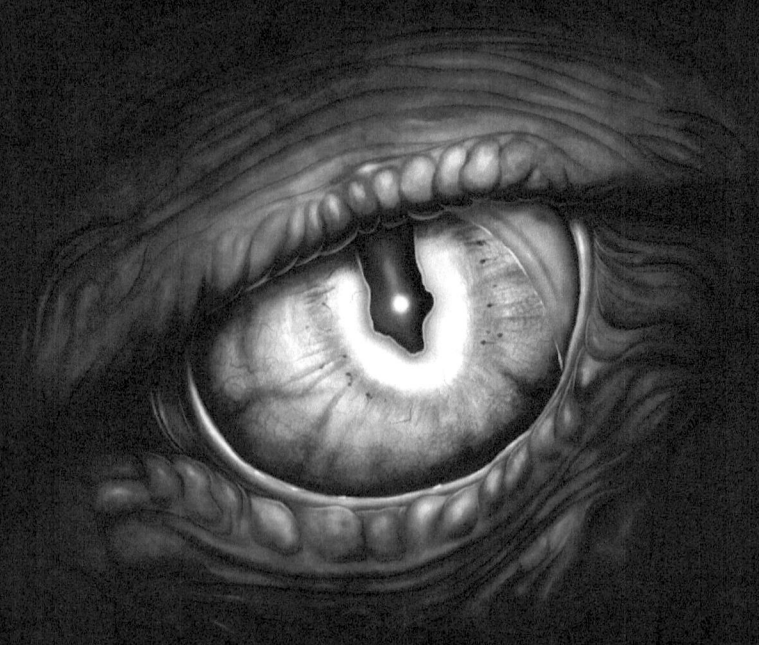

ACKNOWLEDGEMENTS

THE THING TOO HIDEOUS TO DESCRIBE…
BY DAVID J. SCHOW
FIRST APPEARED IN 'BORDERLANDS 5' EDITED BY THOMAS F. MONTELEONE AND
ELIZABETH E. MONTELEONE (BORDERLANDS PRESS, 2003)

WE ALL MAKE SACRIFICES
BY JONATHAN MABERRY
FIRST APPEARED IN 'WHAT THE #@&% IS THAT?: THE SAGA ANTHOLOGY OF THE
MONSTROUS AND THE MACABRE' (SAGA PRESS, 2016)

SEALED WITH A KISS
BY OWL GOINGBACK
FIRST APPEARED IN 'SOUTH FROM MIDNIGHT' (SOUTHERN FRIED PRESS, 1994)

MIDNIGHT HOBO
BY RAMSEY CAMPBELL
FIRST APPEARED IN 'NIGTHMARES' EDITED BY CHARLES I. GRANT (PLAYBOY PRESS 1979)

MAMMY AND THE FLIES
BY BRUCE BOSTON
FIRST APPEARED IN 'SCARE CARE' EDITED BY GRAHAM MASTERTON (TOR, 1989)

THE CITY OF SIXES
BY EDWARD LEE
FIRST APPEARED AS A PROMO CHAPETTE IN 'INFERNALLY YOURS' (NECRO PUBLICATIONS,
2008)

ALL THE OTHER STORIES ARE NEW TO THIS COLLECTION

INDEPENDENT
LEGIONS
PUBLISHING

AVAILABLE BOOKS

CHILDREN OF NO ONE
by Nicole Cushing

THE ONE THAT COMES BEFORE
by Livia Llewellyn

ALL AMERICAN HORROR OF THE 21ST CENTURY: THE FIRST DECADE
Edited by Mort Castle

BENEATH THE NIGHT
by Greg Gifune

SELECTED STORIES
by Nate Southard

DIGITAL PUBLICATIONS

TALKING IN THE DARK
by Dennis Etchison

THE BEAUTY OF DEATH VOL. 1
Edited by Alessandro Manzetti

THE HORROR SHOW
by Poppy Z. Brite

DOCTOR BRITE
by Poppy Z. Brite

USED STORIES
by Poppy Z. Brite

THE CRYSTAL EMPIRE
by Poppy Z. Brite

SELECTED STORIES
by Poppy Z. Brite

THE USHERS
by Edward Lee

SELECTED STORIES
by Edward Lee

DREAMS THE RAGMAN
by Greg F. Gifune

THE RAIN DANCERS
by Greg Gifune

WHAT WE FOUND IN THE WOODS
by Shane McKenzie

THE HITCHHIKING EFFECT
by Gene O'Neill

SONGS FOR THE LOST
by Alexander Zelenyj

Our publications are available at Amazon and major online
booksellers. Visit our Website: www.independentlegions.com

FORTHCOMING BOOKS

BOTH PAPERBACK & DIGITAL PUBLICATIONS

TRIBAL SCREAMS
by Owl Goingback

DARK MARY
by Paolo Di Orazio

FEARFUL SYMMETRIES
by Tom Monteleone

CROTA
by Owl Goingback

HORROR CALCUTTA
by Poppy Z. Brite (graphic novel)

DARK CARNIVAL
by Joanna Parypinski

THE MAN WHO ESCAPED THIS STORY
by Cody Goodfellow

COYOTE RAGE
by Owl Goingback

000 INDEPENDENT LEGIONS
PUBLISHING

INDEPENDENT LEGIONS PUBLISHING
DI ALESSANDRO MANZETTI
Via Virgilio, 10 – TRIESTE (ITALY)
+39 040 9776602

WWW.INDEPENDENTLEGIONS.COM
WWW.FACEBOOK.COM/INDEPENDENTLEGIONS
INDEPENDENT.LEGIONS@AOL.COM

Horror Writers
ASSOCIATION
SPECIALTY PRESS AWARD RECIPIENT